Supernatural Tales

PATRICK LYNCH

Paperback Published in the United Kingdom
in 2022 by aSys Publishing

eBook Edition Published in the United Kingdom
in 2022 by aSys Publishing

Cover Photograph: Stockhill Wood © Dave Reed

Disclaimer

This is a work of fiction. Names, characters, businesses, places, events and incidents are either the products of the author's imagination or used in a fictitious manner. Any resemblance to actual persons, living or dead, or actual events is purely coincidental.

ISBN: 9798438304999
aSys Publishing 2022

In Memoriam
John Lynch Mackle
1929 - 2020

Contents

The Unspoken Call 1

Down by the River 41

A Strange Story 88

The Tattooist 127

The Tree Keeper 173

A Voice from the Grave 211

Jocelyn's Revenge 262

THE UNSPOKEN CALL

The bright sunlight of a late October afternoon dazzled the woman when she stepped out into the garden. Pulling the kitchen door shut behind her, she paused to let her vision clear, then crossed the lawn, weaving her steps around the small, clipped yew bushes dotting its surface. The wooden gate in the garden wall, overgrown with ivy and standing half open, gave her entry to a lane at the back of the house. She made her way along this, taking care to avoid slipping on its muddy surface, and, after a journey of some seven or eight minutes, turned left into a field of uncut grass. Climbing upwards from here by the slightest of inclines, she headed towards the tree line above.

Feeling the wind rise and ruffle her hair, she became vaguely aware of a shadow growing in the vegetation around her. Surely not rain, she whispered to herself, beginning to wish that she had taken an umbrella from the stand in the hall. And yet the sky had been clear all day; she had made a point of checking. Shivering, she turned up the collar of her coat, and hastened onwards.

The track which she followed led her deep into the forest, into a space of ever-changing shadows and sounds. She shivered for a second time, but it was now a feeling of exhilaration which coursed through her, as her mind and body began to slough off the lassitude resulting from her morning labours.

A clearing opened up among the trees, and she found herself walking through grass, shrubs and mixed flora. Rabbits or deer had been at work, as she noticed that saplings had been stripped of their bark, and, where the vegetation was short or patchy, droppings were visible, and hoof prints, in the softer ground around the small pools of standing water. A grey squirrel, which had been foraging for nuts among the dead leaves, stopped to watch her pass.

She moved forward in an unhurried manner, pausing to savour a scent or to try to recollect the name of a flower which she had learned as a schoolgirl. It was when she reached the centre of the clearing, that she became aware of something not quite normal in this woodland paradise; but it took her some seconds to realise this, perhaps because the change was so unexpected, and so incomprehensible: the light was rapidly dimming. But this couldn't be, she thought, letting a stalk of wild grass slip from her hand. She had left the house a little after three, as she always did. There was more than enough time to get back home before evening fell. The confusion this created in her mind grew to a panic, when a noise, as of a great rushing wind, filled her ears. Then all confusion ceased, and all sound stopped, as the darkness became complete.

The following morning, at ten minutes after eight o'clock, Inspector MacGovern stood looking down at the woman's remains. In spite of the number of people who had arrived on the scene in the last quarter-hour, there was little movement about the clearing, so it was in an eerie silence that he circled round the corpse, while trying to avoid treading on the shreds of clothing, and other things, which lay scattered over the ground. Noticing something red and tattered hanging from the foliage of a bush, he merely glanced at it before moving on. The barking of a dog broke in upon his thoughts, and he turned to see its owner, the young man who had made the awful discovery an hour earlier, being questioned by a policewoman half his size.

Tall, and with a physique that was naturally trim, and which he kept so by exercise and careful eating, the forty-three year old Inspector had a full head of black hair and eyes as green as the meadows on which his Irish ancestors had lived. There was a stillness about him, a spareness of word and gesture which some thought a shyness, an assessment they found hard to reconcile with his commanding manner when he did choose to speak or act. This reserve of his, which was really a watching and listening from a distance, often allowed him to peep behind the facade that fronts so much human behaviour. The inscrutable look which he presented to the world effectively discouraged any accurate reading of his own character. This combination of traits, along with his imposing height and unflinching eye-contact, tended to disconcert many of those with whom he had dealings.

Unsettled by what he had been witness to and chilled to his bones by the damp forest air, MacGovern returned to his office in the Central Police Station a little after one-thirty. What he needed was a warm place in which to satisfy his hunger, but the thought of a shared table in the canteen, cramped and noisy with a never-ending stream of chatter, was particularly unappealing to him at that moment. Without taking off his coat, he headed for the main stairs.

Located at no great distance from the police building was a cafe which he often used as a place of refuge, especially when he wanted a quiet space in which to think over the details of a case. It was a popular spot, but now that the offices were filling up again after lunch, he had no trouble finding an empty table. He chose one in the corner by the window, a position which looked out upon a quiet street of splendid old town houses, most of which were now occupied by businesses of one sort or another. The messenger-at-arms he had never had occasion to visit, but the antiquarian bookseller and wine merchants had both benefited from his custom. While waiting to be served his coffee and sandwich, his thoughts drifted off, an involuntary detachment made easier by the tiredness which had crept over him since returning from the forest. He fancied he could hear tradesmen calling out to one another, and servant girls chatting at a corner, and the iron-shod hooves of horses clattering over cobblestones. Then, through the greyness of a late autumn afternoon, ill-lit by street lamps and a weakening sun, a man turned out of a side-street and came walking in his direction.

When the cafe door opened and MacGovern saw enter that same figure who had appeared in his daydream only a moment earlier, the jarring of fantasy and reality left him unable to register anything about the newcomer, other than that he was wearing a hat and carrying a walking stick. The waiter appeared to know the him, as a greeting passed between the two men, and was followed by some minutes of conversation, accompanied by a good deal of suppressed laughter. MacGovern watched them until he caught the waiter's eye and signalled for his bill. He might have continued his observation, too, had not a recollection of that morning's events proved a more powerful draw on his attention than his nascent curiosity. When a voice sounded in his ear and dispelled these musings, he realised that the other man had already left.

'That was Dr. Philbert,' said the waiter. 'He comes in for a coffee and a chat two or three times a week in the afternoon about this time, and always buys a packet of our chocolate wafers to take away with him. Only when he's back in the country, of course. He seems to spend a lot of time abroad, if his stories are anything to go by. A very learned man. Lives just across the road, at number 174. Top two floors. See the green curtains in those windows up there?' The waiter pointed with his ballpoint pen, and MacGovern, turning to follow the direction indicated, saw the figure disappearing in the main door of perhaps the most impressive building on the street. He dropped a few more coins into the plate to show his appreciation for this unsought information. The waiter mumbled a word of thanks, and moved off to begin clearing away dishes from another table.

There being no urgency for him to return to the office at that moment, MacGovern hesitated on the pavement outside the cafe. Anything important could wait for an hour, he thought, and his assistant could deal with anything that wasn't. Besides which, and more importantly, there was something mysterious about this man Philbert, a feeling which he could not shake off. And so it was that, unable or unwilling to resist this strange attraction which had taken hold of him, a few minutes later the Inspector found himself standing looking up at the facade of 174 King Street and wondering whether to ring the bell or not. However, the sudden and prolonged buzzing of the entry system decided the matter, and, accepting the invitation, he pushed open the door and stepped inside.

The entrance hall was very grand, by any standards. A wide stone staircase with wooden balustrade, intricately carved and faintly shining in the dim light of the interior, curved round to the right. Through a small, circular skylight in the ceiling high above, he could see clouds passing by.

When he reached the first floor, a door opened directly in front of him and a man stepped out onto the landing. Absent hat and overcoat, it was the same one he had seen in the cafe.

'Good afternoon,' said the man. His voice was low and soft, and had the undeniable richness of tone and effortless charm which only good breeding could produce. 'I have been expecting you.' The gentle smile and extended hand drew the policeman forward. 'My name is Lemming Philbert.' His grip was strong, and MacGovern felt a twinge of pain in his knuckles. He squeezed back and replied with a simple 'Charlie MacGovern.' The man stepped aside and, holding open the door, bade him enter.

The rich decoration of the residence's interior drew a gasp of pleasure from the Inspector. Paintings and drawings hung on the walls, statues and *objects d'art* stood on every flat surface.

The room into which he was led had bookcases reaching almost to the ceiling on three sides. Along the top of these were busts, in plaster and marble, he supposed, of classical figures, and some large and very fine porcelain vases. Rugs, faded and threadbare with age, covered the floor. As he trod on one, a vision flitted through his mind, of towers and sunlight and heat, and of people in strange dress and speaking strange tongues. The fire burning in the grate of a huge stone fireplace gave off an almost irresistible warmth which seemed, finally, to promise him relief from the persistent chill which still hung about him.

Directing his guest to a leather armchair at the fireside, Philbert settled himself in another opposite. The two men sat looking at one another for some minutes, neither embarrassed by the silence which grew up between them nor feeling any need to break it.

The Inspector reckoned that Philbert was in his mid-fifties, perhaps a little older. A scholar and a gentleman, certainly. The collar of his pale blue shirt fitted perfectly at the neck, and his suit must have cost a small fortune, MacGovern thought. No doubt cut by a master tailor. During the course of his career, he had had occasion to be in the company of other men of wealth and standing. Few of them had Philbert's taste and elegance. Fewer still, his learning, if the size of his library was anything to go by. Inherited wealth, probably. The idea of a private bank entered his head, but why he should have thought so, he couldn't say.

It was Philbert who spoke first.

'You must be wondering why you are here, Mr. MacGovern. Allow me to tell you. When I noticed you in the cafe this afternoon, you seemed greatly troubled. The impression which you made on me was far greater than any I have previously experienced from a member of the public. There was an undoubted air of sadness about you and, if I am not very much mistaken, I saw you shudder several times. Was it horror or fear? There are times when I cannot tell. These are marks of a troubled soul, and are easily picked up by the more sensitive among us, particularly when one is on the lookout for such signs, as I always am. It is difficult to control these very natural responses to emotional stress, and often the sufferer is unaware that he is communicating in such a way. It was the cafe owner who informed me that you are a policeman, and so I assumed that you were involved in an investigation.'

'It's Inspector,' MacGovern said in reply, not without a touch of testiness, 'and I'm always investigating. It's my job.'

'Perhaps I can be of help to you, Inspector,' Philbert continued. 'I have experience in dealing with the unusual which exists in our world and beyond, and have, on more than one occasion, been able to assist the forces of law and order. It's unlikely that you would have heard of me before, as the cases on which I have worked are known to only a few, but my name will most certainly be familiar to some of your superiors.'

'It is kind of you to offer, Doctor Philbert,' MacGovern replied, 'but at this moment in time I am in need of no assistance. I have every resource necessary to help me bring a successful conclusion to whatever I might be working on.'

Philbert watched his guest admiring the fine detail in the carving on the ceiling. When he began to speak again, he did so with a touch of hesitancy, as though uncertain whether he was doing the right thing, by revealing what he now proceeded to do. 'For some time now, Inspector, I have had a presentiment of evil. My sleep is often disturbed by images of violence, but of an indefinite kind. The colour red predominates in my dreams, the colour of blood. When I take a book down, the page at which I open it invariably contains a depiction, in words or images, of an act of destruction. Even during the daylight hours I find it difficult to be free of the feeling that black clouds are gathering above and that a storm is building. The frequency and intensity of such sensations has been increasing for the last months, and I suspect that soon, very soon, the climax will arrive, a point at which action will be required to try to stem the flood or, failing that, to clean up the mess which it produces.'

MacGovern could detect a sense of relief in the other man's voice, as though of a burden finally relinquished.

'I am still not sure what this has to do with me, Doctor. A flood of what? I deal with facts, not dreams. I hope you will forgive me, but have you considered seeing a psychiatrist?'

Philbert appeared amused by the question, as he smiled and his eyes lit up. 'No, no, Inspector. I do need help, but not of that sort. A psychiatrist can do me no good, for he would only refer me back to things which happened in my childhood, or other such nonsense. The problem is not in here,' and he tapped the side of his head, 'it is out there, in the wider world. I am looking for someone who can help me deal with the unpleasant events which the future will bring to birth. A man of experience, a good and honest man. Resolute, unwavering in his commitment to justice. And one invested with the power of the state. A man like yourself, Inspector.'

MacGovern looked at his host, his brows contracted and his head nodding faintly, but Philbert could tell that he was not convinced. The policeman was on the point of rising to his feet when a thought occurred to him.

'How will you know that it has begun, this breaking through of the flood, as you call it?' he asked.

'The strangeness of the event will be apparent to anyone who cares to look. An unusual killing, perhaps, or a seemingly inexplicable series of happenings. More than this, I cannot say.'

A sequence of images passed before MacGovern's eyes, as though his memory had decided, at that moment, to present a slide-show of some of the choicer scenes from his investigations. Scenes which it had retained, but had kept hidden behind a veil, and which now appeared in full colour, complete with sounds and smells. When still a young policeman, after one particularly brutal experience had left him ashen-faced and trembling, an older and more experienced colleague had taken him aside and told him to put all that he had seen out of his mind. If he didn't, the man had said, the horror would gradually invade his private life, and he would never last on the job. MacGovern had listened to those words of wisdom and had walled off the past, pretty effectively, he had thought. And yet here they were again, those images of crime scenes and violent death playing out in slow motion in front of him.

Philbert saw his guest turn pale, and sensed that something was wrong.

'May I offer you a drink, Inspector? Tea or coffee? Something a little stronger, perhaps?' he asked, reaching out to a small bell which stood on the table at his side. MacGovern held up a hand, like a constable on traffic duty stopping a stream of oncoming vehicles, a gesture of his which sometimes appeared in moments of stress.

Philbert pushed himself up from his chair and walked over to the middle of the three large windows, where he stood looking out onto the street below for some minutes. If he had hoped for a continuation of the dialogue, he was disappointed, as the policeman remained silent.

'Perhaps it would be best if we were to bring this meeting to an end, Inspector MacGovern,' he suggested, returning to the fireside. 'The very last thing which I want to do is put you in an awkward position. I am a private individual, after all, and have no official standing of any sort. Allow me to assure you that I shall not mention our meeting or the things which we have discussed, and I hope that you will rest easy on this point. I do feel that we shall meet again, and, if I am not mistaken, rather soon, too. If you wish to contact me in future, I shall give you my phone number. Should you prefer discuss things in person, I shall be at home for the next few weeks and would be pleased to receive you here.'

The Inspector returned home from work sometime after seven. As he climbed the stairs to the bedroom, he could hear his wife, Margaret, in the kitchen finishing preparations for the evening meal. Stripping off his clothes, he stepped under a hot shower, until he felt clean and refreshed. This ritual ablution signalled the end of his working day and the beginning of the few hours of leisure which were left to him.

The children were in their bedrooms. His son Mark, a lean thirteen year old, was sitting at his desk with his nose in a book. He barely registered his father's presence, except to give a thumbs-up sign, when asked how his day had been. Ella was in a cross-legged pose on the floor of her room, her headphones on and a textbook open in front of her, and was so engrossed in her studies that he had to resort to flicking the light off and on to get her attention. She blew him a kiss.

'I had a strange day today,' MacGovern said, uncertain himself whether he was referring to what he had seen in the forest or his subsequent meeting with Philbert. Marge was sitting at the kitchen table with a glass of white wine in her hand. He wondered whether the slight flush on her cheeks was only from the heat in the room.

'Anything to do with that incident reported on the evening news?' she asked, looking up from a recipe book. 'The forest thingy.'

'Hmm,' was his only reply.

Was he really going to ask her if she thought it a good idea that he should share the details of a murder investigation with a man he had never met before and who professed to be some kind of psychic detective? Even as the question formed itself in his mind, he knew it was silly.

'Darling, you're being rather mysterious,' said Marge, closing the book and taking another sip from her glass. 'Do I have to tease it out of you? Why not leave it until after dinner? And have some wine. It's that Merlot that you like so much. It'll help you relax.'

The Inspector remained largely silent throughout the meal, content to let the buzz of noise produced by his wife and children wash over him, and interjecting a comment every now and then. Marge made no further mention of the matter, so he decided to let things take their course. If Doctor Philbert showed up again, he might be prepared to reconsider his offer of assistance.

The next morning, MacGovern rose early and was on his way before the rest of the family were awake. He drove with the window down, and the stream of cold, clean air blew away the last remains of a sleep which had left him rested. He felt ready for whatever the day might bring.

The enquiry was begun, but there was little material to go on.

The constables who had broken the news to the victim's husband were impressed by his composure. His smile seemed genuine and had not the least trace of sadness in it, the female officer remarked, when she returned to the station. Mr. Mellon said that he would be more than willing to help the police in any way possible, but had been unable to offer even the faintest clue as to why someone would want to harm his wife.

Rather than wait for the autopsy report to arrive on his desk, MacGovern decided to pay Dr. Fischer, the medical examiner, a visit in his office at the hospital.

'MacGovern, how very good of you to drop by, and at such a opportune moment,' said Fischer, glancing up from the task in which he was engaged. 'I'm preparing a speech for the Police Surgeon's bi-annual meeting which takes place this evening. There's nothing like working at the last minute to get the creative juices flowing. Please, make yourself comfortable. I take it that you're here about the corpse in the forest,' he added, as an afterthought.

MacGovern removed a brown leather doctor's bag from the only other chair in the room and sat down.

Fischer was in his early fifties, and was of middling height and slimly built, but there was a solidity to his figure that suggested fitness and physical strength. Skiing and diving, holiday pursuits which he was said to enjoy, had given a healthy tone to his complexion. Although balding, what remained of his silvery-grey hair was combed back from his forehead, adding an unmistakable touch of elegance to his already distinguished appearance.

'I'm looking for something out of the ordinary in this case,' said MacGovern, recalling Philbert's words, when he saw Fischer screw the cap on his pen and lay it to one side. 'Something strange.'

'You mean, apart from the bestial savagery of the assault?' replied the medic, leaning forward and resting his elbows on the desk.

He opened a file which lay before him and began to read.

'Cause of death was a heart attack, brought on by massive trauma. There is extensive bruising of the shoulders, head and neck. What could have caused such injuries, I have no idea. About the torso, the flesh appears to have been torn apart, as evidenced by the ragged nature of the wounds. Great physical strength would have been required for that. There is also evidence of something sharp penetrating the flesh to a considerable depth, perhaps with a serrated edge. A knife, possibly. The problem, you see,' the doctor continued, with a slight frown of disappointment contracting his brows, 'is that so much of the body has simply disappeared. I have never seen anything like it. Whatever else might be said,' he went on, shaking his head in seeming disbelief, 'it is clear that you are dealing with an unusually brutal individual. Death occurred in the early hours of the afternoon, as the remains of partially digested salmon were found in the victim's upper intestine. What was left of it, hanging from a bush. This is one lady who won't be lunching again. Other than that, there is little I can add.' He closed the file over and took up his pen again.

There was a note of finality in these last words, so MacGovern muttered a word of thanks and left the doctor to finish writing his speech.

Sergeant Frank Lindsay, whose appearance presented the starkest possible contrast to that of the elegant Dr. Fischer, was MacGovern's assistant. He was a head shorter than his superior and several years younger. He wore glasses which were too small for his face and clothes which did nothing to flatter his plump figure. The razor-burn on his neck was perhaps the most visible sign of a carelessness which extended to almost every part of his being. Ten or twelve years earlier, Lindsay had been transferred from another department, or had been promoted, MacGovern couldn't remember which, but that happy circumstance had been the beginning of a productive working relationship.

The two policemen were sitting opposite one another at a small round table in the Lord Rochester pub, a bottle of beer, still untouched, before each.

'What did the autopsy reveal, sir?' Lindsay asked, sounding only mildly curious.

'The flesh appears to have been torn off the body and the lacerations may have been made by a knife with a serrated edge,' MacGovern replied, keeping his summary to what he considered the salient points.

'And the missing organs? We're not dealing with a psychopathic cannibal are we?'

The question remained unanswered, as both men began to sip their beer. The exchange of facts and ideas between the two, which was a regular end to their working day, or as regular as events allowed, often assumed such an unhurried aspect. There was no knowing what might pop out of those long pauses.

Lindsay was the first to continue.

'Could she have been attacked by an animal of some kind? A bear, for instance?'

'A bear? They disappeared from the wild centuries ago, Frank,' MacGovern replied, turning from watching a customer at the bar to look steadily at his colleague. 'I suppose there might still be one in a zoo or private reserve somewhere hereabouts,' he then conceded.

'They're big, powerful beasts,' Lindsay added, untroubled by the look of incredulity which had appeared on his superior's face, a look which he had seen. 'One could easily tear a person apart. It might account for the appalling state of the remains.'

Some of his suggestions were thought-provoking, at least that could be said for them, MacGovern reflected. What next, though? A wolf? Flesh-eating bacteria? He stopped himself laughing, but couldn't prevent a smile from appearing on his face, which he hoped didn't seem mocking. 'As far as I'm aware, they haven't found any footprints or tracks, other than Mrs. Mellon's, and those belonging to the chap who found the body. And his dog. The surrounding ground is soft, but much of it is covered by grass or leaves.'

Lindsay accepted this information with a shrug, which was as much as to say, it was only a suggestion; and took another sip from his bottle.

Later that evening, as MacGovern lay listening to a collection of Mahler's songs, perhaps moved by the beauty of the music, he felt a twinge of remorse for having treated his assistant's suggestion with such levity. It was always worth considering what he had to say, and the wild animal hypothesis did merit further investigation, especially since there appeared to be so little else on which to work.

He remembered reading newspaper articles telling of exotic pets, big cats and such like, which, having grown unmanageably large, dangerous or too expensive to feed, had simply been released into the wild by their owners and left to fend for themselves. Some claimed that these were the source of the alleged sightings of strange wild beasts which were said to roam the more remote areas of the countryside. Experts called in to investigate more often than not concluded that it was only a large dog or, even more infuriating for those inclined towards the fantastic, a trick of light and shadow in the undergrowth playing on the over-wrought imagination of the explorer, who was perhaps a little frightened by the solitude of the area in which he found himself. Still, the rumours persisted.

He closed his eyes and tried to imagine what an unexpected encounter between beast and woman might look like. The damp smell of the forest grew strong in his nostrils and he could feel its chill on his face. Then the darkness of the trees gave way to a sunlit glade. And into this silent vision broke a scream of terror, so loud and nerve-shredding, he awakened from his sleep with a start and rolled off the couch onto the floor. The music was still playing, and the victim's scream was only the soprano enjoying a thrilling crescendo. Shaken by the dream, he lay on in the blackness of the unlit room until the last haunting sounds of the lieder ended.

***

Wilbur Mellon, the husband of the deceased, had just settled down to an hour or two of quiet study when he heard the doorbell ringing the following morning. He supposed it must be the police, as he was expecting further visits from them. But they wouldn't stay long, he told himself, with a quiet smile. After all, there was nothing for them to find here.

As he rose to answer the door, he reflected on how his wife's study could, with little effort, be adapted to his own needs. He would clear away all her accumulated junk and rearrange the shelves. Perhaps he would treat himself to a new desk and computer. Perhaps. A bonfire in the garden would be just the thing. He saw himself feeding her books and clothing into the flames. Cathartic, in more ways than one. And when the police released her body, he could arrange to have it brought back to the house, and burn that too. Make a job of it.

As Mr. Mellon led the Inspector into the front room of the cottage, Lindsay hung back in the hallway, his sensitive nose having picked up the faintest of smells lingering in the air. The scent was stronger in the living room, and, noticing a squat glass candle holder on the mantelpiece, he had taken a step towards it, when he heard his boss ask, 'Would you mind very much if Sergeant Lindsay had a look around upstairs, Mr. Mellon? And perhaps you'd be good enough to show me where your wife did her writing.'

Lindsay's search of the upper floor yielded nothing of interest, other than the fact that the couple appeared to have slept in separate beds, although not in different bedrooms. When he returned downstairs, his examination of the candle holder revealed traces of a sticky residue in a groove carved into the base. He was still sniffing his fingertip as he entered the study next door. A curious aroma, he thought, feeling an unusual sensation stirring in his head. Attractive and exotic, certainly, but not something that one would want too much of.

MacGovern was sitting at Mrs. Mellon's writing desk, his head cocked to one side, reading the titles on the spines of the books arranged on a shelf. Mellon had offered to make tea for his uninvited guests, and could now be heard in the kitchen arranging crockery and humming snatches of a melody to himself, the sound of a teaspoon tapping on ceramic providing a percussive accompaniment.

'Listen to that,' said MacGovern, turning towards his assistant. 'A bit upbeat for funeral music, if you ask me.' After continuing to give ear to the impromptu performance for some seconds, he inquired, 'Find anything?'

Lindsay described the sleeping arrangements, and then mentioned the unusual smell, almost as an afterthought.

'Perfume, potpourri?' MacGovern suggested.

'A scented candle, I think. This looks interesting.' Lindsay picked a weighty volume up from the desk. He turned it over in his hands, then blew along the top edge, stirring up a cloud of dust, which made him wrinkle his nose and cough. 'I wonder how many people have looked into these pages over the years.'

'It could have been a best-seller in its day, Frank, for all you know.'

'Printed in the year 1876, if my knowledge of Roman numerals is correct,' Lindsay ventured, with a certain diffidence. Apart from the date of publication, the rest of the information on the title page, written in what he knew to be gothic script, was incomprehensible. Probably German, he conjectured, and continued to flick through the thick, rough-cut pages. A bewildering array of unusual signs and symbols covered the surface of each.

MacGovern, meanwhile, had turned his attention to the desk itself, and was pulling out each of the drawers in turn and rummaging among the contents—bottles of ink, writing implements of every sort, paper, old notebooks with pages torn out or scored through, and other odds and ends of the writer's trade. The bottom drawer on the right appeared to be locked, as it resisted his initial attempts to open it. By bracing his knee against the edge of the writing surface and applying much greater force, his second attempt proved more successful. The drawer began to move, millimetre by millimetre, and then shot out, revealing a cardboard box, the crumpled top of which seemed to indicate that it had only gotten stuck. The box contained a pile of type-written sheets, which he had begun to leaf through when Mellon returned, bearing a tray of cups and saucers and a plate of sliced cake.

Indicating the find, the policeman asked, 'Do you mind if I take this away, Mr. Mellon, to have a look through? It might contain something of interest, something to help the investigation. A person, a place, you know?'

For some seconds, Mellon appeared to give his full attention to finding somewhere to set down the tray. His response, when it came, had a mixed note of curiosity and surprise in it, neither one of which emotions he had been able entirely to conceal, if that had been the purpose of the pause.

'Did you find that in the desk, Inspector? It must be the book Miranda was working on. I hadn't realised she had proceeded so far with it.'

'You needn't worry, Mr. Mellon, I'm a fast reader. I'll make sure it's returned to you in a few days,' said MacGovern, adopting his most reassuring manner.

'We would like to take her laptop, as well,' added Lindsay.

'If you think it will be of any use, then please do so. Take them both, and anything else, too.' Mellon was still holding the tray. 'Shall we sit in the front room? There's more space next door and it's a little more comfortable. As you can see, it's rather cramped in here. There's room for a desk and shelves and not much more.'

The remainder of their visit, which lasted until the refreshments had been consumed, consisted of rather stilted conversation, now about Mrs. Mellon, now about entirely unrelated matters.

'There was just one other thing, Mr. Mellon,' said Lindsay, as the two policemen rose to their feet, preparatory to leaving. 'The glass candle holder. Did your wife . . . ?'

'She liked to burn one in her study while she was working. Said it helped her creativity,' he answered, with a smile which remained fixed on his face for longer than was natural.

Wilbur Mellon stood at the front door and waved them off.

'Charming manners,' remarked Lindsay, as he fastened his seat belt. 'Your discovery of the manuscript unsettled him. You saw that, I take it?'

'He probably thought the desk drawer was locked, which was a piece of luck for us. Finding the key must have been on his to-do list.'

***

MacGovern divided his investigating team into two groups. The first was to search for reports of encounters with or sightings of large or unusual wild animals. This task completed, they were to contact all zoos and safari parks within a radius of one hundred miles to inquire about missing animals, those which had escaped or were suspected of having been stolen.

Their concerted labours produced one nugget of information.

Several years previous to the events described herein, the occupants of Wellbeck, a village on the edge of an area of mixed woodland and farmland some thirty miles distant, had been terrified, over a period of months, by sightings of a large ferocious beast. One man had been gored in the leg. Another was chased along a lane and only managed to escape by throwing himself over a hedge. People walking their dogs in the evening reported hearing grunts and howling. Pets had gone missing, and the remains, if discovered at all, were said to have been in a shocking state. No one had been able to provide a clear description of the creature, but all who had encountered it remarked on its glowing red eyes and the stench which hung in the air long after it had gone. Some of the farmers said it was nothing more than a wild boar; others were less certain.

'A wild boar?' said Lindsay, after he had listened to the report of their findings. 'I hadn't thought of that. A likelier candidate than a wolf or bear, I think, but still ...'

A second group of investigators had been instructed to station themselves at the different access points to the forest, for the purpose of speaking to anyone who passed, in the hope of picking up information about possible suspects, persons acting strangely, any unusual faces, that sort of thing.

Since nothing in the office required his immediate attention, MacGovern decided to leave early and take the manuscript with him. If he was lucky, he would have the house to himself for a few hours and might be able to get through the bulk of it by the time his wife returned from work.

Settling himself in an armchair in the lounge, a spacious room at the back of the house normally used only for entertaining guests, he began to read Mrs. Mellon's tale. It was written in the first person, by a woman recording life in her country village: the various characters who make up the community, their comings and goings, and so forth. Only after finishing the early chapters did it occur to him that it read more like a diary of real-life events, than a work of pure imagination. When he reached the first passage in which she appeared to describe her own domestic situation, he stopped skimming and began to read with greater attention. The pleasure and satisfaction which her growing success as a writer brings in its train is evident, as is her contentment with life in general. It is only as the tale progresses, that mention of anxiety and a very real sense of dread occur with increasing frequency. The cause of this sudden change in her happiness, she searches for in vain. When out of doors, she is plagued by a compulsion to look back over her shoulder, as though something were rushing at her from above, only to find nothing there. She no longer finds respite in sleep, as her dreams, previously the source of much material for her stories and novels, have changed into the most unsettling of nightmares, from which she not only obtains no inspiration, but which also deny her the boon of rest. The figure which appears in these recurring horror shows is so indistinct as to be incapable of description, although she is able to identify the colour yellow. She writes of the confusing noise which seems to accompany this figure, or creature, as she begins to describe it; a strange, soft whirring sound, which she likens to the flapping of wings, and which grows louder until she feels she is being suffocated. At this point, she wakens.

Glancing at his watch, MacGovern realised how late it was. Darkness had fallen, and there was still no sign of his wife. He couldn't remember hearing the front door opening, but there were sounds from the floor above which indicated that his son and daughter were already home. Not wishing to interrupt his progress, he decided to try and finish the story, even if it meant reading into the night. If it was a diary, or largely factual, as he was now inclined to believe it was, the information which it provided might prove crucial.

Towards the end of the manuscript, the writing became increasingly difficult to understand and, in some places, was entirely incomprehensible, even after repeated attempts at elucidation. Sentences broke off half-way through, all punctuation and sense of order disappeared and, in many places, single words were all that remained, and often these were misspelt or written backwards.

It was 1.30 am when he laid aside the last of the pages. The house was silent. A rumbling in his stomach reminded him that he hadn't eaten since lunchtime the previous day. Then he realised that he had seen none of his family either. He reached for his phone, and saw a message from his wife. She had popped her head into the room to say hello, but he had been so engrossed in his reading that her greeting had gone unacknowledged, so she decided not to disturb him further. His dinner was in the kitchen, whenever he wanted it. That was five hours ago.

When MacGovern entered his office the following morning, Lindsay was sitting on the edge of the desk reading an official document. He rose and nodded a greeting to the older man.

'Any overnight developments, Frank?' asked MacGovern, as he removed his coat and hung it behind the door. He opened his briefcase and removed the bundle of manuscript.

'Not a thing, sir,' was Lindsay's reply. 'Do you want Holland's team back out at the forest today? They're ready to go.'

'What did yesterday's enquiries produce?'

'Some of those questioned appeared to know nothing about the incident and were shocked when told. Those who had already heard commented on the fact that there were visibly fewer walkers out and about, and that they were all in twos or threes. Holland said that they had finished for the day and were heading home, when they passed a young chap on foot on one of the quiet back roads. When they pulled over to speak to him, they found out that he was in and out of the forest on a fairly regular basis, recording ambient sounds for relaxation videos—waterfalls, wind in the trees, that sort of thing. Turns out that, on the day of the attack, he was in the same part of the forest where the clearing is located and, around about three o'clock in the afternoon, the birds stopped singing. He thought it was a problem with his equipment, but, when he took his headphones off, sure enough, the forest was absolutely silent. It was at least thirty or forty minutes before things started returning to normal.'

'Did he suggest any reason for the sudden silence?'

'Only that he thought that there must have been a bird of prey active in the area at the time. There are kites and buzzards nesting in the forest.'

'And this happened about three o'clock? That corresponds to the estimated time of death that Fischer gave, more or less.' After reflecting on this piece of information for a minute or so, MacGovern decided that it would do no harm for Holland and his team to spend another day or two in the field. There was always the chance they might turn up further snippets of useful information. Lindsay was on the point of leaving the office in order to pass on this instruction, when MacGovern pointed to the printed manuscript on his desk.

'This made for interesting reading last night. No wonder Mellon looked a bit upset yesterday. It gives us something very definite on which to proceed. Was there any word back from the computer boys upstairs? You did tell them it was urgent?'

'The report's on your desk, sir. It seems they had no problems accessing the laptop, because she hadn't bothered using any kind of security. They'll send the machine down later this morning when they've finished checking it. Some files had been deleted during the last months, but most were no more than a few pages in length. Only one of them was of any size, and that was deleted and then scrubbed the day before Mrs. Mellon died. They were unable to recover any of it.'

'A file of some size?' said MacGovern. The two men looked at the pile of paper, then at one another. 'I think it's time to pay Mr. Mellon another visit.'

***

As he drove, Lindsay listened to his boss summarise the salient facts which he had gleaned from reading Mrs. Mellon's manuscript. The recollection of that faint stirring of something unsettling which he had himself experienced in the living room forced itself on his thoughts, but he made no mention of it.

There was no answer when Lindsay knocked on the front door of the cottage. He waited for a moment and then disappeared round the back to see if he could find entry there. MacGovern was about to try the door again when he heard a voice calling to him from the garden of the neighbouring property. The sound was so faint that he almost missed it.

He turned to find an elderly woman waving at him, her head and face just visible over the top of the hedge which separated the two gardens. The fluttering of her hands and the tremor in her voice suggested considerable agitation.

'Good morning, madam. Can I be of some help?' he asked, moving towards her.

'I know it's none of my business,' the woman replied, 'but I've had rather a troubled night on account of the noise.'

'Noise?'

'Yes, I was awakened sometime after midnight by the most dreadful screaming. From my bedroom window, I could see a light on at the back of the house, and I assume that it came from there. I was going to phone someone, but I didn't know who. I am so glad that you're here. I feel that something awful must have happened. Do, please, go and have a look, won't you? It would set my mind at rest. I get so easily frightened these days. That's why I keep all the doors locked, don't you see?'

MacGovern assured her that he would look into the matter and that she wasn't to trouble herself further about it.

As the Inspector reached out a hand to ring the bell once more, the front door opened. Lindsay stood back to let him enter. 'He's in the study. It's not a pretty sight,' was all he had to say.

Mr. Mellon was sitting at his wife's desk. His head was thrown back, and the sight of his staring eyes and contorted features had an unsettling effect on both men. That he was dead, there could be no doubt.

Nothing much appeared to have changed in the room since their last visit. There were a few more old books on the desk, some of them open, lying one on top of the other. Standing on the desk and propped up against the wall was a single sheet of stiff white card, the whole of one side of which was covered by markings in black and red ink. Those on the lower half bore a strong resemblance to musical notation, but the signs and symbols on the upper part MacGovern could make nothing of, other than that they looked like a script of some kind. A cardboard box on the floor contained a jumble of paperbacks penned by one E J Mellon, the very same, he was certain, which had been neatly arranged on the shelf by the desk the day before.

'Didn't take him long to begin clearing out his wife's things,' MacGovern remarked, tapping the box with his foot.

Lindsay went down on one knee to examine the musical instrument lying on the floor at the side of the deceased. 'It looks like a guitar of some kind, although the body is much smaller and it has an unusually long neck.' He strummed the two strings and was visibly surprised by the richness of the tone. 'Sounds nice. I wonder if he made it himself. It looks like the work of an amateur.'

He ran his hand over the body of the wooden instrument. 'The finish is a little rough in places, and the jointing uneven.'

While Lindsay conducted a cursory examination of the house, MacGovern stepped out into the back garden for a breath of fresh air. A crow digging for worms in the grass flew off at the sound of the kitchen door opening. It alighted on the wall, from where it watched the solitary figure make an unhurried circuit of the lawn. Its raucous call, perhaps an expression of its annoyance that its foraging had been interrupted, seemed to chide and mock the policeman at the same time. Admitting that it was a fair comment on their progress in the case thus far, he decided, then and there, to pay Philbert a visit later in the day. It was possible that he might, after all, be able to assist in the investigation. What was it the Doctor had said about the coming flood? "The strangeness of the event will be apparent to all who care to look," or something of that sort. Well, now they had two strange deaths, a sheet of card covered in strange markings, and a strange-looking homemade musical instrument. There was strangeness everywhere he turned.

The autopsy revealed that Mellon had died from massive heart failure, which came as no surprise to Fischer, as the victim's arteriosclerosis was far advanced. Only a matter of time, Fischer had remarked, in spite of previous surgery and probable medication to relieve the symptoms. Death must have occurred in the early hours of the morning, as *rigor mortis* had set in to such a degree that he had had to use considerable force to get the corpse to lie flat on the mortuary table before beginning his medical investigations.

***

The man who opened the door to MacGovern at 174 King Street was not Philbert, but he greeted the Inspector by name. As he was led into the library, the Doctor made his appearance, dressed in a dark suit, and looking as though he had just stepped out of a board meeting.

'Good afternoon, Inspector. You are most welcome. Please, make yourself comfortable,' Philbert said, indicating the chair by the fireside in which the policeman had sat on his earlier visit.

A heavy silence filled the room, undisturbed by noise from the street outside. Half-drawn blinds kept out the glare of the declining afternoon sun and, in the resulting shade, MacGovern was able to get a better impression of his surroundings. He wondered why he hadn't noticed the grand piano before. It was impossible to miss the enormous black shape, over in the corner by the window. A volume of music stood open on the music desk and there were others stacked in piles on the lid. In their midst was the bust of a composer, he supposed.

'I'm not detaining you, I hope, Dr. Philbert,' he began, recollecting the reason for his visit. 'You look as though you're on your way out.'

'Not at all, Inspector. In fact, I have just this moment returned from paying a visit to an old friend. One of the spirituality. Reverend Father O'Toole, SJ. You have made his acquaintance, I think? He seemed to know you.'

'Father Aloysius O'Toole?' MacGovern was surprised by the mention of the name. 'Yes, we've met once or twice. A good man, by all accounts, and a faithful servant of the church. Had an interesting life. Spent a lot of time as a missionary priest in Africa and the Middle East. He must have seen all sorts of unusual things in those places.'

'Yes. We touched on some of those things this morning, as it happens,' said Philbert.

They sat looking at one another for some moments, MacGovern wondering how best to begin, and Philbert all expectation, his hands resting in his lap, the intertwined fingers in ceaseless motion.

It was the Doctor who broke the silence.

'I take it that our meeting of some days past has a bearing on your present visit. Some event has occurred, yes? Of a sort which

I outlined.' Not waiting for a sign of confirmation from his guest, he continued, 'In that case, perhaps you would be good enough to share the details with me.'

MacGovern proceeded to describe all that had taken place during the course of the previous days.

Philbert interrupted his narration at several points, in order to clarify his understanding of the sequence of events or to press the policeman on a detail which he felt might be of particular importance.

'This is certainly a most intriguing affair, Inspector,' was Philbert's comment, when MacGovern had finished speaking. 'I don't suppose you could arrange to have . . . ', but he was forestalled by the policeman handing over a brown envelope containing photographs taken at the crime scenes.

The Doctor studied these for a short while.

'Well, this is remarkable,' he said. He sounded cautious, but there was also a note of conviction in his voice. 'Does this not remind you of anything?' he asked, holding out a coloured photograph of the carnage in the forest on which the unfortunate dog walker had stumbled. 'Nothing at all?'

MacGovern replied in the negative.

'Have you never seen the remains of a dove or pigeon that's been knocked out of the sky by a raptor of some sort, a kite or a kestrel, say? The extremities are untouched, likely because they contain no substantial flesh, and the chest area is often entirely absent. That's what I see when I look at this photograph. And then there's the clothing strewn around the corpse, like the plumage plucked off the victim before consumption takes place. Remarkable.'

He paused and then, looking full at MacGovern, continued: 'And you did say that you have, as yet, been unable to find any distinct footprints or tracks in the soil. In that case, I am prepared to say that it looks as if the poor woman was visited from the skies above on that fateful afternoon. The slashing and tearing to which

Dr. Fischer made reference in his autopsy report could have been produced by a large, a very large and tremendously powerful bird.'

'A bird?' An image of the crow which he had seen in the back garden of the Mellon house reappeared in MacGovern's head, but enlarged to a fearsome degree. The huge corvid lunged at the watching policeman, and proceeded to tear him apart with its massive beak. 'It is fair to say that the savagery of the assault is not consistent with human activity. We had begun to entertain the idea that it might have been a bear, possibly a wolf or wild boar, but the absence of an identifiable trail is, as you suggest, problematic. There was something else,' the policeman added, 'something which I haven't mentioned.'

He related the experience of the young sound recordist.

'The presence of a large winged predator frightening the bird life of the surrounding forest into silence. Yes, it is a useful piece of information.' That the attacker might have come from the air had never occurred to the Inspector, but now that Philbert has raised the intriguing possibility, he then said no more about it, and turned his attention back to the photographs. 'Would you care to comment on this?' he asked, indicating, with his forefinger, the contorted features of Wilbur Mellon, which stared out at the observer in close-up. 'It looks like he had rather a difficult time of it when the end came.'

'It's the face of a man experiencing a moment of terror. The autopsy report said that it was a heart attack which killed him. He may have been frightened to death, quite literally.'

'I agree, Inspector. The key to the puzzle, if there is one, has yet to be found. In other words, what was the source of the terror? Was that same source responsible for the death of his wife? You said that the first thing which struck you, when you arrived in the forest clearing, was the look of horror on her face.'

'There are photographs of the books which were open on the desk, Doctor. Also a few of the musical instrument found on the floor by the body. It's like a guitar, but with only two strings. And some of the sheet of card as well.'

'It is essential that I see these objects,' exclaimed Philbert, not for the first time revealing a trace of excitement in his voice. 'Especially the books. I do have some knowledge of such things, as you can see.' He raised a hand to indicate the bookshelves, almost as though he thought his visitor might have failed to notice them. 'As for the stringed instrument, I have acquaintances who may be able to help, experts in ancient music and instrument reconstruction. I'm certain that they'd be only too happy to lend their expertise. A series of detailed photographs would be all that was required, although it would be good to get the instrument itself, if that can be arranged. But I know how you like to hold on to evidence, Inspector.'

Philbert moved away from the fireside over to his desk. He picked up and examined a number of volumes which lay there, but in a such a way as to suggest a degree of abstraction. The sound of coals popping brought him back from wherever his thoughts had taken him. Tapping the cover of one of these volumes, he asked, 'Do you know what this is, Inspector?'

Perhaps the question had been merely rhetorical, a verbal device he used to reconnect with his guest after his mental absence, or perhaps the briefest of reflections was enough to tell him that the policeman would be unlikely to know anything about such a rare item, for he straightaway continued speaking.

'It's an incunabula dating from the thirteenth century. One of only a very few extant copies. How it came into my possession is a story all by itself.'

He undid the metal clasp and opened the ancient book. The thick, heavy pages crackled, and a not unpleasant musty odour reached the Inspector's nose.

'That doesn't look like paper,' he commented, uncertain whether to say anything at all.

'No, it's parchment. The specially prepared skins of sheep or calves. It'll last for ever. Paper is, of course, much cheaper and easier to use, but it can be rather fragile. Here's a book that was published in the 1970s,' Philbert said, holding up a slim paperback, 'containing a fine investigation into psychic phenomena. The pages have already turned a disgusting shade of yellow and it's coming apart at the spine. It'll have to be treated and rebound, or it'll not last another five years. I don't understand it. It shows a complete disrespect for the art of bookmaking and the process of transmitting knowledge, all for the sake of a saving a few pennies.'

He had turned his attention back to the incunabula, and now stood pressing it open to reveal a diagram covering both of the pages. The colours remained startlingly vivid, even after the passage of so much time, and the amount of detail which the artist had included was a testament to his skill.

'That must have taken a long time to produce,' remarked the policeman, who had followed his host over to the large mahogany desk. He bent forward to get a closer look at the drawings which decorated the margins of the outsize pages, but his curiosity changed in an instant, and he hastily drew back, almost as if he felt he had been exposed to a noxious substance and was in danger of being polluted. His discomfiture did not pass unnoticed.

Philbert's tight-lipped smile was followed by the faintest of sighs.

'Yes, it sometimes has that effect on me, too, Inspector. It has to be treated with the greatest of care. Contained within these pages are a medieval monk's dreams and visions of what lies beyond the veil, shall we say.' He raised his free hand to draw back an imaginary curtain, and once again drifted off for some seconds. 'Not a vision of the damned, you understand; paintings and descriptions of that sort were all too common, at every period of the church's history. This is different, really quite unique, in my experience. From a reading of the accompanying text, it seems that the author had been experimenting with mind-altering substances, hallucinogens. There also exists the possibility that it is a collection of material dating from an even earlier time, copied from different sources, of which we now know nothing. Very likely a combination of both. All the same, it is a stunning pictorial and verbal record of some rather terrifying journeys into the unknown.'

Philbert was still holding the volume open with the outspread fingers, but the tendons on the back of his hand were now standing up, as though he were resisting an inexorably increasing force. Finally giving up the struggle, he quickly withdrew his hand and let the book snap shut.

'I do believe there are times when it positively resists my attempts to open it,' he said, looking up at his guest. 'Almost as though it doesn't want to reveal the knowledge which it contains, either because it is too powerful, in the wrong hands, or because it somehow senses that the seeker is insufficiently prepared or respectful. One of the profane, the uninitiated. A merely casual enquirer.'

He had taken out a handkerchief and was rubbing his fingertips. A look of unease had appeared on his face. 'You will forgive me if I draw our meeting to a close, Inspector, but I have begun to feel rather unwell. Renning will show you out.'

With these words, the Doctor turned and left the room.

***

The telephone was ringing when, some quarter of an hour later, MacGovern entered his office.

'Inspector, I must ask you to treat the sheet of card with the very greatest of care. It is imperative that as few individuals as possible touch it. I feel it is, almost certainly, the single most important clue to the successful solving of the mystery, so you must ensure that it is not damaged in any way.'

MacGovern instructed a team of officers to box up and bring into the station Mellon's musical instrument and library of books.

If there was any doubt about which books were his, they were to bring all of them. He singled out a reliable young constable and assigned to him the particular task of looking after the card with the strange markings. Before being moved, it was to be photographed, front and back, full size and in close-up.

No sooner had the objects arrived at the station, than he sent them on to Philbert.

Several days passed before MacGovern heard anything from the Doctor. He was making his way to the car park when he received a text message asking him to stop in at King Street, if it was convenient. Although having to abandon thoughts of a relaxing evening at home with his family, which was always more than usually appealing at the end of a stressful day, he was not unduly disappointed by this change to his plans, as his curiosity about what Philbert might have discovered amongst the effects of Mr. Mellon had been a persistent presence at the back of his mind.

Renning, rather than lead him into the library, as was his custom, on this occasion opened the door, then stood back to allow MacGovern to enter.

The air in the large room was heavy with the scent of citrus, which he recognised, and other, more exotic ones, which he did not. As he inhaled, he felt an unusual sensation in his head, as of something slipping out of place. From where he stood, he noticed candles burning about the library. What was Philbert doing with candles, he asked himself, hesitantly moving forward several steps from the closed double doors behind him. The reoccurrence of the mental dislocation pushed the question out of his mind, and, fearing that it might be the prelude to a fainting fit, he grasped at the back of a nearby chair for support. He realised then that what he was experiencing was not physical debility, it was a growing anxiety or rising nervous tension.

As these strange sensations, and the thoughts which accompanied them, flitted through MacGovern's head, a dry, twanging, jangling sound broke the silence. The music, for it was music which he heard being played, seemed to speak to him from ages past, and from a place far removed from that in which he then stood. Guessing that it was the sound of a stringed instrument, he wondered whether it might not be the same one which they had found lying on the floor beside the body of Mr. Mellon. Whether it was or not, it was undoubtedly the case that the performer played upon it with great skill, alternating passages of slow tempi, in which the simple and bewitching melody seemed to float along the air, with others, in which there were so many notes, and played so quickly, he was stunned by the artist's virtuosity. A pause in the music was succeeded by a strumming of such ferocity, he wondered that the instrument didn't break asunder. This appeared to be a prelude, as the tempo relaxed, the volume fell away, and a female voice of great power and dynamic range, singing in a language full of guttural sounds, rose up over the accompaniment.

It was only at this point, after he had been in the library for a period of some minutes, his senses having been overwhelmed by the unusual sounds and smells that filled the space around him, that he noticed Philbert sitting slumped in an armchair, his head moving faintly from side to side. As MacGovern stepped round the furniture to greet his host, he saw Philbert's hands rise up trembling before his face and heard him moaning and mumbling in a voice so low, it could only be heard through the gaps in the music. His unsettling appearance, suggestive as it was of some kind of alcoholic or narcotic stupor, only added to the dread which MacGovern felt spreading to every part of his person.

Burning candles stood all round, on plates, in candle holders, on any and every flat surface, and the dribbles of molten wax which had collected around their bases seemed to indicate that they had been alight for some time, almost certainly hours.

Uncertain how best to proceed, he reached out to take hold of Philbert's raised hands, in the hope that this might awaken the other man to his presence and perhaps dispel whatever influence lay over him. As they touched, and connected, a vision filled MacGovern's head, a vision of a winged creature, hovering above him in the sky, like a great black shadow hanging in front of the sun. This vision faded, to be replaced by a second, that of the head of a bird, massive, and with a monstrous, serrated beak, and heavy-lidded yellow eyes flecked with red and green.

Startled by the sight of the creature's dreadful head turning towards him, and the huge beak snapping and tearing, MacGovern dropped the Doctor's hands, started back, and stumbled against a table, knocking it over and scattering candles onto the rugs which covered the floor. As he moved about picking these up, he heard a click, and the music stopped.

Turning about, he saw that Philbert's hands were now resting in his lap, his head was erect, his eyes open, and a smile of satisfaction was spreading over his face.

'Good evening, Inspector MacGovern,' the Doctor said, pushing himself up out of his chair a little unsteadily. He began to move around the library pinching out the flaming wicks with wetted fingertips. 'Did you enjoy the musical interlude? Was it sufficiently mysterious? A remarkable performance, was it not?' he asked, proceeding to open doors and windows, in order to ventilate the room. 'Very effective too, if I'm not mistaken. That was a taste of what Mrs. Mellon experienced, in the days before her death. Just a taste of it. But please, Inspector, take a seat, and let me explain.'

'The instrument which you heard being played just now was Mr. Mellon's,' resumed Philbert, when the two men were seated opposite one another by the fireside in their accustomed armchairs. 'It was a replica of one used in ancient Mesopotamia, three millennia ago. As far as I am aware, none of the originals have survived, because they were made of wood and animal gut, but there are images of them on painted pottery, in carvings and the like, which show us how they may have looked. Mellon took great pains to recreate one, even going so far as to acquire cedar wood. That he received help from a luthier is a distinct possibility. In any case, it was a remarkable piece of work.' He reached out to ring a small bell standing on a table at his side. 'I think the air is sufficiently clear now, Renning,' he said, pointing to the windows, when the housekeeper appeared. 'And some refreshments for the Inspector, if you please.'

MacGovern could only think of asking where the instrument was at that time, a question to which Philbert replied, 'Ferenc Olbert, an acquaintance of mine, from my days at university, has it. He is an expert in the field of ancient music. You were correct about the sheet of card. It did contain musical notation, but it was a rather weak composition, perhaps written by Mr. Mellon himself. Olbert added a little something to increase the richness of the melody, and add a touch of the mysterious.'

As the housekeeper reentered carrying a tray, the two men fell silent. MacGovern watched Philbert massaging his temples, slowly and deliberately. He also remarked the pallor of his host's face, an unhealthy colour which the heat of the fire did nothing to dispel; and the faint shaking of his knees. He himself could feel the beginnings of a headache, and he had been in the room for only ten or fifteen minutes. He wondered how the Doctor had been able to sit for such a long time in that toxic smog.

'The effect of the instrument, as beguiling as it can be on its own,' said Philbert, holding out a cup of tea to his guest, before resuming his seat, 'is immeasurably enriched by a vocal accompaniment. Olbert's daughter trained as an opera singer, although she is currently employed as a restorer of old paintings, a much more lucrative way of earning a living than by warbling arias from Verdi and Puccini. Magdalena has, however, lost none of her considerable talent. It was she who sang the accompanying text. The language was Sumerian. Not many people know Sumerian well, Inspector, but it was a language on which I spent many hours of study in my younger days, so I was able to help with the pronunciation of the text and whatnot. The musical interpretation was all Magdalena's own. I think you will agree, she sang with great feeling.'

MacGovern did agree, and indicated this with a single nod of his head, his mouth being full of cake at that moment.

'What Mr. Mellon accomplished was really out of the ordinary,' continued Philbert, raising his eyebrows, as if to express his disbelief that a mere amateur could have achieved what he appeared to have done. 'This is only a conjecture, Inspector, but I feel that there are sufficient facts to support it. It would seem that, perhaps casting around for something to occupy his time after retirement, he took up the study of history, and became fascinated by that of the ancient Near East. This is understandable, as it is a time which is shrouded in mystery. In his reading of the legends and gods of the various peoples who inhabited the region, that of Imdugud, a winged demon, seems to have made an unusually strong impression on his imagination. The name appears frequently in his notebooks. You were, perhaps, unaware that some of those volumes which your constables collected from the house were notebooks belonging to Mr. Mellon. These also contain many drawings of just such a winged creature. Now those volumes over there,' Philbert pointed to a stack of old books sitting on his desk, 'are ones which Mellon borrowed from the university library. They contain the cuneiform texts and scholarly translations of clay tablets which had lain buried in the sands of Mesopotamia for three thousand years or more. Yes, Inspector, three millennia,' he repeated, seeing a look of astonishment flit across his guest's face. 'He seems to have taken fragments of texts from different sources and stitched them together to create a prayer to this demon Imdugud. But, instead of a prayer that was propitiatory in nature, that is to say, written to appease the demon and keep it in a dormant and passive state, he constructed one which would have the opposite effect. What I am saying, Inspector, is that Mr. Mellon set about trying to conjure up a demon, and appears to have succeeded, even beyond his wildest dreams.'

MacGovern having nothing to add at that point, Philbert continued with his elucidation of the mystery.

'When your constables were preparing to set out to collect the contents of Mr. Mellon's library, your capable assistant, Sergeant Lindsay, asked them to include the candles which he had noticed sitting at the back of a shelf. He had good reason for this. These were the source of the scent of lemons which you must have smelled when you entered the library this evening. However, they are no ordinary candles, Inspector. Chemical analysis of the wax revealed the presence of a hormone, almost certainly added by Mr. Mellon. This hormone acts upon the brain to produce a feeling of anxiety and dread, if used in sufficiently high doses. Mrs. Mellon's burning a candle during her working hours every day for months on end meant that she was continually exposed to the drug's toxicity. Hence, the rising anxiety and terror which she described as persisting for some time, sensations consistent with an accumulation of the hormone in her body.'

The room was now clear of the smell of citrus, but MacGovern could still feel a trace of that unease which had so disturbed him. He wondered how Mrs. Mellon had managed to cope with what must have been a paralysing fear, attendant even on such everyday activities as opening a door, climbing stairs or turning a corner, when she moved into the unseen and unknown.

'I deliberately lit all of the candles, in order to saturate the air with the drug. I wanted to see what effect it would have,' said Philbert.

'And what effect did it have, Doctor? What did I see?'

'In sufficient quantities, the drug induces fear, unease, anxiety, call it what you will. This, in turn, produces a disordering of thought, as evidenced by the confusion of the later entries in Mrs. Mellon's manuscript. You yourself may have experienced that this evening. A strange . . .', but he was unable to find the right word to describe the sensation, and moved his hand in a vaguely circular manner, a gesture intended to indicate a mixing-up of the mental processes. This action, or the degree of bodily animation which accompanied it, seemed to upset Philbert, as he stopped speaking, and his head began to move faintly, as though he was experiencing a fit of dizziness. 'Fear and confusion,' he went on, struggling to regain mastery of his mind and body, 'fear and confusion, acting together, can create an entrance for all sorts of unknown entities. They are like a magnet for spirits that would do us harm, in a very real and physical sense. In this case, a bird-headed monster with a beak like a saw and wings large enough to block out the sun, which Mellon's prayer of invocation summoned up from wherever it resides. Truly terrifying. That is what you saw this evening,' he concluded, setting down his cup and saucer. He rose from his armchair and took up the poker to stir the fire.

'So first he induced a persistent state of terror in his wife, by repeatedly dosing her with a toxic drug, then invoked a winged demon to exploit this fear?'

'Precisely so.'

'And why would he want to do this?' asked MacGovern, passing over, without the slightest demur, the fantastic nature of the Doctor's claims, and landing on familiar territory: motivation. 'Was it just to see if he could? Did he have another purpose in mind?' An image of Mrs. Mellon's mangled remains in the middle of the forest clearing flashed through his head. He had to try to explain two deaths, not just one.

'Resentment of his wife's success as a writer, I imagine. A common enough motivation, to be sure. Perhaps he knew that his heart was about to give out. It is not unusual for people to have a presentiment of their own death. Angered by the fragility of his health and the thought of his wife enjoying a long widowhood, he . . .'

'Then why didn't he put a pillow over her face when she was sleeping, or push her down the stairs?'

'Well, yes, I suppose he could have done that,' agreed Philbert, somewhat nonplussed by the question, as though the idea of someone committing a "normal" murder had never entered his head. 'Then again, Inspector, maybe it was an experiment.'

'And why did the demon appear on that particular day? Why not a week earlier?' asked MacGovern, questions of all sorts now beginning to occur to him.

'For two reasons, I think. First, the disordering of Mrs. Mellon's mind was at its greatest. Secondly, Mr. Mellon was now master of the invocatory prayer and music, after so many weeks of practice. The two came together on that day.'

'And his work as a chemist would have given him access to any drug that he wanted?'

'Yes, I think we can assume that.'

'Why not choose some fast-acting poison? There are some which leave little or no trace in the body of the victim.'

'Very effective, certainly, but perhaps not quite so satisfying to the intellectually curious, or those with a taste for the unusual, both of which I think well describe Mr. Mellon.'

'And his own death, Doctor?'

'It looks very much like he was invoking his winged demon again. All of the drawings which he made of the creature in his notebook are different, which suggests that he had no idea what it looked like, or only the vaguest of notions. Perhaps he wanted to see it for himself, up close and personal. In which case, it was for the first and last time. His heart gave out at the shock. We will never know for sure, Inspector.'

MacGovern spent several days preparing a report. An hour after he submitted it, he got a telephone call summoning him to his superior's office. When he entered, the Chief was sitting at his desk, the report open in front of him. A second man stood off to one side, leaning with his back against the wall. He was formally dressed, grey haired and bespectacled.

'I have read your report, MacGovern,' said the Chief. 'The final pages, in which you describe your experiences and state your findings, make for interesting reading, but they cannot be allowed to stand. An alternative has been substituted.'

He slid a single sheet of paper across the surface of the desk for MacGovern to read. Death of Mrs. Mellon, by person or persons unknown. Death of Mr. Mellon, heart failure brought on by drug use. There was no mention of his last visit to King Street or of Dr. Philbert's elucidation of the mystery.

'Philbert's conclusions are unimpeachable,' said the unknown man, 'but such information cannot be allowed to remain on an official file within the reach of anyone curious enough to go searching for it. A copy of your own summary will be kept, of course, but not here. There can be no disagreement on this matter. It is for the best. Good afternoon, Inspector.'

DOWN BY THE RIVER

'I thought we had reached an agreement that your involvement was to go only so far.'

'We had, but now I'd like it to go a little further.'

The first speaker paused for a moment to look at his reflection in the window. He adjusted the white handkerchief in the breast pocket of his grey suit jacket, straightened his tie and smoothed down his hair. From where he stood, he could see the river down below, running from left to right, a ribbon of deepest black in the growing darkness of evening, its surface broken, here and there, by gently shifting, multi-coloured reflections of the lights running along the riverside pathways. Another hour or two and it would be time to get things underway, he thought. At last. Hansen had seemed greatly pleased by the offer of the boat, in lieu of cash. It would be ample compensation for the Norwegian's labours, and it would also save him the trouble of having to dispose of it when their operation came to an end. There was, however, one other matter which might have to be dealt with tonight, he then reminded himself, a returning thought which somewhat diminished his feeling of satisfaction and pleasure. He had anticipated the almost certain failure of this exchange now underway in his office, and had prepared for it accordingly. The old seaman hadn't batted an eyelid when he had shared his plan with him.

'Is it a question of money?' the first speaker asked, turning back from the window to face his guest, a small red-haired man. 'If so, we can review the fee.'

'No. It's not about the money,' came the reply. 'You have been most generous,'

'What then?'

'The research was interesting, certainly, but it's the sort of thing I do all the time. What I'd really like, is to be involved in the rest of the business. You know, what happens next.'

'I thought I had managed to convince you that your talents were best employed in the library and that you should leave everything else to those with the requisite experience,' said the grey-suited individual, employing his powers of dissuasion one last time, and trying not to let a hint of the frustration which he felt enter his voice. 'What you are asking is not impossible, but I feel that it is unreasonable of you. It would upset my careful planning. I really don't want to be compelled to introduce complications, not at this stage, not when we are so far down the line. You are putting me in an awkward position, you do realise that?'

'In an awkward position, Mr. Fields? All I'm asking for is an opportunity to be of further assistance. An extra pair of hands, so to speak.'

'It's a small operation. No more help is needed,' said Fields.

'I could keep an eye on things here in the office,' suggested the little man, leaning forward in his seat and smiling insincerely, as though he knew he would get his own way in the end. 'Maybe I could update the details on the computer.'

'There is no question of your having access to the computer. That is my business and mine alone.'

'Well then, I could help ensure that the orders are dispatched in good time.'

'Orders? What do you know about orders?' retorted Fields, his voice rising almost to a shout, as he struggled to maintain his normally polite and restrained manner. That insinuating and insistent manner of his! It was like a small dog yapping at his heels, demanding attention and never letting up. What a scourge! His discovery of the information had been a stroke of luck, he would grant that. A really inspired piece of research. But now . . . enough! An extra pair of hands? Keeping an eye on things? Yes, he thought to himself, he could see how it might work, after all.

'I shall need some time to consider your request,' Fields said, calm once more, and moving round behind the seated figure, as though casually talking a turn about the room. 'If you return at the same time tomorrow, I will give you a definite answer.'

'Tomorrow, same time, same place. I knew you'd be agreeable. You seem like a reasonable man, Mr. Fields.'

'I am, yes. May I remind you, it is imperative you speak of this matter to no one? It is essential. Yes?'

'I haven't said a word about what I've been working on these last weeks. Not a soul knows I'm here just now.'

'Then perhaps we had better ensure that that remains the case, don't you think so?'

'What? What are you doing? Leave hold of me. Stop . . . Stop . . . STOP!'

***

'Mark, here are two boys from St. Michael's,' said Marge MacGovern, passing her son the newspaper which she had been perusing. 'Do you know them?'

The teenager laid aside his book to study the coloured photograph. 'I've seen them about the school,' he said, 'but they're in fifth year, so I don't have anything to do with them.' He was handing the paper back, when his father entered the room and took it from him.

'Anything interesting?' MacGovern asked, glancing at the headline of the article which accompanied the photograph. 'St. Michael's Academy in the news again? What have they been up to now?' he said, in a mock serious tone. '"Two senior boys have received a thank you and a handshake from the Italian consul for helping an elderly Italian tourist. In Church Street ..."' He continued reading in silence to the end of the article. 'They're a credit to the school, son. The Headmaster seems pleased,' he remarked, his face creasing with a smile.

'He wasn't quite so pleased last time the school got a mention in the papers, dad. Fun and high jinx at the Halloween party. Remember?'

'Yes. Something about an altercation in the school hall, which ended with the brutal slaying of a large number of pumpkins.'

They all three laughed at the recollection.

Mark returned to his book and his mother to her reading of the week's news. MacGovern settled himself in his chair by the window and was soon lost in a volume of poetry.

The Inspector was sitting alone at a table in the cafeteria in the Central Police Station at 11.00 am the next day, an overcast, wet Monday morning. Before him was a cup of coffee, a doughnut, and a file of official material on which he was trying to focus his attention, even as it kept drifting off to other, entirely unrelated and much more interesting matters. He was giving serious consideration to putting the whole lot through the document shredder in his office and then making up a story of its getting lost, as an excuse for his not having attended to it in good time, when he became aware of an unfamiliar voice speaking at the table directly behind his own. Grateful for a distraction, any distraction at all, he was unable to resist listening to the speaker's narration, although managing, at the same time, to maintain the pretence of being engrossed in his own affairs.

'...she was with her daughter and they were taking the dog for a walk. A two-year old Weimaraner pedigree bitch, a very nice looking dog. Really fine. The mother had decided to try a different route from the one they normally take and so they ended up somewhere down by the river, Cemetery Lane or thereabouts. The dog wanders off into a side street—it's not on a leash, because the place is so quiet and there's hardly any traffic about—and everything is fine, until she starts to go haywire, really wild, barking like mad and throwing herself against one of the doors. This goes on for a minute or so, then the dog turns and comes haring back up the street, runs straight at the woman, knocks her to the ground, and then stands over her, snarling and growling, like she was going to chew her face off. The mother is screaming. The kid has got hold of the dog's collar and is trying to pull it away, but hasn't the strength. At this point, a passing motorist stops to lend a hand. While driving the dog off with an umbrella, he shouts to the woman and kid to get into the car. He finally manages to get in himself without being mauled, and away they go at full speed. By the time he's calmed the woman and kid down, checked them for injuries and driven them home, the bloody dog has found its way back and is sitting on the front steps waiting for them, like nothing has happened. At the father's request, we went over to check on it this morning...'

More people arrived, and the assorted sounds of the cafeteria, chairs legs scraping on the floor and the rattling of crockery and cutlery, made it impossible for him to hear any more of what was being said, so he gathered up his papers and headed back to his office.

The hours of the afternoon passed away in a series of tedious meetings with senior staff, and further vain attempts to clear away some of the files which stood on his desk. He had just finished reading one, and was making notes in the margins with a red biro, when Lindsay appeared, and began to relate, with his customary irreverence, how he had spent the whole morning looking into the disappearance of cats and dogs from a well-to-do suburb of the city.

'A lot of expensive pedigrees among them. And their owners spend considerable sums of money, in addition to the cost of purchase. Insurance, dog walkers, and so on. Pampered pets. Not a mongrel among the lot of them. You know,' Lindsay continued, scratching his ill-shaven chin and frowning, 'I never really saw the attraction of having one about the house, dog or cat. Claw marks and hair everywhere. And as for scooping up poop and bagging it, no thanks. You'll never guess what I saw in the park at the weekend, sir. Some joker had hung small bags of dogshit on a bush at the side of the path. All neatly packaged and carefully arranged, like decorations on a Christmas tree. Considerate, don't you think?'

MacGovern, merely raising an eyebrow in answer, thought it unlikely that any creature on earth could add one iota to the chaos in which his assistant lived, but kept the observation to himself. This talk of pets reminded him of the story he had heard in the cafeteria earlier, and, while continuing to listen with half an ear to Lindsay's animated chatter, he took a street atlas down from a shelf and flicked to the index. The map on the page indicated revealed that Cemetery Lane and Church Street ran parallel to one another and perpendicular to the river, and that they were connected by Bank Street, which ran horizontally between them. They formed a letter H, with Bank Street as the bar joining the two verticals.

Two unusual events occurring in the same area of the city only days apart, he thought, beginning to wonder if the mad Italian gentleman and the crazy German bitch might be connected in some way. As he was beginning to dismiss the idea and ascribe it likely to nothing more than coincidence, a memory flashed into his head.

When still a young constable, he had, over the course of several weeks, found himself returning again and again to a particular area of the city, where an odd mixture of old run-down tenement buildings, empty lots piled high with the rubble of demolition, and assorted business premises were located. No two incidents had been the same: domestic abuse, burglary, arson, and teenage suicide had been some of the more serious cases which had involved the police. He had thought nothing of it himself, neither of the lengthening roll call of misery, nor of the fact that the incidents had occurred within the compass of just three or four streets, until a casual remark made by a fellow constable, a rather taciturn individual with a strong interest in religion, had hinted at the possibility of their being some kind of malign influence at work in the area. A withering look from a senior officer had put an end to the constable's speculations, but the idea had lingered in MacGovern's mind.

The silence in the office, as Lindsay's flow of words finally ceased, interrupted MacGovern's recollections at that point. As he returned the book to its place on the shelf, he resolved to look into the matter, when he could find a few minutes to himself.

***

Leaving his wife and children to tidy up in the kitchen after the evening meal, the Inspector retreated to his study, a spare bedroom at the very top of the house. Framed police certificates and original movie posters covered one wall. His small library of reference books, works of non-fiction, and a growing collection of poetry was neatly arranged on homemade shelves fixed to another.

As he so often did, partly from curiosity and partly from habit, he opened the skylight in the sloping roof and stood looking out over the neighbouring houses and gardens. He could see figures moving around inside lighted rooms, the windows as yet uncovered by drawn curtain or blind. One or two indistinct shapes, the sound of their footsteps fading with every second, strode along darkening lanes and disappeared into the gloom. The headlights of cars passing by on the main road, the noise of the engines muted by distance and the intervening houses, seemed like so many pairs of disembodied eyes hastening through the blackness. The smell of burning coal hanging in the damp air reminded him that he had to order wood for the stoves in the lounge and the day room.

He closed the window again and sat his desk, the sole material relic, so far as he knew, of his father's long and happy career as a teacher of mathematics. After typing some words on the computer keyboard, he leant forward to study the images which appeared on the screen. Cemetery Lane and Clyde Street featured in any number of coloured photographs, many of which appeared to have been taken in the recent past. The comparatively few featuring Bank Street were somewhat older, judging from the style of clothing worn by those who appeared in them. As he scanned through the search results, two photographs caught his attention. These had been taken along Bank Street looking from the Church Street end. In the first, some children are seen playing with a ball. In the second, which appeared to have been taken some moments later, the children are formed into a group and are looking towards the camera, evidently pleased that they have become the centre of a stranger's attention. That is, all except a little boy standing behind the rest of his companions. His head is partly turned round, as though something has distracted him, something unnoticed by the others. What this might be is unclear. The only obvious difference between the two photographs, apart from the arrangement of the children themselves, is that, in the later one, a door has opened at one of the premises, a small door placed within a much larger one. MacGovern felt his eyes growing strained from peering at the bright screen, and the resulting blurring of his vision persuaded him to leave further research until the following day. His last act was to email the two photograph to the technical department and ask for a magnified and enhanced copy of both to be made as soon as was convenient.

When he entered his office at seven the following morning, the desired copies were waiting on his desk. Lindsay was there too, asleep in a chair in a corner of the room. MacGovern wondered whether he had arranged a meeting with his assistant for this early hour of the day, but a glance at his desk diary revealed none such. Perhaps the cleaners had disturbed him in his own office farther down the hall and he had fled here for refuge. How could a man take such care in the polishing of his shoes, he asked himself, admiring the military shine on the Oxfords, and yet think that wearing the same shirt for two days was somehow acceptable? The flecks of dried blood on the collar, where it had come into contact with a shaving nick, were a giveaway. He reached out a hand to give the sleeper a gentle shake, but let it fall again. He would leave him to waken of his own accord.

The details on the images were as sharp and clear as modern technology could make them. The second photograph, the one of the group of children, revealed what might have been a look of surprise on the little boy's face. Or was it fright? His mouth was open, as though in the act of calling out, and he appeared to be grasping at the arm of the larger boy standing in front of him. Not so much to attract his attention, was the thought which occurred to MacGovern, but rather to have something to cling to in a moment of uncertainty. His eyes focused and refocused on the space which the open door created. There was something there, lurking in the shadows of the interior, he was certain of it. Had the unknown photographer caught a ghostly presence with his camera? Merely forming the question in his head was enough to weaken the strength of this conviction. There was a name for it, when the brain saw patterns that didn't exist, but he couldn't remember what it was.

He glanced up to see that Lindsay had awakened from his doze and was watching him with eyes that could hardly stay open. MacGovern passed the photograph over to him and drew his attention to the little boy.

Lindsay looked at it closely for a time.

'Maybe he was just startled by the sound of the door opening, sir. Perhaps they shouldn't have been there. Who knows? It needn't be anything more than that. And the doorway?' Another pause ensued while he peered at the photograph again. 'A pattern formed by the interplay of lighter and darker areas of shadow. Pareidolia, I think they call it. All in the imagination, sir. Why this interest in an old photograph anyway?' he inquired, handing it back. 'You've got enough to do at the moment.' This was accompanied by a wide-eyed look at the stack of files on the desk.

'It might be something, Frank, or it might be nothing at all,' MacGovern replied, with a smile. Pareidolia! How the hell had he known that! There was a word for just such a stroke of good fortune: serendipity. He scribbled both down in his diary without bothering about the spelling. He could check that later. 'If you can manage it today, what with all those other things you've got to do, perhaps you wouldn't mind visiting the public library. See if you can find out anything about Bank Street and its environs. Ok?'

Lindsay accepted the commission without any sign of demur, pushed himself out of the chair like a man twice his age, and shuffled off to get himself some breakfast.

MacGovern didn't move from his desk for the rest of the morning. He had a secretary provide him with all that was necessary to sustain him through his long battle with the accumulated paperwork. It took him the best part of three hours, but he was finally able to scribble his signature on the last of the files, close the brown card folder with a sigh of pleasure, and push it away from him. That annoying task completed, he decided that, as a reward for his efforts, he was going to give himself some time in the afternoon to the other matter that was on his mind, the unusual events centred in those streets near the river.

He picked up the telephone, made a couple of enquiries and, twenty minutes later, a young constable entered his office and stood to attention before his desk. MacGovern asked him to recount all that he remembered of the affair involving the elderly Italian gent who had gotten himself into some difficulty down by the river.

'Well, sir,' the constable began, 'the gentleman's name was Marco Benedetti. He was 73 years old, recently widowed, and was visiting theses shores for the first time. The spot in question being located not far from the central station, we arrived only a few minutes after the call for help was made. Mr. Benedetti was silent during the short car ride back, but seemed to have recovered from whatever it was that had upset him by the time we got there. He appeared more embarrassed than anything, to be quite honest, sir. Anyway, he politely refused all offers of help, saying that he felt much improved. When I asked him what had happened, he shrugged his shoulders, and said that he had begun to experience a confusion in his head. Those were his own words, sir. And this was accompanied by a feeling of sickness. He had eaten something at lunchtime and was, as far as he knew, in good health.'

Asked if he had been able to ascertain where exactly this feeling of confusion had begun to manifest itself, the constable shook his head. 'I did ask, sir, but all he said in reply was, "Il magazzino. Molto strano, molto strano," which means, "the warehouse. Very strange, very strange." He spoke English well, but when we first got to him, it was like he was talking gibberish. I hadn't the faintest idea what he was trying to say. And we couldn't get him to release his hold on the schoolboy. We almost had to prise his fingers apart.'

MacGovern thanked the constable and allowed him to return to his duties. He couldn't remember if they were obliged to inform the consulate when a problem involving a foreign national occurred. Maybe the old chap had, after all, needed help, and had made contact with his own people.

The Inspector then called St. Michael's Academy and asked to speak to the Headmaster. After the briefest of introductions and repeated assurances that the boys were not in any trouble, the Head granted his request for an interview, and an appointment was made for two o'clock that same afternoon.

The two boys arrived at the Headmaster's office at the same time, although coming from different parts of the school campus. They were both seventeen years old, in their second last year, and were well-mannered, capable scholars, with reputations for honesty and hard work.

When asked by the Inspector to describe the events of that day, the more talkative of the two said that they often passed along Church Street on their way home, having crossed the river by one or other of the foot bridges. They occasionally took a different route, just to add some variation to their homeward journey, but they had found that Church Street was usually very quiet at that time in the afternoon and they didn't have to bother about the noise of traffic, which was good, as they always had something to talk about.

On the day in question, they were chatting about a book which they had both been reading. They heard someone calling out, and had crossed the road to see if they could offer help, but had approached the elderly man with a degree of hesitation, as his rambling speech and agitated manner seemed to indicate that he was considerably distressed. They wondered if his strange behaviour might be the result of alcohol or drugs, as such a sight wasn't exactly uncommon on the city's streets. But his clothes looked expensive and he was well-groomed, so they thought probably not. By the time they had plucked up enough courage to speak to him, he had wandered farther up the street. It was at this point that they had called the police.

When MacGovern asked if he was absolutely certain where they were when they encountered the man, the lad replied that they were approaching the entrance to Bank Street, and had assumed that he had come from there.

The other schoolboy, the quieter of the two, appeared to have nothing to add to this narration of events, and would in all likelihood have remained silent, if it hadn't been for his friend's prompting. Seeing his hesitation and embarrassment, the Headmaster added a few words of encouragement and urged him to say whatever was on his mind, however trivial or silly it might seem. With the slightest of stammers and blushing furiously, he said that he had felt rather uneasy about passing Bank Street in the days and weeks before the incident. It had seemed eerily silent and deserted, and not only to the eye—it had also felt empty, desolate. He then went on to say that this feeling had seemed unusually strong on the days when they had football practice after school, which he found puzzling. When MacGovern asked in what way those two days differed from the others, the only thing which the boy could think of was that he never bothered changing back into his uniform before heading home, as it was too much hassle.

MacGovern thanked the boys for their assistance, gave each of them a card with his details on it, and asked them to contact him if they remembered anything else at later date, however insignificant it might appear to be.

As he was about to leave the Headmaster's office, the quieter boy blurted out, 'He calmed down a little when we got near him. I thought at first he was trying to lean on Davie's shoulder, but he just seemed to grasp at the pocket of his blazer and hang on, as if he needed someone to hold him up. He stood like that till the police came.'

***

Lindsay returned from his errand in the late afternoon, just as MacGovern was beginning to think him lost. There was an air of satisfaction apparent in his manner, and he placed a buff-coloured folder on his boss's desk with the words, 'I think you'll find the contents interesting. I had an enjoyable few hours in the company of a female librarian. She was very helpful.'

The folder contained copies of old maps and photographs of the area around Church Street, architectural plans, and sundry other pieces of related information. Several black and white photographs, which appeared to have been taken in the early 1900s, from a position on the opposite side of the river, showed an assortment of craft of various types going about their business—coal barges heading upstream towards the centre of the city, a small ferry midway between one bank and another, skiffs and cargo boats. Also visible was the rear of the buildings on the river side of Bank Street and the double doors in each, used to transfer goods into and out of the trading premises. A wooden jetty or platform, at which several smaller craft were moored, ran along the full length of the buildings. On the brickwork above each set of doors was painted the name of the trading concern, and fixed above that, a pulley system, used for lifting heavier cargo.

The oldest of the maps dated to the middle of the eighteenth century and revealed a very different scene from the present day. In the approximate site of Bank Street was a prison, with courtyard and walls. Much of the surrounding area was open fields, with, here and there, a small wood, roads, or a cluster of houses.

Lindsay tapped this map with his forefinger.

'They used to hang prisoners here,' he said. 'They had a real problem with river pirates at different times, believe it or not. The gallows was a permanent fixture well into the 1800s, by which time the prison had fallen into such a state of neglect and disrepair that they demolished it and sold the land to developers for building. The desire for riverside trading premises had increased along with the prosperity of the city. Much of Bank Street, which is a shorter form of Riverbank Street, dates from that period of construction. As far as can be made out from written descriptions of the area and from the few eyewitness accounts of public executions that exist in diaries and whatnot, the gallows were located somewhere within the premises of number 11, it being the centre of the row.

Boats used to gather on the river to watch the executions. It was considered a form of entertainment for the masses. Have you heard of the expression "hanging in chains"?'

MacGovern shook his head.

'Once the condemned had been executed, the body was put in a metal cage called a gibbet and then hung up again. There was one such device at the end of the prison property, about here,' he said, tapping the map again. 'The corpse remained on display, as a warning to other would-be malefactors, until it fell apart, at which point, whatever was left was thrown into the river.'

'Malefactors? A good word, Frank, but we now call them criminals. Is there much more to it than what you've already told me?' asked MacGovern, putting the various documents back into the folder. 'If there is, I'll take it home and read over it this evening. Unless you want it yourself. You seem quite taken with the history of the place.'

'No, no. I've got other things to do,' Lindsay replied, with a laugh and a wave of the hand. 'But you have to admit it is fascinating. The librarian was quite excited when she returned from her searching and handed me that folder. There must be a whole lot of lost knowledge about the city buried in those old books. An interesting job, working in a library like that.'

'Sounds like you enjoyed the experience. You're not considering a career change, Frank, are you? At your age? What about your pension?'

'What about my pension? Another ten years of this work and I might never see any of it.'

'It's not the job that's wearing you out, Frank, it's all your high living. You need to settle down and get some order into your life. Are you still renting that tiny flat in Overhill?'

Lindsay shook his head. 'I'm staying at a friend's for the time being. He's working abroad, so I've got the use of his place until he returns.'

'And then what?'

The conversation, touching on other matters of a similarly personal nature, went on for another twenty minutes or so, at which point, the colleagues separated.

It had never been MacGovern's intention to take the file home with him, partly because he was unwilling to let an informal investigation, however interesting it might appear to be, eat into his private time. His main reason, however, was that he knew someone else who would do a far better job of examining its contents than he ever could, and with twice as much pleasure.

As he climbed the winding staircase inside 174 King Street, the Inspector felt a touch nervous at the prospect of meeting Philbert again. This wasn't helped by the fact that he had not bothered telephoning ahead to say that he was coming, preferring to drop in unannounced, on the off-chance that he would find the Doctor at home.

He was, and was sitting at his desk when MacGovern was shown into the library. He rose to greet his guest, with a handshake that had lost none of its strength.

'It is a pleasure to see you again, Inspector. Have you recovered from out last meeting?'

'I have, thank you, Doctor. I stopped by some weeks ago, but there was no answer.'

'I was out of the country for a spell, and Renning was spending time in Germany with some of his relations, so that is why you found nobody home.'

'It was nothing important. Just a social call. Were you engaged in research?' MacGovern asked.

'Exactly so, Inspector. I wanted to examine some recent discoveries, pieces of papyrus and unusual carvings of particular significance uncovered in the desert near Abydos. That sort of thing. Most enjoyable. Have you ever been to Egypt?'

MacGovern answered in the negative.

'Fascinating place. Ancient history everywhere you turn. And the natives are very accommodating. I was able to purchase one or two choice artefacts for my collection, and at no very great cost. But please make yourself comfortable, Inspector,' he said, indicating a chair by the fireside.

They had just sat down, when the butler entered the library carrying a tray of tea and comestibles. He set it down on a low table bedside the Doctor, then left as silently as he had come.

'Black and no sugar, I think,' Philbert said, lifting the lid off the teapot and peering into the interior. Apparently satisfied by what he saw, or smelled, he replaced the lid again and poured a cup of the aromatic brew for himself and his guest. 'Do try the cake, Inspector. Butterkuchen, I think they call it in Germany. If you find it a touch dry, dip it into your tea. I sometimes do.'

MacGovern placed Lindsay's file down on the table and slid it over to Philbert.

'Perhaps you might find an hour or two to have a look over the contents, Doctor. By themselves, they're an interesting piece of local history, but I feel they may also have a bearing on a case which is developing.'

'Are you inviting me to a mystery, Inspector?' Philbert asked, his eyes glowing with pleasure. 'I do hope it will be as interesting as our last one.' He hesitated for a moment, as though undecided whether to open the folder and straightaway proceed to an examination of the contents, or leave it till later. MacGovern looked on with concealed amusement, and no small degree of pleasure himself, that the Doctor should appear so genuinely interested in his meagre offering.

'This is an unexpected treat, Inspector,' Philbert finally said, 'but it is one which I shall savour alone, if you don't mind. It will be a welcome interruption to the studies which I have been prosecuting this afternoon. Tibetan manuscripts are all very interesting, but one can get too much of the sublime and the spiritual. It is unfortunate that the monks didn't see fit to turn their attention to comedy, like the Greeks. There is nothing like a touch of Aristophanic scurrulity to bring one's mind back down to earth.'

Then, to MacGovern's surprise, Philbert made no further mention of the folder. For the better part of the next hour, they sat chatting easily in the splendid surroundings of the library, the policeman about himself and his family, the Doctor about his recent sojourn in Egypt.

'I must say, Inspector,' Philbert remarked, intrigued by the thought of his guest spending his leisure hours reading poetry, 'I don't think I've ever met anyone who is familiar even with the name of Beddoes, never mind his work. That is certainty a surprise. In my younger days, I read him avidly. *Dream-Pedlary* is a bewitching poem, don't you think?'

MacGovern experienced a momentary disappointment when he realised that his attempt at literary name-dropping had come to nothing, but the feeling was immediately succeeded by one of embarrassment, when it occurred to him that the Doctor might very well be able to recite, in whole or in part, the aforementioned work from memory. He loosened his tie a little, in the hope that Philbert might be persuaded to attribute the bloom of colour on his cheeks to the heat in the library, rather than to any consciousness of having been caught out.

When the conversation paused once more, as it had done so many times before, something in Philbert's manner, an almost impalpable sense of his reluctance to continue speaking, suggested to MacGovern that the visit was at an end and that it was now time to go. He thanked his host for his hospitality and rose from his chair.

'This has been a delightful impromptu visit, Inspector, and I do hope that you will repeat it soon. It has been such a relief to leave aside my studies for an hour. Thank you for the file. Pass on my regards to Lindsay. You will keep me informed of any developments?'

Philbert accompanied him down to the street door, where they shook hands again and parted, the policeman to pursue his informal enquiries regarding the mysterious Bank Street, time and the demands of the job permitting; and the Doctor to return to the comfort of his library and his arcane studies.

Some days after this meeting, at the end of a particularly hectic and wearying afternoon, the Inspector was turning out of the car park, when he remembered that his wife was working late and wouldn't be home for some hours yet. Rather than proceed with his homeward journey, he decided, on the spur of the moment, to drive down towards the river. Although it was already getting dark and he thought it unlikely that there would be much to see, it might at least refresh his memory of a part of the city which he hadn't visited for years. He might even get a feel for the area, or come across someone, a resident or a caretaker perhaps, who could add to his small store of information about it.

Diversions resulting from construction work ongoing in different parts of the city, and slow-moving evening traffic, meant that it was some fifty minutes later when he reached his destination.

A heavy mist had risen from the river and hung in the cold night air. This, and the almost complete absence of working streetlights, made visibility difficult, so he switched the headlights onto full beam and reduced his speed to not much more than a crawl. When he turned into Bank Street from Cemetery Lane, the powerful light disturbed a group of individuals collected at some distance ahead of him, as they separated and seemed to fade away into the swirling mist. Initially surprised that people should be standing around in the dark, it then occurred to him that they must be employees enjoying a few moment's conversation at the end of their working day, or were perhaps preparing to start the night shift. Still, whatever they were doing, he thought, they were rather strangely dressed. Waistcoats were all very well, and were coming back into fashion among some of the younger male detectives; but the knee-breeches? It had to be a uniform of some kind.

Not wishing to blind them with the full beam, he switched it off and continued slowly moving forwards. He became aware of other figures flitting about in the shadows at the edges of the field of light, but they turned away and vanished as he drew closer. Something was glinting in the headlights, but what it was, he couldn't say. Metal of some kind, certainly. Silver? A silver buckle? Were some of them wearing buckles on their shoes?

He had reached about the middle of the street, when, without warning, the lights and engine cut out, and the car rolled to a stop in a darkness so inky black, he was unable to see anything of his surroundings. He sat unmoving, straining his ears for the least noise, but all he could hear was the sound of his own breathing, which seemed unnaturally loud. Thinking that the car must have stalled, he tried to reach for the key in the ignition, but found that he was unable to move either arm any more than a few millimetres. As he began to struggle against the invisible restraints, something was forced down over his face and pulled tight against his neck. Then the floor of the car opened up beneath him and, to a noise which sounded like a muffled cheering, he began to fall, and fall, and fall . . .

The descent ended with a jolt so violent, he felt as though his head was being torn off his body.

The brightness which filled his vision an instant later was not some heavenly light, in which angelic beings bathed; it came from the instruments on the dashboard. He was still in the car, and the engine was softly purring.

He tried to remain calm, and told himself that he was fine and that he would sit for a minute or two until the beating of his heart was no longer thudding in his ears. But there was gap in his resolve, a tiny hole born of the night and its shadows, through which entered, first as a trickle, and then as a raging torrent, a blind panic. At a stroke, it washed over him, smashing his resolve and crushing all the air out of his lungs.

He rammed the gearstick into position and stamped on the accelerator pedal, but the car began to slide sideways, as the tyres could find no purchase on the wet and filthy cobblestones. The noise of metal grinding against stone told him that the wheels had struck the kerb on the passenger side, where they must have found traction, as the car then began to pick up speed at a fearsome rate. His senses still greatly confused by what had happened, he somehow had the presence of mind to stamp on the brakes as the car shot out of the far end of the street, and, spinning the steering wheel, managed to bring it to a halt before it struck the wall of the building opposite. Even after it had skidded to rest, he continued to depress the brake pedal with all the strength in his leg and foot, as though unaware, or unwilling to accept, that he had gained control of the vehicle. When he drove off, some moments later, it took a supreme effort to keep the car moving in a straight line, as he was unable to prevent himself from overcompensating for every slight move it made to one side or the other. His driving instincts beginning to return, he glanced in the rear-view mirror, and saw the figure of a bearded man, only partly revealed by the dim light of a street lamp, watching him from the shadow of a doorway.

When the car entered traffic once again, he had to pull over to the side of the road, until he no longer felt overwhelmed by the lights and noise and movement around him.

Marge noticed his subdued manner when he arrived home, but she made no comment on it. Nor did his children, when they saw how detached their father was during the evening meal.

***

Next morning, under a grey drizzling sky, MacGovern was standing midway along Bank Street silently surveying the buildings on both sides of the street. Lindsay, his facial expression changing between scowl of annoyance and puzzled frown, was leaning against the car watching him. The boss was certainly behaving strangely this morning, he remarked to himself. He had been very quiet on the journey over, for one thing, and, for another, he hadn't shaved. Lindsay could not remember when he had last seen him come to work unshaven. It was unheard of. And his collar was unbuttoned. He had been wearing a tie when he entered the office, but, after repeatedly loosening it and then doing it up again, had finally taken it off, rolled it up and stuffed it into the pocket of his jacket. And there he was rubbing his neck again. That had been going on all morning, too. Must be nerves or a skin rash, he thought.

'I don't think I've ever been along here before,' Lindsay said, hoping that this might get MacGovern to tell him what was going on and why they were standing out in the cold and wet, when they could be sitting warm and dry in the car. 'It seems like the urge to clean up and renovate old buildings didn't reach this far. Straight out of a Dickens's novel, Victorian filth and all.' He moved some rubbish around with the toe of his shoe, uncovering a plastic doll's head, crushed flat and barely recognisable. A breath of wind stirred the blonde hair, revealing a face with only one eye and a forlorn smile.

There were ten or so premises on each side of the street, and they had halted before one with a large, heavy wooden door, its dark purplish paint faded, peeling and covered with a layer of dust. It bore the remnants of a bill poster, an advertisement for the forthcoming visit of a circus, but in such a state of disintegration, it was impossible to say how old it was. Along the bottom edge of the door were five iron wheels, each five or six inches in diameter and spaced about two feet apart. A much smaller door, for pedestrian ingress and egress, was cut into the larger, its lower edge eighteen inches or so above the level of the ground. A keyhole and the flap of a viewing port were visible in this. Both doors were locked, the larger one with a chain and padlock. The inscription on the lintel, Kuhn, Loeb and Frankel, Furs and Precious Metals, although still legible, was, like everything else in the street, grimy and looked at least a hundred years old. Three windows in the brickwork above the door indicated the possibility of there being an upper floor inside the premises.

'This is where the group of kids was standing when their photograph was taken,' said Lindsay, recognising the arrangement of the two doors, which appeared to be unique to that particular premises. 'The place you thought was haunted, or something.' Having made the connection, he now found his boss's behaviour a little less inexplicable.

'Frank, I want you to move the car in as close to the wall as possible. Then get up on the roof and see if you can get a look through that window there.' MacGovern was pointing to the window on the far right.

'Even if I stand on the roof, sir, I'll not be high enough. Why don't we look for a ladder? There's bound to be one around here somewhere.'

'I would like it done now,' came the testy reply, 'and I don't want anyone else knowing that we're here, for the time being. What about using that down pipe? There are places which you could use as toe holds.'

Lindsay, taking exception to what he felt was an unreasonable request, was beginning to grumble, when he appeared to remember something, as he got into the car, rummaged around under the passenger seat, and emerged again holding a plastic rod.

'A selfie-stick. It's not long enough to use from the ground, but it should give me the extra length required.'

It was the work of a few minutes to manoeuvre the car into position. Rather than use the roof of the vehicle, which was unlikely to provide much support for a man of his weight, Lindsay rolled down the driver's window, placed his foot on the sill and pushed himself up. With his left hand jammed between the pipe and the wall, and both feet rather precariously resting on a joint in the piping, he was able to take a number of photographs and a short video clip through the window.

He passed the stick and phone down to MacGovern, and had begun his descent, when his foot slipped from its hold and he fell to the ground, ending up crushed into the narrow space between the car and the wall of the building. A burst of profanity expressed the measure of his annoyance, not just with this latest incident, but with the whole morning's adventure.

MacGovern paid no attention to the commotion, nor did he step over to help pull the other man to his feet, as he was busy studying the images of the warehouse window and what lay in the dark space behind the filthy glass. When Lindsay hobbled over to his side, still quietly cursing and brushing muck from his trousers and the sleeves of his jacket, he handed the phone back.

'Here, Frank, have a look at your handiwork. You did well. These'll need to be cleaned up and magnified. Make sure you send them to the tech boys when we get back. And have them make two sets of copies.'

They were turning left out of Bank Street into Church Street, when MacGovern pointed to an individual on their right, who was, at that moment, disappearing through the wire-mesh gate of a temporary car park. He couldn't be certain, but he thought it might be the man he had seen watching him the previous evening.

'Just a couple of questions, Frank, and we'll head back to the office. Then you can get one of the female constables to bandage your hand and rub some antiseptic cream onto that graze on your forehead. Okay? If you ask her nicely, she'll maybe even kiss it better for you.'

The muttered reply to this pleasantry, if MacGovern had paid it the least bit of attention, would almost certainly have constituted a breach of police discipline and been subject to punitive measures.

As the two policemen got out of the car, the man MacGovern wanted to speak to exited the parking lot pushing an old wooden chest on a flat trolley. He stopped to watch them approach.

'Good morning,' said MacGovern.

'Good morning to you,' the man replied. There was a lilt in his voice and a certain something in his pronunciation which suggested he was not a native speaker of English: the word "good" sounded like "god". Scandinavian, perhaps, thought the Inspector, also remarking the man's very blue eyes, and the light honey-brown colouring of his hands and face.

Lindsay showed his warrant card. 'Do you mind if we ask you a few questions?'

The man barely glanced at the photograph. 'Okay.'

'What's your position here?'

'I'm the car-park attendant,' the man answered, the sing-song sounding very clear, 'and I do other things as well, odd jobs, general maintenance, that sort of thing.' MacGovern watched his head bobbing slightly, as though he was agreeing with his own description of himself.

'We're looking into two incidents that happened hereabouts during the last week or so,' MacGovern said. 'The first involved an elderly foreign gent and the second, which took place some days later, involved a woman and a dog. Did you see or hear anything of either incident?'

'I heard the dog barking and went over to have a look,' the man replied, indicating, by a movement of his hand, the entrance to Bank Street. 'Other than that, no.' It wasn't just the head that was moving faintly, it was his whole body, thought MacGovern, turning up the collar of his coat and rubbing his hands together. And it wasn't booze, as his eyes were steady and his speech was coherent.

'Is there much activity along there, in Bank Street?' Lindsay inquired. 'It looks pretty much abandoned.'

'Some of the buildings are still in use, I think. Mainly for storage.'

'Such as?'

'These two at the end here.'

'What about the one with the purple door? Number 11. Down on the left. Have you seen any activity about it? Any coming or going?'

The man shook his head, then began fumbling with the zipper of his jacket, which, after several false starts, he finally managed to do up.

'It must get cold standing out here all day,' said MacGovern.

The man looked at him steadily for a moment, then shrugged. 'I have been in much colder places than this, believe me.'

In the silence that followed this statement, the attendant turned to look past both policemen, in the direction of the river, some thirty or forty yards distant.

'When do you finish here?' the Inspector asked.

'This carpark closes at nine, but I sometimes stay on. If there is work to be done, it is better when nobody's around.'

'Overtime must be useful.'

'Mr. Fields, the owner of the site, always makes sure that I have something extra in my pay at the end of the week. He's good that way. A bonus for helping out when it's needed.'

'And is it needed very often?

'No, just once in a while.'

The sound of a voice coming over a walkie-talkie interrupted the exchange.

'I have to go. I'm wanted elsewhere.'

'Thanks for your time,' said Lindsay. 'If you remember anything, you could let us know, Mr. . . . '

He held out a card with his contact details on it.

'Hansen. Pal Hansen. Leave it inside,' said Hansen, gesturing towards a wooden booth that stood just inside the car-park entrance. Lindsay slipped the card inside the pocket of the man's jacket as he turned and moved away from them.

The telephone was ringing when MacGovern entered his office the following morning. It was Philbert on the line.

'Good morning, Inspector. I hope you are well. I have studied the photographs of the premises at 11 Bank Street which you were good enough to send me yesterday. Is it convenient for me to speak about them just now?'

MacGovern replied that there were no other claims on his attention and that the Doctor could take as much time as he wanted.

'Good. So, what we can see positioned behind the glass of the window is two severed human hands, probably male, and a little on the small side. And nestling between the fingers and palm of each hand is a human eyeball. No idea what colour the eyes are, but they're certainly human. And, from what I can see, although it is not very clear, each hand-eye combination appears to point towards a different end of Bank Street. Both ends of the street are covered, so to speak. Now the first thing to note is that the fingers of each hand were deliberately arranged to look as they did, I am sure of it. It was not by chance, not an effect of *rigor mortis* or anything like that. And each shows a different arrangement of the fingers, which is to say, each hand creates a different hex or curse, for that is the reason they were made to look as they do. To cast a spell. The second factor is the eyes. I think that they were intended to watch over each end of Bank Street and to ward off unwanted attention. You have heard of the expression "to give someone the evil eye", yes? That, I think, is their purpose.'

Philbert paused, as though anticipating a question or remark, but MacGovern, who had been listening with interest to this unusual exposition, had nothing to say. He was, if anything, slightly annoyed by the ensuing silence, and mentally urged the good Doctor to proceed.

'There is a third factor. Were you aware that there was something written along the crooked forefinger of each hand? Perhaps not, as the text is small and rendered somewhat illegible by the dirty and discoloured skin. I was able to make out what it says: "*Ut mentos suos perdant qui prope veniunt*. The Latin means, "that they may lose their minds who come close". Which is to say, that anyone approaching the door, from either direction, would be likely to experience a reaction of some kind, a disordering of the senses perhaps, a feeling of anxiety or unease. A feeling strong enough to turn them away from the premises or discourage a second visit. Something of that sort.'

'What you're saying is that there is a triple hex in action at the site. That's a lot of negative energy, Doctor,' said the policeman.

'Yes, it is. To some extent, the effect of this hex will depend on the constitution of the individual who approaches the premises, and I do not mean their physical make-up. Some people are more spiritually susceptible to influences of this sort than others. The question which follows is, why put a hex on the property? In order to keep people away, is the obvious answer. But away from what? What is going on there?'

'That, I do not know, Doctor. There was no sign of activity when we visited the place yesterday morning.'

'It was just as well that you had company,' said Philbert. 'I would not like to be alone in the presence of such a powerful malign force. There is no knowing what effect it might have.'

MacGovern knew, but made no mention of his unsettling experience. Realising that his hand was making its way to his throat once more, and annoyed that this gesture was in danger of becoming an automatic and unconscious response to any mention of Bank Street, he thrust the offending limb into his trouser pocket.

'Was there no obvious sign of confusion or upset when you were there? No headache or nausea?'

Replying in the negative to Philbert's question, the policeman then related the details of the two incidents which had originally aroused his curiosity about the location.

'The hex does seem to have worked,' Philbert commented, 'in that it has undoubtedly produced confusion, in both man and dog. It strikes me, however, that this has had the unintended effect of drawing attention towards the place, rather than keeping it away. I wonder if there have been other such incidents.'

'One of the schoolboys did remark that he hadn't seen anyone in Bank Street for a number of weeks. There was little sign of life. It was never busy before that, whenever they passed on their way home from school, but the boy said that it had never seemed quite so deserted. I think the word he used was "desolate".'

'Probably the result of the hex.'

'It occurs to me now,' added MacGovern, 'that its effect on the dog may have been unusually pronounced. After all, they are sensitive creatures, and pedigrees even more so, from what I understand. I'm not sure about the foreign gentleman. The report said that he was recently widowed, but whether that could have any bearing on his susceptibility to such a malign influence, I couldn't say.'

'Perhaps, yes, as he must still be experiencing a degree of emotional disturbance. Well, whatever else is going on down there, Inspector, it is almost certain that you will have to add murder to your list of things to investigate. The congealed blood which can clearly be seen on the wrists of the severed hands would seem to indicate that the victim was still alive when the wounds were inflicted. They did not come from a corpse.'

MacGovern said that he had already accepted that probability, when he had first seen the images on Lindsay's phone.

'Before you visit the place again, and I assume that you intend to do so in the near future, please stop by King Street, as I have something you can use to nullify the effects of the curse and ensure your own safety.'

It was some days later, when MacGovern had managed to find a few hours to himself, that he took up Philbert's invitation.

'A simple countermeasure in order to protect you from further spiritual interference, Inspector MacGovern. It would be best to read it before attempting to enter the building,' said the Doctor, picking up and laying aside a number of volumes in his quest to find the one which he wanted. 'I remember leaving it down here only ten minutes ago.'

While Philbert continued his search, MacGovern wandered over to the piano to have a look at the bust which stood amidst the stacks of music. Fashioned in plaster, the subject's prominent nose and hollow cheeks, and the mass of hair swept back from the forehead, made for a striking effect. There was, however, no name on the sculpture, which only served to pique the policeman's interest even more. Turning his attention to the volume of music standing open on the piano, he saw pages black with notes, and muttered a single word: 'Impossible!'

'Found it!' cried Philbert.

MacGovern took the proferred book, and read aloud, "Do not fret because of those who are evil or be envious of those who do wrong; for like the grass they will soon wither … "

'The 37th psalm. It will dispel or nullify any existing negative influences. Recite it from either end of the street, before proceeding.'

When MacGovern suggested that he might like to join the expedition to Bank Street planned for the following morning, Philbert politely declined.

'I feel my time will be better employed in seeking further information about this cursed spot. There are always other sources, but one must know were they are and how to access them. That will be my task for tomorrow. If I find out anything of interest, I'll be sure to let you know.'

***

'How good are you with padlocks, Frank?' asked MacGovern as he fastened his seatbelt.

'I've never met one yet that was able to withstand the attentions of my bolt-cutter,' came Lindsay's reply. 'What are you thinking about?'

'A spot of breaking and entering. I'd like to get a look inside number 11. There's something going on in there, and I want to know what it is.'

'Easier to cut the padlock than try to open the mortice lock in the small door. That might take a lot of time.'

'Which is exactly what I don't want. I checked the padlock when we were last there. It was rusted over, which means that it's not been used in a while. Whoever's working there is probably using the other door, the smaller one. Less hassle.' Then, unwrapping a cloth-covered bundle which was resting on his lap, he continued: 'I found this old padlock in the garage in a box of tools that belonged to Marge's dad. It's about the same size and should do as a replacement.'

MacGovern followed Philbert's instructions with regard to neutralising the hex, watched from the car by Lindsay, who made no attempt to hide his scepticism, from his voice or looks. He had already seen enough of the strange, during the course of the previous days, not to feel greatly troubled by this latest manifestation of it.

They left the car in Cemetery Lane, parked between a flatbed lorry trailer and a large camper van, and made their way into Bank Street on foot.

It was the work of half a minute for Lindsay to cut the padlock and unwind and draw out the chain. He pushed the door open as far as it would go and then stepped back, turning to his superior to await further instructions.

Perhaps it was the expression on MacGovern's face that warned him that something was wrong, the look of expectant curiosity morphing into one revealing the beginnings of fright. Maybe it was the sound of movement coming from within the darkened interior, the creaking of a rope under strain or the hissing of displaced air. Whichever it was, Lindsay's reaction was to throw himself to the ground. He landed heavily on the cobblestones, knocking the wind out of himself, but his evasive action very probably saved his life.

Through the open doorway, at a height of about three feet above the level of the ground, a huge beam of wood came swinging out of the darkness. It missed MacGovern, who had leapt to one side at the first hint that something was not right, and whistled over the prone form of Lindsay, striking a glancing blow at his hand, which he had raised to protect his head.

When the beam swung back inside the warehouse, Lindsay pushed himself up and, his feet sliding on the cobbles, managed to scramble to safety. MacGovern tied a clean white handkerchief around the bruised and bleeding hand.

An examination of the beam, when it had come to rest, revealed that the ropes on which it swung were attached to the rafters high up inside the building, and that it had been secured by a simple retaining mechanism which had been released when the warehouse door was opened. They would have been safe had they used the smaller access door.

Located in the right-hand corner of the premises, just inside the entrance, was a circular iron staircase which gave access to the floor above. It was here, on the window sill, that Lindsay found the gruesome artefacts which his camera had first given a hint of. The smell of decaying flesh was strong and, when he prodded one of the hands with the tip of his pen, he found that there was no give in the flesh.

'There's no knowing how long it's been here. Fischer might be able to tell,' he said, referring to the police surgeon.

'Leave them where they are, Frank,' said MacGovern from below. 'I don't want anything moved, unless we can be sure of putting it back exactly as it was. What else can you see up there?'

'One empty rusting filing cabinet, a desk with no drawers, and that is it. Must have been an office when the building was in use.'

In the rear wall, opposite to the main entrance, was a second set of doors, smaller in size and opening inwards on hinges. MacGovern, trying not to get any more grease on his hands than was absolutely necessary, slid the locking bolt easily to one side and pulled them open. Cold, damp air rushed into the warehouse, and the sound of water lapping against the brick wall below his feet broke the silence. Directly in front of them and moving gently with the current was a small boat. It was secured by a rope which ran under the doors and was attached to a vertical iron column, one of the supports on which the roof structure rested.

The daylight which now flooded the interior from both ends revealed an industrial lamp and diesel generator, a diving suit draped over a chair, and breathing apparatus, the dial of which indicated that the tank was three-quarters full of air. In the corner, to the right of the doors and covered by a tarpaulin, was an old campaign-chest, fashioned out of dark wood and reinforced with bands of brass. Scarred and battered by years of use, it looked old enough to have been a relic of the Crimean War or some military campaign of even earlier date, and heavy enough to require the strength of two men to move when full. When MacGovern raised the lid, which was unsecured, he found himself looking at a jumble of small bones covering the base.

'What have we got here?' Lindsay asked, rejoining his boss.

'A treasure chest, Frank. But I don't see any gold or jewels.' MacGovern closed the lid again, and turned his attention to the other items. 'Looks like a diving operation. River salvage or what have you. I wonder why they didn't leave the bones where they found them. It doesn't do any good disturbing the remains of the dead.'

'They often find them when they start digging in these old places,' Lindsay remarked. 'Happens all the time. They'll rebury them in another spot, in hallowed ground. A local cemetery, most likely.'

'I suppose it could be archaeological work of some kind,' MacGovern conjectured, moving away from the chest. 'On the river bed.'

'Or structural. Replacing water-damaged brickwork.'

'Where's the cement? And the bricks? Why the desire to keep people away, if that's all they're doing?'

'Well, if they are hunting for treasure,' Lindsay replied, kicking the chest, 'they haven't been very successful.'

He climbed onto the boat and disappeared into the cabin, re-emerging some moments later with the information that there was more equipment below deck, another generator and some rubber hosing.

There was nothing else for them to see.

It took them the best part of twenty minutes to reset the booby-trap, but fixed in such a way that the device would fail to trigger, should anyone try to enter by the main door.

***

MacGovern and his wife were sitting in the kitchen later chatting over the day's events, when Mark popped in to say hello, his late arrival home the result of after-school sports practice. He kissed his mother on the cheek and gave his dad a fist-bump. As he turned to go, his dad caught hold of the bottom edge of his blazer.

'Just a minute, sonny. Let's have a look.'

On the breast pocket of the blazer, an elaborate Celtic cross was embroidered in gold thread, below which were the words *Spes Unica*.

'What does that mean?' he asked.

'Only hope. Sole hope,' said the boy. 'I thought you knew.'

'I had forgotten, but something happened the other day to bring it back to mind. I just wanted to check.' So that was the reason for the old man clinging to the schoolboy's blazer, he realised. The cross. As a protection against ... mental disturbance, evil? And when the boys wore their sports gear home after training, because it didn't have the school insignia on it, they were left open to the malign influence of the triple hex? 'Okay, champ, off you go and change. Dinner will be ready in ...?'

'... twenty minutes,' said his mother, 'so make sure you're not still in the shower or on the phone. And tell your sister.'

***

Philbert's second call to MacGovern came almost a week after his visit to Bank Street, towards the end of a busy afternoon in the Central Police Station.

'I decided to focus my attention on the period during which the prison was in operation, Inspector, as it seemed to me that, if anything unusual had occurred in that location, around Bank Street, it would most likely have been at that time. Before the prison was built, the site was open fields. When it stopped being used as a prison, it was allowed to fall into a state of ruin, before being demolished, and the land used for building the riverside trading premises which exist to this day. Having exhausted all available historical sources, I then began burrowing around in the religious archives of the city. Those in the Cathedral and the university were of some use, but it was in the library of the Bishop's Palace that I finally found what I was looking for. Are you still there, Inspector?'

MacGovern murmured an affirmative.

'The Reverend John Frederick Evans, D.D., preacher and scholar, was chaplain in Bank Prison for many years, and his name was the one constant in everything which I read pertaining to the establishment. However, his long tenure came to an unexpected close, when he put an end to his life. *Vitae finem fecit*, as the phrase is. He killed himself, Inspector. After his death, the records show that the prison chaplain was replaced every year, without fail, and that visits from the ecclesiastical authorities were conducted at least bi-annually. It seemed clear to me, from this sequence of events, that something had gone wrong, something which the bishop was taking pains to ensure could never happen again. What that was, I determined to find out. I continued my search. While working my way through a fifteen volume set of bound religious tracts and pamphlets, I struck gold. The last four volumes of the set were handwritten, not printed, and appear to have been bound at a later date, as minor differences in the style of the binding are apparent. They are a diary, Inspector, written in an elegant and educated hand, and in a condensed, but literate and comprehensible Latin. The diary of the Reverend Evans, begins in the year 1756 and ends with his death in March of 1772. Towards the end of the fourth and final volume, I came upon a book mark, a single sheet of A5 paper, printed on one side and folded in half. A copy should be sitting on your desk even as we are speaking.'

MacGovern shuffled through some files and memos. The brown envelope containing the aforementioned copy was hidden in their midst, hence his failure to notice it before.

The printed side gave details of forthcoming meetings of the city's Historical and Spiritual Society. A series of proposed talks, to be delivered at regular intervals over the winter, included one entitled Praying for Rain: The Gardener as Shaman.

'Inspector MacGovern?'

'I was looking over the leaflet. I had no idea that such a society existed. Some of the talks sound as though they might be rather interesting.'

'I have attended a number of the society's meetings over the years. The quality is really quite good, often rising to excellent.

And many of the speakers are amateurs, like myself. Have you examined the reverse yet?'

MacGovern turned the sheet of paper over and saw a series of tally marks covering much of the surface.

'Someone keeping a score?'

'Permit me to continue, and you shall be enlightened. My first reading of the diary produced nothing more than a feeling of disappointment, as it contains nothing of very great interest. The subject matter is really rather trivial—observations on the weather, tea-parties, house visits and such like. It was during the second reading that it occurred to me that the writer has employed a simple code. He has used an exclamation mark at the end of sentences where he has no business doing so. For example, "Afternoon tea with the Bishop!!" or "Cloudy again!!!" There is nothing exclamatory about such entries, and certainly nothing deserving of two or three exclamation marks. It was that which first caught my attention. I think that the exclamation mark is to be read as a number. I shall not detain you much longer, Inspector, I am almost there. The diary begins in May 1756, but it is not until July of 1758, two years later, that the writer begins to employ his code. The entries for that month contain a total of five exclamation marks. You will see that there are five tally marks at the top of the paper you are holding, yes? Then six and four, for the months of August, September; and so on. Quite why this code was employed, if it is indeed a code, I do not yet know. What I can say with certainty is, that the sheet of paper which you are holding is proof that someone else has recently been reading the Reverend's diary, and has kept a tally of those same exclamation marks, as their study of it progressed. It is easy to conclude that the individual is in some way connected with the Historical and Spiritual Society, perhaps a guest speaker, a private individual or an academic. That will be for you to determine, as I have other work to do. I shall be in touch later. Good bye, Inspector.'

MacGovern counted a total of 124 tally marks on the paper.

The next morning, postponing other work which he had intended to do, he spent some time pursuing enquiries into the Society. From the chairperson of the organising committee, a Miss Vigdis Birgisdottir, who was not at first inclined to be helpful, and then answered his enquiries only with a certain reluctance, he acquired the names and contact details of that year's speakers. The first three on the list presented no problems. The fourth, a Mr. Peterson, who had been scheduled to give a lecture entitled *Excavating the Pain: Revisiting Sites of Desolation*, didn't answer his phone, so he moved on to the remaining names. There was still no answer from Peterson when he tried a second time. He called Miss Birgisdottir again, in the hope that she might have Peterson's address or the number of his landline.

'No, I don't have any more information about him, Inspector, other than that he was an annoying little man. He was always rubbing someone up the wrong way. He badgered me until I agreed to let him give a talk to the Society. He was supposed to speak last Tuesday evening, but didn't turn up. There was no telephone call. Nothing. It was fortunate that one of the other speakers was able to take his place, as there was a room full of expectant attendees.'

'Do you happen to know what he meant by "Sites of Desolation"? It sounds like a strange title for a lecture.'

'It had something to do with those places in which the trauma of the events of an earlier age could still be felt in the present. A battlefield, say. Something of that sort. Yes, it does sound intriguing, doesn't it? Quite a number of the society's members said they were looking forward to it. Too bad he didn't show. Was there anything else?'

MacGovern thanked Miss Birgisdottir, and rang off. He wondered if the "excavation" of the title might include underwater work. And was Mr. Peterson missing, or just careless about attending to commitments and answering his phone?

There were other police matters to occupy his attention for the remainder of the day, so he thought no more about this puzzle.

Shortly after he had arrived home that evening, and was sitting in the car listening to a music broadcast on the radio, his mobile phone rang.

'Any progress to report, Inspector?' asked Philbert, coming to the point with unaccustomed frankness.

MacGovern shared the information which he had acquired.

'Yes, that is interesting,' Philbert remarked. 'And now it's my turn. The last two pages of the diary were stuck together, a fact which, unaccountably, appears to have been missed by whoever was making the tally marks. Although it occurs to me now, as I'm speaking to you, that they may simply have thought that trying to separate them was more trouble than it was worth. Anyway, Inspector, the pages were stuck together with blood. There was other matter present as well, probably tiny fragments of bone or brain. It looks as though an attempt was made to wipe some of this mess away, as it was smeared over both pages.'

'That sounds gruesome, Doctor,' MacGovern said, mildly surprised by the matter-of-fact manner in which this information was delivered. 'So the Reverend Evans and his diary came to a bloody end. Evidence of his suicide, I take it?'

'Yes, at a time when the balance of his mind was disturbed.'

'You mean, he was mad. You sound doubtful.'

'Well, you see, the very last word in the diary is incomplete. Evans has begun to write it, in his normal, neat and fluent hand, but it finishes in a mess of blotting and scoring, as though the hand which held the quill was suddenly no longer under control. A man does not shoot himself half-way through a diary entry, Inspector.'

'You think he was murdered?'

'The spattering of the blood on the paper suggests to me that he was shot in the head from behind and above, but that might only be my overactive imagination.'

'By whom and for what reason?'

'I cannot say, at the moment. There may be other pieces of the puzzle yet to be discovered. I'll let you know.'

As MacGovern slipped his phone back into his jacket pocket and opened the car door, he wondered at the note of weariness which had been audible in Philbert's voice. Dismissing the idea that he could be tired of the investigation so soon after its commencement, he concluded that, in the excitement of the moment, he was perhaps going at it too hard, and would have to learn to pace himself.

***

MacGovern's greeting was either unheard or ignored by Lindsay when he entered his superior's office the following morning.

'The knots in the rope which held the beam in place. Did you notice?' he asked, immediately coming to the point.

'I didn't pay much attention to them, Frank, I have to admit,' replied MacGovern, shaking his head. 'I was more interested in what we might find inside the building.'

He had an informal appointment to speak with a senior colleague about a matter which had been on his mind for some time, and had been gathering documents pertaining thereto.

'They weren't tied any old way,' Lindsay continued. 'They were very effective. That was a lot of weight they were keeping in place. I tried to undo one of them, but it was impossible. Whoever tied them must have known what he was doing.'

'The art of tying knots. I suppose it would be all of a piece with the boat and the diving gear. Someone with a nautical background. So what?'

'The chap we spoke to, the car-park attendant. Did you notice anything unusual about him?' There was the slightest of stresses on the last word of this question, which suggested to MacGovern that his assistant might not forgive, quite so easily, a second failure in the use of his powers of observation.

'I did say to you in the car, as we were driving off, that I thought he looked and sounded like a Nordic. Now that you mention it, though, he wasn't dressed like a janitor or odd-job man. Those heavy rubber boots and the waterproof overalls did seem out of place.'

'And all the while we were talking to him, he was in constant motion. He was unable to remain still. It was like he was . . .'

'. . . still on board a ship and moving with the waves. Well, yes, I did notice that. Hadn't got his land legs back.'

MacGovern picked up his folder and was moving towards the door. When he saw that Lindsay had nothing more to add, he said, 'He's maybe the one to speak to about the knots. Give me an hour or so, and then you can drive us both down there.'

They arrived at Church Street to find the gates of the car-park locked and the place deserted, apart from a regular client who was standing peering through the fence, apparently in the hope of finding someone who could tell him what was going on. He shrugged when asked if he knew where the attendant was.

The building, at the rear of which the car-park was located, had an entrance on this same street and, the main door being open, they entered. An examination of the ground floor revealed nothing of interest, so they climbed the stairs to the one above. Here they found a suite of offices, all of which were vacant, except for the last one on the right.

There were finger marks all over the glass panel of the door, and the office itself was shabby and in need of cleaning. The desk and chair were functional, but looked cheap, perhaps second hand, and rather poor at that. On the desk was a laptop computer and printer. The whole set-up had the appearance of a temporary base for a short-term operation, that might be packed up and moved in an instant, should the need arise.

Lying on the floor behind the desk, invisible to anyone passing along the corridor, was the body of a man. His hands, feet and neck were bound together with a single piece of rope, and in such a way that, should he move either of the former, the rope would gradually tighten about his throat, until he choked himself; which he appeared to have done. He wore a grey suit. A white handkerchief was visible in the breast pocket of the jacket. The bruise on his left cheekbone was evidence of an act of violence, likely intended to subdue the individual before trussing him up. How long the body had lain there, was impossible to say, but there was, as yet, no smell of decay.

When Lindsay examined the knots in the rope, he found that, although different from those used to secure the beam in the warehouse, they were as intricately worked and unusual in appearance as to suggest that the same person might have tied both sets.

In the room to the rear of this office, on a longish table by the window, they found a number of cardboard boxes laid out. Some were long and narrow in shape, others small and compact, and a very few, three in total, were large enough to contain an object about the size of a football. Those already wrapped in brown paper bore a handwritten address label, stuck on with clear adhesive tape.

MacGovern removed the top from one of the unwrapped boxes to reveal a black velvet bag, closed by a drawstring of the same colour. He opened this, and slid the contents, a long, heavy thigh bone, out onto the table. Lindsay lifted a bag from one of the large boxes and set it down. Loosening the drawstring, he drew off the covering to reveal a human skull, complete with lower mandible.

Something thudding against the window caused both men to start.

Then MacGovern's phone began to ring. He put it on loudspeaker and set it down beside the skull.

'Morning, Doctor. Sergeant Lindsay is here with me,' he said, and proceeded to describe what they had found.

Philbert's own researches had turned up material that was no less curious.

'One of the Reverend Evans's tasks was ministering to the spiritual needs of the prisoners in Bank Prison, especially those in the condemned cells awaiting execution, in order to ensure that they were prepared for the journey which they were soon to make. The sister of one these prisoners, a James Wilton, received a small package of his belongings in the days after he was hanged. It appears that Wilton had paid a handsome bribe to one of the gaolers to smuggle the bundle out of the prison and deliver it into her hands. Hidden in this was a letter, written by the unfortunate man in the hours before his execution, in which he lays an awful charge against Evans. He describes his horror at discovering that the Reverend, instead of committing his soul to the mercy of God, appeared to be dedicating it for eternity to the service of the Master of Lies. Wilton had been a scholar in his youth, before his life went awry, and was able to follow some of the Latin prayer which Evans spoke over him. This information, when it was noised abroad, caused an outcry. It was suspected that the Reverend's perversion of his religious office had been proceeding for some time, but for how long, no one was able to say with any certainty. We may never know how many souls were lost, although I might be able to hazard a guess.'

'124?' said MacGovern.

'Exactly so. The number of exclamation marks in the diary, and the number of tally marks on the paper.'

'So the condemned were damned for eternity by this Reverend Evans before they were hanged. Their corpses were gibbeted in public, and, when they had rotted away, their mortal remains were thrown into the river,' said Lindsay. He noticed MacGovern rubbing his neck again. The discomfort, whatever it was, clearly hadn't gone away. 'And what we are looking at now, is the bones of some of those prisoners?'

'Just so, Sergeant,' said Philbert.

'This is the treasure they were digging for on the river bed?' asked MacGovern. 'What possible use could they have for a lot of old bones?'

'There is a market for such gruesome artefacts, Inspector,' Philbert assured him, 'and they fetch considerable sums of money among collectors.'

'Collectors? Of old bones?' MacGovern, in his twenty-odd years of service as a policeman, had seen all manner of criminal activity, but this was certainly a first.

'Imagine you're an occultist and are having friends round in the evening for a seance. Candles and burning incense may help create an atmosphere, but there's nothing quite like a human skull to add a touch of the macabre. And if the skull happened to belong to a man, condemned and hanged for his crimes, so much the better. It adds a certain caché, don't you think? The poor fools! They can have no possible idea of the horror which lies in wait for them when they begin their silly games. A soul consecrated to the service of the Evil One, eternally restless, yet longing for peace. And summoned back to be a Friday evening's entertainment. Lord, save us!'

They could hear the tremor in the speaker's voice.

'Or teenagers playing with a Ouija board, using a finger or rib bone as a counter? That's likely to be an occasion they'll never forget.'

'I think I can imagine what might happen,' said MacGovern, his own recent experience recurring to mind with unusual vividness. 'Do you have any idea why Evans acted as he did?'

'I cannot be certain, Inspector. The judge who presided during the time when Evans was chaplain, was Augustus Milne, a man of vast legal learning, and a hanging judge, if ever there was one. He acquired a reputation, among his servants and his subordinates, for savagery, and there were suggestions that he was involved in "dark matters", which I take to mean that he was an occultist. Hypothesis, my hypothesis. Evans and Milne move in the same social circles.

They were, after all, men of learning and position. The Church and the Law were two of the three accepted occupations for men of good family, if they had no inheritance of which to speak. The other was the Military. The Reverend is somehow corrupted by his association with Justice Milne, and is persuaded or compelled to act on his behalf, that is, to ensure a regular supply of sacrificial victims to sate the hunger of Milne's demonic masters.'

'Why?' interrupted MacGovern. 'What does Milne get from this?'

'Forbidden knowledge, the assistance of infernal powers, who knows? Years pass. By accident or an act of providence, Wilton's letter and its contents are made public. Fearing exposure, the Judge has Evans murdered.'

'Or commits the murder himself,' suggested MacGovern. 'Tidying up a loose end.'

'A relative of one of Evan's many victims taking revenge?' Lindsay suggested.

Until a team of forensic officers arrived on the scene, the three men continued to discuss various aspects of the case, many of which would remain unclear.

MacGovern was allowed to see the list of clients which the tech department found on the computer. It was not extensive, but it did contain some interesting and well-known names—that of an Italian prince, for example, and an American billionaire; and those of politicians, academics, and so on, both domestic and foreign. The financial records indicated that the business had been active for some weeks, likely from about the time that the schoolboy had noticed the near complete absence of people from Bank Street, and that it had already taken in a surprising amount of money.

And what do we know of Mr. Peterson, the annoying little man with the red hair? The heavy chain bound round his legs keeps him weighted down on the river bed, out in the centre of the stream where the water is deepest. His body and handless arms are engaged in a gentle, slow-moving dance, but it is a dance seen only by the eyeless sockets in his head. For all that we know to the contrary, there he remains, to this very day.

Hansen, if that was his name, was never found, and no record of such an individual was discovered on the laptop.

Was Fields murdered, or did he kill himself, was a question that was much discussed in certain legal quarters. Learned journals of the law continue to publish, every so often, the considered opinions, pertaining to the case, of eminent men of that profession.

***

Some weeks after these events occurred, the Inspector paid Philbert a visit at his residence in King Street. As the two men were chatting, the Doctor opened a book which was lying on the table at his side and passed it over to the policeman.

What MacGovern saw was a colour reproduction of an oil painting. The figure in the portrait is resplendent in full wig and gown.

'Look at the name, Inspector,' said Philbert, the hint of a smile playing about his lips.

'Augustus George Milne, Lord Fyfe,' MacGovern read out.

Milne's right hand rests on a skull, about the base of which a coil of rope can be seen, although it is largely hidden, by the skill of the painter, or the intention of the sitter. The face is pale and narrow, the nose long and hooked, the eyes dark and menacing. The tension visible about the mouth looks like the grimace of a hard and brutal man. The sight of the knee-breeches, not plus-fours, and the silver buckles adorning the black leather shoes made MacGovern's eyes open wide. The ghosts of the dead and damned which he had seen in Bank Street had been so attired. And now here he was, looking at a depiction of the man who had sent them to their deaths. For what? Stealing an apple or a loaf of bread? Forging a signature on a cheque? And how many among their number had been innocent? He had noticed the indistinct faces of women and children disappearing in the swirls of mist. Young, old. Male, female. Guilty, innocent. All fodder for the hangman's noose. The Stealer of Souls had been well provided for during those years.

'Look at the right hand,' said Philbert, his voice cutting in on the policeman's reflections. 'Can you see that the fingers form the letter M? Now, is that M for Milne, or M for Mason? It is possible that, by such a hand signal, he is indicating that he is a brother of the lodge and a possessor of occult knowledge.'

***

For months after the conclusion of the investigation, every morning at 7am, a black Audi turns into Bank Street and comes to a halt outside number 11. Renning leaves his position in the driving seat to open one of the rear doors and assist his passenger out. This ageing man, stooped, and clad in the vestments of a Norbertine monk, his head covered by a cowl and the fingers of his right hand telling his beads without cease, enters the warehouse and prepares to say mass, at a makeshift altar, for the repose of the souls of the departed. Every day, for 124 days, this process repeats. 124 days, 124 masses, and 124 souls finally given their eternal rest.

A STRANGE STORY

'And now we go to the Shelbourne Hall,' says the female news reader, smiling into the camera, 'where, in little over an hour, Sir Archibald Menzies will receive his award of Freedom of the City from the Lord Mayor. Good evening, Maurice. What have you got for our viewers this evening?'

'Evening, Marion,' comes the confident reply. The image on screen changes to that of a young man, smartly attired in a blue suit, white shirt and elegant tie. He appears relaxed in his role as roving presenter, and his every word and gesture bespeak the professional. 'And a good evening to all of those who are watching from the comfort of their homes. I'm standing here on the steps of the Shelbourne Hall in the company of Sir Archie and Lady Frances Menzies,' he says, turning to the elderly couple. 'Sir Archie, it is good of you to give us a few moments of your time.'

'Always a pleasure, Maurice,' replies Sir Archie, great in stature, if not in inches. He is considerably shorter than his wife, but she is standing one step lower then he is, for appearances' sake. A flush of pleasure suffuses his cheeks and his eyes are bright and laughing.

'You must be proud that the city has chosen to honour you in this way.'

'It is certainly a very great honour, and I shall treasure the memory of the occasion.'

'Perhaps, for the benefit of our viewers and listeners, you would be good enough to share with us what you think it takes to be successful.'

'Well, Maurice, I am of the opinion that there is nothing which a man cannot accomplish, if he is prepared to work long and hard. And if he has the love and support of a good woman, so much the better.'

Sir Archie turns to his wife and smiles with great tenderness, raises her hand to his lips and kisses it. Cheering and clapping can be heard coming from members of the public who have gathered for the purpose of seeing this great son of their city. His display of affection has moved them.

'When I was a young man, not so long ago,' he chortles, 'I worked fiendishly hard. No matter what I did, I gave it my best. And, you know, it wasn't easy. I had the very devil of a job sometimes. Hell! Pardon me. Heck! If your viewers knew what I had to do to get where I am now, they would turn pale. I made a pact with the . . . eh . . . with myself, that, if ever I was successful, I would give back everything I had to him, to the people of this city, without whose help I could not have accomplished even a fraction of what I have.'

'Those are inspiring words indeed, Sir Archie. And it is a remarkable act of generosity, one entirely in keeping with your extraordinary record of charitable donations, I might add, that you have pledged your fortune to the city.'

'Maurice, money is not the root of all evil. The devil is, the devil of it is, that a man can do a lot of good with his money, and the best thing that he can do with it, is to give it all away. And that's what I'm going to do.'

'A wonderful gesture, Sir Archie.'

At this moment, a disturbance can be heard occurring somewhere off camera.

'Sir Archie? Is everything all right?' the interviewer asks, noticing a look of consternation appear on the old man's face.

'I'm . . . I'm fine, yes, yes. I was . . . ,' the old man replies, his voice trailing off.

'Recollecting a particularly sweet business deal, Sir Archie?' Maurice suggests, moving the microphone a little closer.

'Sweet? Yes, Maurice, life is sweet. Very sweet. It has been a wonderful journey . . . but I must be off now.'

Lady Frances appears concerned. She places a reassuring hand on her husband's arm, but he seems not to notice the gesture. He keeps looking off to one side, as though he has seen, perhaps among the crowd of onlookers, someone whom he recognises.

After repeating a question several times and getting no response from Sir Archie, the reporter hears the producer's voice in his earpiece telling him to bring the interview to a close.

'Well, there you have it, ladies and gentlemen. Sir Archie and Lady Frances Menzies. And now, back to you in the studio, Marion.'

***

Doctor Prenson is standing on one side of the bed, Doctor Robinson on the other. Their patient is lying perfectly still: no rising and falling of the chest is visible, no indication of life apparent in the trembling of an eyelid or the twitch of a limb. Robinson had tried holding a mirror to the patient's nose and mouth, but no misting appeared on its surface. The last of the bruising, if it could be called such, for it was unlike any that they had seen before, was disappearing before their eyes. The livid colouring about the jaw and neck faded, shrunk in size and gradually took on the pallor of the rest of the face, a whiteness that was made all the more striking by the contrast which it formed with the blackness of the patient's hair. The deep lacerations on the thighs were closing up of their own accord, and the lighter wounds on the arms and chest had already healed to such an extent that it was impossible to find any trace of them.

'What did the paramedics say?' inquired Prenson, the senior and more experienced of the two medics.

'They had problems getting a pulse,' replied Robinson. 'Then his heart rate was all over the place. Blood pressure up one minute and down the next. They couldn't get a needle into his arm to attach a drip.'

'And the wounds, what did they say about them?'

'Extensive, but . . . '

'But what?'

'There was no bleeding.'

Prenson nodded his head, not so much to indicate that he understood this latest odd fact in an increasingly odd case, or had a medical explanation for it, but simply to indicate that he had heard what his colleague had said. Uncertain how to respond to this information, he could only manage another question.

'Did you try to get a sample of blood?'

'Yes, several times. At first I thought the needle had failed to pierce the skin, as unlikely as it sounds, but when I looked closer, I could see that this wasn't the case. However, when I drew out the plunger, the tip of the needle seemed to come with it. It was as though the body was expelling it.'

'So no blood from the wounds and none from the body either. And what do the x-rays show?'

'Nothing.'

'Nothing?'

'They're all blank.'

'What do you mean "blank"?'

'They show nothing. No skeleton, no organs, nothing.'

'Are you telling me that the x-ray machine is not working?'

'No, it's working fine. At least, it was this morning, before we looked at the patient. What I'm saying is, that the x-rays we took of him are blank. It is not that they reveal no injury, it is that they reveal nothing at all. Blank.'

'But this is impossible. And the ECG? Surely that can give us something to work with.'

'Confusion. Noise. A signal so jumbled that it is, to all intents and purposes, meaningless. The MRI scan was no better. Same for the CT scan. We haven't done a PET scan or ultrasound yet, but I'm prepared to bet the result will be no different.'

Robinson waited for his senior colleague to make a suggestion as to how they might proceed, but he waited in vain. The older man moved over the window of the room and stood there, his hands in his trouser pockets, looking out over the hospital car park at the hills in the far distance, as though a possible solution to the enigma might be found there. When he turned back, he could only shrug his shoulders.

'I have no idea what to say. I've never seen anything like this before. Is it possible that all the equipment could have failed? Should we move him to another hospital and see if they can do any better? What do you think?'

***

'Fancy a walk along the riverside, sir?' asked Lindsay, sticking his head round the office door about a quarter after one o'clock. 'Fresh air and a sandwich. Get you away from the desk for an hour.'

'Sure,' replied MacGovern, with a sigh, laying down his pen and sitting back in his chair. 'What's the weather doing, Frank?' Yes, it would be good to get out for a while, he thought, yawning and stretching.

'Cold and dry,' came the reply. 'No need to bring your brolly.'

As an alternative to the staff canteen, with its noise and stodgy food, the idea couldn't be beaten.

They had reached the half-way point of the circuit, having stopped to satisfy their hunger at a stall selling hot rolls and snacks, and were about to cross over a footbridge to the other bank and begin their return, when MacGovern turned aside to lean on the railing for a moment and watch a vessel moving past them on the water. It looked like a private craft. The passengers inside were enjoying a celebration of some sort. A birthday party, by the sounds of it, he thought, as the clinking of champagne glasses and another wave of laughter reached his ears, both muted by the chugging of the boat's engine and the noise of water slapping against the hull. His musings were interrupted by a shout of 'Watch yourself!'

Lindsay had started forwards to try to intercept a man who was staggering towards the metal railing, with enough apparent momentum and so little control of his movements, as to be in danger of tipping over it and falling into the river. Lindsay had taken only a few steps, when the individual collapsed onto the pavement, his head striking the ground with a thud that could be heard by everyone in the vicinity.

It took a considerable effort on the part of the two policemen to get the fallen man to his feet again and half carry, half drag him to a nearby seat, one of many located at intervals along the riverside walk. The problem wasn't his size or that he was unduly heavy, but that he seemed to be incapable of coordinating his actions, and that his legs had turned to rubber and were unable to support him, so that he was, in effect, a dead weight to those holding him up. Their task was made all the harder by his apparent insistence on holding onto his umbrella, which served only to encumber his steps and those of his helpers.

'If you could just let me have the umbrella until we get you to this bench, you can have it back again,' said Lindsay, gently trying to ease it out of the man's hand.

'You're the second person to try and take it from me this afternoon. Get one of your own!' the man barked in reply.

His appearance made it difficult to estimate his age, but to Lindsay he looked to be in his fifties. The greyness of his face, drawn and badly shaven, his unkempt hair and dishevelled clothes all tended to create an air of despair, and no doubt made him look older than he was. When they finally got him seated, they had to continue holding him up, in order to prevent him from collapsing forward onto the ground again.

'Someone tried to take your umbrella, did they?' asked Lindsay.

'In broad daylight. But he didn't get it, as you can see,' the man said, with a faint note of triumph in his voice. He tried to raise the umbrella to reinforce his point, but hadn't the strength to do so.

'And why would someone want to steal your umbrella, sir? Much easier to go into a shop and buy one, don't you think?'

'He wanted to steal it, I'm sure of it. But . . . ' He broke off, as though to reconsider the veracity of this statement. 'He took a firm grip of it. That's what drew my attention to his presence.'

'I see. Well, why don't you tell us what happened, Mr. . . . ?'

'Fehler. Brian Fehler.'

'Take your time, Mr. Fehler. There's no rush,' said Lindsay, in his most reassuring manner.

Fehler appeared to engage in a silent debate with himself, as if to weigh up the pros and cons of this suggestion. His hands moved ceaselessly, appearing at first to dismiss it, then to express hesitation. After a minute of such deliberation, he gave himself a thumbs up.

'I haven't been quite myself for some time now,' he said, after clearing his throat several times. 'When things aren't going so well, and they've been pretty bad today, I come to the cathedral to speak with Father Gilbert. You know, the old priest with the beard and glasses, the tall one.' He raised up his free hand to reinforce this part of his description. 'We talked for a while, and then he suggested that I sit in the sun and fresh air for a half hour. He thought it might help clear my head. And that's when it happened.

That's when I felt the tug on the umbrella. I looked round and this chap is sitting right next to me. Just where you are now,' he said, half turning his head towards MacGovern.

Lindsay noticed that Fehler seemed unable to look at either of them directly, jerking his head away when he came close to making eye contact, a prospect which seemed only to increase his agitation. The reason for this strange behaviour Fehler then made clear.

'His eyes locked on mine. I couldn't look away. And then I could feel him climbing into my head and rummaging around in my thoughts. It was like he was picking at the stitches that were holding my mind together and everything was falling apart. I could feel the energy draining out of me.'

He slumped over to one side, his head sunk on his chest, and remained silent and inert for some minutes.

'Would you like us to take you somewhere?' MacGovern asked, when he began to show signs of life again. 'Shall I call a cab to get you home?'

Fehler shook his head.

'I'll be fine. I'll sit on here for a bit. Thanks, I'll be okay.'

'Before we go, Mr. Fehler,' asked MacGovern, rising to his feet, 'could you give us a description of this individual? We are police officers, and may want to pursue this matter.' He was doubtful of a coherent reply, given the confusion which the encounter seemed to have caused, but a smile appeared on Fehler's face, the first they had seen in their brief association.

'Lots of dark hair. He kept pushing it back from his forehead, I remember that. And his face was very pale.'

'You got a good look at him?' MacGovern said.

'I did,' Fehler replied, looking the policeman full in the face, if only for a moment. 'Today was the second time. I saw him yesterday morning as well, at the hospital.'

'Which one? The Northern General?' asked Lindsay.

'Yes. I was attending my fortnightly appointment with Dr. Humboldt, my psychiatrist. I normally come down in the lift, but it was full when the doors opened on the tenth, which is where Humboldt's office is, so I used the stairwell and walked down a couple of floors. I felt myself getting tired and decided to wait for the lift on the eighth. It was there that I saw him.'

Fehler steadily refused further offers of help, so they left him there, a scruffy, solitary figure, hunched over, his eyes closed, one hand still clutching his rolled up black umbrella; and turned their steps towards the footbridge.

'You know, when I passed the front desk the evening before last,' said MacGovern, when the two men had proceeded on their way in silence for some minutes, 'there was a bit of a rumpus going on. A woman complaining about someone trying to steal her scarf.'

'I don't see the connection,' said Lindsay, turning to look at his superior, and wondering if, while daydreaming about the pleasures of living on a houseboat, a pleasure in which he indulged whenever he came near the river, he had missed the relation of a relevant fact linking the two incidents.

'She was wearing the scarf round her neck. A dark blue silk one. It was elegantly tied and tucked into the collar of her coat. At least, it was when I saw her. There was no way someone could have stolen it without first unwinding it, or pulling her head off. The desk sergeant had quite a job trying to calm her down. Said that she should consider herself lucky he hadn't managed to get it.'

'Still not sure that I follow,' Lindsay replied.

'It was what the woman said next that stuck in my mind. She seemed to imply that she wasn't certain, after all, that it was the scarf that he wanted. Which I thought was strange, considering the vehemence of her former assertion.'

'Like Fehler, you mean?'

'Yes.'

***

Several hours later, when MacGovern was looking in the fridge for something to nibble on before his evening meal, he heard the news reader on the radio, after reporting on the day's main events, mention an accident which had taken place on the river. The report said that a middle-aged man had fallen into the water, and had been rescued from almost certain drowning by a boat which had been in the vicinity at the time.

Only one of the local newspapers made any mention of the incident in its next day's edition. "Brain Fehler, 44, a married father of two, and formerly employed as an accountant in the Menzies' Group, was pulled out of the river by . . ."

It was Lindsay who drew his attention to a second report, this consisting of a few column inches in an inside page of the previous day's edition of the same paper, of the arrest of a woman for trying to steal an expensive handbag from Olivia's Luxury Emporium.

'It's the same woman who reported the attempted theft of a scarf the day before yesterday, sir, the one you mentioned. I checked the name with the desk sergeant.'

'Well, this is strange,' was all that MacGovern said in reply. 'Was there a description of the suspect, the alleged scarf-stealer?' he asked, wondering if there might be a connection between the two incidents.

'It looks like it might be the same guy who tried to take Fehler's umbrella. Pale complexion, with a full head of dark hair.'

'So, we have two attempted thefts occurring on two consecutive days, in each of which, the supposed object never really seems to have been in serious danger of being taken. That is to say, the scarf and the umbrella. A fact which is unusual in itself. Why pretend to steal something? What is more, . . .' MacGovern mused, rubbing the pads of his forefinger and thumb together, as though testing the strength of a conjecture which yet remained unspoken.

'Each of the victims is then involved in a more serious incident sometime later, as the principal actor,' said Lindsay.

'It is rather curious. There does appear to be a pattern here, Frank, but we've only got the two incidents to go on. See if you can find out a bit more about the woman's background. Give her a call. And keep an eye open for anything even remotely similar happening. I'm going to drive over to the hospital and make a few inquiries of my own. See you later.'

A nurse at the reception desk on the eighth floor of the Northern General confirmed that an individual, matching the description which Fehler had given, had indeed been admitted on the evening of Monday the 16th, shortly after 9pm. He had been registered under the name Smith, because they had found no identification on him, and had been assigned to the care of Doctor Robinson, to whose office MacGovern was then directed.

The doctor's office was empty, but MacGovern found him in the corridor leaning against a vending machine and sipping a cup of coffee. He had just finished his shift, and said that he would be more than happy to give the policeman a few minutes of his time, then led the way to a quiet corner where they would be able to talk without being interrupted.

Robinson needed little prompting to tell his story, and MacGovern listened to the narration with increasing disbelief, a feeling which he was unable to prevent manifesting itself on his face, which in no way appeared to discourage the doctor. What he was hearing was impossible, to medical science and common sense, and yet here was this experienced and rational man telling of it in a manner so matter-of-fact as to suggest that what he had seen was almost an everyday occurrence. The doctor finished by saying that the decision to move the patient to another hospital for further testing had been forestalled by his sudden disappearance.

MacGovern thanked Robinson, left him to finish his coffee, and was already some way along the corridor in the direction of the lifts, when he heard a male voice calling his name. He turned to find the doctor following him.

'Would you mind stepping in here for a moment, Inspector?' Robinson asked, pushing open the door to a room full of medical supplies. 'There was something else which I wanted to say to you.'

He closed the door and stood with his back against it, his feet planted on the floor in such a way as to make it clear that he wished to prevent anyone else from entering and perhaps inadvertently overhearing what it was that he wanted to say.

'Are you a religious man, Inspector?' he inquired.

'Not especially, Doctor. Why do you ask?'

Robinson was nervous and appeared unsure how to begin.

'The eye reflex test which I did on the patient when he was brought in is a standard test. Shine a light on the pupil to see how it reacts, yes? Well, that's not what happened.' He broke off and looked over MacGovern's shoulder, unwilling or unable to meet the policeman's eye.

MacGovern waited in silence, watching the doctor shifting his weight from one foot to another.

'I had an affair with one of the nurses. Jean,' Robinson began, after taking a deep breath and letting it out slowly. 'It went on for three months. It's over now. My wife didn't know anything about it, I'm sure of it. Jean promised me that she hadn't told anyone. I've no reason to disbelieve her. It ended amicably.'

'It happens,' said MacGovern. As to the ending being amicable, he felt less certain, but said nothing to that effect.

'He seemed to know. The patient, I mean. When I looked into his eyes, it was all there. Jean and me together. In her flat. In the restaurant. It was all there, like someone had filmed us together.'

The disbelief was evident in his voice and there was a puzzled look on his face.

'How could he know? I don't understand,' he went on. 'And that wasn't the worst of it. First it was Jean and me, then me and the wife and kids. Back to Jean and me holding hands, kissing. Then me and the family. Back and forth. Jean, the wife. Jean, the kids. Just to drive home my deceit, I suppose, and make me feel even worse. At that point, Inspector, something strange happened. I could feel something beginning to stir within the patient. There was no movement, you understand, no visible reaction. I could feel . . . a certain . . . energy.'

'And you think that all this happened as a result of your conducting the test?' MacGovern asked. He wondered if the doctor's nerves weren't simply overwrought as a result of tiredness, and that he was imagining things, this notion that he had been found out, that he had been watched by a third party. Was it a case of blackmail, by a colleague jealous of the nurse's attentions? Had the doctor's wife or family suspected him of marital infidelity and employed a private detective to film the lovers together? And what he had seen was simply a playback of the evidence, which had caused him so much guilt, he had unburdened himself to the first person whom he thought he could trust? If that was one possible explanation for the occurrence, why concoct such an improbable story? But, even as he asked himself this question, he remembered the reason for his visit in the first place. What the doctor had just described to him was similar to Fehler's experience; similar, but not the same. Robinson, apart from the guilt which plagued him, appeared to be fully functioning at a high level in his demanding job, whereas Fehler had given every indication of being a physical and mental wreck of a man. 'Were you the only one to do the test?' the policeman asked. If he could find someone else who had had a similar experience, he might be more inclined to believe this tale of a man's misdeeds being revealed to him in the eyes of another.

'As far as I know. Maybe Doctor Prenson did it as well. You should speak to him.'

MacGovern did, but Prenson had nothing unusual to tell, or, if he had, was not prepared to share it with anyone.

***

In the afternoon of that same day, shortly after three o'clock, no further reports of strange encounters having come to his attention, MacGovern made his way on foot from his office to Philbert's residence in King Street. When shown into the library by Renning, he found the Doctor sitting in front of a computer screen, so absorbed in what he was doing, it was some moments before he realised he had a guest. It was the quiet buzzing of the Inspector's mobile phone in his jacket pocket that broke the Doctor's intense concentration.

'Hello, Inspector,' Philbert said, in rather a distracted manner and without looking up. 'Your visit is timely. I had thought of calling you, but you have saved me the trouble. There is something which I want you to look at. I am going to show you television footage of Sir Archie Menzies, taken a couple of nights ago on the steps of the Shelbourne Hall. You were aware, I suppose, that he was to be the recipient of an award?'

'Yes. It's been all over the papers for the last week.'

'Difficult to miss, I suppose. There were two cameras from the TV studio present at the ceremony. One recorded an interview with the great man, and the other, located farther back in the grounds, filmed the building and gardens, the arrival of guests, and such like. I have managed to obtain a copy of both. The studio were initially reluctant to comply with my request, so I called the MD.'

'Friends in high places,' murmured the policeman.

'It can prove useful.'

Philbert brought two images up on screen and arranged them side by side, the better to allow comparison. They are magnified images of Sir Archie's eyes, taken from different parts of the interview, when he was looking directly into the camera. In the darkened room, the effect is somewhat startling.

'What do you notice?' asked Philbert, shifting to one side to allow his guest to get a closer look at the screen.

He watched MacGovern glance from one image to the other and back several times, but saw no look of discovery appear on his face.

'The light has gone out of his eyes. Can you not see it?' Philbert said, pointing to the second of the two stills. 'I saw it immediately when I began examining the footage, although I dare say I already had some inkling about what was going on. One can also see how the healthy colour of the skin has drained away. A greyness has set in, and the eyes have taken on a blank look. If you study the interview, his whole body seems to collapse in on itself. It is as though the life force has gone out of him, physically and mentally.'

'Now that you mention it, the difference is striking,' said MacGovern. 'But why the interest?'

'You are aware that he did not receive his award from the Mayor? Straight after this interview, he returned home. A passing ill-humour, was how the press described it.'

'And this temporary indisposition was the reason you asked for the camera footage?' asked McGovern.

Philbert shook his head. 'His physical health is of no interest to me, Inspector, except in so far as it might be an indication of something else which is going on inside the man.'

'Something else?' MacGovern was feeling increasingly lost.

'I have met Sir Archie on a number of occasions in the past. He is a regular at charitable events, musical evenings, that sort of thing. I don't know him at all well, but a nodding acquaintance has grown up between us over the years. In consequence, I received an invitation to attend the Lord Mayor's award ceremony. I decided not to go, as I had rather a lot of work to be getting on with. I did, however, listen to the radio broadcast. Have you heard it, Inspector? The interview does not last for very long, just a few minutes, but it was most interesting. Arresting, in fact. I couldn't quite believe what I was hearing. I had to stop what I was doing and listen to it again.'

Philbert then played an audio recording of the broadcast.

'It is not just the strange ending to the interview that caught my attention. Listen to how flat his tone of voice has become and how drawn out his words are. The thing which struck me most of all, however, was the number of references to the diabolical.'

'Surely only figures of speech,' suggested MacGovern. 'Nothing more serious than that. He's only being humorous, as I believe he is want to be. It's one of the traits that so endears him to the public. An eminent man who has managed to retain a boyish sense of humour.'

'I cannot agree with you there, Inspector,' replied Philbert, frowning and shaking his head. 'One such remark would have been neither here nor there, I grant you that, but there were at least half-a-dozen. The devil, hell, a pact, evil. They are all there, for everyone to hear, although I would be surprised if more than one person in ten thousand noticed it. No, I am convinced it is significant.'

'And what do you think that he is signifying?'

Philbert remained silent, tapping his fingertips on the surface of the desk. It was unlike him to be reticent, MacGovern thought, beginning to suspect that it might herald something out of the ordinary.

'I think that he is signifying the source of his worldly success,' Philbert finally replied, 'nothing more or less. It is as clear as the summer sun, Inspector. Sir Archibald Menzies owes his vast wealth and all that goes with it to a power which is not of this world. And it is a power which has now, I think, decided to claim its reward.'

'You're saying that his success is owing to a pact which he made with . . . ?' The question remained incomplete. MacGovern was a man who was accustomed to dealing with the real problems of a real world, one to which his five senses were attuned. In spite of his past dealings with the Doctor, and all which that had entailed, he still felt a certain reluctance about venturing into other realms. That it was always best to search for the simplest possible explanation covering all of the known facts, and an explanation which could be verified, had been a lesson that was dinned into him, during his years of training, by men of experience. But, even as these words from the past echoed in his head, the tale which Doctor Robinson had told that very morning rose up to silence them.

Philbert narrowed his eyes at the policeman for a second.

'…with the Evil One, my dear sir. When still a very young man, yes. Listen again to what he says.'

Replaying the significant part of the recording several times, the references are indeed unmistakable.

'And his apparent confusion and the other changes that you noticed?' asked the policeman, prepared to accept the possibility that the doctor's point had some validity.

'I think that something happened, during the course of the interview, to make him aware that he is shortly to pay the price for his success. He knows or suspects that his time is up. The cup which once overfloweth has now run dry.'

'I wonder,' MacGovern murmured. 'Replay the recording one more time, if you would, Doctor. Can you hear that noise in the background? There!'

'I had not noticed it. A minor commotion among those who have gathered outside the hall, perhaps. Or are you going to tell me otherwise?'

'It was the sound of an accident, I am pretty sure of it. And the victim has proven to be more than a little unusual, from a medical point of view.'

Philbert listened with unwavering attention, his elbow resting on the desk and his chin on his hand, to MacGovern's description of the two unusual incidents which had taken place on the city's streets during the previous days, and of his visit to the hospital and what he had learned about the accident outside the Shelbourne Hall on the evening in question.

'And this individual, the victim of the accident, appeared from where exactly?' was Philbert's first question, this narration of events complete, as he turned his attention to the computer again.

'Out of the shrubs to the right of the hall. The driver of the vehicle said that he appeared out of nowhere and came running straight at him.'

'Out of nowhere? He must have come from somewhere. If we're lucky, the cameras may have captured something. Let's have a look at the footage from the second one.'

The Shelbourne Hall appears on the screen. The camera pans left, pausing for a moment on the shrubs, the manicured lawns and the imposing bronze life-size statue of Lord Shelbourne, the long-dead benefactor, a part of whose fortune had been the source of the building fund. It then moves slowly right, so that the viewer is able to appreciate the magnificent frontage, comprising two impressive towers at either end of a long, central section. Guests and members of the public are seen gathered around the spot where the interview is taking place.

It was MacGovern who noticed the change first, in the night sky, some distance above the right-hand tower, where the darkness appeared to become less black, less inky. The air is in motion, a movement not unlike the roiling of clouds. When Philbert increased the zoom and slowed the footage down as much as possible, this same small area of vibrating air was seen to move downwards. In two or three seconds, it has disappeared behind the tower.

Philbert played the footage over and over again, some eight or ten times, his eyes never moving from the screen. He finally paused the film, rose from the desk, and moved over to the fireside, where Renning had set down a tray of refreshments on the low table beside his armchair.

MacGovern thought the tea unusually good, even beyond what he had previously tasted there.

'Darjeeling first flush, with a hint of lemon, Inspector,' said Philbert, in answer to his guest's unspoken question.

MacGovern took another sip. The temperature was just right, and not the least hint of tartness. And there was a plate of the most inviting looking iced gingerbread as well. 'So, now we also have something falling out of the night sky to contend with, in addition to everything else. What could it be?' he asked.

'The very same which collided with the vehicle, if I am not much mistaken,' replied Philbert, 'although in a considerably altered form. The change in Sir Archie's behaviour begins a moment after the vibration appears in the sky above the Shelbourne Hall. That much is clear from synchronising the footage from both cameras. I would be prepared to bet that the two things are connected.'

He stirred his tea slowly and with an unusual degree of concentration for some moments, then continued, 'I think that what we have just seen might be the instrument of his demise. An angel of darkness come to do the bidding of its master. I think that it has come to collect the sum owing.'

'What sum?'

'His soul, Inspector. Sir Archie's soul. What else?'

In the silence that followed these words, MacGovern realised that he had well and truly moved beyond the realms of the everyday, and was about to comment to this effect, when his mobile phone began to buzz once more. This time he felt unable to ignore it.

'Just an update on the woman with the scarf, sir.' It was Lindsay on the other end of the line. 'She worked as a secretary for the Menzies' Group. Resigned last year, after six years with them. Hasn't worked since.'

'Did she say why she resigned, Frank?' MacGovern inquired. 'Did something happen? I'm going to put the phone on speaker, so that Doctor Philbert can hear you.'

'It was a good job. Well-paid, reasonably interesting work and so on,' Lindsay replied. 'But she said that she just couldn't continue working there. She wasn't overworked or harassed or bullied, anything like that. One day, she felt that she just had to leave, to get away. And it was only when she finally did so, that she realised just how low her energy levels had fallen. She described it as being like a slow decline, but isn't sure when it began. There was no one incident which stands out in her mind as being responsible, no argument with a colleague, nothing like that. And the change from day-to-day, from week-to-week was so slight as to pass unnoticed.'

'She didn't have another job to go to and hasn't been in work since then?' MacGovern asked.

'No, she hasn't felt well enough. Her GP thinks it might be a depression, and has offered medication and counselling, but she has, so far, refused all offers of help. She is recovering, of that she is convinced; but progress is slow. The world has begun to take on colour again. She hadn't been aware of just how grey everything had become, even her clothing. Used to wear bright colours all the time, reds, blues, greens, what have you. You known the way women dress. Took to buying darker colours, flat shoes, and left off her brooches and other jewellery.'

'And what did the lady have to say about the theft of the handbag, Sergeant Lindsay?' inquired Philbert, who had been listening to the foregoing details with his arms folded over his chest and his head cocked to one side.

'She has no idea what happened, Doctor Philbert. Called it a moment of madness,' came the reply. 'Can't quite believe it. But she is certain that it had something to do with the encounter with our pale-faced stranger. Is convinced of it.'

'Thank you, Sergeant Lindsay,' said Philbert and, turning to his guest, 'Perhaps, Inspector, you would be good enough to allow me to ask the sergeant to contact this Mr. Fehler and find out about his experiences working for the Menzies' Group?'

'Yes, Frank, that's what to do now. Thanks.'

'What do you make of that?' Philbert asked, when MacGovern had returned his phone to his jacket pocket.

'You think it's relevant, all that stuff about her suits and shoes?'

'Oh yes,' said Philbert, without a second's hesitation. 'Very much so. Do you remember what I said about the change in Sir Archie's complexion? The loss of colour. The lifeless grey pallor. But in his case, the alteration was instantaneous; it did not take five or six years to appear. And it was real, not just a metaphor used by a lady to describe the effects of her low mood on her surroundings. You have seen it for yourself, Inspector,' he said, gesturing towards the computer on his desk.

Their meeting ended at that point, as Renning entered the library to announce the arrival of another guest.

'I'll be off now, Doctor, and I'll let you know of any further developments,' said MacGovern, over his shoulder, as he turned and walked to the door.

'Good afternoon, Inspector,' Philbert replied, rising from his desk. 'Renning, would you be good enough to show the Inspector out?'

***

Even as they were engaged in this discussion, a third incident of a similar nature was taking place in the city, within fifteen minutes' walk of King Street. A young woman, described by the solitary witness to the event as behaving in an erratic manner, stepped off the pavement into the path of an oncoming bus. The driver hit the brakes and pulled down hard on the steering wheel, causing the vehicle to veer into the other lane, where it skidded to a stop, its front wheels mounting the pavement. As chance would have it, the lane was empty of traffic at the time, and the pavement of pedestrians. Investigations revealed that this woman fitted, in every way, the emerging pattern.

'Employed as a currency analyst in the investment arm of the Menzies' Group,' said Lindsay, reading from his notebook. 'A Miss Brampton. Left seven months ago, after working there for four years. Interesting job, great salary, good prospects. Arrived at work one morning, but was unable to enter the building. Said her legs wouldn't carry her forwards. She stood on the pavement outside watching her colleagues going in through the doors, then returned home. Emailed in her resignation. She's had no contact with any of her former workmates since. Has taken to doing gardens, not for the money, though, as she's fairly well off.'

'One more casualty of the Menzies' Group,' remarked MacGovern. 'And the accident?'

'She had been lunching with a friend in the city centre, and decided to walk home. She took one of those quiet streets that lead down to the river, Octagon Street, I think,' Lindsay continued, referring to his notebook again, but he was unable to find the information which he sought. 'Anyway, she was half-way along the street when she felt a hand on her shoulder, which gave her a fright, as she hadn't heard any footsteps behind her. When she looked round, she locked eyes with our dark-haired friend. The encounter didn't last any more than a minute or so.' He closed his notebook.

'And . . . ?'

'Five minutes later, she nearly walked under a bus. Very lucky woman.'

***

With each day that passed, the tally of incidents of a similar nature increased by one, and the newspaper reports grew in length, from a few inches in a side column to a quarter of a page, all the while moving inexorably towards the front of the paper.

Since none of the victims was subject to a physical assault, and the witnesses, as few in number as they were, became confused when giving whatever details they could of the different events, even to the point of contradicting their own statements, MacGovern, at a loss as to how to proceed, told his officers to be on the look-out for anyone matching the description which Fehler had given him.

He wakened every morning, wondering when and where the next incident would take place, certain that it was only a matter of time before he would be dealing with a fatality. It was this growing anxiety that occasioned his next visit to Philbert.

Their discussion picked up at the point where it had left off, some days previously.

'Are you still convinced that this thing, this . . .' MacGovern began, uncertain how best to describe the alleged perpetrator.

'. . . demon, spirit, an imp of Satan. It is permitted to use such words, Inspector,' said Philbert, with the faintest trace of a smile on his face.

'Are you still convinced, Doctor, that this demon has come for Menzies, and, if so, why? And why is it attacking other people, and in an apparently random manner?'

'In answer to your first question, I am as certain as I can be that Menzies is the key to this mysterious sequence of events, Inspector, for the reasons which we have already discussed. Is it possible that he was unwilling to fulfil his part of the bargain, supposing such a compact was indeed made? Even old men, men who have tasted many of the pleasures that life has to offer, to the point of satiety and beyond, can be reluctant to leave behind their grand houses and beautiful mistresses, their art collections and fast cars. Let us say that he has decided to avoid paying the bill which has now become due. What would you do, as a tradesman, say, if one of your clients was unduly tardy about paying up, MacGovern? Hmm?'

'Send in a debt collector,' the policeman ventured.

'Precisely so. A debt collector. Now think of what Doctor Robinson told you. Medical anomalies do exist, but, however distorted and grotesque they may be, they are still human beings, with blood, bones, internal organs and so forth, all of which can been seen. Spiritual creatures, on the other hand . . . spiritual creatures, good or bad, are an entirely different matter, if you will pardon the pun. This would explain why none of the medical tests at the hospital worked. What we have here is a hostile spirit, not incorporeal, like you read of in books or see in horror films. Nor is it occupying another human body. It is not a demonic possession of some kind. Rather, it has simply created for itself a carapace, a covering which has every external resemblance to a human body, but it is a resemblance which is literally only skin-deep.'

The intensity evident in the Doctor's manner of speaking at this moment was so great that MacGovern found himself hanging on his every word.

'To answer your second question, Inspector. It is attacking them. That is exactly what it is doing. Like all beings, it requires sustenance, but the demonic thrives on negative sources of spiritual energy, such as sadness, despair, anger. We can now say, without the slightest doubt, that the victims of its predations are all former employees of one of Menzies' many companies, except for Dr. Robinson, and that all of them appear to have suffered, to a greater or lesser degree, a psychological trauma of some kind. I cannot say that this was a result of the work which they were doing, as none of them were employed in what we might call a difficult or particularly stressful capacity; they were simply doing what they were paid to do, as a secretary, accountant, analyst, what have you. No, I am inclined to think that there is a toxicity in the environment, an unwholesomeness, to which they were particularly susceptible and from which they could not escape, except by terminating their employment. For some of these unfortunates, the process took five or six years, while others were unable to endure as many months. And not one of them has been able to say what triggered this decline, that there was one incident which could be said to have been responsible, or even that they were aware that something untoward was taking place.'

'A subtle malign influence. Stemming from what, do you think, Doctor?'

'From Menzies himself, if I am not much mistaken. Directly, in his daily intercourse with his staff, or indirectly, because whatever he touches receives the mark of his own corruption. He would not be the first man to have hidden his nefarious deeds behind an outward veneer of respectability.'

'And why are there not more of these damaged people?'

'I imagine that there are a great many of them, moving around this city, slowing recovering from the effects of the spiritual poison to which they have been exposed, and soon to be prey to this entity, this demonic spirit.'

'What I don't understand is, what happened outside the Shelbourne Hall on the Monday evening? Why did it not take down Sir Archie then, if he was its principal target?' asked MacGovern.

'In its physical form, it was involved in an accident, a collision with a lorry, which resulted in a temporary incapacitation, and a running down of its battery. It was the doctor's guilt about his affair which provided the energy which it required to get moving again. That's what Robinson meant when he said that he felt a stirring somewhere within the patient. His negative emotional energy got the motor running, if we could put it that way. If it hadn't been Robinson, it would have been someone else, a nurse, an auxiliary. You are asking me what would have occurred if this accident had not taken place. I cannot imagine. Something utterly horrifying. Like . . .'

Philbert paused, as though trying to find a satisfactory analogy, but he was unable to do so, and remained silent.

'And what better time could there be?' mused MacGovern. 'The man is at the very height of his worldly fame. Universally honoured and esteemed. His fall from grace would have been very great.'

'And it will be yet, although there may be no one around to see it.'

Here the conversation broke off, and Philbert sank back into his armchair.

The only light in the room came from the coals glowing in the grate, all that remained of the splendid fire which had greeted the policeman on his entry. Unseen by his guest, in the lengthening shadows, Philbert closed his eyes and retreated within himself.

In the stillness of the library, the silence disturbed by the soft ticking of a clock in a far corner of the room, MacGovern's attention was caught by a movement on a tapestry hanging on the wall immediately to his left, at the side of the marble fireplace. It may have been his tiredness, or a trick of the firelight playing on the silver and golden threads woven into the tapestry's design, but he seemed to see the figures shifting and the colours changing. The hunting scene which it depicted came alive, and he could hear the distant sound of a horn and the baying of dogs getting louder and louder. He was moving quickly, but his limbs were growing heavy. Branches struck his chest and face, and a huge hunting spear, its broad, razor sharp blade glimmering in the half-light of the forest, flew past his head and embedded itself in the trunk of a tree, the shaft vibrating and humming from the energy with which it was propelled. It was then that he realised that he was the prey, he was the one they were pursuing. He felt a searing pain in his leg and another in his back. The hounds were on him and they were tearing at his flesh. He raised his head and bellowed, like the stag he had become.

'I see you're enjoying my tapestry, Inspector.' Philbert's voice, sounding strangely disembodied and distant, although its owner was sitting only eight or ten feet away, dispelled the vision in a trice. 'The next time you visit, if you're feeling curious, do have a look at this one,' he added, indicating, by the merest flicker of his index finger, the tapestry on his own side of the fireplace. 'It shows the martyrdom of a mediaeval saint.'

'A hanging?' asked MacGovern, resisting the desire to raise a hand to his neck, as the memory of a previous experience flashed through his mind.

'No, a burning at the stake. And a most convincing depiction.'

This reply was followed by a heavy sigh, as the speaker stretched out and crossed his legs. Listening to the sound of Philbert's soft regular breathing for some moments, the Inspector, thinking his host must have fallen into a doze, rose from his armchair, set down his cup and saucer on the tray, and quietly stepped over to the middle of the three large windows. He stood there for some time, looking down at the pedestrians passing by on the street below. A shabby suit, shiny at the knees and elbows, might reveal a man for whom dress was not important, or one who had not the means to improve his attire; dyed hair and a heavily made-up face, a woman trying to make herself look ten years younger than she was. These external indicators he could read, with varying degrees of success; but what was it that allowed this being to "see" or feel a potential source of energy? And, if the forces of law and order were unable to track down and apprehend the offender, how would they be able to prevent any harm coming to Menzies himself?

'There is nothing that we can do to save Sir Archie from his fate, Inspector,' said Philbert, his voice breaking in on the policeman's cogitations. 'That was decided the moment he sold his soul for the proverbial thirty pieces of silver. The outcome is inevitable.'

This interruption served, in part, to answer the second of these questions, and, since it was not the only occasion on which Philbert appeared to have been able to read his thoughts, it surely required no great stretch of the imagination to accept that there might also exist those who could read a person's mental state. Quite how they might profit from it, was another question entirely, but one to which his own experiences suggested an answer. During his years on the force, he had witnessed the rapid rise of a certain female officer into the senior ranks. He had been asked to assist on some of the investigations which she had led, and, being present at the morning briefings which she had given to her teams of officers, had marvelled at the change which took place in her demeanour, during that short period of ten or fifteen minutes. The small, slim woman, whose first words to the assembled group were always a hesitantly mumbled "good morning", had then seemed to suck up all the available energy in the room, until she quite dominated everyone in it, becoming the centre of all attention and the source of all ideas. If her diminutive size did not increase, in consequence of this change, her bearing certainly did, so that even the most physically intimidating of male officers were quick to step out of her way when she approached. In that case, yes, he could see how it might be possible that this strange entity could be sustained by its predations.

'And can we be sure of what that outcome is, Doctor?' asked MacGovern, his thoughts returning to the matter in hand. The prospect of this series of psychic attacks extending indefinitely into the future was beginning to make him a little uneasy, a feeling not likely to be mitigated by the admission that his officers stood little chance of apprehending the offender. 'Is it possible that Menzies is not the target, but that the aim is, rather, to draw public attention to the corruption at the heart of his business empire?'

'I must confess that I had not considered that possibility, Inspector,' came the reply. The suggestion seemed to give Philbert pause for thought, as he pulled out a white handkerchief from the cuff of his suit jacket and mopped his brow, a gesture which also just happened partly to conceal the look of consternation which passed over his features at that moment.

'We can already see the effect which these incidents are having on the news media,' said MacGovern, continuing to develop his thesis. 'Another half dozen such, and reports are certain to begin appearing on the front pages of some of the city's newspapers. After that, who knows what might happen?'

'Calls for an inquiry. Falling share prices. Yes, it is possible.'

***

And, just as serious questions were beginning to be asked about Menzies and what lay at the heart of his success and why so many of his former employees had begun behaving strangely, the attacks stopped, the journalists lost interest, and the ever fickle attention of the newspaper reading public shifted to the astonishing revelations of the affair involving the Duchess's maid and the electric toothbrush.

MacGovern's reaction to this unexpected cessation was more relief than anything else, and it was a relief which grew with every passing day, no further assaults occurring to suggest it might be premature. So he placed the file in a drawer of his desk and, there being no shortage of other acts of a criminal nature to claim his attention, quite forgot about it.

Philbert, on the other hand, seemed only to grow more curious, and he began to devote ever greater periods of time to the affair. As was often the case, he felt it likely that the city archives might hold at least a part of the explanation to the mystery, and spent hours sitting at a small desk in the reference library, scrolling through microfilm.

The research was slow and required repeated visits to the library. When he felt his eyes growing strained from peering at the screen, or his back and shoulders beginning to ache from sitting hunched over, he went for a wander, and lost himself among the miles of shelves of books. He discovered, much to his delight, an edition of the Sanskrit text of the *Meghaduta* of Kalidasa, published at Bombay in the middle years of the nineteenth century. Onto one of the pages of this volume, the cover rubbed at the extremities and the binding a little loose, a librarian had secured, by means of a paper clip, several slips of yellowing paper, on which the erstwhile amateur scholar had begun to list items of vocabulary. A rare treasure in itself, it was the details scribbled on the title page which intrigued him, when he read them for the first time, revealing, as they did, that the individual, whose study of the work seemed not to have progressed beyond the first half-dozen pages of text, had been a resident of the very same village in which Philbert had spent much of his early life. How was it possible, he asked himself, that I should uncover, by chance, such an unlikely association of place and interest in the midst of so many forgotten old volumes? This happy discovery not only pleased him greatly, it also inspired him to persevere in his search, and even seemed to promise that he would eventually find the information which he was looking for and was certain did exist, however elusive it had, thus far, proven to be.

***

If the Inspector was able to find a half-hour to himself, he liked to slip out of the station and go for a walk along the city's quiet back streets. The fresh air helped clear away the fog from a head made heavy by the combination of central heating, bright ceiling lights and computer screens; and the exercise stimulated a circulation sluggish from hours sitting behind a desk. It never ceased to surprise him that, in such a large and populous city, at certain times of the day, a man might have the streets to himself, by and large. What a contrast with the ceaseless noise and coming and going of his place of work!

On this occasion, however, he directed his steps to a small art gallery which he had discovered, located no more than five minutes from his office. The city's museum, a great sprawling, red sandstone Victorian building, while closed during a period of renovation, had moved some of its treasures to this vacant site, just off one of the pedestrian precincts; and it was in this oasis of calm that we find him, seven or eight days after the last of the unusual events described above.

There were never many visitors, in spite of the gallery's central location, a fact which initially surprised MacGovern, indicating, as it seemed to do, a lack of public appreciation for the treasures on display, and a lack of awareness of the mentally calming and cleansing effects which were to be enjoyed there on even the briefest of visits. On later consideration, however, he was inclined to attribute this simply to the fact that there was an almost complete absence of external indications to its presence; he had himself stumbled upon it purely by chance.

He was in a room hung with a selection of oil portraits, and was reading an information panel at the side of one of these, when he felt his arm bumped. Turning a scowl of annoyance on the possessor of the offending limb, he found himself looking into the brown eyes and smiling face of the Doctor. Philbert raised his hat by way of apology for the intrusion.

'I propose to visit Menzies, Inspector,' he said, when they had taken a seat on a padded bench, provided for the benefit of those who wished to enjoy longer periods of artistic contemplation, 'and reveal to him what I know and what I surmise. I also intend to give him a description of this strange creature which has been creating minor havoc on the city's streets, a description which, I am certain, he will recognise.'

'Recognise?' MacGovern was unable to conceal his surprise.

'Yes, recognise, Inspector. While you have been chasing pick-pockets and bicycle thieves, I have been busy burrowing around in the archives. And look what I found, hidden away in their midst.'

So saying, he opened the envelope which was resting in his lap and, drawing forth the single item which it contained, presented it to the policeman. What MacGovern saw, was a black and white portrait photograph of two men, one seated at a rather imposing desk, the other standing several steps behind his companion. They are young men, perhaps in their early twenties, and are dressed in three-piece suits of dark, heavy cloth. There is a faint smile on the face of the sitter, which may be a mark of the contentment which he feels with the success that has begun to accrue to his hard work. His companion's visage reveals no such satisfaction; it is, rather, one of intensity and purpose, drive and ambition; all of which MacGovern seems to see in the hard set of the mouth and the tension in the hand which clasps the high back of the chair in which his companion is sitting. This standing figure, although much altered in appearance by the passage of many years, and as many travails, is immediately recognisable as Archibald Menzies. But it is the seated figure's mass of dark hair, swept back from a face of unusual paleness, which arrests the policeman's attention. After looking at it for some seconds, he turns to Philbert, and sees him quietly nodding his head.

'Yes, indeed, Inspector,' comes the reply to the unspoken question. 'Cuthbert Morris, former owner and principal partner of the Morris Iron and Steel Foundry. And standing behind him is his second in command, one Archibald Menzies. It is an interesting tale, and I shall tell you as much as I know, for some aspects of it yet remain unclear.'

***

'I had no idea that such a photograph existed, Doctor Philbert,' said Menzies, holding it close to his face and looking at it intently. His eyes grew moist, and a heavy sigh escaped him. 'It may be the only one of Cuthbert which exists. He was killed shortly thereafter. You do know that he was an orphan, yes, and had no other family?' When he continued, it was in a voice which trembled with emotion and was scarcely louder than a whisper. 'His face has haunted my dreams for these sixty years and more.' Menzies was lying on a sofa, in the study of his splendid suburban villa, his body swaddled in blankets, like a baby in a cradle. Bottles of tablets and a glass of water stood on a nearby table, within arm's reach of the invalid. The male secretary who had shown Philbert into the room, had placed a chair close to the sofa, so that he might sit at the old man's side.

'It was taken at the height of our success. A modest success it was, to be sure;' Menzies said, shrugging inside his cocoon of blankets, 'but it felt like we were on top of the world. Between us, we had little education to speak of, and hardly money enough to pay the rent for the premises. But what we did have, was boundless energy, and a hunger to succeed. At least, one of us did. From then on, however, it would all have been down hill, if things hadn't changed.' So saying, he handed the photograph back to his guest.

'A steel works was a dangerous environment in those days. We lost a number of good men.' Menzies's voice faded away, and he moved his head to stare past his guest and out the enormous bay window of the room, as if recollecting the names and faces of some of those unfortunates. 'I used to hope, Doctor, that something would happen to Cuthbert. Just enough to keep him out of the way for a couple of months. Nothing serious, though. A bump on the head, a broken leg. Then I would step into his shoes, and show him what I thought we could really do. Take that contract with Grabble & Co., for example.' The name rolled off his tongue, then he hesitated, realising that he was speaking of matters which had occurred so long ago and were so particular to his own history, that nobody else could possibly know anything about them. He was pleasantly surprised, however, to see the look of recognition which appeared on Philbert's face. After his hours of research, there was little about Menzies and his past which the doctor did not know, at least of that which could be gleaned from the extant printed sources. 'They wanted us to make something that was really beyond our capabilities; it was too big and too complicated. And they wanted it on credit, for a month or two. Cuthbert wouldn't take the job on. He said we couldn't manage it, technically or financially. I thought we could, and told him so. I tried to talk him round, but nothing would make him change his mind. We had a disagreement. Voices were raised, and things were said that shouldn't have been.'

Here the old man paused to moisten his lips with a sip of water.

'I had just come out of the office, where I'd been doing paperwork, and caught sight of Cuthbert high up on the gantry which ran from one side of the premises to the other. He always liked to keep a close eye on what was going on, and used often to stand up there and watch the cauldron coming out of the furnace and the molten steel being poured into ingots. It seemed to fascinate him, all that heat and light, all those elemental forces at work. I remember thinking how strange his face looked, glowing orange in the reflected light of the furnace. There was something unearthly about it.'

'And that's when it happened?' asked Philbert, leaning forward, to make sure that no word from the old man's lips was lost.

'Yes. He was standing leaning over, his right hand gripping the iron railing. And then, even as I watched, the hand began to slide away. His other was deep in his trouser pocket, and he wasn't able to get it out in time to stop himself. He tumbled over the handrail. Instead of landing on the pile of wooden pallets and tarpaulins below, which I ... which would have broken his fall, he managed to grab hold of a hanging chain. The momentum carried him right over the cauldron, and the searing heat and sparks ... his clothes caught fire, and ...'

'... he fell right into it, into the cauldron of molten steel.' A blood sacrifice, to be sure, albeit unintended, thought Philbert. No wonder he's had so much success in business. Death would have been instantaneous, but oh! the horror of it. A descent into a hell on earth. While hoping for a minor accident, for his plan to go so badly wrong, he must have been praying for something a whole lot more serious, he told himself, watching the old man's eyelids slowly close and a tear run down his cheek. Or, perhaps, whoever heard his prayer decided to give him more than he bargained for. Bruising, concussion, and a couple of broken limbs, injuries warranting a stay in hospital and a long period of recovery, would have cleared the way for Menzies to take control. After that, what? A steady and continuing modest success? Perhaps a little more. And Morris would have been suitably recompensed for his accident, not just financially, from the growing profits, but also by seeing his business expanding. Instead, Menzies damns himself, and sends his friend to an early grave.

The old man's voice broke in on his thoughts at this point.

'When the steel had cooled, I had the men load it onto a lorry and move it to the cemetery. It took them hours of digging before they had a hole large enough to bury the ingot. And from that moment, everything I laid my hand to was successful. Nothing ever failed. The unlikeliest of business ventures turned profitable, sometimes wildly so, in spite of the predictions of my accountants and advisors. My competitors used to say I had the luck of the devil. But it wasn't his luck which I had, it was his assistance. I had a supernatural helper. And all,' he said, his trembling hand making a gesture which seemed intended to encompass not only the room in which they were talking, or the house, but the whole extent of his business empire, 'for what?'

'Your soul, Sir Archie,' said Philbert. 'And now the bill has come due. You are aware, I take it, that someone, or something, I should say, with more than a passing resemblance to Cuthbert Morris has been stalking the streets of this city, preying on your former employees? You are aware of that?' he asked, eyeing the old man closely. 'There must be a reason for such a series of occurrences happening now, after all these years.'

'It is the most closely guarded of secrets, Doctor, that I am a very ill man. But perhaps you already knew that, you who appear to know so much else about me. Or have guessed it, perhaps, from the condition in which you see me now, and from these bottles of tablets. I do not wish to die. I wish to go on living.' The passion with with Menzies spoke these words cost him more energy than he could afford to expend, and, his head falling back onto the cushion, he lay still and silent for some moments.

'How long do you have?' asked Philbert.

'Months. Weeks. I can feel it slipping away, even as we speak, the life force. A year or two, perhaps more, if I have a transplant. It might give the scientists and medical men time to come up with a cure. I've spent an enormous sum of money funding research in different parts of the world. Unfortunately, there is no liver available, or none which the doctors think would be suitable. Besides, it is not only the liver ...'

'Perhaps they don't want to waste such a scarce resource on an old man near the end of his life and unlikely to receive much benefit from it, especially when there are so many young people dying for want of a replacement.'

'Scarce?' Menzies' reply was followed by a laugh, which turned into a cough. He took another sip of water. 'Do you know that one can buy organs, Doctor? Kidneys, livers, eyes, even hearts. When money is no obstacle, everything is for sale. And provided one asks no questions, one need never trouble oneself about the source. An executed convict, an accident victim on life support ...'

'A criminal gang preying on street children? Is that what one of your doctors was doing in Haiti, Sir Archie? Were you really prepared to go to such lengths?'

Menzies merely shrugged, and the hint of a sneer passed across his features. Philbert had to restrain himself from evincing signs of the revulsion which rose up inside him.

'Is that why this entity has been roaming the streets of the city, to remind you to keep your part of the bargain?'

'It was on the evening of the award ceremony,' said Menzies in reply, 'as I stood in front of the Shelbourne Hall, that I finally made the decision to go ahead with the operation, however risky it might be, and however ... illicit the source of the organs. I had been hesitating for weeks, in spite of the growing seriousness of the disease and the persistent urging of my personal doctor. I told myself that I didn't have to leave it all behind, not just yet. And I am not talking about the material aspects of fame and fortune, Doctor, although they make life very pleasant. It is that feeling of being on top of the world of which I am speaking, that sense of power, invincibility, call it what you will. What man would blame me for wishing to preserve, for as long as I could, by fair means or foul, this blessed existence?'

A blessed existence? Stemming from such a beginning? 'And that was the moment when the visitor appeared?' Philbert asked.

'I knew that something was wrong, the moment I made the decision,' Menzies said. 'I could feel it in every part of me.'

'I was listening to the live radio broadcast, and could hear the change in your voice. I am assuming that it, the entity in the external form of Cuthbert Morris, came to fetch you, if we could put it that way, to take you away from this world, when you were at the very summit of your worldly acclaim, before the eyes of the assembled guests, and those watching and listening in their homes.'

'What a spectacle it would have made! What a display of infernal power! Who would have thought that a simple accident could have occurred to disrupt the plan!'

'And the series of assaults which it went on to commit about the city, was for what purpose? To bring attention to the pollution at the heart of your empire? To reveal to the public just how many victims of your progress there have been, even in this one city? Was that its secondary purpose, having failed in its primary objective?'

'As more and more newspapers took up the story, I realised that, if I did proceed with the operation, it would only be to see everything for which I had worked torn down before my eyes. The humiliation would have been unendurable.'

'And when you reconsidered, when you decided not to go ahead with the transplant, the attacks stopped, and public attention moved away to other matters.'

'The irony of it, Doctor,' Menzies said, a tight-lipped smile appearing on his face, 'is that neither my son nor daughter has any interest in taking over the reins when I die. One is employed as a music therapist in the most deprived area of the city, the other is making her way as an artist. My empire will fall into the hands of my generals.' He spat out this last word.

'And like those of Alexander, after his death, they'll squabble and fight amongst themselves, until your business empire falls apart.'

'The collapse has already begun, Doctor Philbert. Every day I receive reports of internal strife, directors in the boardroom having to be pulled apart before they could pull one another to pieces. The cracks in the foundation are growing, and the vermin are coming out into the daylight. Not that I didn't know they were there, or even that I had created them, in my own image.'

'I suppose,' said Philbert, wishing to draw his visit to a close, as he saw the old man's strength fading, even as they were speaking, 'the demon's appearing as Morris needs no explanation.'

'A reminder to me, if any were needed, of the source of my success, I imagine. His fall, my rise. His wretched death, my charmed life.'

Philbert was now satisfied that all the loose ends of the puzzle had been tied up. 'I shall be going, Sir Archie,' he said, rising to his feet; but the old man had already drifted off to sleep. He watched the faint pulse beating in Menzies's neck, and asked himself how long it would be before he would begin his final journey.

Menzies held on for some weeks, his bodily strength draining away with every passing day, although he remained mentally alert enough to deal with matters related to his business and the contested succession, right up until the very end.

One morning, he asked his male secretary, Michael, for his help. There was something which he wanted to do, which he must do, was what the old man said. His gentle protest unavailing, Michael had taken the old man's arm, and had supported him as he slowly climbed up and up, and round and round the wide central stairway, until he stood on the top floor of the splendid mansion, leaning with his frail body against the polished mahogany banister, looking down, through a great expanse of open space, onto the stone flags which paved the hall sixty feet below.

'Leave me now, Michael,' Sir Archie said, clasping the bannister with both hands until his knuckles turned white. 'Leave me,' he repeated, in a firmer voice, his flashing eyes quelling the rising murmur of concern.

Michael was half-way down to the floor below, when he heard the old man say, in a voice that was surprisingly loud and free of any trace of a quaver, 'This is for you, Cuthbert, and for the oil which I smeared on the handrail. We're quits now.' And as he turned to look back up, he saw the old man silently falling past him into eternity.

THE TATTOOIST

Inspector MacGovern was sitting in his office at the Central Police Station, his legs stretched out beneath the desk, his hands behind his head, enjoying ten minutes shut-eye. He had not slept well the previous night, nor for some nights before that, being troubled by a recurring image of violence which he had witnessed on one of his recent cases, and which thrust itself into his dreams with unusual vividness about three hours after midnight, causing him to start awake. Rather than lie tossing and turning, which served only to disturb his wife, he had tried to read himself back to sleep. The attempt had failed, as it almost always did, but he had become so absorbed in the volume of stories, that the sky was lightening when he finally closed the book and laid it to one side.

An hour later, at twenty-five minutes after six o'clock, by means of a door which led from the underground parking lot, he entered the main building, and climbed the three flights of stairs to the floor on which his office was located. Striding past empty desks and chairs, his rubber-soled shoes squeaking on the cream-coloured tiles, he spoke a word or two of greeting to members of the night-shift whom he recognised. The second floor was often chilly at that hour, a coolness exacerbated by the air-conditioning, which never seemed to stop blowing, and the effect which this had on the Inspector, acting on his tiredness, was mildly depressive in nature. On such occasions, the first thing which he did on entering his office, was turn up the thermostat of the vertical radiator by the window, and stand pressed against it, looking out over the still slumbering city, and feeling the heat burning his backside.

After some hours spent attending to paperwork, a seemingly endless task, which he punctuated, on this occasion, by an uncommonly large number of lengthy pauses, he closed the file before him, and then closed his eyes. Drifting off into a half-sleep, he found his thoughts turning to Doctor Philbert, whom he hadn't seen for a month or more, since the affair involving Sir Archie Menzies had come to such an unexpected end. What a mess that was, he reflected, seeing once again, in his mind's eye, the condition of the magnate's body after his fall from the uppermost story of the house. The secretary, who was with Menzies at the time, insisted that the old man, in his weakened physical state and light-headed from the exertion of climbing the stairs, something which he never did, as there was a lift in the residence, had simply lost his balance and, unable to stop himself, had tumbled against the bannister and fallen over. The coroner had accepted this narration of events and had recorded the death as an accident. In the weeks since then, MacGovern had, from time to time, made a point of turning to the business pages of the newspapers to see if there was any further mention of the Menzies' Group of companies, a casual enquiry which revealed that the whole concern appeared to be slowly coming apart, a view supported by the fact that the value of the group's shares had fallen by more than a third in that short interval of time, and that the downward trend, according to those in the know, now looked irrecoverable, whoever might take charge at the helm.

He was asking himself why it was that, at this particular moment, the Doctor's distinguished face, with its long, finely shaped nose, the right eyelid slightly drooping, should fix itself in his head, when his musings were interrupted by a single knock at the door, which heralded the entrance of his assistant, Frank Lindsay.

'Morning, sir,' Lindsay said, his appearance in the room accompanied by the faint scent of aftershave. Without waiting for a reply to his greeting, the sergeant straightaway proceeded to the purpose of his visit. 'A woman's body has been found, sir. Doesn't look like murder, but the circumstances are sufficiently unusual as to require your particular attention.'

MacGovern received this information in silence and unmoving, apart from his right eye flickering open. He had gained a certain notoriety among his fellow officers, and a growing respect from his superiors, as a result of the three cases on which he had already worked with the learned Doctor, so it was no surprise that, should anything out of the ordinary present itself at a crime scene, his name was now the first to be suggested as the one best suited to deal with the case. With a nod of his head, he rose, fetched his coat from the hook behind the door, and followed the sergeant out into the corridor.

After a journey of twenty-five minutes, a good part of which was spent sitting at traffic lights, Lindsay turned the car into Nightingale Street and pulled up outside a block of tenement flats, a three-storey red sandstone building dating from the later years of the Victorian era. MacGovern knew this area of the suburbs only from the afternoon walks which he took with his wife at the weekend, when they would explore some of the more elegant parts of the city, occasionally accompanied by one or both of their children, if they could be persuaded to join their parents. The small gardens belonging to the ground-floor flats were, all of them, neatly kept, the railings painted and the hedges trimmed. One of the better areas, no doubt, he thought, as he picked out a number of new and expensive cars parked on both sides of the quiet road. A low crime neighbourhood, too, he then reflected, which might explain why this was the first time he had been there, in his capacity as a policeman.

The victim's spacious and well-appointed flat was on the second floor. Bookcases full of paperbacks, a selection of art prints on the walls, elegantly framed and tastefully arranged, and a cello and bow in a stand in the smaller of the two bedrooms, suggested that the inhabitant was an educated person. And now deceased, MacGovern reminded himself, as he stepped into the main bedroom.

The woman was lying in bed, her dark hair scattered over the off-white linen pillows. The vacant stare of her eyes and the pallor of her smooth skin gave her a strange appearance, not unlike that of a manikin, which her raised right hand, frozen in a position near her face, only added to. The fingers of this hand were clenched, not tightly enough to make a closed fist, but just so much as to suggest that she might have been clutching at something.

Much of the left-hand side of her body was exposed to view, as the quilt had been thrown back, perhaps indicating that she had tried to rise from the bed, before being overcome by whatever force it was that had taken her life. The tattoos which covered her skin caught MacGovern's attention immediately. Why did women choose to mar their natural beauty with such monstrosities, he asked himself, as his eyes took in one dark, inky design after another. There were multi-coloured geometrical patterns, quotations in more than one oriental script, and the finely worked head of a sphinx on that part of the body which was revealed to his view.

'Who found the body?' the Inspector asked, addressing the question to a young male constable standing at the foot of the bed, whom he vaguely recognised from a previous case.

'Friend of the victim, sir,' the constable replied, with a slight backward movement of his head, thereby indicating where the said friend was to be found. 'Girlfriend. Has a key to the flat. They were to meet here, and then go for a coffee. When she rang the buzzer at the main door,' the direction of which was indicated by another movement of his head, this time sideways, 'and got no answer, she used the key to get in.'

The friend was sitting on the couch in the living room, her arms folded tightly across her chest, her body rocking backwards and forwards, and her unblinking, unseeing eyes focused on some distant spot. That she had been weeping was clear, but she seemed calm when MacGovern introduced himself to her and began, as gently as he could, to question her about the deceased lying in the next room.

He learned from this woman that she did not, in fact, have a key to the flat, but that she had used the one which her friend, Miss Martina Connaught, the occupant, left hidden under a flower pot in the garden of her downstairs neighbour, just in case she locked herself out, which had happened on more than one occasion. (This was an arrangement which the neighbour knew about.) When she had repeatedly pressed the buzzer at the main door of the close, just before ten o'clock that morning, the time at which they had agreed to meet, and which had been confirmed by text the previous evening, and there was no answer, she buzzed one of other residents in the close and asked to be let in, and had then used the key to enter the flat. As far as she could tell, after a cursory look round, nothing appeared to be out of place since her last visit, some five or six days earlier.

'Couldn't have been a suicide, sir?' Lindsay asked, a half-hour later, when the two men stood together in the kitchen talking over the details which they had so far established. 'You did see the bottle of sleeping tablets on the bedside table?'

'Possible, I suppose,' replied MacGovern, without much conviction, reflecting on the unusual arrangement of the quilt and the pose of the corpse, which seemed to suggest that the body had been in motion at the point of death.

'As for the spare key, any one of the neighbours could have known about it.'

'You can ask them about that when you speak to them, Frank. They'll need to be told what's happened,' said MacGovern. 'It's not just the neighbours, though. Anyone passing could have seen either the victim or her friend, or anyone else who knew of the arrangement for that matter, hiding the key or taking it out. They could have been overheard talking about it, in a shop or cafe, and then followed to the location. The possibilities are endless.'

Hearing a commotion in the hallway, MacGovern stepped out to ascertain its cause, and found Fischer, the police surgeon, edging his way past a rather large female constable who was inadvertently blocking his access to the bedroom.

'Morning, MacGovern,' Fischer said.

'Morning,' MacGovern replied, watching the doctor disappear through the bedroom door. He was wearing a blue silk bow tie with narrow white stripes. Ever the dandy, MacGovern thought, with more than a touch of admiration for the older man's sense of style. Even his fawn raincoat looked expensive and elegant, in spite of its being rumpled.

'What do you think of women with tattoos, Frank?' he asked, withdrawing to the kitchen again and closing the door. 'Do you find it attractive?'

'Never thought about it much, to be quite honest, sir,' Lindsay replied 'People do what they want with their bodies. I tell you what, though, my niece got one. Her mother nearly blew the roof off when she saw it. I was visiting at the time. I thought she was going to murder her. And it was only a small butterfly on the inside of her wrist.'

'I think I'd probably react in the same way, if either of the kids got one,' MacGovern said, sympathising with the mother's response. 'I sometimes wonder if Ella has one, hidden beneath her clothes' line, where I can't see it.'

With that, the Inspector left his assistant to begin the task of informing the victim's neighbours, took the car keys from him, and drove himself back to the station.

Fischer had just completed the autopsy when MacGovern arrived at the Northern General Hospital, late in the afternoon of that same day.

'She was asphyxiated, in the early hours of the morning,' the doctor said, peeling off his surgical gloves and removing his gown, which he rolled up into a ball and deposited in a waste bin. 'But whether it was by accident or design, is for you to determine, MacGovern. Some of the bones of the neck were crushed, but there's no haemorrhaging present in the tissue consistent with an act of manual strangulation. Nor are there any residual marks on the external surface of the skin, no redness or bruising produced by the pressure of fingertips.'

'Could the murderer . . . could a rope or something similar have been used?' asked MacGovern, as the doctor began to wash his hands at the sink. He had noticed a dark red dressing gown lying crumpled on the floor, at the foot of the bed. Its chord was missing. Would it be found in the flat, he wondered, or had it been removed by the assailant?

'There were no ligature marks either,' the doctor replied, 'but that might only mean that, if one was used, it was released at the point of death. The scratches on her cheek were produced by the fingernails of her right hand, likely the result of her attempts to remove whatever was choking her. She had a leather strap on the other wrist, the left one,' he continued, after a pause, during which he put on his suit jacket.

'Which means what? Bondage? You think she liked being tied up?'

'Not necessarily. I saw the cello in the back bedroom. It might have been a support for the tendons in her wrist, if she had strained them with too much practice. It's not uncommon with musicians.

Especially if they have small hands, which she did, and are trying to play difficult music. Pieces that require wide stretches.'

Fischer spread his fingers out, looked at them for some seconds, then vigorously rubbed his hands together, as though his recent occupation had left them chilled and in need of a heat.

MacGovern left him to write up the autopsy report. At least that ruled out suicide, he thought, as he made his way back to the car. That the death might have resulted from bondage gone wrong was not something which had occurred to him. Absent any other leads, it was worth considering.

Subsequent investigations revealed that the deceased was an intelligent woman who had no known enemies. Why anyone would want to harm her was a mystery on which none of her family or friends could shed any light. The neighbours, those who were able to be contacted, because two of them worked abroad for longer or shorter periods and were not then resident in the building, when quizzed about the hidden key, knew nothing about it; nor had they had seen any strangers in the close or hanging about the main door.

The enquiries soon reached a dead end.

Six days later, no further progress having been made in the Connaught case, the body of a second victim was discovered on the edge of a patch of woodland, in the largest of the three parks located within the city boundaries. A couple out for an early morning jog had passed a man lying on the ground, and had thought, at first, that he was sleeping rough, but when they stopped to check, and the husband got close enough to see the ground soaked with blood, he called the police.

It was a few minutes after 7.30 am when MacGovern arrived at the scene. Lindsay was already there, standing bent over and examining the corpse from a distance of about two metres. The bottoms of his grey trousers were soaked from walking through the dew-sodden grass.

'He may have been too drunk to go any farther, sir,' he ventured, nodding a morning greeting to his superior, and then indicating the open can of lager still clutched in the victim's right hand, 'and simply collapsed here. Or thought that the long grass would make a comfortable bed for the night, until he was sober enough to make his way home in the morning.'

'And he was assaulted as he lay sleeping?' MacGovern said. 'Or the assault took place as he walked past these trees, and he was then left lying here.' His attention distracted by the whirring of wings, he raised his head to follow a pair of wood pigeons which flew out of the copse at that moment, likely disturbed by the increasing movement around their overnight roost. The sun was struggling to break through a bank of grey clouds, and was spreading a strange diffuse light over the sky. It would be some hours yet before it was strong enough to burn off the dew, he thought, feeling the dampness beginning to soak through his shoes. He normally carried a pair of wellingtons in the car boot, but his wife had taken them out to clean them, after their last muddy country walk, and hadn't put them back. Shivering in the chill air, he turned up the collar of his sports jacket and thrust his hands into the patch pockets.

'Those tracks were made by the jogger,' said Lindsay, pointing with his index finger. 'No other tracks are visible in the grass, either leading to the body or away from it. Which means that nothing, neither man nor beast, has been near it since dewfall.'

'Which was when?' asked MacGovern, turning a look of mild astonishment on his assistant.

'At a time yet to be determined,' Lindsay replied, straightening up. He moved back, as the forensics team approached.

The corpse was discovered to be that of Henry Litton, a married man in his mid-fifties, with three grown-up children.

'After enjoying an evening of celebration with a group of male friends,' read Lindsay from his notebook the following day, 'all of whom appeared to have been in an advanced state of inebriation,

Mr. Litton separated from the rest of the party, with the intention of making his way home alone. The shortest route took him through Bellfield Park, which was where his body was found. The assault must have taken place sometime after he parted company with his friends, at about 1.30 am, if the testimony of the bouncer on the door of the pub in which they had their last drink is credible, and before 3 am, which the university's department of Meteorology estimates to have been the time when the dew began forming. Apart from that around the corpse, forensics were unable to find any other traces of blood on the ground.'

'No bloody footprints leading us directly to the murderer,' said MacGovern.

'No footprints of any kind.'

'Yes, that is very strange. A self-inflicted wound, perhaps,' the Inspector mused aloud.

'A man might accidentally wound himself in the neck, if he was to fall heavily while under the influence. But the head wounds . . .'

The telephone ringing at this point interrupted their speculations.

'Fischer here, MacGovern,' said the police surgeon, in his customary brusque manner. 'The victim was subject to an attack of unusual brutality, which resulted in the crushing of his skull and windpipe. These injuries, by themselves, were serious enough to have been fatal, in my opinion. However, it was the loss of blood from the puncture of the carotid artery which killed him. Death could have resulted in ten to fifteen minutes. One other thing,' he added, hearing the Inspector beginning to speak. 'There exists the possibility that he was comatose at the time of the assault, as the alcohol content of his blood was so high.'

'What could have caused the wound in the neck?' MacGovern asked.

'It was a smooth, sharp object,' came the reply.

'A stick?' suggested MacGovern. He wondered if the attacker had broken a branch off one of the surrounding trees, or had used one that was lying on the ground. Forensics had been unable to find anything of that sort, although their search had extended well beyond the location of the body.

'The wound was clean. There were no splinters of wood present, but I couldn't rule out that possibility.'

An hour or so later, when a copy of the autopsy report arrived on his desk, MacGovern's curiosity was aroused by one of the tattoos which the photographs of the victim's corpse revealed. On the impressive expanse of the man's muscular right forearm, he could make out a copy of Friedrich's painting *The Abbey in The Oakwood*, which he recognised at once, as it featured on the cover of a collection of the horror stories of M. R. James which he had in his library. He made a mental note to look out the volume when he got home, as it had been years since he had read any of them.

Inquiries revealed that Litton had recently enjoyed a spell at Her Majesty's pleasure, a five-month sentence for affray, reduced for good behaviour. It was this early release from prison which he was celebrating, with a group of friends, on the night of his death. On learning of his association with a number of career criminals, one of whom was suspected of being involved in the supply of drugs in the city, MacGovern began to consider the possibility that he had been the target of a revenge attack, perhaps between rival gangs, rather than the victim of a random assault; and he instructed one team of officers to focus on this line of inquiry.

A fortnight passed without progress in either case, when a further incident of a similar nature occurred.

'The father is insistent that there was someone in the room with his daughter, sir,' the constable who had attended the emergency call explained. 'And I've just been on the phone to the hospital again. The doctor says that the lab has detected traces of a toxic substance in her blood.'

'I see. Thanks,' said MacGovern, somewhat puzzled by these two disparate pieces of information. 'Which ward did you say the woman was in?' he asked, as the constable turned to go.

'Ward eight, sir.'

MacGovern wasn't on duty that evening. His wife was dining with friends at a restaurant in the city centre, where he was to pick her up about midnight, but returning early, he had decided to wait for her telephone call at the station, rather than sit in his car. Fortunately or unfortunately, the Inspector who was on duty had been called away to another case.

Checking his watch, and thinking it more likely than not that his wife would call later than arranged, he slipped on his jacket and headed for the door.

The roads were quiet, and he arrived at the hospital in little less than ten minutes.

MacGovern found Mr. and Mrs. Coyle sitting at their daughter's bedside in a small room near the reception desk on ward 8. The father rose to greet him when he entered; Mrs. Coyle remained seated, briefly raising an anxious face, over which the fleetest of smiles passed.

Their daughter was lying unconscious in bed, propped up on two white pillows, her breathing assisted by a ventilator. The drip in her right arm must be to flush out toxins, or for administering an antidote, MacGovern thought, recollecting the information which the constable had given him. Almost at the same moment, he noticed that the young woman was wearing a sleeveless nightdress, for no other reason, than that it revealed a tattoo on her left shoulder. It was small in size, but the considerable artistry and vibrant colours of the design made such an impression on him that he had to resist the urge to step closer to the bed in order to get a better look at it, at least until he had spoken with the parents. What kind of spider it was, he had no idea.

Before he could speak to either the mother or father, a doctor entered the room. Holding the door open, he smiled at MacGovern and asked if he could speak with him outside in the corridor.

'Miss Coyle was almost certainly poisoned last night, Inspector,' the doctor said, coming straight to the point. 'When she arrived here, she was in considerable pain and was showing signs of a strong allergic reaction. She was also having problems breathing on her own. That's why she was put on a ventilator. There were other symptoms as well, but I needn't go into the details with you. Analysis of her blood discovered traces of highly toxic substances. Peptides, and other things. They have an effect on some of the important chemical channels in neutrons.' The doctor grew animated when conveying this latter piece of information, as if it were a source of particular medical or scientific interest. 'Although the concentration was small—there wasn't a lot of it in the blood—what was present had a significant detrimental effect on her health.'

'The father thinks she was assaulted, Doctor,' said MacGovern. 'Someone entered the bedroom through the open window.'

'Well, something happened last night, otherwise she wouldn't be in the state she's in. As to its being someone, I couldn't possible say. More likely to be something.'

'Such as . . . ?'

'The likeliest source of the toxin is arachnic. From a spider,' he added, with a touch of emphasis, seeing the look of incomprehension on the policeman's face.

'And the bruising on her face?' MacGovern inquired, raising a hand to his cheek, although not entirely focused on the question he was asking, as his thoughts were beginning to move along other tracks.

'It's not bruising, Inspector,' came the doctor's reply, 'although it might look like it. Perhaps that's why Mr. Coyle thinks that she was assaulted. The site of the wound has already begun to show signs of necrosis, as evidenced by the red, white and blue colour of the skin. It's not that the blood capillaries were damaged, which is what happens when a bruise appears, as the result of being struck, say.' He gently punched the palm of his left hand with the balled fist of his right. 'It's that the skin tissue around the location of the bite is dying, as a result of the effects of the poison in her blood.'

'Okay, Doctor. Thanks,' said MacGovern, the quietness of his response a result of his abstracted thoughts.

The doctor smiled again, pulled a stethoscope out of the pocket of his blue medical top, and moved off in the direction of the nurses' desk.

MacGovern reentered the one-bed room, and, addressing himself to Mr. Coyle, said that he would be in touch sometime the next day, as there were details of the case which needed clarifying.

As he approached the main door of the ward, a man dressed in the dark green uniform of a paramedic, who was standing leaning against the wall of the corridor, pushed himself off and took a step forward. 'Are you the policeman who came to speak to Maria's parents?' he asked, in a hesitant manner.

'Miss Coyle? Yes,' replied MacGovern.

'Do you have a few minutes?'

'Of course.'

The paramedic led him into a waiting room, which was furnished with chairs and a water fountain, its walls plastered with posters on every imaginable aspect of health and hygiene, and which, at that time of night, was empty of visitors.

'Maria is a friend of mine,' the paramedic began, when they were seated. 'I recognised the address when the information came through from the controller. This is going to sound strange,' he continued, after a brief pause, as though uncertain how best to express what he had on his mind. 'I've known her for a long time. We're sometimes in the same company of an evening, at the pub. Her left shoulder . . . ' and he clamped his hand over his left shoulder, 'has a tattoo on it. A spider of some kind.'

'It's very common nowadays,' said MacGovern. He could think of nothing else to say, but hoped that his remark sounded sufficiently encouraging.

'It wasn't there when we arrived at the house,' the man said, looking down at the floor, perhaps intimidated by MacGovern's stern gaze, which never left his face. 'I had seen it before. But it wasn't on her shoulder when we strapped her into the stretcher at the house this evening. At least not as I remembered it.'

'Not as you remembered it?'

'Did you see her when you went into the room just now? You saw that tattoo on her shoulder?' the paramedic asked, vaguely pointing in the direction of the patient. 'That's how I remember it.'

'And how did it look when you saw it at the house?' inquired MacGovern.

'It was . . . different.' He looked up from the floor again, but, unable to hold the policeman's gaze for any more than a few seconds, turned his head to look at one of the wall posters. 'It was . . . much simpler. Basic.'

'Basic?'

'Yes. All the colour was gone. Only the outline was left,' he said. 'Like the ink had been washed away. In the shower, say.'

The paramedic slid back in his seat, glanced uncertainly at the Inspector, and made a gesture of incomprehension.

'And it's not like that now,' said MacGovern. 'I did notice it this evening. It was difficult to miss. What you're saying then, Mr. . . . ?'

'Andrews. Rob Andrews.'

'What you're saying then, Mr. Andrews, is that the tattoo disappeared, seemed to disappear, and has now reappeared. Something of that sort. Is it possible that the tattooist used an ink that reacts differently in different lighting?' he suggested in all seriousness.

But there was no reply to his question.

'Was their something else, Mr. Andrews?' MacGovern asked, suspecting that there was more to come.

'Yes,' said Andrews, but he didn't immediately begin to say what that was. 'We arrived at the hospital. I went round to the back of the ambulance to help lift the stretcher out. It tilted a little, and something slid out from under one of the folds in the blanket. Something black. About so big.' He drew a circle in the palm of his left hand with his right index finger. 'It seemed to cling onto the side of the blanket for a second or two, and then disappeared underneath the stretcher.'

'Could it have been the woman's phone or something like that?'

'I didn't hear anything striking the ground, and I didn't stop to look, as it was already quite dark, and there was a lot going on in the ambulance bay.'

'Perhaps her mother put her purse in her hand before she left,' MacGovern suggested. 'In case she had to buy something when she got to the hospital.'

'There was nothing in either of her hands when I put the blanket round her and strapped her into the stretcher.'

'What exactly are you saying, Mr. Andrews? A tattoo which changes appearance, or disappears and reappears, and a dark shape moving over the stretcher. Are you saying that they are one and the same thing? You think it was the tattoo, or the spider, that slid off the stretcher? Is that what you're saying?' MacGovern tried to keep his tone even and matter-of-fact, for fear of embarrassing the paramedic into silence.

'No idea.' Andrews followed this muttered rely with a shrug of his shoulders.

'Thanks for taking the trouble to speak to me, Mr. Andrews,' said the Inspector, patting his knees and rising to his feet, when it became clear that the man had nothing further to add. 'I can contact you here, at the hospital, if we need to speak again, yes?'

MacGovern took the lift down to the ground floor, and was heading towards the exit, when his mobile phone rang. It was

Marge on the line, looking for her lift home. And would he mind dropping off one or two of her friends on the way?

***

The following morning, MacGovern and Lindsay arrived at the Coyle home, a detached four-bedroom house in the suburbs. Mrs. Coyle had just spoken with the hospital. Her daughter had had a restful night and was showing signs of progress; she was breathing on her own and the drip had been removed from her arm. MacGovern noticed that the anxiety which had marked the woman's features the previous evening had gone, and that the encouraging news from ward eight had brought a note of animation to her voice.

'I told her not to open the window at night,' were Mr. Coyle's first words, when they were seated in the living-room. 'I know the weather's warm, and the bedroom can get quite stuffy, but I warned her against it. After that last time.'

'Why don't you start at the beginning, Mr. Coyle,' MacGovern said.

'We were watching television in here,' Coyle began, with a glance at his wife, 'when we heard one of the girls screaming. It must have been about a quarter to eleven. I knew it was Sam, as she often has nightmares.'

'Nightmares!' interrupted MacGovern, looking angrily at the father. 'You told the officer you thought there was someone in your daughter's bedroom. That someone had come in through the open window.'

Coyle was dressed for work, clean-shaven and suited, although the collar of his shirt was unbuttoned, and his tie was hanging over the back of the armchair on which he was sitting.

'She does have nightmares, Inspector,' Coyle replied, his tone mildly defensive. 'But I didn't say she was having one that night. Anyway,' he said, scowling back at the policeman, 'she was sitting up in bed. Her hands were moving about frantically, like she was trying to keep someone away. You know, fighting someone off. So I seized hold of her wrists and managed to calm her down. As I was holding her, she passed out. I thought maybe she had just fallen asleep again, but the way her body went all soft and she collapsed back onto the pillow alarmed me. And when I couldn't waken her, I called an ambulance.'

'What makes you so sure there was someone else in the room with your daughter, sir?' Lindsay asked.

'Five or six weeks ago, I think it was,' replied Coyle. 'She woke up, and saw a man's face peeping in at the bedroom window. Scared the life out of her. Her bedroom's on the ground floor, so he could have climbed in quite easily. And out again. No problem.'

'So, to be absolutely clear, Mr. Coyle, did you or did you not see anyone in your daughter's bedroom?' asked Lindsay.

'I didn't. But one of Maria's t-shirts was lying on the floor, and got jammed underneath the bedroom door, so I couldn't open it right away. That would have given him time to escape.'

'Mr. Coyle, you are aware that a constable checked the flowerbed just beneath your daughter's bedroom window, and found no footprints in the earth. The bed had recently been dug over, for the purposes of weeding. That's what you told him,' MacGovern said. 'And the bruising on her face wasn't from a blow, from some imaginary intruder, Mr. Coyle. It was the result of a toxin in her blood. Your daughter was bitten on the face by something, sir.'

'Is it possible,' Lindsay went on, speaking in a gentler manner than his superior, perhaps hoping that a calm, firm approach might help dispel the father's persistent delusion, 'that, in the confusion of the moment, you only imagined that there was someone in the bedroom, as unlikely as that sounds, Mr. Coyle? You've been worried about your daughter, since that last occurrence, and, hearing her screams convinced you that your worst fears for her safety had come true. Is that not how it was, sir?'

'Well, yes, I suppose it's possible,' Coyle finally admitted, turning his head slightly, to avoid seeing his wife's embarrassment. 'But there was something there, I'm sure of it. On the bedclothes.'

'Something on the bedclothes?' said MacGovern, nodding his head. At least one part of the puzzle appeared to have been cleared up, he thought. 'Why don't we go through and have a look?'

Coyle led them into his daughter's bedroom. He raised the sash window up some five or six inches and closed the curtains, as they had been on the night in question, then went back out into the hallway, shutting the door behind him, and leaving Lindsay and MacGovern standing in the darkened room. At a verbal signal from Lindsay, Coyle threw open the door and rushed back into the room, his right hand reaching out to flick on the light switch on the bedroom wall. This sudden entry, and the volume of air which the opening door displaced, caused the ceiling light to sway back and forth with considerable violence.

On closer examination, the shade appeared to have been designed in such a way, that the light was thrown out sideways, illuminating much of the bedroom, while leaving a small occluded area directly beneath the bulb. As the three men watched, the patch of shadow which this cast moved back and forth over the bedspread, as the light continued to swing from side to side.

'Is this what you saw, Mr. Coyle?' asked Lindsay, pointing at the circular shadow.

Coyle's head nodded faintly for some seconds, and a look of confusion then appeared on his face. 'Could have been,' was all that he said, before turning and walking back to the living room.

MacGovern lingered in the bedroom for a moment, when the other two had left, and wondered if Coyle had not, in fact, been correct when he had stated that he had seen something moving over the bedclothes, and that it was, perhaps, the very same dark shape which the paramedic had noticed falling out of the folds of the stretcher blanket, some time later that same evening.

'The power of the imagination, Frank,' said MacGovern, as they drove back to the station. 'It's not the first time I've spoken with a witness who was convinced that what they think they saw actually happened, even when video evidence of the incident directly contradicts their statement. Some are even prepared to swear that the footage must have been altered. You must have seen that too?'

'Sure,' replied Lindsay, his eyes ceaselessly scanning the traffic and glancing in the mirrors. 'You're saying that the father's fears of someone coming in through the bedroom window were so strong and so persistent, that he simply imagined the whole thing?' He frowned, as a motorcyclist pulled into the lane directly ahead of them, then suddenly braked, indicated, and turned off.

'Chances are he's read about something like that happening. Perhaps he had a similar experience himself.' MacGovern laughed at a recollection which entered his head. 'I remember as a teenager, waking about three o'clock one summer morning, and seeing a hand coming in at the open bedroom window. Scared me half to death. I woke the whole house with my yelling. My dad called the police.'

'And what happened?'

'I kept the bedroom window closed for a long time after that. Dad used to say that the room smelled like a bear pit in the morning, when he came in to waken me at seven, but there was no way I was going to leave the window open again. Not for a while, anyway.'

In the late afternoon of that same day, the Inspector stood looking down at a series of coloured photographs spread over the surface of his desk. One set of four was of the corpse of Martina Connaught, taken from different positions in the bedroom of her flat; the second set was of Henry Litton's body.

MacGovern had already studied the close-up photographs of Connaught's face and neck, perhaps in the hope of seeing something which would lend support to Fischer's verdict of death by strangulation, but he had given only a cursory look, if even that, at the others contained in the police file. One of these he now held in his hand, a photograph of the exposed right-hand side of the victim's body, showing the tattoo of a snake, the tail of which began just above the right ankle, the top of the head finishing two or three inches below the armpit. It was little more than an outline, with a hint of detailing and colouring here and there. Accurately drawn, as far as his untrained eye could tell, there was nothing arresting about it, like the spider he had seen on Miss Coyle's shoulder, when he had visited her at the hospital; and it was distinctly second-rate, compared with the fabulous multi-coloured geometrical "sleeve" which covered the victim's right arm.

After examining this image for some moments, he laid it down and picked up another, this one of Litton's corpse, lying on its side in the long grass of the park. The victim's bloodstained shirt is rucked up, revealing the lower half of his back, and part of a tattoo thereon, which MacGovern thought looked very much like the muzzle of a tiger.

It was the work of a few minutes to telephone Fischer and ask him if the injuries sustained by Litton could be consistent with an attack by a large predator.

'You mean a large dog, MacGovern?' Fischer asked, and, without waiting for the Inspector's reply, continued, 'No. No canine that I know of has the physical strength to inflict those sorts of wounds. Tremendous force was required to crush the victims head.'

'I wasn't thinking of a dog, Fischer. I was thinking about a large cat.'

'What?'

'A tiger.'

'Good heavens, man! A tiger running wild in the heart of the metropolis. That's a bit far-fetched, don't you think?' Fischer sounded incredulous, and his blustering response, which had initially embarrassed the policeman, now annoyed him.

'I know how ridiculous it sounds,' came MacGovern's increasingly voluble and testy reply. 'I want to know if it's possible? You said that you thought the artery had been pierced by a sharp stick. Could it have been a tooth?'

'Well, I suppose it could. But . . . ?'

'Never mind the "buts". Could Litton have been savaged by a big cat, like a tiger? Yes or no?'

'Yes.'

'That's all I wanted to know.'

MacGovern replaced the handset, and stood pressing down on it, until the feeling of irritation passed. He had also wanted to ask Fischer if it was possible that the first victim, Martina Connaught, had been asphyxiated, not by someone strangling her with a cord or ligature, but by a powerful snake, which had coiled itself about her neck. Instead, he answered the question by himself, and in the affirmative. Which left the spider on the young woman's shoulder. He looked at the wall clock. There wasn't time to waste, if his surmise was correct, but he could afford an hour or so to visit Philbert, and share with him his ideas.

King Street was quiet, as it always was. The traffic which passed along it was minimal, even during the hours of the afternoon, when the offices were beginning to empty, although it was often difficult to find a free parking bay anywhere along its length after 8 am. MacGovern recognised the black Audi, parked fifteen or twenty feet from the front door of 174, its alloy wheels and bodywork spotless and polished to a high shine.

He could hear the piano as soon as he reached the first floor. It was a faint, but unmistakable sound, muffled by the intervening walls and undisturbed by any other noise, from inside or outside the building.

Renning's knock on the library door was so quiet and the volume from the piano so great that, when he opened it to admit the Inspector, Philbert continued to play, unaware that he now had a guest. The door closing behind him, MacGovern moved forward a pace or two and then stopped, rooted to the spot, as a great wave of sound washed over him. The rocking accompaniment played by the left hand, unchanging and growing in volume, suddenly ceased, and the fingers of the pianist's right hand flew down the full length of the keyboard, to stop with a succession of bass notes, which thundered out, with scarcely less power, it seemed to the listener, than the great bell in the minster tower tolling three o'clock. The silence which followed was hardly less overwhelming, and MacGovern felt himself reeling, as though he had been buffeted by a storm.

Philbert bent forward, and appeared as though about to place a kiss on the top of the instrument, when the creaking of a floorboard, as his guest shifted his weight from one foot to the other, startled him. The frown of annoyance on his face immediately softened to a smile, when he turned and saw the Inspector standing there, half-hidden in the gloom.

'Welcome, welcome, Inspector MacGovern,' he said, rising from the piano bench. 'Do, please, come in. I was just giving my fingers a little exercise. Nothing quite like an hour or two of...'

At that moment, the library door opened, and Renning entered, carrying a tray, on which MacGovern could see light blue china teacups.

'I've been involved in a number of puzzling cases over the last weeks, Doctor,' the policeman began, when the two men had taken their accustomed armchairs at the fireside. 'I think I know what might be happening, but it's so strange, that I thought you might be able to help shed some light on the matter.'

As the Inspector related the details of the three cases, Philbert poured tea for himself and his guest, and, knowing how much he enjoyed Renning's baking, placed two slices of walnut cake on MacGovern's plate before handing it to him.

'Very unusual indeed, Inspector,' Philbert remarked, sounding greatly intrigued. 'Enchanted tattoos. I don't think I've ever encountered such a phenomenon before. And how do you plan to proceed?' he asked, slowly stirring half a teaspoon of honey into his tea.

'I had thought to try to persuade the young woman, Miss Coyle, to get her tattoo removed, if she has recovered sufficiently from the attack. Failing that, I have no idea.'

'Getting rid of it would be best, I agree. I'm not sure how easy it'll be to convince her that the tattoo is possessed by a demon spirit. That is what we're dealing with here, you do realise that, don't you? Primitive magic of some kind, I shouldn't wonder. I would very much like to see the object in question, if that can be arranged, and to witness its removal, if you do manage to persuade her.'

'If it's convenient, Doctor, we could visit the hospital this afternoon,' MacGovern replied, feeling relieved, and reassured, at the thought of Philbert's presence at his side, in the face of such danger. 'Your own experience of such matters may make a far greater impression on Miss Coyle than I ever could.'

'Agreed, Inspector. But first, there are other matters to attend to. Have you tried the cake?'

***

They found the young woman sitting up in bed reading a magazine.

'Miss Coyle, allow me to introduce Doctor Philbert, an acquaintance of mine,' said MacGovern.

'Very pleased to meet you, Miss Coyle,' said Philbert, bowing his head graciously. 'I do hope that you are recovering from your ordeal. From what the Inspector has told me, it sounds as though you had a close escape.'

Miss Coyle smiled at her visitors, but it was an odd, lopsided smile, as the muscles on one side of her face were still suffering the effects of the poison. The bruising or discolouration looked to have worsened somewhat, since MacGovern's visit of the day before, but the healthy pinkish colour visible elsewhere in her visage seemed to indicate that the medical treatment was working, and that her recovery was proceeding apace.

These words of introduction and greeting over, Philbert began to address the young woman directly.

'Miss Coyle, what I am about to say to you will sound very strange indeed, but I want you to listen to it, carefully and with an open mind.' He had taken a seat at the bedside, and was sitting with his hands pressed together, as though pleading his case. 'We, the Inspector and I, have very good reason to believe that the tattoo on your shoulder is enchanted, and not in a good way. Quite the reverse, in fact. There is no need for you to be alarmed about this,' he continued, reaching out a hand to reassure the young woman, when he saw a look of fear pass over her features, 'but we must act to undo the spell. And the best way to do that, in my opinion, is to remove the tattoo.'

Miss Coyle tried to smile a second time, but the smile faltered, and, as she shivered, it was replaced by something very like a grimace.

'I realise that you may have spent a lot of money on the tattoo, and may be particularly proud of it, but its continued presence on your body is dangerous. If I'm being perfectly honest, it may prove fatal. We know of at least two other cases in which a tattoo of this sort may have resulted in death.'

Miss Coyle's hand had moved up her left arm during this short speech, and was now resting on her shoulder.

'It was expensive. And isn't it beautiful?' she asked, in a faint voice, pushing up the short sleeve of her hospital gown.

'A terrible beauty, to be sure,' said Philbert, recoiling slightly at his first sight of the tattoo. He then leant forward, and moved his head from one side to another, in order to look at it from different angles. 'The work of an undoubted master. The skill is remarkable, and the colours and detail equally so. Do you know what kind of spider it is? Although I hardly think that matters,' he added, as an afterthought.

'No,' came the reply.

'Could you tell us where you got the tattoo, Miss Coyle?' MacGovern asked.

'In Windmill Street,' she said, somewhat clumsily, and trying not to dribble. 'South of the river. Close to where the old public school building is; the one that's falling down. The name was Visual Ink Tattoos. I think that's right.'

'And why that one? There must have been some reason,' said Philbert, glancing at the woman's face, before returning his attention to the tattoo.

'The designs in the window display looked so real,' she replied. 'They were like nothing I had ever seen before. There was one of a bird with purple plumage and green eyes. I bumped my head against the glass trying to get a closer look at it. And that's when he opened the door and invited me in.'

'And in you went,' said Philbert, with a smile.

'In I went. I told him that I wanted something special, something out of the ordinary. He kept nodding his head, but I wasn't sure that he fully understood me. He didn't have books of designs, like the other places I'd visited. There were nature books. Books of photographs of animals and birds. So I sat down and flipped through the books, until I found the one I wanted. The spider.'

'And why choose the spider?' asked Philbert, watching her closely from his chair at the bedside.

'I'm not sure I did choose it,' she said. 'I rather think it chose me. It just seemed to come out of the page.' As she spoke these words, she made her right hand scamper over the blanket, a five-fingered imitation of an eight-legged arachnid.

'It chose you, you think?' murmured Philbert. 'Hmm. Interesting. Do you know why it might have chosen you, Miss Coyle?'

Whether it was that her eyes shone unusually brightly at that moment, or her face grew unnaturally pale, the effect was striking. 'It is strange,' she replied. 'I was always afraid of them. You know, creepy things in dark cellars.' The same hand which had, a moment before, scampered over the bedclothes, now made an agitated gesture, as though hastily brushing something off her face.

'A common enough feeling, I imagine,' Philbert remarked, a note of disappointment audible in his voice. He had been expecting her to tell a tale of childhood trauma, perhaps involving a terrifying encounter with a huge bird-eating spider in some tropical paradise. 'Would you say it was a strong fear, Miss Coyle?' Philbert had taken out his mobile phone. After tapping on the screen, he held it up for her to look at. 'Strong enough,' he said, in answer to his own question, as he saw her shiver at the displayed image. 'What about this one?' he asked, repeating the experiment, and getting a similar result. 'I really can't imagine why you would choose to have an image of the one thing which frightens you so much tattooed onto your body, my dear young lady. It is beyond me. Unless ...'

'I can't explain it,' she replied, interrupting Philbert. 'There was something there, in that back room, a voice in my head, maybe, which seemed to say that it had to be the spider. Anyway, I can't see it very well.' Raising her arm, she twisted her head round to look at the design. 'Most of the time I don't even remember that it's there.'

'In that case, perhaps you won't miss it when it's gone, Miss Coyle,' said the Doctor.

The door opened at that point in the conversation, and the doctor, with whom MacGovern had spoken on his previous visit, entered the room, followed by a second medic, pushing a trolley of equipment.

'Right on time, Doctor,' said Philbert, rising from his chair. 'Miss Coyle has agreed to the removal of the tattoo, but there are some precautions which I think should be taken, if the operation is to proceed safely and successfully.'

'Such as?' Doctor Ascot inquired, turning to his colleague, as if to check that he was listening.

'Two things only,' said Philbert, holding up the same number of fingers. 'A covering of some kind for Miss Coyle's face and upper body. It should be strong, tear-resistant, and impermeable.' Seeing Dr. Ascot reaching down to the lower shelf of the trolley, to take up just such an item, he proceeded to the second stipulation. 'It is essential, doctor,' he continued, directing these words to the dermatologist who was to perform the procedure, a Dr. Anwar, 'that the laser be directed right at the head of the spider. Aim for the brain. In that way, the creature will immediately be rendered harmless. After that, you can remove the remainder of the tattoo however you want.'

'Off with its head,' returned Doctor Anwar, with a look of unconcealed scepticism on his face. 'I would normally begin with one of the extremities, and work towards the centre of the tattoo,' he said, looking at his colleague for confirmation.

'I must insist that you begin with the centre of the head,' Philbert stated firmly.

Anwar shrugged, when he saw Doctor Ascot nod in agreement.

The necessary arrangements made, Anwar donned his protective googles and switched on the laser's power unit.

MacGovern and Doctor Ascot were standing at the foot of the bed. Philbert stood at Anwar's left side, so that he could watch the proceedings from close-up.

What happened next is not entirely clear. Philbert insisted, afterwards, that things began to go wrong the moment the doctor placed one gloved hand on the patient's arm and raised the laser pen in the other. Perhaps the destructive impulse inherent in the doctor's action was conveyed to the demon in the tattoo, as, in a matter of seconds, and to the horror of all those watching, the inky design, rising out of the patient's skin, took on a three-dimensional form, then lifted and waggled its forelegs, and scurried up onto the patient's face.

Miss Coyle began to scream and wriggle, an action which threatened to shake the surgical covering free and expose her flesh.

'It's trying to bite her through the sheet,' shouted Philbert, starting forward. 'My hat! MacGovern, throw me my hat!'

The policeman seized the hat up from the chair on which it was sitting and tossed it over to Philbert, who caught it by the brim, intending to swat away the hideous form. Doctor Anwar, momentarily nonplussed by this spectacle of horror, straightaway regained his composure, and calmly followed the spider with the laser pen. As the point of laser light moved over its body, Anwar was unable to keep his hand steady enough to allow the powerful instrument to render the creature harmless. Instantaneously turning its attention away from the young woman, the spider launched itself from her covered face and landed on Anwar's cheek, knocking off his plastic goggles. The doctor screamed, and, dropping the laser pen, began flailing at his face with his gloved hands. In a few seconds, however, in a very few seconds, there was enough poison in his bloodstream to ensure that the outcome could only be fatal. His hands continuing to strike at his face to no avail, he sank to his knees, and then collapsed backwards onto the floor of the room.

It may have been the fact that the three men were seeing something far beyond their comprehension, which had a dampening effect on their reactions. Doctor Ascot had already moved backwards away from the bed, when the spider had first manifested itself in three-dimensional form, and he continued to move in that direction, with increasing haste, as the horror unfolded. MacGovern, perhaps stunned by the speed of events, or unable to overcome his own natural revulsion of such creatures, remained rooted to the spot. Philbert, however, appeared mesmerised by the black shape, as it sat there on Anwar's swelling face. The twitching of the doctor's body slowed, his trembling right hand fell to the floor and lay still, and a last gentle breath, scarcely louder than a sigh, escaped from between his parted lips. As the life slipped from his body, so the animating force also left that of the spider, which shrunk in size and appeared to dry up, until it was nothing more than a husk, such as might be seen in the window corner of any garden shed or garage. The slightest movement of air, produced when Philbert bent over to look at it, blew it under the bedside table and out of sight.

'Look!' exclaimed MacGovern, finally recovering his senses.

On the woman's shoulder, there was now the most basic of tattoos, little more than a crude outline, in fact. Easy enough to identify as that of a spider, it had lost all the magic of the original.

Later that same day, Miss Coyle returned home.

This tragic sequence of events provided Philbert with much that was useful for his investigation.

'By some process,' he said tentatively, as Inspector MacGovern drove them both back to King Street, 'a demonic spirit is captured. Where and by what means, I have no idea, as yet. This demon is constrained to animate the tattoo of a deadly creature—a snake, a tiger, and a spider. At some point, during the hours of darkness, it would seem, when the wearer of the tattoo is sleeping, the demon becomes active. In taking the life of the individual, it regains its own freedom.'

'What on earth could the motivation for such a series of murderous attacks be? Revenge? Money? Just because?' MacGovern asked.

'That will have to be examined,' Philbert replied, and, turning to the Inspector, said, 'You're not taking me home, are you? Should we not be heading for Windmill Street? What was the name of the place?'

'Visual Ink Tattoos, I think she said,' MacGovern answered, flicking on the indicator, before cutting across two lanes of evening traffic.

They found the place, near the dilapidated remains of the public school building, but the name painted on the window was Varua Ino Tattoos.

Lindsay, whom his superior had called en route from the hospital, was already there, sitting in his car at the kerbside.

'"What's in a name?"' murmured Philbert, when he read the words on the glass. 'Rather a lot, I imagine.'

It was only after repeated knocking on the door, that the proprietor appeared, but he stood some way back, in the shadows of the interior, and seemed not to want to come any closer. Lindsay rattled the door handle a few times, but still the man hesitated before finally granting them access.

A small room at the front of the premises, bare of anything which might suggest to what use it had been put, if any, led into a second, somewhat longer than the first, in which the artist performed his work. The books of animal photographs, of which Miss Coyle had spoken and from which she had selected her design, were neatly stacked, one on top of another, on a low table in a corner. A reclining couch for the client, a seat for the tattooist and a second table for his instruments, inks and a CD player was all the furniture which was to be seen there.

The tattooist was little more than five feet tall, and stood looking up at his three guests, turning his head from one to the other, as they positioned themselves about the room. He wore a t-shirt and shorts, and a pair of sandals on his feet, a garb which revealed to the eye a multitude of designs covering his arms, legs, and much of his face and neck; but the darkness of his skin made it difficult to see what each represented.

It became clear, when Lindsay tried speaking with the little man, that his knowledge of English was basic. Realising that there was little chance of obtaining any useful information from him, MacGovern decided to take him back to the station, where he would be detained, until they could find out what his native language was, and then secure the services of a translator. If what he had seen at the hospital an hour earlier was anything to go by, it would unprofessional, to say the least, to leave him at liberty.

'I wonder if I might stay on here for a while,' said Philbert, when the Inspector was preparing to leave. 'I'll lock up when I'm finished, and can drop the keys into the station later.'

MacGovern had no objection to the Doctor's request, and, after one last look around the room, a look which took in the bare walls and the painted wooden floorboards, left him to his devices.

An idea had formed in Philbert's head, when he heard Miss Coyle say that she felt that the design for the tattoo had chosen her, and not the other way around; and he wanted to test his hypothesis. If she had been frightened by spiders in her childhood, it made little sense to him that she should want to have one tattooed on her skin, however beautiful it might be.

He picked up the topmost book of nature photographs, sat himself on the tattooist's chair, and began to leaf through the pages, taking time to let each of the images fill his thoughts. After an hour or so of such study, and having worked his way through several of the volumes, he was beginning to grow a touch bored with the endeavour, when he turned a page and found himself looking at a photograph of a tree. A momentary confusion followed, during which he asked himself what this was doing in the midst of a series of portraits showing animals in their natural habitats, when he realised that the tree had an unusual light green foliage, which covered not only the tree itself, but the ground on which it grew, and the surrounding area. When he finally realised that he was looking at a swarm of locusts, which appeared to have engulfed the landscape, leaving little that was recognisable to the eye, the effect which it made on him was instantaneous, and he almost dropped the book on the floor, so great was his revulsion. And yet, this shock was succeeded, after a few seconds, by a strange feeling of attraction, even of desire. Yes, he said to himself, almost without realising it, this would be his sign: the locust; and he looked up and smiled, as though the tattooist was still present, and was silently watching and waiting for his decision.

Many years prior to this, during the summer following his graduation from university, Philbert had been engaged in the excavation of an archaeological site in northern Iraq. It was a small, private operation, not entirely legal, but granted permission to proceed, after substantial sums of money had passed into the hands of local government officials. His interest in the languages and history of the region, and his father's friendship with the wealthy collector who had provided the funding for the expedition, had secured him a place in the team. It would be his task, as well as assisting with the digging, to translate any clay tablets which they might find. Such discoveries, if any such were made, although of undoubted historical interest, were to be considered incidental, the man had said, as their main focus was the statuary, thought to be located in whatever remained of the temple complex, buried beneath three millennia or more of earth, sand and vegetation.

The excavation had entered its fourth week. The temple precinct had been found, but there was, as yet, no trace of any statues. Philbert was in his tent, stretched out on his camp bed enjoying a brief nap during the impossible heat of the afternoon, when he heard his name being called. He lay on for some minutes, until the voice called again, this time with greater urgency.

On reaching the dig site, Philbert found three of his companions standing in silence looking down into the trench, in which the last of the group had been toiling since early morning. This individual, Durward by name, was sitting back on his heels in the bottom of the trench, trowel in hand and his hat resting on his lap. The light sandy soil in which he had been digging was littered with shining yellow objects, which Philbert initially thought were gold coins, or perhaps examples of the very temple statuary which they had been seeking. Handed one by Professor Hendon, the leader of the expedition, he found that the nugget of gold, cuboidal in shape, approximately three inches long, one inch wide, and a quarter of an inch deep, had been worked to represent a locust. Whether it had been carved or cast in a mould was a question which remained unanswered, as his attention was seized by the cuneiform marking on the underside, for the interpretation of which his presence had been sought. The inscription read "Avenger". That on another, "Devourer", and the third which he was handed had a combination of signs which he could only hazard meant "Death-dealer", or something similar.

'Locusts. One of the ten plagues of the bible,' remarked Hendon. The light blue linen shirt which he was wearing was stuck to his back with sweat, and a fine layer of dust covered the lenses of his glasses, which he was forever pushing back up his nose.

'From the Book of Exodus,' added Merrill, the Hebraist, whose knowledge of the languages of the region extended even to Khotanese. The only child of wealthy parents, who spent much of their time travelling, leaving him in the care of a nanny, from an early age he had found consolation for his loneliness in the study of the arcane and the difficult. It was the discovery of a grammar of Ge'ez in the school library, a book written by a former pupil and bearing his dedication on the fly leaf, which had kept him company through a long, solitary summer vacation at home. From that day forth, Merrill was never again lonely.

'Did they not devour everything in their path?' asked Durward, after scooping up another handful of golden nuggets and depositing them on the side of the trench. The tallest and most athletic of the group, his great reserves of strength and stamina allowed him to work the whole day through, with barely a pause for a meal at noon. When the sky darkened, as the evening came on, he surrounded himself with paraffin lamps and continued to dig. He had invested heavily in the expedition and was determined to make his investment pay.

'Every last thing,' whispered Philbert, continuing to pick up and examine the golden insects. "Stripper-of-flesh", "Gorger", "All-consuming". Each one had a different name, as far as he could tell, and they must already have dug out over two hundred of them, at the very least.

'The ground hereabouts must be full of them,' said Durward, his excitement growing by the second. 'We're sitting on a fortune. Each one of these must be worth what?'

But his speculations were interrupted by Gough, who asked, 'Do you not think we should leave them where they are?' Gough's forte was organisation. He also had an uncanny ability to read people, animals, the energy in places, all sorts of things, in fact, particularly at a moment of change, from good to bad, from rain to sun, from strength to weakness, or vice-versa. With little effort of inquiry, he had discovered in which order the local officials were to be bribed, and with how much; and had managed to play one off against another, to the considerable advantage of the group. His knowledge was of men, and their weaknesses, not of long-dead languages. He had read Durward and the Professor at a glance. The one wanted all the loot which he could carry back with him, the other academic accolades; and neither one cared much about how they got it: plunder or sacrilege, it was all one to them. 'Might they not be guarding the place, or something of that sort?' he continued, trying to effect a lightness of manner, so as not to cause upset, but deadly serious all the same.

'Are you mad, Gough?' scoffed Durward, his head appearing above the level of the trench again, his face displaying a scowl of annoyance. 'Has the sun addled your brains, man? Do you think I laid out all that money just so that you could get some colour in your skinny legs? If you want to help, fetch me down a basket. If not, stay out of the way.' Gough took this rebuke with a shrug, turned on his heel, and headed off to where the stores of equipment were located.

Philbert's contribution to the day's digging had taken place during the early hours of the morning, from just after it was light, when the air was so much cooler, as he was recovering from sunstroke and a stomach upset, a combination of maladies which had left him in a weakened state. Speaking a word to Hendon, to let him know where he was going, he left them there to continue their work.

The sun was well past its zenith when, after an hour's walk from the camp, the wet sponge under his hat keeping his head cool, and stopping every so often to rest or look about the empty land, he reached an outcrop of rock. Much of this was covered with vegetation, consisting of short, thick bushes, small trees whose growth was stunted from lack of water, and such like. Since their arrival in that place, he had taken to exploring this geological feature whenever time permitted, partly because of the oddness of its shape, but mainly in the hope of finding an object of value hidden in one of its many caves, some of which, in his opinion, were too regular in appearance to have been formed by natural processes.

He scrambled up the sloping side, using rocks or branches for purchase, and, when he reached the top, turned to look back in the direction from which he had come. A veil seemed to have been drawn over the camp, which he thought must be a cloud of dust blown up by a passing storm, or a dust devil whipped up by changing currents of air, a common enough phenomenon in those parts, and one which plagued their progress from time to time. What a piece of good fortune to have missed that, he thought.

Feeling that further exploration was beyond his still recovering strength, he sat there up on the crest in the shade, content to enjoy the warm breeze on his face and bare limbs, until the lengthening shadows told him that it was time to begin his return journey.

It was Gough whom he came upon first, just beyond the campsite. He appeared to have tried to wrap himself up in a canvas tarpaulin, in the hope that this would form an effective shield.

The stout material covered his torso, which was still intact, as far as Philbert could tell, but the exposed parts of his body—his head, neck, arms and legs—were stripped to the bone of flesh.

The remains of Durward and Hendon—he could tell which was which, the one, from its size; the other, from the glasses which lay beside it in the sand—he found lying at the bottom of the trench. As he stood looking down at the pinky-white skeletons, his brain struggling to comprehend what he was seeing, a locust crawled out of the eye socket of Durward's skull and, bloated after its feast, struggled to take wing and fly off. While watching another crawling over his foot, he realised that all of the golden nuggets which had been dug out of the ground had disappeared. He looked up into the sky above, then back to the distant spot in which he had rested and from which he had seen the veil obscure the campsite. It was a storm of locusts which had blown across the sky, not a cloud of dust. Gough had been right, after all, Philbert thought. He had sensed that something was not right, and had tried to warn the others. He shook the locust off his boot and trod on it. The body popped and blood squirted over the pale dry sand.

Merrill, the last of his companions, had disappeared.

The isolation of the place, and the silence, unbroken by bird song or other animate sound, but which seemed to ring in his ears nonetheless, sharpened his bewilderment and horror, feelings which alternated with one another as the darkness came on.

Quashing the almost overmastering desire to leave at once, Philbert hurriedly buried the remains of his three associates by the light of paraffin lamps, then packed away as many of their possessions as would fit into one of the two jeeps which they had brought, leaving enough room for his own gear and several cans of diesel fuel and one of water. He was already far, far away from that mysterious spot, when the sun of a new day peeped over the horizon.

The sound of voices passing by on the street outside the shop brought Philbert back from his dreamland. He closed the volume over, and was returning it to the stack, when several sheets of paper slipped out of it onto the floor. As he bent down to gather them up, he saw that they were photographs of the tattooist. One in particular seized his attention, revealing, as it did, a tattoo showing bats flying in front of a full moon in a cloudy sky, on the inside of his right forearm, beginning just above his wrist bone and reaching up to the bend of the elbow. As he studied the image, an alarm bell began ringing in Philbert's head, a faint but insistent warning that MacGovern and Lindsay were in danger. There was no answer when he called the Inspector's mobile number.

It was, in fact, already too late to help the policemen.

Some ten minutes or so into their journey to the Central Police Station, MacGovern, who was sitting in the passenger seat, heard a murmur coming from the back seat, which he assumed was only the tattooist talking to himself in his own language. The noise of the car engine, and of the traffic through which they were then moving, and the design of the interior of the vehicle itself, had the combined effect of considerably muffling these sounds, which were already rather indistinct. The Inspector's first thought was to ask himself where on earth they would find an interpreter. His second, immediately following on from this, was to remind himself that they had no idea what language the man was speaking, and until that was known, there was no point in looking for a translator. However, the increasing volume of these incomprehensible sounds cut in on his reflections at that moment, and he turned round in his seat in order to check that everything was okay in the back of the car. As he did so, something soft and warm struck his face, and collapsed into his lap, where it lay wriggling and flapping its wings, its claws catching in the material of his trousers. It was a vampire bat, and its black eyes where staring up at him. It opened its moist, red mouth to reveal two very sharp white front teeth. This bat was followed by another, which struck the dashboard and bounced back into Lindsay's chest, so shocking the driver, that he let go of the steering wheel and raised his hands in fright.

In less time than it takes to read these words, the inside of the car was full of their small dark furry bodies and flapping wings, and the sound of their chittering mouths and scratching claws.

Heedless of all other considerations except how to get away from this pestilential swarm, Lindsay stamped on the brake pedal, causing the vehicle to slew across the road. It was still moving when they flung the doors open and threw themselves out, flailing about with their arms and filling the air with shouts of disgust. They ran off in different directions, and kept running, until they found places of refuge from the creatures flapping about their heads, MacGovern shutting himself in a phone box, and Lindsay dashing into a newspaper shop.

When, some fifteen minutes or so later, having assured themselves that the sky was clear, they returned to the car, it was empty, their passenger and his bats gone.

They received medical attention when they got back to the station. A nurse administered tetanus jabs and applied antiseptic cream and plasters or bandages to the scratches and bites.

Philbert, when he managed to contact MacGovern by phone, was relieved to hear that they had come off so lightly.

'I don't think it was his intention to cause serious harm, Inspector,' he said, referring to the tattooist. 'It was a means of ensuring his escape, should the need ever arise. I imagine that the murmuring sound which you heard was a chant of some kind, which he used to call up a demonic spirit. A tattoo on his other arm appears to show what looks like a swarm of killer bees. I cannot even begin to imagine how awful an encounter with them would have been.'

MacGovern took some consolation from this information. He had received a number of particularly nasty bites on his hands and face, but it was reassuring to know that he was, after all, still alive.

A watch was kept on the tattoo parlour for some weeks, but nothing was ever seen of the small man again.

Some days after these events occurred, a technician arrived at MacGovern's office.

'I had a look at it, sir, just as you requested,' he said, depositing the CD player and discs, which had been taken from the tattoo parlour during the subsequent search of the premises, on the Inspector's desk. 'There was a disc in it when it arrived at the workshop,' he continued. 'I couldn't make anything of it at all, sir. I tried them, one after the other, and none of them made the least bit of sense. So I handed them over to a colleague who works in audio-visual. He tried speeding up the recordings. It's a man's voice on the discs, that's for sure, but he's speaking in a foreign language. Maybe someone at the university could help you work out what's being said, sir.

MacGovern nodded his thanks, and returned his attention to the file open before him.

'There was one other thing, sir,' said the technician, turning back with his hand on the door handle, 'which I almost forgot to mention. You can hear the sound of the sea in the background of the recordings. Waves lapping on the shore. Must have been recorded on a beach somewhere.'

Summoning his secretary, MacGovern had her send the discs round to King Street, pursuant to the Doctor's request to have a chance to examine their contents.

A day or two later, hearing nothing from Philbert, and his curiosity getting the better of him, MacGovern took time off from the case on which he was then working, and walked round to the Doctor's residence in the early hours of the afternoon.

'What is clear, Inspector,' said Philbert, leaning forward in his armchair and staring into the fire for some seconds, before turning to face his guest again, 'is that each of the attacks took place when the victim was asleep. That is point number one. The bottle of sleeping pills on the first victim's bedside table suggests that she was in a drug-induced sleep when she was strangled. It was a considerable quantity of alcohol which rendered Mr. Litton comatose, during which time his head was crushed. As for Miss Coyle, she woke up in the nick of time, when the attack had only just begun. Perhaps she is a light sleeper, and would have wakened at the slightest disturbance. Or it may be that the nightmare she was experiencing was so frightening that her mind's only remedy for the situation was to jolt her awake. You see, Inspector, the nightmare is the key to the mystery, of that I am certain. The key to a part of it, at least.'

At this point, Philbert related to MacGovern his own experiences in the tattoo parlour.

'The fear, irrational or otherwise,' he went on, 'which resides in the person's psyche, a fear which recurs during the hours of sleep in the form of nightmares, is both the source of the inspiration for the design of the tattoo, and the trigger for the activation of the demon associated with it. How this is possible, I have no idea,' he said, shaking his head, a puzzled frown contracting his brow. 'There was something there, in that back room, which, in spite of my own horror, seemed to be urging me on. One voice telling me that it was the locust, only the locust, which I should have tattooed on my skin; while another, fainter voice said no.'

'And the CDs?' asked MacGovern, his eyes resting on the CD player which stood on the table at the Doctor's side. 'Did you find out anything from them?'

Philbert, pressing the play button, said, 'Listen to this.'

The voice was different, but MacGovern thought the sound of the words was similar to what he had heard coming from the back seat of the car, in the moments before he and Lindsay had been attacked by the bats.

'One of the Polynesian or Micronesian languages,' said Philbert, speaking over the recording, 'as far as I have been able to ascertain.

The scholar with whom I have consulted on the matter, knowing nothing of these strange languages myself, informed me that it is a prayer of some kind. My own conjecture is that they are the words of a spell which binds a demon spirit to the form of the tattoo, and were played while that tattoo was being done. I suspect that the recording was slowed down and was played at a very low volume, so as not to disturb the tattooist's client, but that is only a surmise. You see,' he said in continuation, 'there are among the peoples of these islands a class of priests, called *Po'i 'Uhane*—I think I have the name correct -, who can catch a spirit and force it to do their bidding. Please don't ask me how that is possible, Inspector,' he said, with a shake of his head, as he saw his guest beginning to form that very question.

So there were things which even Philbert didn't know, MacGovern told himself. Wise and learned, but not omniscient.

'Can you hear the sea in the background?' Philbert asked, returning his guest's attention to the recording. The sound of lapping waves conjured up an image in MacGovern's mind of a deserted length of warm, golden sand, basking under skies which were forever blue in some exotic land. Wherever it was, MacGovern wished himself there, at that moment. 'And that noise,' said Philbert, breaking in on the Inspector's daydream, and turning up the volume as far as it would go, 'is the call of a bird. A Kuhl's lorikeet. A species of seabird native to French Polynesia and the Cook Islands. So there!'

With these words, Philbert pushed himself up out of his armchair.

'If you would be good enough to follow me, Inspector,' he said, moving towards the door of the library, 'there is something else which I would like to show you.'

The back garden of the residence was surrounded by a high brick wall on three sides. Near the bottom of the garden, and as far away as possible from doors and windows, Philbert's own and those of his neighbours, Renning had lit a fire in a brazier, and was feeding it twigs and dried leaves. He smiled at the Inspector, as the two men approached, then moved away to a stand watching from a distance.

One by one, Philbert dropped four of the compact discs into the fire, immediately stepping back six or seven paces after doing so. The billowing black smoke and strong chemical smell which filled the air as each disc burned had him covering his nose and mouth with a pocket handkerchief. He offered no explanation for his actions, so MacGovern had to be content to watch the proceedings in silence, standing with his arms folded across his chest, and directing a sideways glance at the Doctor every time he stepped back from the brazier.

After watching the yellow and orange flames curling around the fourth disc, and unable to contain his curiosity any longer, MacGovern was on the point of asking what it was that the Doctor had hoped to see, when Philbert began his explanation.

'Consider this, Inspector,' he said. 'The demon is not on the compact disc, but is constrained by the prayer or incantation which is. Now, if we suspect that two of the tattooist's clients have already succumbed to the animal designs on their bodies—the Connaught woman and Litton, the man in the park. Miss Coyle survived, although the unfortunate Doctor Anwar did not. That makes a total of three victims. But I have burned four discs, without anything happening. This means that ...'

'There may be a victim unknown to us.'

'I think it likely,' said Philbert, smiling at the Inspector, his head nodding slightly. 'A fourth demon has already been released from its constraining spell. It is possible that the body of the victim has not yet been found, perhaps someone living alone, without family or friends to notice their absence. Or ...'

'The body has been found, but there was nothing suspicious about the death,' interjected the policeman.

'Quite so. There were no records in the shop?' Philbert asked. 'Nothing that could give you details of former clients?'

'Nothing at all. No computer. No written records,' replied MacGovern.

'That really is too bad.'

'What about the last disc?' asked MacGovern, pointing at the CD which the Doctor was still holding. 'Would you mind if I tried?' He reached out a hand to take it, and felt a slight resistance, as though Philbert were uncertain about the wisdom of acceding to his request.

MacGovern dropped the disc into the flames, and would have stood close by the brazier watching, in spite of the pungent, swirling smoke, if Philbert had not called him back, a note of urgency clearly audible in his voice.

It was perhaps ten or fifteen seconds before the heat of the fire began to melt the plastic, causing the disc to warp and its edges to curl up, at which point, a powerful scream or roar was heard coming from the midst of the flames, immediately followed by a violent movement of the air, which was strong enough to knock the brazier over and buffet the watchers.

MacGovern's face registered a look of astonishment and bewilderment.

'That,' said Philbert, 'was what I was looking for.' He was clearly pleased that the experiment had succeeded, as his eyes were glowing and he was unable to repress a smile. 'The constraining spell was destroyed and the demon has been released. If the prayer on that last disc has already been used to bewitch a tattoo, the wearer of the tattoo is now safe. If not, we have prevented a tragedy, of that I am certain.'

'I was not joking, Inspector,' Philbert said, indicating the properties on either side of his own residence, as they walked back up the house, 'when I said to you earlier, that, after he announced your arrival, I got Renning to visit my neighbours and ask them to ensure that all windows looking onto the garden were closed this afternoon. The last thing I wanted was for an evil spirit to find its way into their midst. I don't think I mentioned it before, but the words *varua ino* mean just that, evil spirit.'

The next day, shortly after 9.30 am, a young man arrived at the Varua Ino tattoo parlour. MacGovern was on the premises at the time, looking into odd corners to see if any evidence might have been missed. He had instructed a constable to go through all of the photographic volumes and ensure that every page was checked, in case they contained something that might be useful.

The young man was angry, and pushed past a second constable standing at the door. In a loud voice, he insisted on speaking to the tattooist.

MacGovern introduced himself, and informed the visitor that the owner of the shop had disappeared.

'I paid a lot of money for this tattoo,' the man said, and smacked his hand against his left thigh. 'And when I got undressed for bed last night, I noticed that it had gone off.'

'What do you mean "gone off"?' asked the Inspector.

'Gone off! It's lost all its colour. Look!'

So saying, he undid his belt and dropped his jeans.

'What do think of that?' he said, pulling up his boxer shorts and pointing at his leg. 'That was supposed to be a wolf.'

'It still looks like one,' MacGovern replied, eyeing the design.

'But it didn't look like that yesterday morning,' the man said, his voice rising almost to a shout. 'It looked like this.' He pulled his mobile phone out of his coat pocket and held it out for the Inspector to look at. On the screen was a photograph of the most ferocious wolf which MacGovern had ever seen. It wasn't life-like, it was hyper-real. The beast's head was lowered, and its eyes, flashing fire and rage, looked up at the beholder from beneath a furrowed brow. The bared teeth in the snarling mouth looked sharp enough to tear away and devour great hunks of flesh. The male constable who had been flicking through the books of photographs, but had stopped to watch the proceedings, took a step back when he saw the image. MacGovern looked at the man's thigh again, where barely a fraction of the astonishing detail remained; there was little more than the outline and some shading; not quite the work of an amateur, but not much better.

'I see what you mean,' said MacGovern. 'Are you frightened of wolves, sir?' he asked, putting Philbert's hypothesis to the test. 'Do you have nightmares of them attacking you? Anything like that?'

'No;' came the growling reply, 'but my wife does. She can't bear to look at it. That's partly the reason I got it done. To scare the hell out of her.'

'In that case, sir, I think there's something you need to know,' MacGovern said. 'Have a seat, and I'll try to explain.'

THE TREE KEEPER

Billy Albright was fourteen years and three months old when he left school for good. He came home one afternoon and told his mam he wasn't going back, and that was that.

His grandpa suggested that he might want to try getting a job on the de Winton estate. Better than school, anyhow, the old man had said. No point in sitting in a classroom all day, unless you were a scholar and intended to go on to the university and study Greek.

'The first day they tried to teach me to say "How d'ye do?" in French,' said grandpa, 'was my last day at school.' He laughed out loud and slapped his knee at the memory. 'There's different types of learning, Bill. Some folks learn best in the classroom and some learn all they need to know out of it. Learning for school and learning for life.'

Grandpa had worked on the estate himself long years ago, when he was about the same age as Billy was now. He used sometimes to speak of the glorious weather of those few months, a time which he had spent working out in the summer sun from early morning, hoeing and reaping. As brown as a berry he was then. He might still have been there to this day, if the gamekeeper hadn't caught him poaching fish from the river and rabbits from the fields down by the remains of the old Roman settlement, where the soil was sandy and the hedges overgrown. When they told him not to come back, he merely shrugged, and found a place as an apprentice with Grigg, the stone mason. Over the years, he had worked on both the de Winton's grand country house and on the other estate buildings, and had gotten to know Walter Lambert, the Head Gardener.

'I'll speak to Wally Lambert,' said grandpa. 'You leave it to me, Bill.

A week later, Billy was told that he was to be at Mr. Lambert's hut the following morning at eight o'clock sharp.

'So don't be late, son,' said his mum. 'And make sure your boots are polished.'

***

Walter Lambert was a man in his middle sixties, still hale and active after a lifetime spent working for the de Wintons. The old hat which he always wore, hail, rain or shine, covered a bald patch in his grey hair. From below its floppy brim, battered by a hundred storms, a pair of deep blue eyes, set in a face the colour of hazelnut, looked out at the world. Some noticed a touch of sadness in those eyes, a statement which caused surprise, as Walter's speech was full of gentle humour and his laughter came easily. Still, it was remarked, all that time which he spent alone in the silence of the forest among those great trees was sure to have an effect on him. There were even those who swore that they had seen him leaning against a tree, so quiet and still, it looked as though he had become part of it.

Walter's kindness and honesty were as much a part of the man as the nose on his face. Patient with even the most dilatory of his staff and unfailingly courteous to everyone with whom he had dealings, he was loved by many and respected by all. But it was his vast knowledge of all things horticultural, already impressive when he had started on the estate as a lad of thirteen and greatly enriched by the older generation of men with whom he worked, that marked him out. Lord de Winton himself had often had occasion to thank the young gardener for the fine quality of this or that piece of work which he had done; it might be a repair to one of the greenhouses or a particularly attractive arrangement of flowers in the beds before the drawing room windows. The peer had even gone so far as to ask his advice on a point of botanical lore, which was an unheard of mark of esteem. The result of all this was that, when the opportunity for promotion arose, it was generally accepted that he should be the one chosen. And so, by slow degrees, Walter Lambert, known as Wally or Old Lam to his friends, rose steadily upwards until, just shy of his forty-third birthday, he was asked to take on sole charge of the estate grounds.

His hut, for it was little more than that, although built with the skill of a craftsman, and comfortable and pleasing to the eye, stood distant from the main house, in the shade of a grove of chestnut trees. Only in the coldest weather was the door closed. On the morning when Billy arrived for his interview, it stood open to the world. A thin column of grey smoke rose from the chimney, and the sound of tapping could be heard coming from inside.

The lad knocked on the doorframe and stood back, taking one last opportunity to make sure that the shine on his boots was undimmed and that his tie was straight.

Mr. Lambert appeared in the doorway with his pipe in hand. He smiled and nodded a greeting to the lad.

'Morning, Bill. How's your grandad?'

'Morning, Mr. Lambert. He's doing fine. He sends his regards. And my mother sends her thanks for the vegetables which you gave him to take away. I brought the basket back,' replied Billy, with a touch of nerves, setting the empty wicker basket down on the ground.

'Tell your mother she is most welcome, my lad. The ground hereabouts is good for growing, so whatever we plant, we're sure to get a fine crop. In spite of all the mouths to be fed up there,' and he waved his pipe in the direction of the big house, 'there'll always be plenty to spare. You tell her I'll send her fruit, too, damsons and apricots, and anything else that's in season. Then she can make some of that famous jam of hers.'

Mrs. Albright's reputation as a maker of fine preserves was well known, in the village and beyond. The fact was, there was nothing that she couldn't do in that small kitchen of hers. She was always cooking and baking, for the family, first of all, as they were all hard-working country folks with big appetites and bodily strength to keep up. If there was anything left over, she might share it with the neighbours or sell it in a local shop or at the market. The income which she earned from this, she saved in an account at the Post Office. It was always good to have something put by, just in case it was needed, she used to say.

Of all the things that his mother made, Billy liked her jams and chutneys best. A slice of freshly baked bread, still warm from the oven, covered in a thick layer of creamy, salted butter and spread over with some of her cherry curd was just about the tastiest thing he could imagine. The very thought of it was enough to bring a smile to his face. And if he was to wash it down with a mug of strong tea, sweetened with honey from the hives in the garden, so much the better. Only her meat pies could make the smile on his face even wider.

Mr. Lambert watched the lad's eyes light up and his gaze drift off to some other place. We've got a dreamer here, he thought. If what his grandad says about him is true, he'll do just fine. He's still a bit on the short side, but he's got strong hands, and his shoulders and thighs will fill out with all the heavy lifting and laying that's to be done.

'So, Bill, your grandad tells me that you've finished with school and are looking for a job.'

'That's right, Mr. Lambert,' Billy replied, drawing himself up and pushing his shoulders back. It was a grown-up world of work which he was entering now, even if he wasn't fully grown himself. And with that came responsibilities and a wage. He'd be able to contribute something to the housekeeping. At that moment, and not for the first time, he experienced a pleasurable feeling of freedom, like an animal released back into its natural habitat from the cage in which it has been living a cramped existence.

'And it seems that you don't fancy an apprenticeship with Griggs. You don't want to be a mason like your grandad. It's a good and honourable trade. Steady work and whatnot,' continued the gardener, watching Billy closely. He saw a look of uncertainty pass over the boy's face.

'Well, no, I . . .' Was he being told that there was no place for him on the de Winton estate? He hadn't exactly set his heart on it, but the idea had grown on him over the past week or so. As for following in his grandpa's footsteps, Billy had seen the work that he had done with his hands, the statues and columns and tracery which he had carved for the old churches all around, work that would last for hundreds of years, just like the originals had. But he also remembered watching his mother using a carpet beater to beat his grandpa's work jacket and overalls, and the clouds of stone dust that went billowing up into the air. The dust had made Billy sneeze until his head ached. And now, as an old man, grandpa would sit by the fireside of an evening, coughing and wheezing and trying to catch his breath.

Billy drew in a lungful of cool, clean, fresh morning air, and felt how good it was.

'No, Mr. Lambert. That's not for me.' He shook his head and, embarrassed that he had spoken so decidedly, stirred the gravel underfoot with the toe of his boot.

'So tell me about this garden of yours back home,' said Mr. Lambert. 'What are you growing in it?'

'Well, it's trees mainly,' replied Billy. 'From seed. Silver birch, larch and elm. I've also got oak and chestnut saplings which are coming on well. The only problem is, they're getting big and are taking up too much space. Mam said that I should try to sell them at the next farmers' market.'

'That's not a bad idea, lad. It's not an easy thing to do, you know, growing trees from seed. And you'll not find many for sale hereabouts. I imagine there are some folks who'd be only too glad to buy them from you. They'd look fine when newly panted in a garden.'

At that moment, Billy became acutely aware that each of the large chestnut trees which surrounded and overshadowed them had or had taken on a very distinct existence. They were no longer just trees, growing in the background, but a council of elders, old and wise, and very much present, alive and listening to every word which he spoke. And they were not silent. He had the strangest idea that they were talking about him and that they found him . . . approved. Yes, he was eminently suitable.

Now that the decision had been made, Mr. Lambert drew the interview to a close.

'Well, there's lots of work to be done on the estate, Bill, and you look like just the lad to do it. You'd have to work all over, you understand? And you'd have to learn all sorts of other things, too, so working with the trees wouldn't be the only thing you did. How does that sound?'

'That's fine with me, Mr. Lambert,' the youngster replied, a broad smile breaking out on his face.

'In that case, you can start tomorrow morning.'

***

Months passed, and young Billy soon forgot about school. He liked working outside in the fresh air, even in the wind and rain, so long as he was wrapped up well and his feet didn't get cold and wet. It didn't take long for the other staff to recognise that his interest and enthusiasm were genuine, and they easily accepted the newcomer as one of their company.

***

'You need to pay special attention to the trees, Bill,' said Mr. Lambert.

He had found Billy potting seedlings in one of the greenhouses and had suggested that they go for a stroll, as there was something important which he wanted to say to him.

'Although you may not think so, because of their age and size, they need just as much care as the flowers. I don't mean that you have to water them every day or ensure that the ground in which they're growing is free of weeds.'

'That would be difficult,' said Billy. 'Sure, they get all the water they need from the rain, anyway, don't they?'

'As long as the soil can hold on to it and it doesn't simply run off into a nearby stream.'

'They also store a lot of water inside themselves, in the moisture of the wood.'

Mr. Lambert nodded in agreement. The discussion wasn't quite where he wanted it to be, but it was important to put the lad at his ease before attempting to share with him what he had on his mind.

They walked on in silence side-by-side. Billy attempted to measure his stride to that of the older man. As Wally Lambert was tall and had long legs, and an odd way of tapping the toe of his right boot on the ground every dozen or so steps, as though knocking off an accumulation of soil stuck to the sole, this proved difficult. Billy finally gave up and fell a few steps behind.

The old woodsman directed his steps off the gravel drive and into the shadow and coolness of the trees, a mixture of oaks, chestnuts, poplars and other deciduous growing together in a natural harmony. He stopped beside an especially fine old oak tree and placed his hand on the trunk. Billy watched him, and then copied his action. As they stood thus, the older man began to speak once more.

'You know, Bill, the reason that I've brought you here is that I wanted to share with you some of the things which I learned when I was about the same age as you. When I started working on the estate, the Head Gardener was an old man called Bartholomew Wilkinson. Maybe you've heard some of the older staff speaking about him.'

Billy nodded. Charlie Wagstaff, who had been a gamekeeper on the estate all his life and who, at seventy-five years old, was still to be seen tottering about with a loaded shotgun under his arm, used occasionally to mention the name of Wilkinson with something very like a note of reverence in his voice.

'He knew just about everything there was to know about gardens. The names of plants, Latin and English, and the common names by which many of them were known. He could get anything to grow, as well, could old Bart. Every type of fruit and vegetable, no matter how exotic or rare. And those greenhouses and plots produced something for the house at every time of the year. But he had a special love, just like you and I do, Bill. More than anything else, he loved trees. And he planted some of those that are growing round about us at this moment.'

'Not this oak, though,' said Billy. 'It's too old.'

'No, he didn't plant this one, but I can show you many that he did. Just like you, he grew them from seed and, once they were big enough, he moved them out of the nursery and into the ground. And before Bartholomew Wilkinson, there was Joshua Hammersby. And so on, all the way back to the founding of this estate, sometime in the thirteen hundreds. There's written records in the library up there,' and he nodded in the direction of the big house, 'and plans and designs, containing details about what was cut down and what was planted and where. The flower beds and elegant hedges and gravel walkways weren't always here. It was the trees they wanted most of all. They provided an income for the estate when they were cut down for timber; but they had another purpose as well.'

At that moment, at some distance from where the two men stood, a family group moved past them down the drive in the direction of the main house, visitors out for an hour's fresh air and exercise. Two small children, a boy and a girl, laughing and shouting, were chasing a black and white spaniel, which seemed determined not to be caught. Their parents followed behind, watching the fun and high jinks. Every time the children managed to get a hand on the dog's collar or its tail or an ear, off it would go again.

'Look, Bill,' said Mr. Lambert, who had turned his head to watch. 'What do you notice?' he asked, in a quiet voice, so as not to be overheard.

A puzzled look appeared on Billy's face, and he shrugged his shoulders.

'They're having fun,' came the hesitant reply. It was the first thought that had come into his head and, no sooner had it done so, than it was out of his mouth.

'And they look happy.'

A brief silence followed, during which they continued to watch the children's antics, until the group disappeared out of sight around a bend in the drive, then Mr. Lambert went on. 'Here's something that I want you to do, Bill, when you remember. I want you to watch the visitors who come to the park. Discretely. That is, try to do so without attracting attention. Watch how they behave. And when I speak to you again, tomorrow or the next day, you can tell me what you've seen. Agreed?'

'Okay, Mr. Lambert.'

'You don't need to ask me why just now,' Walter Lambert said, when he saw the look of curiosity on the boy's face and guessed at the question forming on his lips. 'Anyway, I think it's high time that you got back to the greenhouse, don't you? Otherwise, Bert Oldshaw will have something to say to you. On you go.'

He watched the boy break into a run, then turned back towards the great oak beside which he was standing. Placing his hand on the trunk again and moving his head closer, he appeared to speak a few words to it. What he said, there was no one close enough to hear.

Was it just the rising wind that caused the tree to move with greater animation? And that sound the branches made, as they rubbed together, it didn't sound like laughter, did it? Just a little like a deep, drawn out "Ho"?

Lambert gave it one final pat and moved on to the next tree, a very tall beech which had lost a branch or two in that year's equinoctial gales and was looking a touch the worse for wear. Its bark was peeling in places and someone had carved their initials into the exposed wood. The woodsman did just the same with this one, too, and, when he had finished whispering some words of friendship or consolation, a few words of encouragement or thanks, he moved on. And so, for the next half-hour or more, he wandered among the trees, stopping to speak with the older among them, perhaps to pull off a dead leaf or two, or knock off a rotten branch. He left the young ones to themselves. It would be a long time, perhaps many, many years, before they would receive a word of greeting. And he himself would be long gone by that time. Besides which, just like the children with the dog, they had their parents or elders to look after them until that time.

As he made his way back to his hut, by a long, roundabout route, through an area of woodland that was particularly densely grown and rather dark, at any hour of the day, and one which, because of the absence of any well-trodden paths, or for some other reason, was seldom explored by visitors, he noticed that the undergrowth had been trampled down. At the centre of the circle of broken stalks and scuffed leaves were the remains of a fire. He picked up a number of empty bottles and assorted rubbish, shaking his head at the very idea that someone should simply have tossed them away. Where was their respect? If everyone treated the park like this, it wouldn't be long before it wasn't fit to be seen. And here was a scrap of clothing, as well, torn and burnt. It had been white, that he could see, but was now dirty and stained with . . . with what? Fruit juice or wine, he thought, stuffing the rag into his jacket pocket. At least they had made their campfire from twigs and branches which had been lying around, as he could find no evidence of axe or saw marks on any of the surrounding trees.

He would have to remember to pass through this spot more often. Camping out in the woods overnight was one thing, and nobody minded it, so long as it didn't happen too often or there was any trouble; but lighting fires was another matter, especially in this dry season of the year. A moment's carelessness and the whole place might go up in flames. Fire and trees did not mix very well.

***

'Well, Bill, did you do what I asked?' Mr. Lambert inquired, when, some days later, he happened on the lad sharpening a hand axe.

Billy said that he had.

'I was hosing down and cleaning the gates at the north entrance yesterday morning, so I had a good chance to watch people as they passed me by.'

'I hope you didn't soak anyone,' said Mr. Lambert, with a chuckle, knowing full well that the lad would have taken great pains to do no such thing.

'No, I didn't,' replied Billy, trying to suppress a smile. 'I did turn the hose on a couple of dogs, though, when their owners weren't looking,' the boy added, uncertain how the older man would react to the confession. 'They only barked and ran off.'

'And what did you notice? Was there anything about the behaviour of the visitors which stood out in your mind?'

The boy's head moved to one side, as if to say "not really".

'There must be something that you noticed, Bill.'

'The noise? There's often a lot of noise. Chatter and laughter. Except if they're on their own, in which case it wouldn't do for them to be seen talking to themselves, would it?'

'It would not, Bill. That it would not. But I dare say there's plenty of them on their own who do just that. Go on, lad.'

'It didn't always happen, but I thought their behaviour seemed to change. Sometimes only a little, but sometimes a lot. It was as if a weight was being lifted from their shoulders when they passed through the gate. They seemed to relax and straighten up and walk with a spring in their step.'

Mr. Lambert, not wishing to interrupt the flow of his young assistant's words, made no comment, but indicated his approval of these remarks with a faint nod of his head.

'The children always seem very happy to be among the trees,' Billy continued, 'and the dogs have great fun, running all over the place, sniffing at all those strange scents, and then disappearing into the bushes. It's as though they can sense that they're now free to do what they want.'

He looked up at the older man, as if for confirmation that what he had noticed was, in fact, the case, but Mr. Lambert appeared to be giving all his attention to filling his briarwood pipe.

When he had lit it and taken a few puffs, he asked the boy, 'And why do you think that is, Bill? Why do all these people, young and old, on their own or in company, want to come here and walk in these woods?'

A silence followed, which neither seemed to want to break.

'You know,' Mr. Lambert went on, 'there's an old legend that says, when a great tree falls or is cut down by man, the store of wisdom and happiness in this world diminishes. There are also those who believe that one of the purposes of the trees, perhaps their main purpose, is to attach the earth to the sky. And when a tree is cut down, one of the giants, mind you, not one the babies,' he said, reaching out a hand to pat the narrow trunk of a small elder, 'the sky becomes detached at that point, and when the very last tree falls, if that should ever happen, the sky will fly off and the world will be left open.'

'Open? Open to what, Mr. Lambert?' asked Billy. He looked up through the leaves and branches to the patches of blue sky above, as if to spot places where it might have become loose and ready to fly off.

'What, indeed, Bill?' came the reply. 'The stories don't say, perhaps because the tellers of those same stories never could imagine such a thing happening. And with people like you and me around, young Bill,' said Mr. Lambert, becoming quite animated and, in an access of paternal affection, placing his hand on the boy's shoulder, 'that's not something we need worry ourselves about. We'll never let that happen, will we? And there are plenty of tree-lovers like us, all over the world, who'll do the same.'

And so ended their discussion for the present. Walter was happy with the progress that he had made. It didn't do any harm to get Bill thinking, but he didn't want to confuse him. Besides which, there was always a lot of work to be done around the grounds, and the young fellow had his tasks to attend to, like everyone else. It wouldn't do for him to be day-dreaming and falling behind.

***

'Do you remember what we discussed last time, Bill?' asked Mr. Lambert. Weeks had passed. The weather remained fine and warm. They were cutting down a tree which had been damaged in the winter storms six months or so earlier. Walter had kept an eye on it since then. The strong, dry wind that had been blowing all the previous night had further weakened it, leaving him with no option but to take it down.

'The healing power of the trees,' said Billy, after landing another powerful blow with his axe. He had been doing a lot of thinking since they had last talked together. He had also been watching the visitors, and was more convinced than ever that he had been in the right.

Mr. Lambert rested on the long hickory shaft of his double-headed axe and took the pipe out of his mouth, as if wishing to make what he had to say absolutely clear. 'They help carry away those poisons which accumulate in our hearts and minds, as a result of the lives we lead. They somehow act as conduits, channels, through which these toxins are drawn out of us and passed up into the air where they are dispersed. Like a chimney, getting rid of the waste from the fire, the smoke, so that you can enjoy the heat. The trees have that effect, Bill, but it is a spiritual cleansing that I'm talking about. By some power which they possess, ancient and magic, they are able to extract those feelings that weigh us down, the bad thoughts, the sadness and such like. And very often, we don't even know that those feelings are there, or that they've been removed. We might feel a certain lightness of mood, or sleep better at night, or laugh easier.'

Billy understood everything that Mr. Lambert said, and knew in his heart that it was so.

'And just as the trees help us, so must we also help them,' continued Wally Lambert. 'I, and you, who will come after me, as keepers of this sacred space, this woody paradise, if you want to call it that and it isn't too poetical a way of describing it, have a duty to nourish and care for the trees in turn. That is what I'm trying to get at.'

In the silence that followed these words of wisdom from the older man, the sound of the wind whispering through the leaves was unusually sweet. Billy felt a tingling all over his body. A magical energy was flowing though him, an energy which made his eyes shine so brightly, that Mr. Lambert burst out laughing.

'That's why people come here, Bill. Just a little of what you're feeling now is enough to help them through, until they can get back here to recharge their batteries again.'

At that moment, Billy realised that he had been elevated to a position of importance, and that, whatever else he might do on the estate, it would be his particular task, along with Mr. Lambert, to look after these huge denizens of the forest.

One afternoon, when Billy had finished weeding and raking the gravel paths in the yew hedge maze, a daily task, if the walks weren't to look untidy and unkempt, he sat himself down on a stone bench to enjoy a few minutes of quiet. Propping the rake against his leg and pulling out a handkerchief, he began to mop his neck and brow. From somewhere nearby, the call of a cuckoo drifted through the warm air; and he began to nod off.

'Taking a touch of the sun, Bill?' Mr. Lambert's voice made the lad start, and he turned to find the old man standing by his side. He was holding something in his left hand, partly concealed by his arm and body.

'Is that for me?' Billy asked, his words sounding rather muddled, as though his tongue hadn't woken up when the rest of him had. 'A gun?'

'It's an air rifle, laddie. If you'll come with me, I'll tell you what I want you to do. Come on.'

Billy pushed himself up, picked up his rake and bucket, and trudged after Mr. Lambert. Trying to catch forty winks somewhere in the garden during the day without being caught was nigh impossible. Old Lam's hawk eyes would find you anywhere.

'The grey squirrels are getting out of hand in some parts of the estate,' said Mr. Lambert, when his young assistant had caught up with him.

'You want me to shoot them?' Billy asked.

'No, I want you to scare them off by making loud quacking noises, but take the air rifle along with you, just in case they don't appreciate your duck impersonations and start throwing acorns at you. They can get quite ferocious when roused.'

Mr. Lambert laughed when he saw the look of confusion on the boy's face.

'I was joking, Bill. Yes, I want you to shoot them. You've used an air rifle before?'

Billy nodded. 'Grandpa has one which he uses for poa ...' He bit his tongue, and the hint of a blush appeared on his tanned face.

'Hmm,' said Mr. Lambert, looking sideways at the lad and trying not to smile. 'It's still a bit early,' he went on. 'Better this evening, when the visitors are gone and the gates are locked. Can you stay behind for an hour or two and do it then? If you're lucky, you'll get some rabbits for your mother.'

'Why shoot the squirrels?' Billy asked. 'The visitors like watching them, especially the children. And the dogs enjoy chasing them around.'

'They're a pest. They may look nice and furry, but they do a tremendous amount of damage to the trees, as they're forever stripping off the bark to get at the sap underneath. It's the sweetness they like, Bill. And they'll also eat birds' eggs, and the chicks, too, if they're hungry enough. Here, take the rifle and this box of pellets. Go and find a quiet spot, set up a few targets, and get some practice. Remember, try to get a clean kill. Shoot for the head or neck.'

This was an altogether unexpected treat for Billy. The last hour of his working day was usually given over to cleaning gardening tools and sweeping out the greenhouses and potting sheds. And now here he was, off for some target practice and a spot of hunting. It would mean being late for dinner, but he thought his mam wouldn't mind, especially if he brought home some fresh rabbits. It had been a while since she had made a rabbit pie or rabbit stew.

The estate grounds were noticeably emptier in the last half hour before the gates closed at six o'clock. The bustle and noise, which had been so much a part of the place during the daytime, grew quieter as the visitors left. And then, almost at a stroke, all was still and silent.

There was something mildly unsettling about the walks and gardens at this time, as the sky began to darken and the shadows to lengthen. It was as if the visitors had taken something away with them when they departed, and the eeriness, which was so strong he sometimes felt it settling about his shoulders like a cloak, was simply the emptiness which remained. He was used to working on his own for much of the day in the distant reaches of the forest, but this silence through which he now moved unnerved him slightly, so that he stopped every so often, as he made his way to the hunting grounds, to reassure himself that his were the only footsteps which he could hear.

In little more than an hour, Billy's bag was almost full of dead squirrels and rabbits. He was admiring their fur and wondering whether there was enough of it for his mother to make him a hat, when he heard the sharp cracking of a branch somewhere nearby. The sound broke the silence like a gunshot and startled him so much that his first thought was to get out of the clearing and find a place to hide. As he darted off, two of the rabbits fell from his game bag.

Kneeling behind a bush and peeping though the leaves, the lad fixed his eyes on the far side of the clearing, some twenty-five or thirty feet away, that being the direction from which the noise had seemed to come. The foliage began to move and rustle, and a figure emerged, the figure of a man, small and thin, his sallow face fringed by a rather scraggy grey beard and his head covered by a high-crowned old hat with a floppy brim. His clothing, all shades of green and brown, allowed him to blend into the background so effectively, that, when he stopped moving, it was almost impossible to pick him out.

The newcomer appeared to scan the open space before him. He moved forward in a hesitant manner, as though leaving the protection of the trees and bushes only with reluctance, stopped at the centre of the clearing, and then slowly turned around in a full circle, all the while examining the trees, the ground, even the darkening sky above, through the canopy of branches.

'A nice spot,' Billy heard him say, in a low, clear voice. 'Entirely suitable, I think. Very quiet and out of the way. What say you?' and he turned his head, as though addressing the question to a second person standing slightly behind him and to his right hand side, although none was to be seen there.

For some moments, he continued to talk quietly in this manner, seemingly in a discussion concerning the merits of the location and its suitability for some unspoken purpose. Then his eyes fell upon the freshly-slain rabbits.

'What have we here?' he murmured, standing stock-still and peering about in the gathering gloom, as though sensing that the hunter might still be somewhere nearby. Billy began to tremble, causing the zipper of his jacket to rattle, the faintest of sounds which seemed to din in his ears. 'Someone out hunting this evening?' the stranger enquired. 'In this empty spot? Won't do at all, no, it certainly won't.' He slowly shook his head. 'We don't want to be disturbed, do we? No, sir.'

He picked up a rabbit with each hand, sniffed them all over and then appeared to lick the drops of fresh blood from the mortal wounds which the pellets had made, smacking his lips in pleasure. Sitting himself cross-legged on the ground, he took out a folding knife and began to gut one of the rabbits, tearing off and throwing away the skin when he had done so.

He made short work of devouring the pink flesh, and tossed what was left of the carcass into the bushes.

'The foxes can finish it off,' he said, licking his fingers and hands clean.

Stuffing the other rabbit into his coat pocket, he took one last look around and then disappeared into the shadows, departing as silently as he had come.

Billy remained motionless in his hiding-place for all of twenty or thirty minutes, straining his ears for even the faintest of noises which might indicate the direction which the stranger had taken. The very last thing which he wanted, at that late hour of the day and in that lonely spot, was to step out from his place of concealment and straight into the arms of a man who liked the taste of raw meat.

When he finally reached home, his mother was more than a little angry, as dinner had been served hours before and there was still no sign of her boy. He managed to placate her, however, with a tender kiss on the cheek, a muttered apology, and a hesitantly proffered gift of two plump, full-grown rabbits. At this, her mood softened and she told him to sit down at the table and she would fetch his tea for him.

***

After a particularly busy morning, during which he had carted tubs of flowers from various sites about the gardens back to the greenhouse so they could be tidied up, refilled with soil or replanted, Billy was looking forward to his lunch break. Instead of sitting with his fellow workers, as he was accustomed to do, enjoying the gossip and the casual exchange of ideas and experiences, he chose to go off by himself.

In addition to the packet of sandwiches which his mother had prepared for him, as she always did, she included several pieces of ripe fruit, one of her small home-made meat pies and a bottle of ginger beer. It was quite a feast for the youngster, but he had had nothing to eat since the early hours of the morning, and all the energy which he had expended in his tasks meant that he was looking forward to it on this day with a particular feeling of pleasure.

During his wanderings through the woods and fields which made up the estate, Billy had discovered a number of spots of rare beauty. Secluded and too far off the beaten track to be disturbed by visitors, they were places in which he might take his ease for an hour. One such was on the bank of a stream, the Faery Burn, as it was called. He had enjoyed listening to the stories about the origin of the name, but had dismissed them as nothing more than that, stories.

Why he chose the Faery Burn on this day, he couldn't say. Perhaps it was the idea of bathing his feet in the cold water which attracted him.

He dropped the bottle of ginger beer into the water among the reeds, threw his jacket on the ground, and sank down, resting his back against the trunk of a willow tree. This was the life, he said to himself, with a sigh of tiredness and long-anticipated pleasure. He could spend all day in such a spot, watching the bullrushes waving gently in the afternoon breeze and listening to the songs which the sedge-warblers and pied wagtails sang. He shivered with delight at the feeling of the sun's warmth on his face, then shook his head, as his eyelids began to grow heavy. It would be a waste if he was to sleep his lunchtime away, he thought. On the other hand, a short nap could do no harm. And with that, his eyes closed.

***

'Hello,' said the figure. 'Fancy finding you here.'

'Hello. It's a lovely spot,' replied Billy, surprised to discover that he was not alone.

'Yes, it is. It's the loveliest spot for miles around,' said the figure, taking a step closer. 'Do you mind?'

'Not at all. Please, help yourself.' Billy opened the packet of sandwiches and offered them to his guest.

'That pie looks nice,' it said, bending forward to sniff the delicious savoury smell.

There were limits to hospitality, thought Billy, who had been longing to scoff the pie all morning. He held it up, all the same. It was only good manners.

'If you don't mind, I'd like that apple.'

Billy watched her, for he was now certain that it was a she, take a small, delicate bite from the ripe fruit. Her white teeth were very white and her eyes were green, a darker shade of green than that of the garments which she wore. He thought it rather unusual for a girl to have such short hair, as all the girls he knew took great pride in growing theirs as long as they could, even down to their waists. And what slender creamy-white arms she had!

'That was delicious,' she said, and licked her lips. She had eaten the whole apple, core, pips and stalk. 'Do you think I might . . . ?' she inquired, reaching out a tiny hand to the two soft, sweetly-smelling golden apricots. Billy only smiled, and the fruit was gone in a flash. She tossed the stones over her head, one after the other, to land in the middle of the stream with a gentle "plop". 'I'm rather thirsty. It's hot work being out in the sun, don't you know,' she said, and delicately patted her forehead.

'There's a bottle of ginger beer cooling in the stream,' said Billy. He tried to sit up, but found the effort too great, and sank back again.

'Yes, I saw that,' the figure replied, and took the bottle out from under her jerkin.

'I've got a bottle-opener . . . '

'Oh, that's alright, I've got strong teeth.' Off came the top, and she took a sip of the ginger beer. 'Hmmm. Cold and sweet. Lovely.' She took two more sips. 'So, what are doing here, you handsome boy?' she asked, and touched Billy on the nose.

'It's my lunchtime. And I like listening to the birds.'

At that moment, a dove and a hedge-sparrow began a duet, the cooing of one and the chirping of the other sounding especially harmonious. A blackbird joined in, to make it a lively trio.

'You like songs, do you? I could teach you one or two, in return for the apple and the apricots,' she suggested.

Billy nodded his head so eagerly, he bumped it hard against the tree trunk. He grimaced and rubbed at the painful spot, and when, a second or two later, he looked up, he found himself quite alone by the side of the burn. The sun was still shining and the birds were still singing. He wondered if he had only been dreaming. The fruit was gone, that was true, but so were the sandwiches, and the empty ginger beer bottle was lying in the grass at his side. It must have been a dream, he told himself. And now it was time to get back to work. He hoped he wouldn't be late, as he didn't like to hear Mr. Lambert grumbling about lazy so-and-sos.

***

Sitting by the fireside that evening after dinner, staring into the coals and thinking about nothing in particular, Billy heard his mother ask, 'Have you taken to music, Will?' She appeared at the door with a bundle held out in her hand. 'I was unpacking your work bag. Pan pipes, I think they're called.' Billy tried not to jump out of his seat. His eyes wide with wonder, he managed to stammer out that he had borrowed them from a friend. 'It's a lovely piece of cloth,' Mrs. Albright said, holding up to the light the large square of green silk in which the pipes had been wrapped. 'See how it shines so. It would make a nice collar for a dress.' She draped it over her shoulder and admired her reflection in the small mirror hanging from the window frame above the kitchen sink.

Seeing how much his mam liked the silken cloth and wanting to please her, Billy told her that she could keep it, if she would make a bag for the pipes, from the rabbit skins hanging in the garden shed. She took little persuading and, in the space of an hour, the job was done.

***

Next morning, when he was leaving for work, he made sure he had the pipes with him, slung over his shoulder in their new rabbit-skin bag. That he didn't know how to play them yet, troubled him not a whit.

The day turned out fine and warm, with skies the colour of cornflower and lapis, and not a cloud to be seen anywhere.

As he reclined beneath the spreading shade of a beech tree during his lunch hour, chewing on a stalk of grass and listening to the buzzing of insects and wishing that he didn't have anything to do that afternoon, so that he might stay there in that spot for ever, Billy heard a charming melody sounding through the trees, a melody which he could not recollect having heard before. Now it wasn't unusual for a bird from some far distant land to find its way into the forest, where it would stay for a time, before disappearing as suddenly as it had come, and leaving behind it, in the minds of those who were fortunate enough to have heard it, nothing more than a fading memory of its song. And if it wasn't a bird? Quite why such a thought should come into his head, he couldn't say; but it was immediately followed by another, which suggested to him that he might like to try to imitate the sound.

He took out the pipes and placed them to his lips, but the melody stopped and, in its place, he heard a single note played, sustained over some seconds and then repeated several times. This he tried to copy. At first, he blew into the wrong end of the pipes, then blew too loudly or with his lips forming the wrong shape. It took many attempts before he managed it.

The note was repeated one last time, fainter, as though coming to him from farther away, and was followed by the sound of laughter. Then the melody began again, fainter still and growing ever more so, until the only sound which he could hear was that of the surrounding forest.

Billy never knew when or where his next music lesson might take place. If he was by himself when he heard the unmistakable strains of the melody once again, he simply stopped what he was doing and picked up the rabbit-skin bag which he carried around with him everywhere he went. At other times, he might hear it sounding to him over the chatter of voices or the clatter of garden tools. On one occasion, Billy tried to draw his friend's attention to the music, but the other lad listened for a moment, then shrugged his shoulders and shook his head.

In this way, over a period of weeks, he learned all the notes to the melody. At odd moments, between finishing one task and starting another, or in the evenings, when his working day was over, Billy practised the tune, until he could play it clearly and without mistakes.

Mid-morning one day, as Billy was making his way back to the walled garden, where he had to spend an hour hoeing and weeding the vegetable beds, his attention was caught by a blur of colour moving about the forest floor ahead of him. A pair of weasels, perhaps engaged in a territorial dispute, were chasing one another hither and thither at great speed. He stopped to lean against the trunk of a horse chestnut and enjoy the thrilling natural spectacle, but the weasels disappeared beneath a rhododendron bush. Only the faint rustling of leaves told him that the contest continued somewhere out of sight. Disinclined to pursue his journey at that moment, he took out his pipes and began to play the only tune that he knew. Again and again he played it, now louder, now softer, now faster, now slower, each time trying to make it sound more beautiful than the last, until a vibration passing through the trunk caused him to stop. The whole tree, all of its sixty and more feet of height, seemed to be humming with energy. He stood back and watched, in growing astonishment, as it began to move, almost imperceptibly at first, but then with increasing vigour, until it might be said to be fairly dancing, in a slow, pliant, elegant tree-like way.

When he put the pipes to his lips once more, over the sussuration of the leaves and the rubbing and creaking of the branches, he heard a voice break into song. It was a pure, high-pitched voice and it kept perfect time with his piping. The words of the song were in a language which he didn't know, but he sensed that it told a tale of tall trees and quiet woodland glades.

When he repeated the experiment with another tree and saw that his playing had a similar effect, he realised that this would be his most important work on the de Winton estate, this would be how he would ensure the wellbeing of those majestic denizens of the forest. He would play to them, singly or in groups, whenever the time allowed. No, he thought, forming a resolution, he would make time for this task, even if it meant arriving earlier in the morning or staying behind in the evening for an hour. He wouldn't do so every day; two or three times a week would be enough. His only wish was that he might learn other melodies to play for them. And, just as he wished, so it happened.

In spite of the fact that the music lessons took place on a fairly regular basis, Billy never did see her again, that small, slender nymph with the dark green eyes and the white teeth who had so enchanted him by the Faery Burn. However, there were times when he might round a bend on one of his woodland walks, and see a bush shaking or a branch vibrating, as though someone had that moment dashed past; or hear the sound of feet scampering away over dry leaves. At others, feeling himself watched, he might look up from the task in which he was then engaged, and see what looked very much like a face peeping out at him from amidst the leaves, only to find that there was nothing there when he went to investigate.

As he made his way along a shady, half-overgrown track which the red deer used to get from one feeding ground to another, he chanced upon a remarkable thing one day. On the forest floor, some paces ahead of him, still gently rocking from side to side, as though it had at that very moment fallen from a branch above, lay what looked like a bird's nest. It was woven from moss, the soft down of young birds and tufts of rabbit fur, all tied about with long lengths of hair from the tail of a horse. As he held it in the palm of his hand, he marvelled at the fineness of its construction, but it was larger, deeper and rounder in shape than any nest which he had seen before. And the long, golden pheasant's feather which was stuck into its side suggested to him, after a moment's reflection, that it wasn't a nest at all, but a helmet belonging to someone with a rather small head. He had half a mind to take it with him and show Mr. Lambert, but decided to leave it where he had found it, in case its owner returned to look for it. On another occasion, while crossing a burn, he noticed the faint impression of a pair of small feet in the soft mud. As he bent down to have a closer look, an acorn struck him on the side of the head, and then another. Thinking it to be only a squirrel, although one with rather a good aim, he went back to his investigations. And there, bobbing away on the slow-moving waters and almost lost to sight among the reeds and grasses was a small boat, made of twigs and bark.

Such strange encounters and the feeling of someone else being present became so commonplace, that he ceased to wonder at them.

There were places of unusual beauty in that large forest. In these, Billy experienced a feeling akin to that of entering a sacred space. The air, often heavy with the scent of flowers, was so still and pure, it was a delight simply to stand unmoving and breathe it in. Aches and pains were soothed away, and a wonderful feeling of calm pervaded his mind and body. If he knew that his work might take him near one of these woodland bowers, he would be sure to bring with him a small jar of honey or jam, or a piece of fruit, or even one of his mother's pies. This he would leave as a token of his gratitude, for all the pleasures which his work in the forest brought him, for the gift of music which he had been granted and the special purpose to which he was to put it, and for the unseen protection which he felt was always near him. When he returned, the present would be gone, but the empty jar would always be there, standing in the same place where he had left it.

One day, late in the afternoon or early in the evening, whichever it might be, when he was finished the last of his tasks, Billy Albright mounted his bicycle and made his way, in his usual unhurried manner, along the gravel drive in the direction of the south gate. The route rose gradually to a high point of ground from where it was possible to survey the whole of the estate and get a fair estimation of its considerable extent. Without thinking, he stopped here and turned to look back along the road that he had just come.

The sky seemed unusually bright for the time of the day, and, in spite of the fact that only the softest of breezes caressed his cheeks, in the far distance, over towards the northern boundary of the de Winton estate, he could see that some of the trees were moving with great energy, changing the colour of the canopy to a remarkable light green, as the underside of their leaves was exposed to the eye. Strange to say, the surrounding forest was entirely still or only very faintly stirring. Why this should be, was a question which began to form in his mind, but a rising feeling of nausea and an overwhelming desire to get home left it barely acknowledged. The last thing which he saw, as he turned to resume his homeward journey, was an expanse of very dark cloud directly above the swirling tops of those trees.

By the time he reached home, his head was aching fit to burst. His mother commented on the paleness of his face and placed a hand on his brow.

'You're burning up, son,' she said. 'I'll run you a bath, and then straight to bed. I'll bring you up a bowl of chicken soup and, when you're finished that, a hot toddy. On you go, Billy boy. Leave your stuff here.'

Billy did as he was bidden.

The bath relaxed his tired limbs, the warm soup filled his belly, and the hot toddy sent him into a deep, but unsettled sleep, in which he tossed and turned without cease. A confused and confusing sequence of fragmented images flitted through his mind. Frightening sounds, of intoxicated laughter, the beating of a drum and the steadily rising cadence of a chant dinned in his ears. And then came a scream, so piercing and terrifying that the boy, still unconscious, frantically tried to pull the sheets up over his head.

A little after one o'clock, Billy's eyes blinked once, twice, and then opened wide. He yawned and stretched, feeling well-rested, if a little queasy in his stomach, which was perhaps only on account of the quantity of brandy which his mother had used in her toddy. She always liked to make it good and strong, she said, or it wouldn't have the effect it should have. Otherwise, he felt in good shape. He threw back the sheets and sat on the edge of the bed for a moment, to see if his head still ached. The pain had been replaced by a sound, which he could only describe as being like a groan, deep and full of sadness. Like the blast of a foghorn, muted by great distance and a dense blanket of fog. Repeating over and over.

He knew it was a warning.

He began to dress, but in rather a distracted manner, as he tried mentally to grasp at and bring into focus the indistinct impression that there was something which he had to do, some task which had been enjoined upon him. What this was remained unclear. But he must remember the hand axe. And the torch, he would need that too.

As he left the house, he tried to prevent the door of the back porch from creaking as he closed it behind him. The hinges would need oiled when he returned. Returned? Yes; but from where? Where was he going at this late hour of the night?

With the hatchet tucked into his belt and the torch in his pocket, he pushed the bicycle out of the garden gate and onto the road. All was silent and dark, apart from a light in an upstairs window at the far end of the street. The Bertram's house.

The note of warning in his head was more urgent. He could hear another sound now, as of the whispering of a myriad of leaves. The message was unclear, but it set his nerves on edge.

And into his head, for the merest fraction of a second, came the image of a face which he had seen before. On just one occasion. It had frightened him then, when he had watched it silently appear out of the shadows, and the sudden recollection of it now caused him to tremble so violently, he nearly lost control of his bicycle and crashed it into the low wall of the bridge over which he was at that moment passing.

It wasn't the blood of a rabbit which dripped from the fringe of grey beard. The certainty of that thought struck him like a hammer.

As his eyes became accustomed to the darkness, he pedalled with ever greater urgency, seemingly unconscious of the dangerous proximity of the stone walls, and the trees and hedges past which he sped. He was almost there, but the South Gate would be locked, and there could be no question of rousing the gatekeeper to let him through. The minutes wasted in waiting and answering questions was time which he did not have.

At that instant, he knew what the confusion of sounds in his head was. The trees were calling to him.

He skidded to a halt, picked up the bicycle and, with every muscle straining, pushed it up the tall iron gate and tipped it over the top. It clattered to the ground on the other side, but the noise didn't worry him. He would be long gone before anyone came to investigate. Then he was up and over himself. That was no trouble. He hadn't yet found a tree on the estate which he couldn't climb.

The speed at which he moved over the unpaved surface of the long drive made the bicycle shudder dreadfully, with the result that his wrists and forearms were soon aching. Every bump threatened to unseat him and send him flying to the ground.

As he flew past the highest point of the drive, he thought he saw a faint patch of light in the darkness far ahead, but couldn't be sure that it wasn't just his imagination playing tricks. It didn't matter now, in any case, as he knew where he was going. The trees had known what was to happen. The sign which they had given him on the previous evening had been a foreshadowing of destruction.

When he reached Mr. Lambert's hut, tenantless and locked up for the night, he dropped the bicycle and pulled out his torch. Before disappearing among the trees, he paused to run his thumb along the edge of the hatchet. Yes, it was nice and sharp. It would need to be for the work which he had to do.

Low-hanging branches and foliage lashed at his face and hands. His feet slid on damp leaves or stumbled over exposed roots, and he was sent sprawling onto the ground or tumbling into a bush or tree trunk. He picked himself up and pushed on, forcing more speed from his tiring limbs, but the uneven ground, suddenly rising up or falling away, made it impossible for him to maintain momentum. Still, he was heedless of everything, except the need to reach his destination before it was too late.

It was as he pushed himself up from the ground after yet another fall, that he heard the sound, a real sound now, not just one in his head. It was still indistinct, but very definitely audible. Turning off the torch, he began to move forward, keeping his eyes fixed on the dimmest of yellowy-orange glows up ahead. The collision caused him to start back in fright. Something brushed against his hand, something soft and warm, but it sped past and on into the darkness and was gone before he thought to try to grasp at it or stop it.

When he reached the clearing, Billy dashed forward without pausing. His unexpected presence there, in that scene of madness, seemed barely to register. The dancers continued to dance around the fire, twisting themselves into all manner of shapes, like rag dolls shaken by invisible hands. The chanting rose and fell, keeping time to the beating of a tambor or drum. Only the figure in the centre of that ring of writhing human bodies seemed to have become aware that there was an intruder in their midst, as it turned to stare at him. The terrible light in its eyes faded and a look of incomprehension appeared on its face. Its hands, which had been raised above waist level, dropped to its sides. Billy saw that one held a knife, its long blade glinting in the light of the fire, and that the other, the one closest to him, held an infant child, gripped by the leg and hanging upside down.

These facts had scarcely registered in the lad's mind, when, in one swift and fluent movement, he drew the hatchet from his belt with his right hand, balanced it for a second, and then struck down. The heavy axe head, honed to a razor sharpness and driven with all the strength which he could muster in his powerful shoulders and torso, a strength augmented by cold fury, cleaved the head in two. The man sank to his knees and fell forwards onto the ground, the axe stuck fast in his neck.

Billy scooped up the child and swung it out of the circle of chaos into the shadows beyond the clearing, hoping that the soft, damp ground would be enough to break its fall and prevent injury.

The dancers danced and the drummer drummed.

As he rose up, a Maenad, her face partly covered by a tangled mass of dark hair, and naked, but for a loin cloth, rushed at him with a crazed scream. She raised her clenched fists and tried to strike at him, but he seized hold of her wrists and, forcing her arms apart, drove a knee up into her groin and slammed his head into her face as it jerked forwards to meet his own. When he released his hold of her, she crumpled in a heap at his feet, writhing and moaning from the pain of the double assault. He lifted his booted foot to crush the life out of her, when he was knocked to the ground by a blow from behind.

Still the drummer drummed and the dancers danced.

Try as he might to shake it off, an immovable weight on his back pressed him into the cold earth. He felt a hand twine itself in his hair, and his head was pulled so far back that he was able to see the glowing sparks from the fire rising up, amidst the smoke, into the darkness above. As the knife blade rested against his neck and the pressure on it gradually increased, he heard a laugh, and a voice whispered into his ear, 'No, this won't do, at all.' It was a voice which he had heard once before, in a clearing such as this, in another part of the forest, on a late spring evening months before.

In the few seconds of life which he knew were left to him, Billy felt no fear, but the image of his beloved mother passing before his eyes brought with it a wave of sadness, for the pain that his death would cause her, and the bewilderment, and the long years of mourning that would be hers.

He opened his mouth to send forth a scream of rage into the night, but it was drowned out by a noise like thunder coming from above, a cracking and splintering and rending of wood. A bough, as thick as a man's waist and heavy beyond imagining, crashed down onto the head and shoulders of Billy's assailant, crushing his skull and knocking him sideways. As the lad tried to free himself from the branches which covered him, he heard voices calling out or crying in pain. A second bough, on a tree at the farther edge of the clearing, groaned mightily for some seconds, a sound that was like the roar of a hundred ravening beasts, then it too splintered and fell, striking down or smothering those members of the nocturnal assembly who still remained standing.

Although entirely covered, the weight which pinned Billy down was not very great, and by wriggling sideways, he was able to free himself.

All noise had ceased, except for an occasional low moan, which, after some minutes, fell silent. From where he stood, Billy could see nothing but leaves, long branches and the two huge boughs, laying crossways, one over the other. How this had happened, he had no idea. These trees had, each of them, broken off one of their limbs, to save him from certain death and to bury the evil which had been taking place beneath their gaze. He could only wonder at it.

He was roused from this contemplation by the crackling of flames and the smell of woodsmoke, both of which were growing stronger. The fire, far from being extinguished, was now burning with increasing vigour. His first thought was for the child. He must get it to safety. Those others, invisible beneath the tangled mass of greenery, he scarcely thought of, other than that they were very likely already dead. If any still breathed, it was now too late to save them, even had he wished to. However wicked they were, whatever awfulness they had been part of, he did not want to hear their screams, when the flames began to lick at their flesh. It was time to go.

His search proved fruitless. Torch in hand, he moved about among the trees and bushes in an increasingly frantic manner, all the while trying to keep calm and remind himself that there was still hope. A wave of despair washed over him when he finally realised that the child was lost and there was nothing more that he could do.

Billy found his bicycle lying where he had dropped it. Tired and sore, he pedalled off into the night, without a single backward glance.

***

The following day, Mr. Lambert was where he always was at that time of the morning, standing leaning against the doorframe of his hut, smoking his pipe and staring off into the distance.

Lord de Winton trudged out of the trees and passed them, unshaven, haggard, and wearing a scruffy old overcoat which made him look more like a tramp than a peer of the realm. He was in company with a man whom Billy did not recognise. Speaking in low voices, they appeared deep in discussion, as neither man paid any attention to the gardener's morning greeting.

'How do, Bill,' said Mr. Lambert, sounding distracted himself. He was watching the two men intently. 'Something happened last night.'

'Really?' was all Billy said in reply.

'Hmm. Lady de Winton and her guests. A party in the forest. A celebration of some sort.' Mr. Lambert frowned. That such a thing should happen anywhere on the estate was beyond thinking, but these rich folks were a law unto themselves. 'There was music and dancing, but it all got a bit out of hand, it seems.'

'Someone was hurt?' Billy asked, trying to inject a note of curiosity into his voice. He was uncertain and frightened, yes, but not curious. Unusually silent at breakfast, which his mother had attributed to the lingering effects of his malady, he had, in fact, been turning over in his mind the possible consequences of his nocturnal actions. It appeared that none of the family had heard him leave or return in the early hours of the morning. The gatekeeper may have caught a glimpse of someone moving around outside his lodge, but the night had been cloudy and there was no light on his bicycle, so it would have been well nigh impossible for him to point the finger at the lad, supposing he had been wakened by the noise at the gate. He hadn't noticed anything strange in Mr. Lambert's behaviour towards him when he had arrived at his place of work. As for Lady de Winton and her guests, they were now silent, for ever. There was only that other presence which he had encountered near the clearing, the one that had flown past him. But it had been as black as pitch among the trees; there was no way . . .

And, just as Billy began to feel a sense of relief displace the nervous tension which had been gnawing at him since he awoke that morning, he remembered the hatchet. The axe-head had his initials on it, a WA inscribed on both faces. He was done for. He staggered, and it was all he could do not to collapse in a heap at the door of the hut.

This sudden movement caused Mr. Lambert to break off his close observation of the two men, whose discussion had taken on a greater urgency and looked to be moving towards a conclusion.

'It was a little more serious than that, Bill,' Mr. Lambert replied. 'The fire got out of control and . . . well, whatever happened . . . they were all burned to death. His Lordship found the remains early this morning, just after four o'clock. When Her Ladyship didn't return, he began to get worried that something might have happened, and went out to try to find her.'

'And did he?'

'What was left of her. Burned to nothing. Just the skeleton.'

A silence of some minutes followed this grim piece of news. Billy wondered what Lord de Winton had seen in the forest clearing. Scorched trees and, lying scattered around amidst the smouldering ashes, bones that were still too hot to touch. He shuddered at the thought, but his curiosity getting the better of him, he began to entertain the notion that he might go and have a look himself. Perhaps later, when all the fuss had died down. If he was still free to do so.

'You know,' continued the old man, 'it must have been quite a blaze, but the strange thing is, it just seemed to burn itself out. The fire didn't spread to the surrounding trees. I had a look first thing this morning. Very odd. The whole place could have gone up like a tinder box.'

Another mystery, thought Billy, to add to all the rest. His equanimity began to reassert itself. Perhaps things would turn out okay, after all.

'Who's the other man?' he asked.

'Chief Inspector Digby. Police.'

Lord de Winton and the Inspector appeared to reach an agreement, as a brief smile flickered over de Winton's face. The peer, whose years of service in the Grenadier Guards had left him with an impressive military bearing, was now hunched over, and a claw-like hand, appearing out of the capacious sleeve, clutched the overcoat tight at his neck. Digby remained impassive for some seconds, seemed as if about to offer his hand, but then nodded his head once, turned on his heel and walked off to his car.

'I can't imagine his Lordship wanting any of that,' said Mr. Lambert, pointing back over his shoulder with his pipe, 'to appear in the papers. I shouldn't wonder if the whole affair was hushed up. Just a few column inches on an inside page.' He shook his head, clamped his teeth down on the stem of his pipe and turned to step inside his hut.

'How could that be?' Billy asked.

'Money and power,' came the reply. 'Them that's got it, knows how to use it.'

***

Mr. Lambert was right. There was only the briefest of mentions in the local press about the tragic events which had occurred. It was suggested that, by some act of carelessness, the tins of paraffin, the fuel which had been used to kindle the fire, had been left too close to the flames, and had exploded from the intense heat. The coroner recorded a verdict of death by misadventure.

Talk of financial compensation for the families of the victims came to nothing, as no-one appeared to know the names of those who had been present at the celebration. After some days of animated discussion, the matter fell strangely quiet. The de Wintons were an old and powerful family in those parts, and had eyes and ears everywhere, and servants and employees ever ready to do their bidding and act in their interest; and they got what they most wanted. Closed mouths. Silence.

Mrs. Bertram, wife of the local GP, was seen driving away from the village on her own early one morning not long after the events described above. A "For Sale" sign appeared on the house that very same afternoon. When young Jenny Potter knocked at the back door of her friend's house, Mr. Wilding, the girl's father, told her that Emily had had an accident and had been taken to hospital in the next county, but wasn't expected to live. Jenny was sure it was Mrs. Wilding whom she heard sobbing as the door closed.

In those small, close-knit country hamlets and villages, nothing ever escapes notice for long. And so it was, that stories were whispered, over back hedges or in quiet country lanes, over a pint of bitter or during a game of bowls, of the disappearance of so-and-so, and what had really happened on that dark night.

That the little boy—it was the boy whom Billy had encountered as he neared the clearing—and his sister had simply wandered off one afternoon and had gotten lost in the wild woods was accepted to be the truth of the matter. There were other, dissentient, voices, who called to mind the fact that a child had gone missing months before from the village of Burton Edge, only ten miles distant, as the crow flies; but these voices, like all of the others, fell silent. If questioned later about their remarks, they shook their heads or feigned ignorance.

The reappearance of the children brought much happiness and many tears of joy. Their mother had left them playing in the back garden down by the stream, on the far side of which began the de Winton estate. When she had gone out to fetch them in for dinner, they were nowhere to be seen. They recovered from their ordeal, the baby girl after a day or two of cosseting and cuddling, although she found it difficult to be separated from her mother for even a few minutes. The boy's return to his former happy self took longer. He was silent and withdrawn for a week or more, and, when he did begin to speak again, all he seemed to want to talk about was of a small, bright-eyed figure which had taken him by the hand on that frightening, bewildering night and had led him to where his sister was lying, hidden under a mulberry bush on a bed of soft moss and scented, dry leaves. Carrying the girl child in a sling about its neck and keeping a firm hold of her brother's hand, it had walked for a long time through the trees and the darkness, all the while quietly singing to them both in a high, sweet voice. The song lulled the baby to sleep, and soothed away some of the little boy's fears and calmed his trembling limbs. When they reached the gatekeeper's lodge, it had kissed them both and then disappeared into the night again. It was some minutes before the boy's soft tapping at the door of the lodge caused a light to appear in an upstairs window.

***

Billy Albright soon ceased to worry about his part in the events of that night. As the days and weeks passed, normality appeared to return to the de Winton estate, at least, among those who had employment there. What went on in the family circle was impossible to fathom. There were comings and goings of strange faces at odd hours of the night and day, and the sound of raised voices could sometimes be heard in the library. But over and around everything, a wall of silence and mystery. Mr. Lambert softly tut-tutted and shook his head, when Billy merely hinted at the affair.

One hot afternoon, thirsty from his labours and seeking refreshment, Billy made his way through the forest to a place where he knew that a spring of cold, fresh water bubbled up amidst a grove of linden trees. The last time he had been there, he had left a jar of his mother's delicious apple and pear chutney. He found the empty jar lying in the grass growing about the spring head, but it was the other object, the blackened axehead with the initials WA on both faces which made him raise his head and smile.

A VOICE FROM THE GRAVE

'Anyone got plans for the weekend?' asked Matilda, setting her glass down on the pub table. She dropped a packet of peanuts into her boyfriend's lap. 'For Jimmy the monkey.'

Annette, a small, silent girl with very blue eyes, whose creamy skin had an attractive sprinkling of freckles, stopped sipping her drink to say, 'I know a place we could go.' She wore her brown hair in plaited pigtails, and the end of one of these she fixed between her nose and upper lip, in the manner of a moustache, her scrunched up face giving her the appearance of a surly teenager. Looking round at each of her friends to see if the suggestion had aroused any interest, but seeing none, she let the braid go and flicked it back over her shoulder. Then realising that they might not have heard her over the noise coming from the surrounding tables, she was on the point of repeating herself, when Frank Miller responded.

'Where?' he asked. He had been admiring his new tattoo from the moment he had taken his jacket off, and was constantly smoothing down the edges of the cling film which covered it; but he now turned his eyes on his friend sitting opposite.

The monosyllabic reply was all that Annie needed. Leaning forward and resting her elbows on the round table, she said, 'My uncle once told me about a place.'

Jordy, who had visited the bookshop before joining the others for a drink, stopped reading the back cover of his latest purchase. The look of expectancy on his face was further sign of encouragement.

Jimmie was too busy feasting his eyes on Matilda to pay any attention, but Matilda seemed intrigued, and registered her approval with a faint nod of the head, and a sigh which seemed to say, "Why not? I'm bored with all this." This being the unrelenting attention of her boyfriend.

'Was that the same uncle who died in mysterious circumstances?' she asked. 'What happened again, Annie?' She swatted away Jimmie's hand, when he tried to push back a lock of hair hanging over her face.

'He fell out of a window,' Annie replied, her voice trailing off as she answered, so that only the first two words were audible. She frowned at her friend.

'Fell. And was impaled on a railing. Rather unlucky, I'd say,' added Beth, the blonde and the beautiful, the faintest of smiles playing about her lips.

'Straight through the heart, wasn't it?' said Matilda, appearing not to heed the warning look. 'But did he fall? Or was he pushed?' She met Annie's stare, and held it for what seemed like an age, then turned her head to direct a withering look at the little man sitting by her side.

Jimmie appeared not to notice the sneer. He would probably whimper and plead, Matty thought, when she told him it was over, like he had done the last time she had tried to break off their relationship. Jimmie the monkey. His close-cropped hair revealed a number of scars on his scalp, and there was turn in his left eye. A googly green eye. He had a good heart, though, she admitted.

A very good heart. Yes, she would tell him at the weekend, she resolved, taking another sip of port.

'Where did you say it was?' Frank's attention had wandered back to the design on his upper arm, and thinking that he had missed the information, he repeated the question.

'I didn't say,' said Annie. 'It's Dardour Forest.'

'What is it with you and forests, Annie?' he asked, smiling at her. 'Are you a woodland nymphette? Or whatever they call it.'

'Nymph, Frank,' interjected Jordy. 'The word is nymph. Nymphette means . . . eh . . . something quite different,' he added, blushing, and seeming to take, at that particular moment, an unusual degree of interest in what was going on at a neighbouring table.

'Sounds exciting,' murmured Beth, in her usual slow, dreamy way. 'Will we need tents? Or shall we rough it, and build a shelter from . . . trees and stuff?' Whenever she spoke, her head moved, as though in time to a music that only she could hear. Like the roll of a ship in a swell. Matilda, watching the graceful movement, had originally put it down to the effect of alcohol, but it happened regardless of whether Beth was drinking or not.

'Wild men of the woods. For a weekend. Weekend wild men. And women,' Jimmie said, with a smirk at Frank.

Matilda's eyes grew wide, in mock horror at this feeble attempt at wit.

'It's only about three hours drive away,' Annie informed them. 'We could hire a minibus. What do you think? Anyone?'

'Why Dardour Forest?' asked Frank. He finished his pint with a long draught and set the glass down. 'Why not the forest over by Lowdown Hill. It's closer, and there's an old ruin we could sleep in. On the edge of the fields. A stone-built barn of sorts. The roof's still on, although the floor was covered with muck the last time I was there. But that was ages ago. We could used it as a base to explore.'

'There's a ruin in Dardour Forest, too,' replied Annie, after a brief pause, lest she sound a little too insistent. She was pleased that the discussion was gathering steam, but wanted to keep it on point. 'A ruined monastery, my uncle said. Pre-Reformation. Dating from thirteen hundred and something.'

'A monastery? Never heard of it,' said Jordy, evincing signs of astonishment that such a place should have been unknown to him. His imagination, stimulated by wide reading and much dreaming, often during the hours of daylight, when he should have been attending to his university lecturers, began forming images of tumbledown walls and silent, hooded figures moving among shadows. To say that he was intrigued by the proposal, would have been greatly to understate how he felt at that moment. His new book could wait, he told himself, slipping it into his bag. A real life adventure beat fiction every day of the week.

'There's not much to see, as far as I know,' Annie continued. 'The monastery church and . . .'

'If there's an old church,' Beth cut in, 'there's probably a graveyard as well.' She turned her slowly blinking grey eyes on Annie, and let them linger there, taking in the flawless skin and the glossy black lipstick and the small, beautiful hand caressing the neck under the chin. 'What have you been planning, Annie?'

Frank, noticing Beth's animation, wondered if that was a double or triple vodka she was drinking. The added cranberries, where they weren't diluted by ice cubes, gave the liquid a deep red colour. Not as dark as her nail varnish, though, which had a plummy sort of richness to it. He couldn't put a name to the colours: arterial red and venous red were the only two reds he knew. He glanced down at his own hands, resting on his thighs beneath the table top, hands which he had soaked long and scrubbed hard before coming out; but still the traces remained, of his day's labours. Big hands, strong wrists, muscular forearms. His thoughts turned back to Beth, sitting at his side. That purple scarf around her neck had to be silk. It reflected the light wonderfully as she moved her head. She looked very fine tonight. Very lovely. Beauty, wealth and wit. She was well and truly out of his league.

'Count me in,' said Jordy, excitement lighting up his face and making his accent more pronounced. The Canadian student's favourite pastime was reading, mainly Victorian gothic fiction, of which he had an impressive collection, but his tastes were catholic, and extended even to Richardson's *Clarissa*, or the *Letters of Horace Walpole*, complete in 9 volumes, with notes and appendices.

'Let's put it to the vote,' suggested Frank, who appeared not the least bit annoyed that his own idea had been passed over without as much as a single comment of interest or approbation.

'I thought we were going to Dave's party on Saturday night,' said Jimmie, looking round at Matilda, and nudging her leg with his knee.

'You can go, if you want, Jimmie,' she replied. 'I'm in.' She winked at Annie, who couldn't prevent a smile spreading over her freckly face.

Only Jimmie held back, but the thought of being separated from his beloved for two whole days was more than he could bear, so, after considering the matter for all of ten seconds, he finally agreed to join them.

'It wouldn't have been the same without you, Jimbo,' Annie said, turning her smile on him. Jimmie flinched when their eyes met, and flinched again when she reached out a hand to stroke his cheek.

A day later, on the Thursday of the week, Frank called Annie to let her know that he had managed to get the loan of a minibus for the weekend. His cousin, who was part-owner of a local garage, had had one on his forecourt for six months or more, without it attracting the interest of any buyer.

'He didn't even ask me what I wanted it for,' said Frank, pleased by his easy success. 'Threw me the keys and told me to make sure it came back in one piece. Even offered to put some diesel in the tank. Said the run would do it good. Open the engine up.'

'Great, Frank,' replied Annie. 'We won't need a trailer, will we?'

'It's a twelve-seater, so there should be enough room inside for all the baggage, if people are sensible about how much they bring. No suitcases, Annie. It's not a fashion parade. Tents, sleeping bags, a change of clothing, and waterproofs, if they have any. And a pair of boots. That's all.'

'I'll call round and tell them. If you can arrange to buy the drinks, I'll get the food. Where do you want to meet?'

'Outside your place, at 4.'

Jordy was so excited at the idea of a weekend's camping in a forest that he was unable to get any sleep on the Thursday night, so he sat up in bed reading, until the birdsong outside his bedroom window heralded the dawn of the new day. His choice of literature was unlikely to have had a calming effect on his fevered imagination, as it involved a forlorn maiden being kidnapped and held captive in an ill-lit dungeon, a disappointed hero, and all manner of gory deaths. He was so tired, he slept through all of his Friday morning lectures, then decided to cut his afternoon classes in order to be at the meeting place on time.

Frank's work at the stockyard was finished by lunchtime on Friday. Annie was employed part-time as an archivist in several of the town's libraries, but her services were not required over the weekend. Jimmie's attendance at college was erratic, even at the best of times. Worried that he might miss the adventure, as a result of some unexpected catastrophe befalling the city's entire transport system, he stayed in bed, drinking weak tea and playing video games all day. Matilda was a talented artist who worked from home, so she could manage her time in whatever way she wanted. She was hoping to get some inspiration from the trip, amongst other things, and packed a sketch book and pencils. As for Beth, her daddy was so wealthy, she didn't need to earn a living. She was an intelligent girl, but had no interest in continuing her academic studies when she finished school, so daddy insisted that she get a job. She did, but her employment never lasted. Working at the same place for four weeks together was her idea of a long-term commitment, and was an achievement which she celebrated, very often by not going back for a fifth. Variety was, after all, she said, with a sniff, the spice of life. Daddy was not amused, and threatened to cut her allowance, although he never did.

'What are you bringing those for?' inquired Frank, when he got out of the minibus to help pack away the bags of provisions which Annie had bought for the weekend. She was standing on the pavement outside her flat, her foot on her hold-all, and a garden spade in each hand.

'I thought we might need them,' she said in reply. 'I expect Jordy will bring his metal detector. There's bound to be something buried in the ground about the ruins of an ancient church. Besides, we might need them at the campsite, for smoothing out the ground or digging a latrine or ... I don't know what.'

Frank accepted this explanation without demur, and the two made short work of packing everything away in the back of the minibus. Annie got in the passenger door, and slid along the double seat. As she leant over to hand Frank a chocolate bar, she noticed that he was wearing his hunting knife strapped to his belt. Taking hold of the handle with one of her small hands, she drew it half out of the sheath, and sat staring at the glinting steel blade for some seconds. Frank's much larger hand, on top of her own, gently pushed it back down into its thick leather scabbard. As their eyes met, her head made the slightest of nods. He devoured the chocolate bar in two bites, a wolfish grin spreading over his face.

They drove to the football pitches on the edge of town, where Annie had arranged with the others to pick them up. The location was only a ten or fifteen minute walk away from where each of them lived, and was roughly central. Better that, she said, than driving about the narrow streets with a long minibus, and waiting outside flats, blocking up the road, and disturbing the neighbours by honking the horn. The playing fields were deserted at that time on the Friday afternoon, apart from a solitary man being taken for a walk by his two dogs, and a little boy flying a red kite. Grey clouds were blowing across the sky, and Frank felt drops of rain on his face when he got out to help Beth with her bag.

'I brought the metal detector, Annie,' said Jordy, dropping everything he was carrying onto the pavement, and pulling out a handkerchief to wipe the sweat from his forehead. 'Just like you suggested.'

Matilda and Jimmie arrived last, she walking ahead, her tall, erect figure making quite an impression on the eye, clad, as she was, all in black; he coming on behind, rather like a small lost dog, stopping to catch his breath, check his pockets or tie a shoelace, and shouting out for his inamorata to wait up a bit. She ignored his forlorn calls, and reached the minibus a good two minutes before he did. As they stood together watching the little man making his way towards them, Jordy saw the three girls exchange the oddest of looks, a wordless stare that lasted for some seconds; but, knowing nothing of the ways of women, except what he had read in his tales of horror and imagination, wondered if they had discovered the means of communicating telepathically. Probably an intrigue of some kind, he thought. In a moment of inspiration, he knew what it was: they had planned to dress up as ghosts and frighten the life out of him and Frank and Jimmie, when it was midnight, and the forest was silent, and they were sound asleep in their tents. That must be it. He decided not to share his idea with the other males, in case it spoiled the fun, but he would keep a lookout for any signs of female mischief. He watched Annie's eyes light up, as she looked again at Jimmie. How fitting, he thought, glancing at each of the girls: they were all wearing dark lipstick and black nail varnish, and their faces were unnaturally pale, as though ... as though ... and his thoughts wandered off into the regions of fantasy, where nothing is at it appears, and mystery lies around every corner.

Annie, who had made most of the arrangements, had also decided on the route, and sat at Frank's side as he drove, with a map open on her lap. Why use the motorway and dual-carriageways, she had said to him, when they could drive on quiet country roads. It would take an hour or so longer to get to there, that was true, but they had time to spare, and they could enjoy the scenery as they went. It made no difference to Frank, so long as he knew when to turn and when to go straight on.

The journey was uneventful. Jordy, overcome by tiredness, fell asleep shortly after they started out, and disturbed everyone with his snoring, until Matilda reached over and pinched his nostrils together, causing him to waken with a gasp and a splutter, which made them all laugh. Realising that he had been the victim of a prank, he blew a raspberry at his friends, turned over in his seat and went back to sleep. Jimmie started feeling sick after forty minutes, the result of his gorging on snacks and sweets, then insisted that they stop the minibus so that he could offload the by-product of the litre of sugary drinks that he had managed to polish off in that short time. It really was too much, thought Frank, initially ignoring the sound of Jimmie's voice bleating in his ear. He could hold it in for a little while longer. Might teach him a lesson. But the bleat became a whine that would not stop, so Frank flicked on the indicator and pulled over to the side of the road. Jimmie was no sooner out and engaged in his business, than Matilda pulled the side door shut, and they drove off without him.

'Do you want me to keep going?' Frank called out.

'No,' the three girls replied together.

'We wouldn't leave wee Jimmie behind, would we, girls?' said Annie. Frank could see Beth and Matty in the rear view mirror grinning and shaking their heads.

The miffed expression on Jimmie's face vanished, when he heard the cheers and laughter which greeted his reentry.

Annie, convinced that they were near their destination, but confused by the map and growing a little anxious that, there being not a single road sign to guide them, they might drive into the forest and lose themselves for hours on the long, silent empty roads which criss-crossed that vast wooded area, finally agreed that they should stop to ask for directions from the first person they met. This happened to be an old man, whom Beth noticed standing half-hidden under a chestnut tree at the side of the road, and whom they had already driven past, when she called out for Frank to stop. He was leaning on a thick staff, a brown tweed hat pulled low over his eyes, and his black and white collie lying curled up on the ground at his feet. Peeping over the top of an overgrown hedge of blackthorn and hazel, the dark red tiles of a cottage roof could be seen. From the chimney stack, a faint column of woodsmoke drifted up and vanished into the evening sky, leaving behind it nothing more than its unmistakable scent. Annie got out to speak to him, and returned five minutes later with the information they needed.

'What took so long?' asked Frank, releasing the handbrake and accelerating slowly away.

'We were just chatting,' replied Annie. 'About this and that. He wanted to know how many we were and where we had come from. And what we wanted with the place. It was lucky that Beth saw him, as his is the only house for miles around. Retired forestry worker, he said. Just him and his old dog. Very sweet. Never took the pipe out of his mouth all the time he was speaking.'

'He's still standing there,' said Frank, looking at the receding figure in the rear view mirror.

Annie, turning her head to look in the wing mirror, saw the old man's hand raised in the briefest of farewell gestures, then fall and rise again, and move from one side to the other, before his figure was lost in the distance and the shadows.

'Did he tell you how to get there?'

'Hmm,' she replied, distracted by what she had seen. 'Keep straight on for three miles or so. There's a turning to the right, not far beyond a humpbacked stone bridge, which'll take us off the main road and onto a forest trail, but the entrance is almost impossible to see until you're right on it, so keep it slow, Frank. And the trail is likely to be muddy, what with all the rain we've had recently, so be careful we don't get stuck.' She patted his hand, which was resting on the gearstick.

Frank's sideways glance at his companion was not intended to express some mild annoyance which he might have felt at these words of caution, as though his driving skills had come under reproach, nor at the gesture of restraint which had followed them: no, he had heard a tremor in her voice as she spoke. Was she really afraid of getting lost, he asked himself, or that he wouldn't be able to manage the minibus on a less than ideal surface?

The track was considerably broken up, and was not only muddy, but was strewn with leaves fallen from the canopy of trees above. It was still passable, so long as he kept the vehicle in a low gear, and his eyes on the shadowy route ahead, in order to anticipate potential difficulties well in advance. After progressing in this manner for some quarter of an hour, the track rose a little and grew firmer, then came to an end, petering off into an area of uneven ground covered by grass and other low vegetation.

At the sound of the handbrake going on and the engine being turned off, the doors of the minibus were thrown open and the young people climbed out into the damp, chilly air. Matilda, finding it too cool for her liking, got straight back in again to fetch her pullover. She gave Jordy a shake as she passed, as he was still snoring quietly beneath the cover of his heavy jacket, his cheek pressed against the window. It took him some moments to realise that they had arrived, and he was then so eager to join the others, he bumped his head as he exited the vehicle.

'Jordy, watch out! We've only just gotten here and you're already wounded,' shouted Matilda, eyeing the cut on his forehead. 'Let me get a plaster for that.'

'We don't have much time to set up camp,' said Frank, glancing at his watch. 'It's already seven-thirty, and it's getting darker by the minute.' Details in the middle distance, which he had been able to pick out only moments earlier, were now disappearing in the increasing gloom.

They chose an area of dry, firm flattish ground for the campsite, located at some thirty paces or so from the minibus. Everyone helped transport the tents and provisions from the vehicle. Frank and Jordy would have the largest of the tents, a bell-shaped canvas construction that was reminiscent of a past age, when young men and women made months-long cycling tours of the Alps or the Schwarzwald. Beth and Annie were happy with their three-man winter tent, which was as dry, warm and cosy as modern technology could make it. Matilda had resigned herself to sharing with Jimmie, but, to her surprise and delight, feelings which she was unable to conceal from her companions, her boyfriend insisted on building himself a shelter for the night. A chord stretched between two trees provided support for a waterproof nylon sheet, beneath which he heaped up as much dry moss as he could find in the vicinity. On top of this base, which kept him insulated from the chill of the forest floor, he unrolled a sleeping mat and his sleeping bag. Twenty minutes after that, while the others were still sorting out their own accommodation, he had sawn up a small tree into logs and built a screen across the opening of his shelter, for the purposes of reflecting the heat of a fire back into the interior of his shelter. This burst of activity rather surprised the others, as Jimmie was always thought to live in a state bordering on chaos, a disorder which reached into every corner of his life. The hand axe, folding saw and compact spade which he produced from his pack perhaps suggested otherwise, and also testified to an interest in the outdoors, an interest of which none of his companions had been aware. Visibly pleased with the results of his labours, he proceeded to cut more wood for the large campfire which Frank was then preparing.

The girls suggested that Matilda share with them, as they still had plenty of room in their tent, even after packing away clothing and wellington boots; but she shook her head, and said that she didn't mind being on her own. She pitched her tent at some distance from the others, on the very edge of the clearing, at the foot of an oak tree, between the trunk and an overgrown holly bush, a position which left only the front of the tent accessible. This, she said, would give her added protection against the cold, and other things. By these words, Jordy thought she meant ghosts or similar nocturnal terrors, and began to relate a story from one of his books which told of just such an occurrence, and of the dreadful consequences which befell the unfortunate individual. However, Matilda had become aware that Jordy seemed to be paying the female element of the company an unusual amount of attention since their arrival at the camp, so her comment was only partly in jest. Thinking it probably nothing more than a harmless curiosity on the part of her shy bookish student friend, whose head she knew was full of the fanciful and the romantic, she was, at the same time, unsettled enough by his uncharacteristic behaviour to choose that particular spot for her tent, given the natural security which it offered. As an added precaution, the heavy stone which she had used to knock in the tent pegs, she hid just inside the flap, so that it might be ready to hand, in case the night should bring her any unwanted visitors.

It wasn't long before the fire was burning, and, wrapped up in sweaters or jackets for extra warmth, they were sitting around it eating bowls of tuna pasta and slices of crusty bread, all of which

Annie had prepared in the twinkling of an eye. Frank took charge of the two portable coolers, which were full of bottled water, beer and soft drinks. Left to their own devices, he thought, casting a placid eye over the assembled company, they would most likely drink the lot in one go. Jimmie could probably finish it all by himself, he added, smiling to himself, and watching the little man, by turns, amuse and annoy Matilda and Beth. With every sip of beer, Frank felt his eyelids getting heavier and heavier. It had been a tiring week at the shambles, as it often was; and the strain of driving the minibus had just about exhausted his last reserves of strength. Finishing his drink, he bade his companions good night, and disappeared inside his tent. Scarcely a moment later, the sound of his snoring could be heard forming an accompaniment to the crackling of the flames and the idle chatter of the happy group of adventurers.

An hour later, and all was silent at the campsite. The fire had burned low, leaving a heap of smouldering ashes, which still glowed in the darkness, and, from time to time, burst out into small, flickering orange and yellow flames, as the rising night breezes fed them oxygen. Jimmie, inebriated by three bottles of double-distilled Belgian beer, which he had drunk as though they contained nothing stronger than water, had tripped over the heap of sawn logs piled up by his shelter and fallen onto his sleeping bag, where he lay, fully-clothed, oblivious to the world. Matilda had thrown a blanket over him, before retiring for the night. Jordy had intended to spend an hour reading Polidori's *Vampyre*, a dog-eared copy of which he had brought with him, stuffed into his jacket pocket, but, much to his annoyance and frustration, found that his electric lamp was no longer working. Somewhat befuddled by the effects of alcohol, and still tired, in spite of his dozing in the minibus *en route*, he tried to fix it by the light of the campfire, but, after five minutes of fruitless fumbling and silent cursing, he gave up the task, zipped himself into his sleeping bag and fell asleep. Little did he know that his tent mate, who was longing for a good eight hour's rest, had simply turned one of the lamp batteries around, thereby rendering the device useless.

Annie lay awake and fully dressed in her sleeping bag, listening to the sounds of night—the soft plopping made by moisture dropping from the leaves above onto the taught fabric of the tent; the hooting of an owl, as it rested between hunting forays; and the bark of a fox. This last, an unearthly screech, which broke on her ears like the scream of a murder victim, came from somewhere close at hand, and so frightened her, it took an age before her pulse slowed to normal and the tension in her body dissipated. When she was sure that Beth was asleep, she would slip out. There was something which she had to do before tomorrow. It would only take . . . , but her train of thought was interrupted by a faint noise, which sounded to her like feet padding over damp leaves. This increased in volume, until a snuffling and wheezing told her that whatever was making the noise was directly outside the tent. It was probably only the fox, she told herself, making a supreme effort not let fear take hold again, an effort which failed even before it was begun. Another bottle of beer after dinner would have knocked her out, but what she had to do required a clear head. And now here she was, lying awake, and terrified by the least sound. Attracted by the strange scents which the visitors had brought with them, the fox had come to investigate. That was all. Beth had zipped the tent flaps up when she had entered, and the zipper was on the inside. Good. And the fabric of the tent? Was it strong enough? Of course, Frank had answered her query, as they were packing the gear into the minibus earlier that afternoon. Unless . . . Unless what, she had interrupted him. He had looked at her askance before continuing. Unless someone was to try to cut it with a knife or . . . and his reply had broken off, to be replaced by a puzzled expression. Or some sharp object, he finally suggested, after he had cast around for another implement likely to be involved in an assault on a tent.

Like a stick? she asked, after a momentary pause, and trying to make the enquiry sound as casual as possible. A stick? I suppose so, he went on, but it would have to be sharp, as the material is as strong as can be. It doesn't tear or pierce easily, even if you attempt to puncture it directly. This is an expensive piece of kit, Annie, he said, slapping the bundle with the palm of his hand. What are you worried about? She shrugged the question off, and busied herself with checking that the plastic bags full of food were securely stowed and not likely to tip over and spill their contents all over the floor of the vehicle when they turned a corner or had to brake suddenly. A second screech or yelp broke in on her recollections, but sounding farther away this time. Much farther away. Beth's regular breathing was barely audible. It was time to go.

Annie stood beyond the circle of tents and the glowing remains of the fire until her eyes became accustomed to the darkness. The torch was only for emergencies, she reminded herself, checking once again that it was in the pocket of her fleece, as there was always the possibility that its powerful beam, when switched on, might alert others to her presence, which she most certainly did not want. At least, not for the time being. This time tomorrow, it wouldn't matter.

***

'Where have you been?' whispered Beth, when Annie crawled into the tent some time later.

'I needed a pee,' came her reply.

'It was only you then. Moving around outside. I wondered who it was. It gave me a fright.' Beth's head sank back and she let out a tired sigh.

'When?' asked Annie, trying to keep her voice even.

'Don't know. A while ago. I thought I heard footsteps outside. Wondered if it was Jordy playing at ghosts or something.' Beth was drifting back to sleep. 'There was a dog, too, I think.'

'A dog?'

'Hmmmm. Heard something growling,' Beth continued to mumble, as she fell asleep, but her words were lost on her friend, who was thinking of other matters.

***

Annie didn't sleep much that night. When it was light enough, she got up and moved around the campsite looking for traces of the nocturnal visitor, but found none. The ground was soft, and there were places where the exposed earth would have carried a footprint, but her detective work was made impossible by the fact that she and her five companions had been walking back and forth over the area all of the previous evening. There were animal tracks near the minibus, but whether they had been made by dog or fox, she couldn't say. As she returned to the tent, her eye, purely by chance, picked up an indentation in the black earth. Hunkering down to examine it, she found it was a hole, circular in shape and penetrating down into the ground to a depth of three or four inches. In diameter, it was about an inch and a half. She couldn't be certain, but, when she slipped her forefinger into it, she got the impression that it had been made by a pointed object. An object that was sharpened at one end. An old man's walking staff, with a pointed end. A thick wooden stake sharpened to a point. Then she realised what that odd farewell gesture of the old man's had been: it wasn't a wave, it was a sign of the cross which he had made. He must have known. Annie felt her stomach muscles tighten, as fear laid a hold on her. There was another sensation now, an ache in her chest. Tension, or …? She laid a hand on her breast, but the hand could neither soothe away the ache, nor feel the beating of her heart.

After a breakfast of porridge, bacon rolls and mugs of coffee, the six friends went exploring. Moving at an easy pace and chatting amiably with one another, they followed the course of a stream through an area of mixed woodland for thirty minutes or so, until they found themselves standing on the edge of a clearing, looking across a sea of long green grass, at the ruined facade of an old church. Jordy commented on what appeared to be a series of tracks in the grass, which was otherwise undisturbed, to which Annie replied, that they were probably those of the fox which she had heard moving around during the night. They did seem rather large for a fox, Jordy thought, but he kept the observation to himself. Walking in single file, as though not wishing further to trample the grass, but in reality because it was still very wet with dew, and only Annie was wearing wellingtons, she led them across the clearing.

'It doesn't look safe,' said Jordy, moving as far away from the external wall of the ancient building as the surrounding trees would allow. Blocks of masonry lay about on all sides, much of it partly or almost entirely hidden by the vegetation, a fact which seemed to indicate that it had fallen long ago, and had lain undisturbed ever since.

'So you won't be climbing up to explore, Jordy?' replied Matilda, who watched his nervous hesitation with a smile of amusement. 'I thought you were the adventurous type,' she added, giving him a gentle push to get him moving again. 'The view from up there must be spectacular.' She stood back to let those coming behind pass, then looked up, her eye following the line of a huge column formed from carved blocks of light grey stone. Perhaps they could get onto a higher level from somewhere inside, she thought, picturing to herself a narrow stair, hidden in some secret corner, and winding up and up. But her musings were interrupted by a sprinkling of fine dust raining down upon her upturned face, and she moved off hurriedly, fearing that this might be the prelude to a far more dangerous dilapidation.

Bethany was right: there was an old graveyard.

Those headstones which yet remained, had long since fallen over, and were broken into pieces and overgrown with grass; some had sunk into the earth to such a degree that only a corner was still visible to the searching eye, and over which one might have to stumble before realising it was there at all. The eye and finger of the curious explorer moved in vain over the surface of the crumbling stone, as the sun and rain and wind, and the freezing frosts and battering hail of half a thousand years and more had effaced all but the deepest of masons' marks.

They wandered about that hallowed space for a while, singly or in pairs, now squatting down to scratch at the earth with a stick or penknife, now standing idly for a moment with eyes closed, listening to the silence, and perhaps wishing themselves back at the campfire, and feeling the heat take the nip from the chilly midmorning air.

Jimmie, for whom it was difficult to be still for any length of time, in mind or body, found the place oppressive. As an outlet for some of his nervous energy, he darted off from the others and began climbing a tree. Losing interest in this, he jumped down and, haring off in another direction, scrambled over the remains of a stone wall and disappeared from view. This wall must have surrounded the graveyard at an earlier age, but was now, like the rest of the site, in a broken down state, and was, in many places, nothing more than a grassy bump in the earth.

No one noticed his absence, until he called out, the note of excitement in his voice so patent, that Beth rushed towards the source of the sound. She found him squatting down in the grass, shifting sideways and scoring the ground with a length of broken branch. He had already marked out a good part of the perimeter of a largish rectangle.

'What is it, Jimmie?' she asked, coming up behind him and looking down over his shoulders, as he continued to edge sideways.

'Look at the ground,' he said. 'Can you not see? It's sunk.'

Completing his work as the last of his companions joined them, he rose to his feet, staggering backwards as the blood rushed away from his head.

'What do you think it could be?' he asked, leaning against the wall until his head stopped spinning and his vision cleared.

The surface of the ground which he had marked out was uneven and had indeed sunk, by as much as six inches in some places.

'Is it just my imagination,' said Matilda, 'or is the grass thicker and greener here?' She moved around the perimeter, trying to find a viewpoint from which to answer her own question one way or another.

'It's a pit,' said Jordy quietly, and folded his arms. 'A grave pit.'

'What? How do you know that?' queried Frank, frowning at his friend. It wasn't that he doubted Jordy's word, he simply wanted to know how he had arrived at that conclusion.

'Well, for a start, the shape is regular, so it must be man-made,' Jordy replied. 'Then there's the width. About six feet, I'd say. Maybe a little more. Wide enough to take a corpse without a coffin. Probably buried just as they were, naked, I mean. Or maybe wrapped up in a burial cloth. The fact that the ground has sunk away so much suggests that there must have been a lot of bodies buried here. As the flesh decays, the ground sinks a little. You often see that in cemeteries. The grave diggers have to add soil to level out the ground. And then ...' and he looked at Matilda, '...you were right about the grass, Matty. It is thicker and greener. All those decaying bodies providing a rich supply of compost.'

Frank appeared more than satisfied by his learned friend's summary, and smiled and nodded in appreciation.

'Why would they need a pit?' asked Jimmie. 'Why not just bury them in individual graves, like the rest?' He waved his hand at the walled graveyard behind them.

'Anyone know?' Jordy waited for a suggestion, but when none came, he continued: 'What if they were simply overwhelmed by the number of the dead?' His studies in history and his wide reading of Gothic fiction were then to yield up one further intriguing idea. 'What could have killed off so many of the monastic community at one time, supposing it is monks who are buried here?' Like a schoolteacher hoping for an answer from his class of students, he seemed prepared to wait for an age. Beth was on the point of saying something, then reconsidered. Her gaze wandered past Jimmie and rested on the trees bordering the far side of the graveyard. Frank fiddled with the handle of his hunting knife.

'Do tell, Jordy,' said Matilda, after a minute or more of silence. 'Don't keep us in suspense any longer, my dear chap.'

'Rats,' came his reply.

'Rats to you, too!' Matilda responded without hesitation.

'Rats and fleas?' Jordy seemed to want to tease the answer out of them.

'The Black Death.' Annie's reply was matter of fact, as though she had known the answer all the time, but had simply wanted to play along with Jordy's game.

'What we might have here,' continued Jordy, 'is a plague pit. We could be standing on the remains of ten, twenty, thirty monks. Maybe even more.' Seeing a look of incredulity flit across Frank's face, he proceeded to explain his thinking. 'Imagine a stranger arriving at the monastery one evening, seeking admittance. Perhaps he . . .'

' . . . or she,' interjected Annie.

'Perhaps they were hungry and thirsty,' he went on, narrowing his eyes at Annie, 'and needed a place to sleep for the night. Monasteries always had accommodation for travellers. A dormitory for them to sleep in. That sort of thing.'

'Maybe it was a monk returning from travels abroad,' added Beth. She had been making her way through Scott's novels, and had found them interesting, although rather hard going at times. 'Or the Father Abbot returning from a convocation.'

'A convocation?' asked Frank.

'A meeting with other abbots,' she answered. 'Perhaps at one of the monasteries on the banks of the Rhine or . . .'

'The individual,' Jordy broke in firmly, 'knows or suspects that there is something wrong with them. He also knows that the monastery has a hospital, as they all did, and that the monks might have a remedy for his affliction.'

'So they let him in, give him food and rest, tend his sickness . . . ,' Beth interrupted again. Her imagination was now fully engaged by the picture that her friend was painting for them. 'And, in return for all their kindness, the infection he is carrying kills off half the community. Or more.'

'Imagine what the following weeks must have been like,' continued Jordy, 'as the infection spread through the community. Dead and dying everywhere. Hell with the lid off. The Last Judgement at hand.' The flush in his cheeks indicated that he, too, had become enraptured by the fantasy which he had woven, from the meagrest of facts, it might be said. He had the makings of a good storyteller, but, as all good storytellers know, the strangest of endings can often result from the simplest of beginnings.

'Very scary.' Mathilda's voice seemed unnaturally quiet. It was hardly louder than the sound of the wind, which stirred the grass at their feet and ruffled a few strands of Beth's fine blond hair, which she moved away from her face and tucked behind her ear.

Frank saw Annie shiver and rub her hands together. It's not that cold, he thought. And it couldn't be the dampness of the ground, as she was wearing wellingtons and long, thick socks.

'Jimmie,' he asked, 'how did you know . . . ?'

'Let's go back to the minibus and get the spades,' suggested Beth, speaking at the same time. She gave Matilda a nudge with her elbow, to see what she thought of the idea. Matty said that she was game, if Annie was.

'Wait,' said Frank. 'You want to dig here?'

'Why not?' Annie shrugged. 'We came here to explore, didn't we? Besides, what else is there to do?'

'Go for walk in the forest,' Jimmie answered, already suspecting that the decision had been made. The unease which he had been feeling since they had arrived at the ruin was growing, and he now wanted to get away from the place. He would go for a walk by himself, if no one else wanted to come. Or sit by the campfire and drink beer.

'I don't suppose it would take long,' said Frank, already prepared to consider the idea from a practical point of view. He squatted down on his heels, and, drawing his hunting knife, thrust it into the ground. 'It's soft. If we remove the top layer of turf, roll it up and set it aside, like they do on the tv, we can replace it when we're finished.'

'This is not strictly legal, you know. We are committing sacrilege, by digging up a grave and disturbing the remains of the dead.' Jordy's comment introduced a pause in the proceedings, as the other members of the group had been on the point of returning to the campsite, thinking the matter settled. They now stopped to ponder his words.

'It's not likely anyone'll know, Jordy,' said Annie. 'As Frank says, we'll tidy up when we're done. If we bring the tarpaulin from the minibus, we can heap the soil up on it, so the grass isn't damaged. Besides, no one ever comes here.'

'No wonder,' muttered Jimmie, wrinkling his nose, as though the air was polluted by the smell of death and decay. 'There's something not right about it.'

No one paid him the least attention, as they were all used to his complaining.

'How do you know?' Jordy asked, sounding mildly annoyed by Annie's certainty.

'Look around you,' she replied. 'Have you seen any signs of life?'

Jordy conceded this point with a shrug.

'And if anyone does turn up,' said Beth, taking up the cudgels in order to drive any remaining doubt from his mind, 'you can show them your university matriculation card. It does say that you're studying ancient history, doesn't it?'

'You can say it's an archaeological dig,' Annie suggested.

'And we're your assistants,' added Frank. 'Paid by the hour. Waged labour. Come on, let's go back and get something to eat.' With that, he turned and headed off, the others following behind.

Now that he had voiced his concerns about the project, and they had been laid to rest by Annie and Beth's powers of persuasion, Jordy felt a little easier in his mind. He was just as excited by the idea of digging up the past as the rest of his friends, perhaps even more so, given his fascination with such old places; but there were responsibilities. That they could leave the site in the same condition in which they had found it was impossible, he knew full well. The signs of their digging, no matter how careful they were about replacing the turf, would be visible to the eye for months afterwards. In a place such as this, though, he reflected, looking at the swaying trees and gently moving grasses and meadow flowers, and listening to the intermittent birdsong and the noise of insects busy with their ephemeral lives; in a place such as this, where humanity no longer intrudes, and nature was left in peace to work her transformation, the marks of their presence would be soon obliterated. Much sooner than the labours of the monks themselves, he told himself, turning his eyes towards the dilapidated stone structures of the monastery church. An ash tree was growing in the chancel, and some of its branches had found an exit through the building's great windows. Others, constrained to grow in the limited space available, were gradually forcing the ruined walls apart. In ten years or twenty, or a hundred, the building would burst asunder, and the tree would emerge victorious. Or it might slowly collapse, weakened by strong winds and heavy rains, by the frosts of winter and the heats of summer contracting and expanding the moisture within the heavy stones and joints, until they cracked, crumbled and gave way beneath the enormous weight of masonry above.

Ivy covered a large part of the building's exterior. This year's growth was easy to distinguish from what had come before, by the size and fresh appearance of the leaves, the lighter shades of green which they wore, and the ease with which they moved in the late morning breezes. And after the tree had done its work, he thought, the ivy would take over, and cover everything with a carpet of green.

The sudden and distant hammering of a woodpecker breaking in upon his daydream, he realised that the others were long gone and that he was alone. Was it only the wind, blowing though gaps in the age old stonework, that made the air around him hum? Or was it something else which he heard there in that solitary spot, and which made the hairs on the back of his neck stand up, and a feeling of dread seize hold of him? His feet had grown cold, and the coldness seemed to be moving up his legs, as though frozen hands were clutching at his flesh and drawing all the heat out of it. Feet, ankles, shins, and now his knees were beginning to lose sensation. Some instinct directing his thoughts, he looked down, to see that he was standing inside the perimeter of the grave. The dreadful idea that there was something down there, beneath his freezing feet, under the layers of soil, trying to get out, flitted across his mind. Overwhelmed by the urge to get away from the place, he tried to run, but found himself stumbling forwards, as his lower limbs failed to respond to the neural impulses flashing down from his brain. It was with a strange hopping, jumping motion, therefore, that he made his way out of the cemetery, passed the monastery ruins, and back to the safety of the trees, a motion accompanied by much flapping of his arms, as he tried to maintain his balance. The fear of falling to the ground, and of not being able to rise again, and of lying stretched out or curled up, a prey to whatever it was that had taken hold of his legs, drove him onwards.

It wasn't just Beth who noticed how close Jordy sat to the campfire, while they ate lunch and talked over the afternoon's labours.

Frank and Annie exchanged curious looks with one another, when they saw him lay aside his bowl of soup, pull off his boots and socks, and begin to rub at his feet and calves. Thinking that he must have fallen into a stream on the way back to camp and gotten soaked, Jimmie offered him a spare pair of thick socks which he had in his bag, but Jordy thanked him and shook his head. He sat taking his soup and sandwiches, with his bare feet resting on a warm stone at the fireside, the flames licking about his shins.

When they arrived back at the monastery in the early hours of the afternoon, Beth and Matilda each brought a spade, Frank had the rolled up tarpaulin over his shoulder, and Annie trudged along in the rear carrying a backpack full of drinks and snacks. Jimmie had slipped away while they were eating lunch, and still hadn't returned by the time they left camp. Jordy had disappeared inside his tent after he had finished eating, leaving the others to tidy up.

'Aren't you coming, Jordy?' Matilda had asked, lifting the tent flap and peering inside. Puzzled by his subdued manner and an uncharacteristic reluctance to enter into the discussion they were having at lunch about the possibility of finding some ecclesiastical treasure during their excavation, she had determined to find out what was the matter with him.

'I'll be along later,' he replied, trying to sound confident and natural, but failing in both. He was sitting on his sleeping bag in his boxer shorts, chaffing his bare feet and calves.

'I'm cold,' he said, seeing a quizzical look appear on Matty's face.

She crawled in beside him, after a backwards glance to check that Frank was close by.

'So, so cold, Matty. Feel here.' He took her hand and placed it against his left calf. 'See?'

Matilda nodded, then moved her hand to a point above his knee, where the flesh was warm to the touch. 'Strange,' was all she said. 'Wear two pairs of socks.' She backed out of the tent, leaving him to wonder why he why hadn't told her what had happened.

Jordy finally did set out to join his friends, but his nerves were on edge, and he was continually stopping to listen, and turn about, and listen again, as though expecting to see someone step out from behind a tree which he had just walked past, or hear the sound of something moving after him over the carpet of leaves which covered the ground. He was so overcome by a feeling of unease, at different points along the way, that he had to dart off to one side or other and hide himself in the shadows, hunkering down behind a bush or pressing himself flat against a tree trunk, until the anxiety eased enough to allow him to continue.

When he reached the graveyard, the tarpaulin, spread out on the grass near the pit, its corners weighted down with stones taken from the graveyard wall, was already covered by an impressive heap of black earth. At its side lay rolled-up lengths of turf. Frank was stopped to have a rest. Beads of sweat stood out on his face and brow, and his grey t-shirt showed patches of damp on the back and under the arms.

The three girls and Jordy all took turns at digging.

Beth uncovered the first bones, which looked like part of a spinal column. She handed the spade up out of the pit and continued digging with a penknife, and was then joined by Annie. The two worked side-by-side in that cramped space, quickly, almost feverishly, one might say. Frank, watching them from above, and surprised by the energy which they brought to the task, thought it was a love of buried treasure which drove them on. He hoped they wouldn't be disappointed.

At the first sign of human remains, Jordy excused himself, saying that he was feeling nauseous. He would return to camp and start getting things ready for dinner, and build up the fire, and chop wood, and heat water for them to wash with, as they were sure to be filthy when they got back.

Annie and Beth, hearing the words tumbling out of his mouth, stopped working to watch him hasten away, and then exchanged glances with Matilda, who could only shrug.

After another hour or so, kneeling on the flat bottom of the pit and digging down only along one edge, they had uncovered a whole line of human skulls, how many deep they couldn't say, but their position indicated that the deceased had been buried facing towards the east, in the direction of the rising sun.

***

The four arrived back at the campsite a little after six o'clock, looking rather worn out by their labours. Grateful for the hot water which Jordy had prepared, they washed up, changed out of their dirty clothes, and were soon seated about the fire sipping bottles of beer.

'Why didn't you stay and help?' Matilda asked Jordy, who moved about handing out drinks and snacks, or busied himself with tending to the fire.

'I never really felt easy about it,' he replied. 'About disturbing the remains of the dead. There might be consequences,' he added, after a pause.

'Legal consequences?' asked Annie, opening another bottle. 'Who's to know, Jordy? Just we six. Where is Jimmie, by the way?'

'Here I am,' Jimmie said, stepping into the firelight. He had been lingering by the minibus listening to his friends' easy chatter, and was feeling a little left out of things, because he hadn't taken part in the excavation. Fetching his portable chair, he set it down beside Matilda.

'Where have you been all day, Jimbo?' Matilda asked, gently tugging his ear. Her enquiry sounded unusually affectionate to Frank, who was used to hearing a certain testiness in their verbal exchanges. Thinking it only the effect of the alcohol, he gave it no further attention.

'Here and there,' said Jimmie in reply. 'I went for a long walk, and did some exploring. Not much to see really. Lots of trees and streams and squirrels.'

'I wasn't thinking about legal consequences,' said Jordy, in answer to Annie's question.

'He means ghosts,' said Jimmie. 'The spirits of the dead. That sort of thing.' He moved his chair a little closer to the fire.

'Well, there wasn't much to see anyway,' said Frank, stretching his legs out and placing his hands behind his head. 'Bones, and more bones. That skull looked interesting though,' he then added. 'The last one you uncovered, Annie. The one with the brick in its mouth.'

Annie seemed to be on the point of saying something in reply, when Jordy cut in.

'What did you say?' he asked in a quiet voice, setting down an armful of chopped logs.

'What?' said Frank.

'Just some old bones, Jordy,' said Annie. 'Complete waste of time. Not a . . . '

'The skull. What did you say about the skull?' he repeated, ignoring Annie.

'The last one Annie uncovered, at the far right of the pit. It had a brick in its mouth, or a stone,' Frank answered, feeling a touch disconcerted by the unfamiliar note of urgency in his friend's normally calm voice.

'What are you so worked up about, Jordy?' asked Matilda. 'You've been acting *so* strange all day. Ever since you got back from the monastery this morning. What *is* going on?'

'Burial traditions,' he said, after a pause. 'As part of a course in medieval history. In a book in the library, there was a photograph of an archaeological excavation in Venice. The academics knew it was the site of a plague pit, because they had found records in the city's archives which gave the location and the date. Fifteenth century. Very early.'

'Is there a point to this story of yours, Jordy?' asked Frank. 'Or are you just going to ramble on for another half hour until we've all fallen asleep?'

'Time for dinner,' said Annie, rising to her feet. 'Beth, can you . . .'

'Wait!' interrupted Frank, sounding annoyed. He was tired, and, although he wouldn't have admitted it to anyone, he was also disappointed that they hadn't found anything of interest or value in the pit. 'I want to hear what he has to say.'

'One of the photographs taken at the site was of a skull. With a brick placed between the jaws, forcing them wide apart.' Jordy thrust his left hand in between the extended thumb and fingers of his other hand to show what he meant.

'So what?' said Frank, and tossed his beer bottle top into the fire.

'I haven't finished yet,' Jordy went on. 'The scholars who found it were convinced that it was the skull of a . . . a female vampire, and that the stone had been placed between her jaws in order to prevent her feeding on the corpses of the plague victims buried alongside her in the pit.'

'You're telling us now,' exclaimed Jimmie, jumping up from his chair, 'as it's getting dark, in the middle of a forest, miles away from anywhere, with the remains of a ruined monastery nearby, that you think we've dug up the skull of a vampire?' The rising pitch of his voice revealed his great agitation. This idea of Annie's was turning into a nightmare. He knew he should never have come.

'Good story,' said Frank, offering Jordy his hand.

'It's not a story,' Jordy replied, giving the extended hand a single shake. He looked round at his friends, one by one. 'It's not a story. It's true. I'm telling you, it's true.'

'Not good,' said Jimmie, fetching another bottle of beer from the chiller. 'No, not good at all. Definitely not so good.'

'The skull of a vampire?' said Beth, her eyes growing very wide, and not appearing in the least put out by Jordy's story. 'What do you say we go back and have a look. All of us. That makes six against one. Safety in numbers and all that.'

'No, no,' Jimmie nixed the suggestion. His speech was beginning to sound slurred. Matty had slipped a little something into his beer, just to give it an extra kick, and the combination of intoxicants was now making itself felt.

'What do you think, Jordy? Frank?' asked Matilda. 'Are you game? Scaredy-cat Jimmie can stay here and make sure the tents don't run away. Annie, are you coming?' She was already up from her seat and heading towards her tent. 'Come on, guys. Get your torches.'

Twenty minutes later, and they were all standing around the edge of the burial pit.

'Oh my Lord!' gasped Jimmie, pointing the beam of his torch down at the skull. 'Oh. My. Lord.'

'It looks like there's a patch of skin on it,' whispered Beth, who had jumped down into the pit for a closer look. 'And hair.'

'Where did that come from?' asked Frank. 'It wasn't there before. The skull was bare when we left to go back to the camp. I'm sure of it. Annie, you were last to leave. Did you see it?'

Annie's spoken reply was indistinct.

'Someone must have given it fresh blood,' said Jordy, stepping back from the edge of the grave. 'The blood from a living human being is needed to begin the process of regeneration. Where did it come from?'

It was Jimmie who broke the silence following this question. 'Annie's got a plaster on her finger,' he blurted out. 'She's trying to hide it. She put her hand in her pocket when you were talking, Jordy. I saw her.'

'It's only a small cut,' replied Annie, drawing her hand out of her jacket pocket and extending the wounded forefinger for all the group to see. A clear plaster was wound about the tip.

'It doesn't matter how big the cut was,' said Jordy, stepping further away. 'All it takes is a few drops.' He was shaking his head and looking steadily at Annie. 'Annie, what have you done? Annie.'

'She cut it on her penknife when she was digging away the soil,' added Matilda.

'It was an accident, Jordy,' Annie protested, but her statement didn't carry much conviction, and Jordy wasn't convinced.

The restraints which had been holding Jimmie together all that day, in the face of this latest frightening development, finally fell away. He began to shake uncontrollably, and, suddenly springing backwards, as though overcome with horror at what he had seen in the bottom of the pit and wanting only to flee, stumbled over the graveyard wall and fell, striking his head against something hard. Frank winced at the sound of the blow.

'That's Jimmie out,' remarked Matilda, revealing not the least trace of compassion in her voice or manner. She remained where she was, standing beside Annie.

'What should we do, Jordy?' asked Beth, and they all turned to look at their book-learned friend.

'Go straight back to the campsite,' he replied, without hesitation. 'Right now. Come back in the morning, at first light, and fill in the pit. Then go home, and forget about it. Otherwise …' But the sentence remained unfinished. Seeing no immediate response from his companions, he added, 'I've had enough. I'm out. You can stay if you want.' With these words, he moved off in the direction of the camp and disappeared into the darkness, only the bobbing circle of light thrown out by his torch remaining visible to the eye for some moments.

'Why don't we conduct an experiment?' suggested Beth, whose soft, sweet voice sounded unusually beguiling. 'Just a little one. It can't do any harm.' Perhaps assuming that Frank could have no possible objection to her idea, or ready to ignore him if he did speak out, she continued, 'Jump down here, Annie.' Annie did as she was bidden. 'Now, let me tear off your plaster. There!' Fresh blood welled up all along the knife cut on Annie's finger. 'Hold it over the skull,' said Beth, 'and squeeze out a drop or two. Squeeze. That's it. Good girl, Annie.' She took Annie's head in both her hands and kissed her full on the mouth.

'Look!' shouted Frank, dragging his eyes away from the osculating couple.

Where the two drops of blood had fallen, skin appeared on the bare white bone, and a tuft of hair sprouted, short and coarse.

'What might we not do with a ready supply of the stuff?' asked Beth, looking up out of the pit at Matilda.

Annie hunkered down to get a closer look at the skull. As she reached out a hand to touch it, by accident or design, further drops of blood dripped onto it. The effect was immediate. The two patches of skin joined together and more hair appeared.

Frank reached down and, one after the other, pulled the girls out of the grave pit.

'I think we should do exactly what Jordy said.' Frank was big, and strongly built, and he would have squared up to any man alive, but there was a hint of a tremor in his voice when he spoke these words. If not afraid, he was unsettled by what he had seen. His hand reached to the hunting knife at his side, as if for reassurance.

'I agree,' said Matilda, resting a hand on his arm. 'You return to the camp, Frank, and make sure Jordy's okay. We'll bring Jimmy back.'

At that moment, a groaning could be heard coming from the other side of the graveyard wall.

'No, really, Frank, it's okay. On you go.' She gave him a gentle push. 'We'll be right behind you. Okay girls?'

Annie and Beth nodded silently.

They watched the tall figure disappear into the night.

'Listen,' said Beth, turning from one friend to the other, and placing a finger to her lips. 'Listen.'

Jimmy groaned again.

Then another sound could be heard, like that of a voice coming to them in a dream, through a long, long stretch of years.

'*Je veux . . .*,' it whispered. '*Je veux . . .*'

'I want,' translated Annie.

' *. . . vivre.*' With a sigh, like the gentle stirring of a night breeze, it fell silent.

'To live.'

They could hear Jimmie shifting about on the other side of the graveyard wall, as though he was trying to get to his feet. The girls looked at each other, spoke not a word, and moved towards the sound.

'Hey, Jimmie,' whispered Matilda.

'Jimbo. Jimbo,' softly sang Annie's lilting voice, as she took the penknife out of the pocket of her jeans.

'Anaesthetised by booze and stunned by a fall,' Beth croaked, her throat dry from an excitement that was making her vibrate. 'Should make the job so much easier.'

'Up you get, little Jimmie,' said Matilda. 'There's a good boy.'

***

Jordy was nowhere to be seen when Frank reached the campsite. He added some logs to the fire, tidied away empty beer cans and bottles, and, after one last look round, crawled inside his tent and drew down the flap behind him.

***

When Frank awakened some time later, he could hear voices, two female voices coming from somewhere near the tent.

'Where are you, Frankie?' said one, low and seductive. He didn't recognise it. It wasn't one of his friends. It sounded foreign. It had an accent.

'Coming out to play, Frank?' That was Beth, he was sure of it.

Where the hell is Jordy, Frank asked himself, looking at his friend's empty sleeping bag. He crawled out of the tent and stood up. There, on the other side of the campfire, which had now burned down, but still gave off enough light for him to see by, was Beth and some other female. They were naked, and were joined at the mouth. Frank could see tongues flickering and hear lips sucking and smacking, and moans of pleasure. Desire rose up in him like a wave. He moved forwards, unzipping his fleece.

'Want to join in, Frank?' asked Beth, holding a hand out towards him.

'*Viens!*' said the other figure, beckoning with a finger. '*Viens!*'

'This is Lilly,' said Beth, turning a lazy, lustful smile on her friend. Their mouths came together again, and they chewed at one another, and bit and nipped, at ears, and noses and chins.

Frank had never seen Beth naked before. She had a flat belly. And surprisingly full legs. No thigh gap, no problem. He remembered reading the phrase in some magazine, a glossy mag, with full-page photographs. Two big nipples stood out from her small breasts.

Lilly was an inch or two taller than Beth. A great mass of dark hair reached down to her shoulders. Her whole body looked soft and warm, and seemed to Frank, as he watched them kissing, to promise the realisation of every erotic dream he had ever had, and of pleasures far, far beyond his imaginings. Beth's fingers toyed with her nipple, rolling and pulling and stroking, which produced such an ecstasy in Lilly, she broke off the kiss, her head lolling back, her mouth agape.

'Want to have some fun, Frank?' Beth asked, in the dreamiest of voices, and with a sultry smile, looking at him from below half-closed eyelids.

They separated, and began moving towards him, one on each side of the fire, like a pair of hyenas going after a wounded gazelle. Then Beth hung back, allowing Lilly to advance on her own. Her lustful look had lost some of its intensity, Frank thought, and he seemed to detect something else behind it. Purpose? Determination? The momentary confusion which resulted from this observation was replaced by the beginnings of suspicion. However, a smile yet played about her lips, and had charm enough to draw him forwards a step or two, in spite of himself. Then he saw the light in her eyes appear again, and her smile widen, and desire surged up inside him, washing away all caution and making him tremble. Sensing his weakness, Lilly lunged at him, covering the distance between them with a remarkable burst of speed. It was only at the very last moment, certain that the prey was now in her grasp, that her smile disappeared, and her mouth opened wide, revealing two unnaturally long teeth.

And what was it that saved him?

In those last seconds, as she launched herself at him, he saw not the face of a woman, but the maw of a snarling dog, like the ferocious guard dogs which he sometimes met on farms, when he came to slaughter pigs or sheep, as a favour to the farmer. Perhaps excited by the smell of blood, which he knew must hang around him wherever he went, one such, a savage Alsatian, had come racing at him from the far end of the farmyard, even as he was engaged in his work. The farmer's gruff words of command, snapped out as he saw the beast make for the slaughterman, had no effect. Letting go of the sheep which he had just taken hold of, and kicking it out of the way so as not to impede his movements, Frank waited until the dog was airborne, then, timing his reaction to perfection, seized it by the throat with one huge hand, seized and held it, and squeezed, and squeezed, gritting his teeth and focusing every ounce of strength which his body contained into his forearm and fist. He first choked the dog insensible, then let it drop to the ground, and stamped on its head and crushed its skull. He would have done more, too, but the old farmer had cried out and seized him by the shoulder and drawn him back.

Just such an instinct for self-preservation saved him on this occasion, too. He was still holding Lilly by the throat, although the sound of her choking had stopped and her body had gone limp, when he heard Beth advancing at a run. Fearful of letting go with his right hand, he used his left to draw his hunting knife out of its scabbard, and, as Beth's hands grasped at his head and face, drove the long blade up into her neck at a point above the Adam's apple. Her body's forward momentum and his powerful counter thrust caused the knife to pass through her head and out the back of her skull as though it were made of nothing more substantial than tissue paper. He let go of both women at the same time, Lilly striking the ground, and lying quite still, Beth twitching for some seconds, until her damaged brain shut down and the involuntary muscle-spasms ceased.

His eyes moved from one beautiful naked female form to the other, his mind unable to comprehend what had happened. Every sensual delight which, only moments before, had seemed to be his for the enjoying, had vanished in an instant. They lay before him now, lifeless, cooling in the cold night air, and growing pale.

Stooping to retrieve his knife, he pulled opened Beth's mouth, and touched the tip of one long canine with the pad of his fingertip. Sharp, very sharp. And deadly.

'Frank. Are you alright, Frank?'

The voice gave him a fright, coming as it did out of the silence and darkness, and from no more than four or five feet away. He started back, holding out his bloody knife, and fearing that he might have to deal with another monster in female form.

'It's me, Frank. It's Annie.'

He could see the firelight reflecting from her eyes, and could smell the scent of her body, but he was unable to make out anything more of her than that. One sense alone had been stimulated by the erotic performance which he had witnessed, only one, and the rest had been dulled, as though subjected to repeated doses of morphine. Perhaps that had been their intention all along, he thought, so that, when the vision of delight changed into something altogether different, he would be unable to defend himself. It had been very nearly successful: he could still feel desire tugging at him, hidden underneath the adrenalin rush which had produced the burst of violence, and which had left his heart thudding in his chest.

'Look, look at their teeth, Annie,' he stammered out, beginning to recover himself.

'Yes, Frank, I can see.' Her voice sounded different. Muted in some way. 'We can't leave them here like this,' she said, moving a step closer. 'We'll have to get rid of them. Bury them. But first . . .'

'What?' he said, rising to his feet.

'Their heads, Frank.'

She knelt down beside Beth's prone form and ran her fingers through the blonde hair, stuck to the face and forehead by sweat and blood. 'You'll have to cut their heads off first, Frank, otherwise . . . they'll have no rest.' She placed her lips against Beth's cheek, stifled a sob that rose up in her breast, then raised her tear-filled eyes to him. 'Best to do it now, Frank. Now!'

Was it the note of mastery in her voice, issuing a command that he was unable to disobey, which made him act without hesitation? Or was it a dawning realisation of the horrible fate which had almost befallen him, and a desire to obliterate it, for ever, to destroy beyond repair the possibility of its arising again from either polluted source?

The razor edge of the heavy steel blade made short work of the slender female necks, slicing through the flesh without effort, and passing between the vertebrae with only the slightest of pressure.

'What about the others?' he said, wiping his knife clean on a tussock of grass.

'Why don't we go and look for them now?' Annie replied, taking hold of his hand and leading him away from the scene of carnage.

It didn't seem strange to him, then or later, that she was able to lead him straight to the place where Jordy and Matilda were lying together on the ground, Jordy on his back and Matilda curled up at his side, her face pressed in against his ear and her left arm lying across his chest. By the light of Annie's torch, they could see the bite mark on their friends' necks.

'They're still alive,' said Frank, after checking each wrist for a pulse. 'What now, Annie?'

The wordless look which she gave him was replete with meaning. Frank drew out his hunting knife and dropped to one knee. He rolled Matilda onto her back, in order to make the job easier, and heard her murmuring from the depths of sleep, as he placed the blade against her throat.

'What now?' he asked again, when the deed was done.

'They'll have to be buried. They can't be left here for someone to find.'

'We can bury them in the pit,' he answered, looking beyond the unimaginable present to the purely practical future. Practical was good. 'No one'll know once it's filled in. Here,' he said, holding out the two severed heads. 'You carry these, and I'll bring the bodies.'

Annie recoiled.

'No, no, Frank, I can't. I'll go back to the campsite and start clearing up. We'll need to be gone from this place in the morning, and there's a lot to do before then.'

'Frightened of getting blood on your sweater, Annie?' he asked. She was wearing a polo neck, and her hand was constantly adjusting the neck of the garment.

'Oh no, Frank. I'm not afraid of that. At all,' she said in reply. She didn't sound disgusted, he thought, trying to see past the beam of the torch which she was pointing at him. Or frightened. There was neither disgust at what she had seen him do, nor fear of what the consequences might be for both of them. Quite the contrary, it seemed to him. Or something like it. Playful. He was puzzled, and dropped the heads at his feet.

'Is there something wrong, Annie?' he asked. 'Your voice is strange.'

'I sometimes get mouth ulcers,' she said, sounding as though she were speaking through closed lips. 'They can be quite painful.'

'Okay, Annie,' he sighed. 'You get back and start clearing up. I'll deal with . . . these.'

She handed him her torch and turned away.

With some difficulty, he got Jordy's headless corpse onto his shoulder, and carried it up through the forest to the monastery graveyard. He was a strong man, and was used to moving carcasses of meat around during the day, but they were stiff from being stored in a refrigerator, not warm and floppy, he reminded himself, stopping to shift the weight a little to one side. It was too bad. He had so looked forward to this weekend, as a chance to get away from the filth of the slaughterhouse, and now here he was again, he reflected, a feeling of disgust rising up in him, still dealing in death, and with the familiar smell of warm blood in his nostrils.

As he slid Jordy's body off his shoulder, the torchlight illumined Jimmie, lying on his back at the bottom of the pit, his eyes wide open, and a great gaping wound in his neck. His first thought was to decry the poor workmanship. A small, blunt knife, wielded by a not very strong or steady hand, he thought, taking in the ragged edge of the cut. Effective enough, certainly; but lacking in skill.

Must have been a frightening and painful death for the wee chap. He had never much liked Jimmie, but he wouldn't have slaughtered a dog like that, never mind a man.

The girls must have dug up the rest of the skeleton after he left them to return to the camp, he said to himself. And before they murdered Jimmie, and used his blood to revivify the creature, or rejuvenate it, or whatever the word was. There was now only a series of hollows in the earth where the skeleton had been, and a small pool of Jimmie's blood lay in the bottom of one of these, perhaps where it had collected in the greatest volume, the rest having long since soaked into the ground.

At least Annie was okay, he thought, striding back down through the trees to fetch Matilda. He wondered how she had managed to get away from the others. Must have run off into the night, when she saw what happened to Beth and Matilda. It was reassuring to know that he was not on his own. Annie would always know what to do, and he breathed easier at the thought. For the briefest of moments, he asked himself just what it was that her uncle had told her about the place, but ever practical as he was, a list of work still to be done edged the question out of his mind. A step or two later and it was as though the thought had never occurred to him.

It took him the best part of an hour to complete the burial of the four bodies, and the work left him very near exhausted. Last of all, he dropped the four heads into the pit as though they were so many cabbages, then picked up the spade and began to fill it in from the pile of earth on the tarpaulin. That done, he replaced the turf as best he could and patted it down with the back of the spade. He dragged the tarpaulin into the bushes growing along the side of the clearing and disposed of the remaining earth there.

When he returned, scarcely five minutes later, and paused to survey his handiwork, the torchlight revealed to his eye movement on the ground. All around the grave, the grass, which had been trodden flat by six pairs of feet and crushed by the heap of displaced earth, appeared to be unbending itself and standing erect once more, as it had been before their arrival. That was not all: the seams in the turf, which he had cut with his knife in order to make its removal easier, were joining up of their own accord, and the uneven ground, which he had tried to level out, could be seen, here and there, moving up or down, to flatten a hump or raise a hollow, until all was perfectly even. First he was amazed at what he saw, then transfixed. And then he was frightened. He was witnessing a different supernatural power in action now, and one which sought to hide what was monstrous and unholy from the eyes of men.

What power it was, and where it came from, were questions which never entered his head. All he could think of, was to get away, from the monastery, and the forest, and back to people and civilisation.

As he neared the ruined edifice, he seemed to hear a low droning noise, unvarying, unceasing, and rising up over it the sound of...what? Voices. Chanting. A chorus? And a line of robed figures, faces hidden beneath cowls, hands hidden in sleeves, moved out of the mists which hung in the damp night air around the broken chancel, and processed towards the pit, all the while chanting, chanting, chanting, from their long-dead throats. The vision made him blink and stare, the sound made every hair on his body stand on end.

Dropping the spade and tarpaulin, he slapped his head with both hands, over and over. It was only a dream, he told himself. One of Jordy's stories come to life in his head again. Because he was so tired. That was all.

What stories would Jordy have to tell him when next they met, he wondered, leaning his weary body against the ancient masonry. Whether he had, in the confusion of the moment, already forgotten the part he had played in his friend's fate, or was referring to some future time, when they would be together again, is unclear. The cold stone helped to cool his blood and to connect him with reality once more. How would he ever be able to apologise to Jordy for what he had done to him? He mouthed the word "sorry", then stooped to pick up the spade and tarpaulin.

***

When Frank awoke the following morning, it was still early, but the dim light of day made its way through the thick canvas of the tent.

Annie was lying at his side, wrapped up in Jordy's sleeping bag, her head covered by a blanket. She stirred when he began to move, and said, in a sleepy voice, 'Is it very bright outside, Frank?'

'Not very,' he replied.

'You couldn't fetch my sunglasses from the minibus, could you? I've got the beginnings of a migraine, and bright light'll only make it worse. I can't bear the pain.'

When he tried to lift the blanket and peer under it, she pushed his hand away.

'It's too bright. Fetch the glasses, Frank. Please.'

He did so, and tossed them into the tent.

He decided to burn everything that could be burned. What couldn't be burned, he would bury in the forest, or dispose of on the way home. Throw it over a bridge or take it to a council dump.

He breakfasted on dry rolls, slices of cold ham, and a bottle of beer. As he raised a roll to his mouth, he realised just how filthy his hands were: the skin and nails were thick with earth and dried blood. He would have to soak in a bath for a week to get clean again, and his clothes would have to be burned. No point trying to wash them, he thought, looking down at the dark stains that covered the legs of his jeans. Best burn the lot.

When he had finished the meal, which may have stopped the growling in his stomach, but barely satisfied his hunger, he rekindled the campfire, and added the last of the cut logs. As he fed his friends' clothing into the rising flames, traces of perfumes and body scents, which yet lingered on the items, drifted up through the strong smell of the woodsmoke and released a flood of memories in his head: faces, fragments of sound, locations. For a second, for one fleeting moment, he felt a surge of happiness, as his memory opened up its store of treasures and selected a few of its choicest gems for his delectation. But the doors of the vault closed as quickly as they had opened, and the visions vanished, and the sadness which followed so completely dashed away whatever reserves of mental and physical strength were keeping him functioning, that he staggered forwards. He threw out his arms, as if in greeting to the fire and the purifying flames and the oblivion which he hoped would quickly follow.

A hand on his belt pulled him backwards, and he turned to see Annie standing behind him, the dark glasses which shielded her eyes forming a stark contrast to the unnatural paleness of her skin. Her other hand was pressed against the neck of her sweater.

'No, Frank,' was all that she said, quietly, and through lips that barely moved.

The tents in which the girls had slept followed the clothing into the flames, then the remaining food. Jimmie's waterproof sheet and wooden firewall came last.

Not far from the camp, in the soft yielding ground beneath a clump of bushes, which Annie pulled to one side to make his task easier, Frank dug a hole for the ashes from the fire. They carried away and hid among the trees the stones which had formed the fire surround, and scattered handfuls of leaves over the blackened earth. For good measure, Frank dragged in a large fallen branch which yet retained much of its foliage, and left it lying on the spot.

Circling out from the centre of the camp and moving in opposite directions, they walked over the site one last time, to ensure that they hadn't missed anything, but they had completed the work so thoroughly, it was almost as though they had never been there, in that silent forest clearing.

'A day or two of rain will wash away the footprints,' said Annie.

When she was satisfied with the work which they had done, they departed.

The road was empty when they turned out of the track onto it.

'Frank,' said Annie, resting a hand on his arm, when they had driven no more than a hundred yards. 'There's one last think that we need to take care of, before heading back to town. Just one, Frank.'

He frowned, but said nothing, nor did he remove his eyes from the road ahead.

'Frank, the old man saw us all together, on the evening we arrived. He has to go, too, Frank, otherwise they'll find out what happened here, and we'll go to jail, Frank, for a very long time. No one would believe us, if we told them what happened, Frank. No one. I know, and you know. No one else will believe us, Frank. The old man has to go.'

He took his foot off the accelerator pedal and let the minibus slow to a halt and stall, in the middle of the road. Still no cars passed them. He was sitting bent over, his hands resting on the steering wheel, staring out of the windscreen at some distant spot. He was filthy and haggard, and stank of smoke and earth.

'Okay, Annie,' he said, nodding faintly. 'Okay,' he said once more, his voice trailing off into silence.

They pulled up outside the cottage, on the other side of the road.

'You take care of the dog, Annie,' Frank said, as he opened the driver's door. 'If it smells the blood on me, it'll start howling. You go first. Get a hold of its collar, and don't let go. If it starts to bark, muzzle it.'

He stood by the minibus watching her go through the garden gate and approach the house. Hearing the gravel crunching beneath her feet, the dog appeared, and came haring along the path towards her, its tail wagging with excitement. Then it slid to a halt on the loose surface, lowered its head, and began to growl and back away.

Annie kept moving forwards, calling out "here, boy" and "good doggie".

Puzzled by this reaction, Frank looked at his friend's crouching figure, but whatever thoughts may have begun to form in his head were swept away by a compulsion to act, to get this last task out of the way.

'Grab it, Annie,' he shouted, starting forwards and clearing the gate at a jump.

As the collie turned to flee, she caught it by the tail and dragged it back, causing it to turn and snap at her hand, and snarl and yelp, in pain and fear. She managed to grab its leather collar, and held on as it tried to wriggle free. When Frank arrived at her side, he first stunned the dog with a punch to the head, and then twisted its neck until the bones cracked and it went limp. Annie let the lifeless form fall to the ground and stepped to one side, and leant her back against the wall of the cottage.

It was the strangest of looks that she turned on him then, a look that was half defiant woman, half frightened teenage girl. Her right hand clasped the neck of her grey cashmere sweater, the other she held up, palm outwards, as though to deflect from its course the storm of rage which she felt imminent. Unable to see her eyes, he watched her mouth hesitating between smile of friendship and sneer of contempt, saw her nostrils flare and her head tilt backwards, as she stared back up at him.

'What happened with the dog, Annie?' he said, balling both hands into fists. Every movement he made caused her to flinch.

'I was frightened, Frank, that's all. Frightened.' Her voice trembled, her outstretched hand trembled. She was trembling all over. 'It must have sensed I was afraid. Dogs can smell fear.'

'What's wrong with your neck?' he growled. 'You're always touching your neck. Is something wrong with it? Let me see.'

'It's an allergic reaction to the wool, Frank,' she murmured, summoning up from some deep hidden well within her the courage to maintain the charade, for just a little longer. 'It makes me itch. I can't wear it against my skin. This is Beth's sweater. She took my fleece.'

He stared straight at where he thought her eyes must be, looking at him from behind the dark lenses, and raised a hand, as though to seize and choke her. But at that moment, the tension went out of her body, she let out a sigh of relief, and gently pushing away his hand, reached out and stroked his face. The touch of her fingertips on his cheek, warm and tender and affectionate, soothed away his rage, and brought him under her control again.

'We'll soon be gone from here, Frank,' she whispered, and stood up on tiptoe to place the most delicious of scented kisses on his cheek. 'Soon. And then we can start getting back to normal. Like it was before. But first . . .' and she took him by the hand and led him round to the rear of the cottage.

They found the old man, the only witness to their arrival in that place, in the small cottage kitchen, sitting with his back to the door, dozing by the fireside, a week-old newspaper open on his lap, a glass of whiskey standing on the table at his side. They left him there, a moment later, asleep for eternity, sitting much closer to the fire, much too close to the fire, the rising flames, fed with newspaper and whiskey, beginning to singe his trouser leg. Frank carried the dog into the house and laid it down on the rug at its master's feet.

They waited in the minibus until billows of smoke began to appear over the cottage roof, then drove off.

They drove in silence for a long time, Annie working on a solution to the puzzle of how to explain the disappearance of their friends, and Frank trying not to fall asleep at the wheel.

'Frank, we'll need to get our story straight. You do understand that, don't you?' Annie asked. She was sitting next to the passenger door, leaving an empty seat between them, the fingers of her left hand casually playing about the door handle. Her right lay on top of the seatbelt lock.

He nodded his head, but kept looking straight ahead. Each pair of oncoming headlights made him grasp the steering wheel tighter, as though afraid that, in his exhausted state, he might not be able to resist their allure and might drive straight into them.

'Jimmie first,' she continued. 'He's always drinking and popping pills, and moving from one bedsit to another. And he's hardly ever at college. I think Matilda was the only person who knew where he was living recently. We needn't worry about Beth either, as she often takes off on her own, for days or weeks at a time. I got a call from her mother last month, asking if I knew where she was. Turns out she was in Spain, on some course. Psychogeography, I think. And if she is at home, it only means her parents are away on holiday. You know how rich they are and how much time they spend abroad?'

'What about Jordy?' asked Frank, appearing a little more animated, as though this tying up of loose ends, one by one, offered them the hope that they might, after all, be able to put the events of the weekend behind them.

'He was always talking about comic conventions, or cosplay adventure weekends and stuff like that.'

'We could say he was homesick and went back to Canada for a holiday,' Frank suggested.

'Best say nothing at all, Frank, unless someone asks. And if anyone does ask, keep it simple. We met up on Wednesday evening for a drink, as we often do, but haven't seen any of them since.'

'Ok, Annie. What about Matilda?'

'Matilda is a bit tricky. Did you know that she was seeing someone else?' Annie asked, moving her right hand away from the seatbelt lock and resting it in her lap. Frank wouldn't be able to get his seatbelt off quickly, she thought, as he was so tired. And his size would make it difficult to get out from behind the steering wheel. She, on the other hand, was small, reasonably fresh after the previous night's rest, and lithe of limb. She could be out of the minibus in a flash.

Frank shook his head. 'Got fed up with Jimmie, did she? No surprise there.'

'Yes, she was seeing some guy. You know how she was into the Gothic scene? Well, she met him there.' She shrugged, which was as much as to say, if anyone comes looking for her, they can look there, among the weird, the wonderful and the grotesque.

They stopped at a set of traffic lights.

It wasn't yet midday. There were still seven or eight hours until it got dark again, she figured, pushing the glasses back up her nose. The light turned green, but the vehicle remained stationary. Frank's eyes were closed.

'Frank. Wake up, Frank,' she called, tapping his knee with her foot.

He awakened with a start, and turned such a look of bewilderment and pain on her, that Annie's hand flashed to the seat-belt lock again. She released it and pushed herself up against the passenger door.

They reached Frank's flat without further incident.

It was a small, rather grubby, dingy one bed flat on the edge of town. The rent was cheap, and the neighbours were constantly changing: people came, and stayed for a while, and then moved on. Annie drew the curtains in the living room, and they stood together in the gloom. She took off her glasses and threw them onto the settee.

'Home again,' she said. 'Almost done. Just the minibus to clean out, and then we can rest. Have you got any bleach in the kitchen, Frank?'

The question triggered something in him, and he began to rage. Was it the casual nature of her enquiry that proved the final straw, conveying to him as it did, the idea of them washing away the remains of their friends with a cloth and some kitchen cleaner? A casual sloughing off of so much humanity, a dispassionate full stop to their years of friendship and the many shared evenings of laughter and warmth?

Annie backed away into a corner of the room, not from any fear now that he would turn on her, but simply to give him all the room he needed to work off his fury, or despair, or whatever demon it was that wanted to get out. She wondered if the avenging spirits of the dead were already haunting him, the furies, the "well-intended ones" the Greeks called them, employing euphemism to try to placate their dreadful power. Were they already buzzing around in his head and making him feel as though his brain was boiling? In her mind's eye, she saw the smiling faces of Jordy, Beth and Matilda morph into something indescribably awful, something laying siege to every one of his senses. A guerrilla warfare of sorts, its combatants emerging out of the depths of the psyche when least expected, clouding every blue sky, chilling every warm day, in reality and metaphor. Worse, probably. Much worse. She smiled back at them; they held no fear for her. Nor did she feel any remorse for Jimmie. Matilda had put two fingers up his nostrils and pulled his head back. Beth had sat on top of him while she, Annie, did her work.

There was no possibility of her soothing away such a storm of violence, by word or gesture, so she stood watching him punch at the door, and punch through it. And tear the shelves off the wall, scattering books and ornaments in every direction. And kick over the table, and stamp the legs off, and use one as a bludgeon, with which to beat at the walls, until the wood splintered and broke, leaving him with nothing more than a shattered stump in his hands.

Overwhelmed by tiredness, anger and sadness, he stood in the middle of the room like a man punch drunk, weaving from side to side, and, unable to keep himself upright any longer, collapsed onto the floor, and rolled over onto his back, his eyes closed and his chest heaving.

Now that the hurricane had blown itself out, Annie moved out from her place of refuge. She sat down straddling his supine figure, and, bending forwards, placed a hand on his cheek and a kiss on his left eye.

'Strong, brave Frank,' she whispered.

Her right hand moved down from the cheek and rested on his neck.

'Good, kind Frank,' she whispered, and kissed him on the other eye.

As she drew her head back, she licked the tip of his nose, and pecked at his dry lips. The heaving of his chest began to subside.

She moved her hand on his neck until the heel pressed against the artery running up from the heart.

Pulse. She trembled with ecstasy.

Pulse. Her head fell back and her mouth opened, full and wide, revealing two long, sharp canines.

Pulse. She drew her hand away and placed her mouth on his neck.

Pulse. Warm, sweet blood.

Pulse. Joy beyond imagining.

Pulse. Life eternal.

JOCELYN'S REVENGE

It was Monday morning, and the rain was bouncing off the pavements in the great metropolis of Glasgow.

There wasn't quite so much bounce in the footsteps of Mr. Frobisher, the Headmaster, when he entered the main building of St. Martin's Academy and climbed the stairs to his office. As he passed a couple of small boys, he gave his umbrella a vigorous shake, soaking them both and causing squeaks of protest. Another successful skirmish in a long war of attrition, he thought. He would emerge victorious, of that he was certain.

Frobisher was a tall, slim man who dressed correctly, spoke formally, frowned a great deal, and, as a rule, tried to keep people at arm's length, if he was unable to keep them any further away. Nature had, however, created a point of weakness in his formidable armour: his luxuriant growth of silvery-grey hair, in spite of a generous application of hair cream every morning, would sometimes stand up on end, without warning and often at a most inconvenient moment. It was difficult to keep a straight face, when speaking with a man who looked like he had stuck his finger into an electric socket.

Mrs. Winifred Burp, the Head's personal secretary, was of an altogether different sort. An inch or two over five feet in height, she was plump and warm-hearted. She beamed an enormous smile at Frobisher as he made himself comfortable behind his capacious desk. Her greeting was as jolly as ever.

'Good morning, Headmaster,' she chirped, her happiness bubbling over to such a degree that she was unable to resist practising a *chaseé*.

'Morning, Mrs. Burp,' Frobisher replied, his tone of voice almost as flat as his feet. 'Anything happening this week?' he asked, sinking down in his chair, as though mentally preparing himself for the worst.

'There is the monthly Monday mid-morning meeting for moaning and mumping,' Mrs. Burp read from her diary.

'Ah yes, the Miserable Mums. And what's on their agenda?'

'Apart from your head, they say that there is something wrong with something somewhere.'

'And they want it fixed, I suppose.'

'They want it fixed. Yesterday would be good, but if you could manage it sooner…And tomorrow you are meeting with the parents of George Caulfield.'

'Caulfield, the light-fingered third year boy. Better a kleptomaniac than an arsonist, I suppose,' said Frobisher, checking that his wristwatch and wallet were where they should be. 'Make sure that anything which he could possibly fit into his pockets has been locked away, would you, Mrs. Burp? The last time I had anything to do with that boy, I lost a rather lovely green silk handkerchief and a silver propelling pencil. What's it to be then, do you think, another suspension, or shall we try the nuclear option?'

'You're not going to blow him up, Headmaster, are you?' said Mrs. Burp, her eyes growing wide with excitement.

'My dear lady, calm yourself. I simply meant that, perhaps it was now time for me to suggest that we, that is to say, the school and the reprobate, part company, and that the arrangement is to be on a permanent basis. Expulsion, Mrs. Burp, is what I am getting at. How many chances has the boy had?'

'At least twenty-eight.'

'There is a certain optimism which never dies,' continued Frobisher, shaking his head, 'and a very great deal of the world's supply of it appears to have been gifted to the guidance teachers of this educational establishment. Expulsion it is then.' And he flicked a paper clip off the surface of the desk.

'On Wednesday afternoon, the second year girls have a hockey match.'

'They have managed to find a team who are prepared to play them?' Frobisher asked, unable to conceal his astonishment. 'I don't believe it.'

'Yes, some of the local clubs have assembled a squad of their biggest and strongest players.'

'The poor fools don't stand a chance. Their size will avail them naught against that bunch of little savages. It might be an idea to contact the hospital and tell them to prepare for the worst.'

'Expect heaps of hockey-stick injuries on Wednesday!!!' Mrs. Burp murmured, as she scribbled a note in her diary. 'On Thursday morning, you have a meeting with Miss Mulvey. She wants to discuss with you the possibility of bringing back capital punishment for some of her fourth year boys.'

'What! Capital punishment! I didn't realise things had gotten so bad. If only she would take a firm hand with those rascals at the beginning of the year, they wouldn't now be locking her in the cupboard every other period.'

'A good whack is all they need,' said Mrs. Burp, in her most affectionate manner, and she pulled up the sleeves of her beautiful pale green cardigan, as though eager to make a start on that very task. 'I did ask, but she was quite certain that it was capital punishment which she wanted to discuss with you. And Friday is Pi Day.

Dr. Forrester would like to speak about it at morning assembly,' she concluded, closing her black diary.

'Pie Day? That sounds interesting,' Frobisher said, visibly perking up and shooting his cuffs. 'Now, what about a little . . . ?'

' . . . something to get you started, Headmaster?'

'Quite so.' A note of hope sounded feebly in Frobisher's voice. It was only Monday morning, and there was a long week ahead. He would need all the support that could be mustered, even if it was only to be found in regular doses of Darjeeling tea and lemon puff biscuits.

Monday, Tuesday and Wednesday came and went, the school remained standing where it had done for the past one hundred and twenty years or so, and none of the staff was murdered.

Thursday's meeting with Miss Mulvey came to rather a dramatic end. The poor lady, distraught beyond measure by the behaviour of her tormentors, had taken a rolling-pin from her handbag and, in a high-pitched, trembling voice, had threatened to "lay it on with plenty of gusto and crack a few pates." Frobisher let the storm blow itself out and, when it was safe to do so, had gently disarmed her. Something would be done about the malefactors, of that she could rest assured.

What a way to start the day, he groaned, sinking back into his chair after she had gone. Still, there was always tomorrow to look forward to. Pie Day. There was solace to be found in a Sheppard's pie, no doubt about it; but a game pie, stuffed full of pheasant, venison and wild boar, baked in a thick, crusty pastry, and covered with hot gravy was a higher order of gustatory delight. And for dessert, it would have to be apple and rhubarb pie, with blueberries, a sprinkling of cinnamon and several large dollops of double cream. That would go down very nicely, indeed. He must find a moment or two to speak to Mrs. Tooke, the cook, and ask her what she had in mind for the special day.

Mr. Frobisher found Mrs. Tooke in her kitchen sharpening a large meat cleaver on a whetstone. Rather like a headsman putting an edge to his axe, he thought, taking a step or two backwards.

'Friday? Pie Day?' she asked. 'I know nothing about it, Headmaster. Let's have a look at the menu for tomorrow. There's carrot soup, fish and chips and peas, and rice pudding with pears.'

'But no pies?' asked the Headmaster, experiencing a momentary deflation of spirits.

'Nope. Pie-free Friday, I'm afraid. I could knock up some custard tarts, if that'd make you happy,' she suggested, after a moment's reflection. The cleaver flew threw the air and thudded into the wall at the other end of the kitchen. A young fellow who was washing a pot at the sink stopped to pat the top of his head, as if to make sure it was still attached to his body.

'Thank you, no, Mrs. Tooke. Fish and chips it is.'

The Head turned his steps in the direction of the Mathematics Department. Dr. Forrester would be able to clear up this mystery. After all, he was a calm and rational man. Serenity dwelt within those green eyes of his.

'Morning, Forrester,' said Frobisher, striding into the classroom. 'Hard at it solving knotty problems, I see. Ah, joining-the-dots!'

'A little light entertainment, Headmaster,' stammered Doctor Forrester, pushing the puzzle under a pile of jotters.

'You're not going to colour it in when you're finished, are you?' Frobisher asked, relishing the confusion which his unexpected entry had caused.

A flush of embarrassment appeared on Forrester's face. 'Ha! Yes, yes. I mean no, of course not.'

'Now, what's all this I hear about tomorrow being Pie Day?' the Headmaster asked. 'I've just spoken to Mrs. Tooke, the cook, and she knows nothing about it.'

'It's the fourteenth of March,' said Forrester, screwing the cap on his fountain pen and rising to his feet. 'The fourteenth of the third.' He picked up a piece of chalk and wrote on the blackboard

March 14 = 3/14 = 3.14

'Not sure I follow you, Forrester.' Frobisher looked from the board to the Doctor and back to the board again.

'The number pi, Headmaster?' said Forrester, raising an eyebrow.

'The number pie is still a pie,' said Frobisher. All was not lost. There was a pie after all, but it was to contain numbers. But how were they to be made? Moulded from mincemeat, perhaps? Cut from pastry and stuck on the outside of the pie? Yes, that was most likely it.

'The Greek letter pi,' Forrester tried again.

'Ah! First a number pie, and now a pie containing letters of the Greek alphabet. How very unusual. Might we not have both? Two pies are always better than one.'

'You fail to understand, Headmaster. Pi, spelt p-i.'

'. . . e. There is an "e" on the end, sir. P-i-e.'

It took some minutes of patient explanation on the part of Forrester to clear up the misunderstanding.

'I see. So, no pies, but lots of pi.'

'Now you have it, Headmaster.'

'Thank you for your time, Doctor,' said Frobisher, with a curt nod of his head, and the briefest and most freezing of smiles.

The Head strode back to his office, his disappointment fading and his anger rising with every step he took. His hair stood up on end, his eyes flashed fire, and he wore a ferocious scowl on his face. Children turned and fled at his approach. Mrs. Burp hastily prepared an offering of tea and biscuits, in the hope that it might soften his mood. It was to no avail.

Later that same day, just after the start of lunchtime, the dreadful news broke.

Florian Dornford burst into the classroom which the Maths Club used for its weekly meeting. Pupils gathered there to talk numbers, do puzzles, or just hang out with other geeks.

'The Headmaster's cancelled Pi Day,' he shouted.

'What! Cancelled it? You're joking,' said Jocelyn Warwick, looking up from the page of hard sums at which he was then working with great concentration.

The other students stopped what they were doing to listen to the news.

'I'm not. I'm deadly serious,' replied Florian. 'Instead of having Pi Day tomorrow, he's decided to make all of next week Cheese Week.'

'Cheese Week! Is the man mad?' Jocelyn almost shouted, snapping his pencil in two, so great was his shock at the announcement.

'Mad on cheese, it would appear,' snorted Ermengarde Farjean, the most talented girl in second year. Ermengarde could solve a fiendishly difficult equation in ten seconds flat, but was experiencing problems with the large cream cake which she had bought at the baker's. She scraped cream from the top of her ear and licked it off her finger.

And so it was. An upset Dr. Forrester passed on the announcement to the department that afternoon. Pi Day was off, Cheese Week was on.

An emergency after-school meeting for staff was arranged for 3.45 pm that same day.

'As you may or may not know,' began Mr. Frobisher, standing before the assembled teaching staff, 'I have decided to make next week Cheese Week. It will be a five-day long celebration of the joy of cheese. For all too long now, I have been of the opinion that cheese is one of mankind's greatest inventions, bar none. The wheel, Penicillin, space travel, all very well and good, I say, but would any of them have been possible, if it hadn't been for cheese? The only reason the wheel was invented, was so that early man could have a means of transporting his cheeses to market. Sir Alexander Fleming, when he sat down to his breakfast every morning before heading off to his laboratory, could be heard to cry, "Never mind the porridge, woman! Where's my cheese?" As for space travel, we need only consider the moon. Why, it's made of the very stuff!'

'Excellent idea, Headmaster. Cheese Week it is then,' simpered Miss Binnie Sonnenblatt, the school's wrestling coach and international yodelling star.

'I realise that it doesn't leave you much time to prepare,' the Headmaster continued, 'but, over the next few days, I would like you to consider how you intend to make cheese a central part of your lessons next week.'

'That won't be a problem at all,' said Mrs. Tooke, the cook. Various dishes rich in cheese were, at that moment, passing before her mind's eye. She particularly fancied a *tarte flambée* or a taleggio risotto. But would her cheese wire be up to the job, she wondered.

Mr. "Bumbly" Blather, the Head of English, was less certain. 'I'm not sure how we'll be able to manage that,' he said, scrunching up his face.

'Well, instead of *The Merchant of Venice*,' suggested Frobisher, who had come to the meeting prepared for all manner of tricky questions, 'why not introduce the students to that great but little-known work, by our very own G. J. 'Kilty' MacSporran, *The Cheesemonger of Paisley*?'

'A touch obscure, Headmaster,' countered Mr. Blather.

'Obscure, yes. But brilliant!'

Mr. Blather nodded his head weakly, in a manner which, at one and the same time, managed to say yes, maybe, no, absolutely no, and never.

'I have an idea,' chirped Mrs. Axminster-Jones. 'Why don't you . . . '

'*Abi et coque tibi caput, caprimulge*,' whispered Mr. Horace Augustus Murple, with as much contempt as he could muster, and that was a lot. Mr. Murple taught Greek and Latin, mainly to himself, but there were a few occasions during the week when he had one or two pupils in his class.

'…put up a suggestions box in the atrium in which pupils and staff can deposit their ideas for Cheese Week? Recipes, games, and so forth.'

'Splendid idea, Felicity,' said Frobisher.

Not all of the staff were quite so enthusiastic. In fact, there was a good deal of resistance to the idea, and one or two were so underwhelmed, they fell asleep during the meeting. However, the Headmaster won out in the end.

***

Cheese Week was full of surprises for the pupils of St. Martin's. Perhaps the biggest of all, was the unveiling of a new unit of measurement in Mathematics. The imperial and metric units were now to be superseded by the cheese unit. A medium-sized boy might be said to be 8 cheeses, 14 slices and so many shavings high. The advanced class experienced tremendous difficulty in differentiating cheeses, until a first year girl told them it was simply a matter of reading the names on the labels.

There was great excitement in the chemistry laboratory, when a group of pupils, after much trial and error, succeeded in creating an unusually cheesy smell. Further investigation, however, revealed that one of the girls had eaten a family size tin of curried beans for breakfast and…well, delicacy forbids further discussion of the unfortunate matter.

The physicists spent hours investigating, amongst other things, the electrical conducting and explosive properties of cheese. Their experiments failed, as all school physics experiments are destined to do, so the class simply ate the cheese and discussed the weather.

Mr. Murple was his usual austere self. 'The writers of classical antiquity are strangely silent on the subject of cheese,' he said, in his most declamatory manner. 'And so, too, shall we be. Anyone who mentions the blasted stuff will be immediately defenestrated.' The empty desks and chairs in his classroom received this severe reproof in silence.

Although everyone knows that the French are a nation of cheese-eaters, that they can make soup, literally out of anything, is a less well-known fact. They are also a very romantic race of peoples, and Mademoiselle Boff, the French language teacher, a short lady with a not unattractive moustache, was no exception. It was with considerable pleasure, therefore, that she introduced into her conversation classes such lines as *Voulez vous mangez du fromage avec moi?, Mon petite fromage, comme je t'adore* or even *Ma Cherie, vous avez des yeux les plus beaux du monde, et un visage comme un fromage.*

Cheese, being a comestible of the tastiest kind, featured to an unusual degree in the refectory. Mrs. Tooke, the cook, went to a considerable effort to ensure that it was present in every item which the kitchen prepared.

A hungry pupil, hoping to feast on a ham and cheese sandwich at lunchtime, found to his horror or delight, that he could now only get one containing cheese . . . and cheese. Cheese porridge, sticky cheese buns, cheese bars, bottled cheese-flavoured spring water. The list goes on and on. A cheese-fest it most certainly was, but there were unforeseen consequences.

The school nurse, who had taken to wearing a hollowed-out Wensleydale cheese on her head, in place of her white nurse's hat, began to notice that quite a number of the pupils were turning a strange shade of pale yellowy-orange as the week proceeded.

The mother of one boy, shocked by the ragged state of her son's blazer, was horrified to discover that he had tried to eat it, so great an aversion had he taken to the unvarying diet of cheese.

It wasn't long before the pushback began.

The janitor, when he opened the school on Wednesday morning, discovered a message chalked on the wall below the window of the Headmaster's office. It read, "Enuff is enuf!" Accompanying the text, was the badly-drawn picture of a booted foot stomping down on what looked very much like a large wedge of gruyere cheese. The meaning was quite clear.

Mr. Frobisher's first reaction on seeing this graffiti was to comment on the decline of standards in spelling in English, and made a mental note to have a word with Mr. Blather. He told Mr. Grinder, the janitor, to scrub the wall clean. It was important that such vile sentiments not be permitted to interrupt the remaining days of festivity.

In the afternoon of that same day, a member of staff passing through the atrium noticed the words "Take down trousers, coat cheese in vas…" scribbled in blue chalk on the wall above the suggestions box. It appeared that the culprit had been disturbed in the act and had been unable to complete his message. This, too, was washed off; but not before it had been seen by a number of pupils and staff. The cryptic nature of the communication inspired much speculation.

These were not the only instances of rebellion, nor the most dangerous. Mrs. Burp informed the Headmaster that she had received a number of telephone calls, during the course of the day, from pet shops across the city. It appeared that pupils, dressed in the uniform of St. Martin's Academy, had been buying up all the mice they could get their hands on. For what purpose, she could not say. Mr. Frobisher realised in an instant what was afoot. He had it announced by special messengers, drawn from among the Prefects, and instructed to visit every classroom, that any boy or girl caught bringing mice into school was to be sent to his office immediately. Hardly had this warning been broadcast, when a small boy, wearing a look of undisguised resentment on his face and dragging behind him a large school bag, was led into his presence. The bag was found to contain a box of 34 mice, white, black, small, large, long-tailed, whiskered, bright-eyed and restless. All very different, except for one thing—their love of cheese. They had a raging hunger for the stuff, an insatiable desire for it.

'What do you have to say for yourself, young Charlie Pilchard?' growled the Headmaster. 'Speak up, boy!'

'I . . . don't . . . like . . . cheese,' replied Pilchard, through gritted teeth.

'I see. And mice do. I suppose you were planning to release them in the refectory and let them eat all the cheese, is that it? Wretched boy!'

Mr. Frobisher wondered how best to punish this surly revolutionary who stood before him and, at the same time, send a message to the rest of the plotters that such behaviour would not be tolerated.

'The mice will be taken back to the pet shop and you, my lad,' he said, wagging a long, bony finger at the scowling rebel, 'will write a one thousand word essay describing a day in the life of a cheese, which you will hand to me tomorrow morning. Pick any cheese you like, or don't like, for that matter. Emmenthaler, Pecorino Romano, Skyr. I don't care. Tomorrow morning, mind. And I'll count the words myself, so make sure that you're not short.'

The Headmaster turned away to look out of the window and give consideration to the likely efficacy of such a punishment. This pause in the proceedings gave Charlie Pilchard all the time he needed to pull a big black rat from the inside pocket of his blazer, let it down to the floor gently by its tail, and nudge it with the toe of his shoe. The rat scurried off and hid under an armchair which stood in a corner of the office.

'You sit nice and quiet, Mr. Pike,' Charlie whispered. 'There's a good chap.'

'What did you say, you young rogue?' Mr. Frobisher looked and sounded very angry.

'May I go now, sir?' asked Pilchard.

'Go? Yes, to the devil! And be quick about it!' came the thundering reply.

***

'I have an idea,' said Jocelyn, when he, Florian and Ermengarde met at morning break on the Thursday of Cheese Week. 'If it works out, it'll put an end to all this nonsense, once and for all.'

'Do tell, Jocelyn,' said Ermengarde, eager to hear what her friend had on his mind.

Jocelyn looked around to ensure that there was no chance of his being overheard, then replied, 'In that case, a little nearer, please.' The three heads moved very close together.

When school finished for the day, the friends met up at the front gate, and headed off together, linked arm-in-arm. After a walk of thirty minutes, they arrived at a shop, on the window of which were painted, in large green letters with an outline of gold, the words

Tuffler and Wheeze,
In Matters of Food,
Purveyors of Cheese,
To the Great and the Good.

'How may I help you?' asked the man behind the counter, when they stepped into the shop. This was Mr. Tuffler, a man with red cheeks, small ears and a head of curly brown hair. His olfactory organ was unusually well-developed, but whether a gift of nature or the result of years of practice in the art of cheese-sniffing, it was impossible to say.

'We want to buy some cheese,' replied Florian.

'You've certainly come to the right place,' said the man with a smile, which could in no way be described as cheesy.

They saw cheeses of every imaginable shape, size and colour, ranged on shelves which reached up to the ceiling, displayed behind glass, stacked on tables and countertops. It was cheese heaven, if you liked cheese.

'Did you have something particular in mind?' inquired Mr. Tuffler, his eyebrows moving up in an inquisitive manner. 'Cheese from a particular country, say? Hindustan? The islands of Fiji? A hard cheese or a soft one?'

'It must have a strong smell,' said Jocelyn, wrinkling his nose.

'Hmm. A niffy cheese. We don't often get a request for that type. What about this one?' Mr. Tuffler asked, holding out a cheese knife. On the end of this was a small yellow cube from which an unusually pungent odour wafted.

'Ooh! I say. That's rather strong, ain't it?' Florian remarked, taking two steps backwards.

'It certainly has character. That much, at least, could be said for it,' agreed Mr. Tuffler, and his nostrils twitched, and his eyes lit up, as though he found the scent particularly beguiling.

Leaving Ermengarde and Jocelyn to sniff and nibble at Mr. Tuffler's various suggestions, Florian's attention wandered off. At the back of the shop, he noticed a door on which the words *Achtung! Danger of Death* were written in red letters. At that moment, the door opened and a figure emerged, a figure clad in a white coat and wearing a face mask, not unlike that worn by firemen when they enter a burning building.

Now, why would someone working in a cheese shop be wearing breathing apparatus, Florian asked himself. Even as he did so, he was sure he knew the answer.

'What is that man carrying?' he called out, pointing in the direction of the white-coated employee.

'That is the head of our research laboratory,' replied Mr. Tuffler, with a note of pride in his voice, 'and I believe he is carrying a cheese of his very own invention.'

'And why is he wearing a mask?' Florian asked.

'Because,' said the cheesemonger, 'he has in his hands what is very likely . . . the smelliest cheese . . . in the entire world.'

'We'll take it!' shouted all three friends together.

'How much do you want?' said Mr. Tuffler.

'All of it,' replied Ermengarde.

'It'll cost you.' Mr. Tuffler sounded even more excited than the children. 'And how do you wish to pay? Cash or . . . ?'

'Cheque,' said Jocelyn, holding out his dad's credit card.

'A word of warning,' the cheesemonger said, raising a finger, and sounding very serious all of a sudden. 'The cheese must be kept cool, at all times, otherwise . . . '

'Otherwise what?' asked Ermengarde the curious.

'Otherwise, my lass, it will get very smelly indeed.'

'And how smelly is very smelly?' Ermengarde remembered her mother opening her sports bag sometime towards the end of a long, hot summer holiday. Mrs. Farjean had discovered three pairs of unwashed hockey socks at the bottom of the bag. Ermengarde had never ever smelled anything quite so awful as those socks.

'Well,' replied Mr. Tuffler, 'the Lord Mayor bought some, just a small piece, for a banquet which he was giving in the Town Hall. For some reason, it was left out all night. An oversight, surely,' he said, with a shake of his head. 'The room was warm, the cheese went all soft and gooey, and . . . and the stink was indescribable. It was so awful, it stopped the Town Hall clock.'

'Stopped the clock!' exclaimed Jocelyn. 'By Jingo, that's the one for us. If it can stop a clock, it can stop a headmaster.' There was an enormous grin on his face, and he did a small victory dance, right there in the middle of the shop, with all those cheeses silently looking on.

***

Ermengarde's classmates noticed that she was carrying an unusual bag in school on Friday. It was a small bag and was very cold to the touch. She kept it close at all times and, if anyone asked what was in it, she replied that it was her next door neighbour's heart, which she had cut out the night before and was going to roast and eat at a black mass at a friend's house after school. There was an unmistakable hint of menace in her voice when she said this. That, and the unwavering stare of her clear, blue eyes so unnerved the enquiring individual, that she was instantly believed. She was also left her very much to herself for the rest of the day.

The three friends met up near the Headmaster's office at the end of school on Friday. They were standing in a corner trying not to look too conspicuous and wondering how to proceed with their plan, when they heard a loud scream. Mrs. Burp came running out of the office at full tilt, waving her hands in the air. A few seconds later, another scream broke on their ears, this one much louder and deeper. Mr. Frobisher charged out into the corridor and fled in the same direction as his secretary. After them both, scurried a large black rat, its long tail slithering along the floor, its black eyes shining with malevolence.

'Now! Go! Quick!' whispered Florian.

It was the work of a moment to hide the cheese in the bottom drawer of the Headmaster's desk, glue the drawer shut, turn the radiators in the room up full, and flee from the scene.

All they had to do now was wait.

Monday morning dawned cold and clear.

Florian, Ermengarde and Jocelyn walked up from the station together. Their conversation touched on all manner of topics, except one. They would not have admitted it, but they were a little nervous. It was possible, after all, that they might be expelled, if they were found to be the originators of the mischievous deed.

When they reached the foot of Glencoe Street, the street on which St. Martin's was located, they noticed a strange smell in the air. As they got closer to the school, the smell grew stronger and stronger. Police cars, a fire engine and several ambulances were parked outside the main gate. Faint screams could be heard coming from the building. A policeman staggered past them, his face pale and his nose covered with a handkerchief. A crowd of pupils stood at a safe distance watching the situation develop.

It was the janitor who first realised that something was wrong, when he opened the school early on Monday morning, but he could do nothing about it, as he immediately fainted from the smell. The assistant-janitor found him lying just inside the main door, but he too fainted, before he could offer any help. The cleaning ladies, who had a key of their own, entered the building from the opposite end, and were happily making their way along a corridor on the ground floor, when they met with an impenetrable wall of stink, and promptly fainted. A passing motorist raised the alarm, then fainted at the wheel of his car.

The fire brigade were called to deal with the problem. Unable to open the drawer where the cheese was hidden, a fireman used his axe to smash the whole desk to smithereens. A splinter of wood pierced his mask, and he was so overcome by the toxicity of the air, that he went on to chop up the rest of the Headmaster's office. His rampage only came to an end when he swung his axe at an open window, and both axe and fireman disappeared, landing outside on the pavement one storey below. The poor man recovered from the effects of the plunge long before he stopped having nightmares about drowning in a morass of stinky cheese.

The offending cheese was finally removed to a safe distance. The authorities were uncertain how to dispose of it, until their deliberations were interrupted by the appearance of a schoolboy wearing a clothes peg on his nose. He held a cheese-knife in one hand and a packet of crackers in the other. The intrepid fellow was prepared to "do his bit for the school and polish the lot off." The general approval of this suggestion turned to a mild astonishment, when the boy sat down cross-legged on the grass, spread a white handkerchief over his lap, and got stuck in. Their astonishment increased when, after five minutes of steady progress, he pulled out a small bottle of white wine. 'Dry work!' he said, and winked.

St. Martin's recovered from the ordeal after a few days. Cheese was not only removed from the refectory menu for the foreseeable future, but was also tacitly avoided in conversation. In some parts of the school, that is to say, anywhere near the Headmaster's office, it was considered a swear word.

Unable to believe that he had been the victim of a prank, and not wishing to expose himself to further ridicule, Mr. Frobisher forbade all mention of *l'affaire du fromage*. He did form a suspicion or two about who might have been responsible, but did not pursue the matter.

It was many months before his office was entirely free from the dreadful smell. He might open a cupboard or draw back a curtain, and there it would be, a cloud of cheesy whiff hanging in the air, and his eyes would begin to water again and his limbs to tremble. Pedestrians passing the school at that moment might hear a window being violently opened and see a head appear, hanging out over the sill gasping for breath. Quite what they thought of this behaviour, no one knows, as no one asked them. Anyway, it was just one of the many unusual sights to be seen in that great city every day.

Printed in Great Britain
by Amazon

16363867R00164